PRAISE FOR
BLACK DUST
LYNN CHARLES

"In this moving and heartfelt contemporary, Charles (Chef's Table) beautifully chronicles the chaos that results from heartbreak and the agonizing efforts one must make to heal after tragedy…. Readers will agonize, sympathize, and empathize all the way from the beginning of their journey to the end."

—Publishers Weekly

"The author is a fine writer who treats everyone with finesse and tenderness…told with skill and compassion by a woman who understands the gay psyche and desires."

—American Library Association GLBT Roundtable

"Armed with a sweetness that reaches the heart, Charles' poignant novel aligns two distressed souls. Music bonds them together and gives them strength individually as Toby and Emmett renew their spirits in her compelling story."

—RT Book Reviews

PRAISE FOR
CHEF'S TABLE
LYNN CHARLES

"Charles has done an awesome job with this delectable tale of two men with personalities that just don't quit."

—RT F

BENEATH THE STARS

BENEATH THE STARS

A NOVEL

LYNN CHARLES

interlude **press** • new york

Copyright © 2017 Lynn Charles
All Rights Reserved
ISBN 13: 978-1-945053-17-7 (trade)
ISBN 13: 978-1-945053-30-6 (ebook)
Published by Interlude Press
http://interludepress.com

Book and Cover design by CB Messer
Source Photography for Cover and Interior ©Depositphotos.com/
dovapi/Nevena/meowudesign

The quotation from *The Little Prince* by Antoine de Saint-
Exupéry is from Richard Howard's new translation published
by Houghton Mifflin Harcourt Mariner Books in 2000.

10 9 8 7 6 5 4 3 2 1

interlude 🧩 press • new york

To Lisa: The brightest star in my sky.

Each night the moon kisses secretly
the lover who counts the stars.
—Rumi

I.
INTO THE NIGHT

FEBRUARY—WYLIE, PENNSYLVANIA

Eddie Garner was in the business of saving people. He saved people from burning buildings and unsteady structures. It was his job to think of others before himself, to save them from whatever disaster had transpired or was about to transpire.

One person remained beyond his saving reach—the one he loved most—Maggie James.

They sat under a clear starlit sky. A blunt crackled softly between Maggie's lips. An afghan crocheted by her mother covered her bony legs and quelled Eddie's concerns that it was too cool—too *February*—to be outside. She had important topics to cover, she had told him. The weather appeared to be the least of her concerns.

Maggie offered the joint to Eddie. He waved it off. "It's for you," he said. "I'm good."

"I don't like to smoke alone," she said, managing a solid pout amplified by her sunken eyes. A breeze blew the ends of the scarf that covered her bald head off her shoulder. It fluttered back in place the way the long, wavy tendrils of her red hair used to.

She put the joint to his lips. He took a deep drag, instantly grateful she had insisted. The last months had been impossibly hard: metastatic cancer, failed treatment options, custody of her son—their son—into his care, new burdens of childcare while maintaining his rank at the fire station. It was too much. And looking ahead at a world without her in it was virtually unbearable.

The marijuana eased her pain and nausea. And now, like the incense she burned in her room, it relaxed him, if for a short time.

In Eddie's thirty-three years, he could not recall a moment he didn't love Maggie James.

They didn't share the romantic kind of love that leads to a white dress and an uncomfortable tuxedo, to family gathering to hear promises of 'til-death-do-us-part. With Maggie and Eddie, promises were understood, unconditional. The sun rose; the sun set. Eddie loved Maggie; Maggie loved Eddie.

In the midst of that love, he agreed to free her from the nonstop heartbreak of finding a man in the dregs of Wylie's dating pool. She hadn't been seeking a life partner, but someone to help her become a mother. After Eddie's donation, Adrian was born. Love led the way, and cancer came—twice—to rearrange the story.

Death would part them soon enough. Eddie would continue to love her. Sunrise; sunset.

Tonight, death was but an onlooker. Maggie took Eddie's hand in hers. Her fingers were no longer recognizable: they were cold, skeletal, long separated from the art she used to create. "I want to give you something," she said, turning his palm upright. She reached into the pocket strapped to the side of her wheelchair where she kept treasured items: small pictures drawn by Adrian, petals from gifted flowers, a queen of hearts card her mother had nicked from a casino in Pittsburgh.

"Maggie, no. Don't start giving things away."

She ignored him. A long gold chain dangled from her fingers.

"No. Put that back on your neck." The calm from the joint left as quickly as the strike of a match. "Please?" In spite of Eddie's protests, she poured the chain into his hand and curled his fingers around the ring that hung from it. She had worn the man's ring on her thumb for years. As her body withered away, the three-diamond ring had moved to a chain around her neck as a cherished symbol of their threesome: Maggie, Eddie, and Adrian. "Maggie, please," Eddie begged. "I'm not ready."

"I am," she said; her steely determination cut through Eddie's fear.

"But this is *yours*. This is *us*. You need to take it with you."

"Eddie." She brought his full hand to her mouth and kissed his knuckles with dry lips. "I won't need it in the sky."

Eddie was a fireman, a rescuer. He was in the business of saving people. But he could not save Maggie any more than he could gather the stars over their heads and bring them to her. Now, he had no choice but to relinquish her to them. He unfolded his hand and ran his finger over the diamonds. "I won't wear it, Mags. I won't."

"Save it for Adrian, then. Or, for when you find another—to make our trio complete again."

"That won't happen."

"Not if you keep dating dunderheads, no."

"I do not date dunderheads," he said, happy to see a glisten of sass in her eyes. "Not always."

"The only time you don't date dunderheads is when you're not dating." She leaned back with a grimace and hiked the blanket closer to her hips. "I'm ready to go in now. Mom left us some butterscotch pudding."

Eddie swallowed his fears, and, unsure what he would do with it, pocketed the ring as he stood. She might give the ring away, but their trio—Maggie, Eddie, and Adrian—was eternal.

Meanwhile—Chicago, Illinois

Sidney Marneaux looked into the glass-enclosed room before locking its door. A lone floor lamp lit the back brick wall. Dim lights from the hall illuminated an empty desk, a conference table with two chairs, and an open sketch pad. A broom, mop, and bucket leaned against a divider wall that hid boxes filled with the tools to make this place come alive.

As of this morning, it was all his. The lease agreement had Sid's company name on it: Bastra.

In time, that word—his brand—would be etched into the glass door of his brand new atelier. It had been etched into his heart since high school when, the night before the spring sports award ceremony, his best friend Dottie had come to him in a state close to tears—the closest to tears he would ever see her.

Everyone was to "dress appropriately" for the ceremony. "Appropriately" translated to dresses or skirts for the girls and anything from khakis and polo shirts to suits and ties for the guys.

"I will not wear a dress," she had said, locked in a state between anger and fear. "Slacks and blouses don't fit right." She picked at the shoulders of her shirt and tugged at the waistband of her jeans. Her upset had no words, but that day had sparked a flame in him. Nothing was wrong with Dottie, her less-than-feminine taste, or her thick, athletic body. The problem rested in the clothes. Clothes he would, over time, design for people like Dottie who slipped into the cracks of fashion's persistent binary system.

And now, after a decade—college first, then running the online business out of a spare bedroom and tailoring suits for wealthy businessmen to make ends meet—his loyal clientele contributed to a successful Kickstarter campaign and allowed his vision to blossom on the fifth floor of a historic building north of Lincoln Park.

Sid and his assistant, Rue, had spent the morning sweeping the cement floors, washing the floor-to-ceiling windows, and sketching potential layouts for the space. They'd subsisted on a cheeseball and stale crackers to avoid a lunch break. Come dinnertime, Sid had insisted on carryout. When she left, knowing his tendency to forget the world around him, Rue made him promise to be out by nine p.m. "We start early tomorrow; sleep *is* a human need, Sid."

It was ten p.m., now; close enough. He reveled in a slow walk to his train station, in the unseasonable spring-like refreshment of the air.

As he approached the station's stairs, his sister phoned. He declined the call and sent a text: Grabbing a train. Give me 30.

Anna: Do not forget, Sid. This is important.

If Anna was the judge of importance, everything qualified. Off the train, he walked most of the way home before he dialed her number and braced himself for something less than important. "Okay, what's the emergency?"

"It's Dad," she said, as if she had been holding her breath her entire wait.

"Fuck, Anna. Why didn't you *say* that?"

"You didn't answer the phone, asshole. And he's fine. I mean, he won't ever be—" She sighed into the phone. Sid heard her screen door close. He arrived at his apartment and sat on the stoop to close the miles between them and stare at the same sky. "It's me," she said. "I can't do this alone anymore. You need to come home."

"Home" meant Connelly—a lovely college town in central Pennsylvania surrounded by the Allegheny Mountains, its forests, and large expanses of farmland. Mordell College employed not only much of Connelly, but also much of Claremont County. Sid's father was a respected professor emeritus in math, his mother had been a research librarian, and his sister was an adjunct professor in statistics taking a sabbatical to care for their father. Sid hadn't lived in Connelly since his first day in college, over ten years ago. Connelly was no longer "home."

"That's impossible, and you know it," Sid said. "Where's Andrew?"

Anna's silence said plenty about their brother. Andrew was being Andrew: self-involved, self-important, self-immersed, all under the guise of being a family man. His wife and mostly grown kids survived happily without him while he spent his time at the lab researching... well, Sid was convinced he researched ways to shirk his responsibilities. His résumé said something about solar energy.

"He's immovable." Anna finally said, "You aren't; you understand Dad." At Sid's continued silence, she added, "And I know you want the best for him."

"Of course I do, but that doesn't change—" Sid bit his tongue. Her lack of interest in his career had a long history; he redirected from emotion to fact. "I signed the lease on my studio this morning."

"Congratulations." If her tone was any indication, she remained uninterested. "I am doing *everything* here. I need a break."

"I can come down for a few days in a couple weeks," Sid said, unsure if it was true. "Can't you hire a nurse?"

"No. You know he treats them horribly," she said. "You have to pull some weight, Sid."

He closed his eyes and tried to explain again. "Anna, when I say I signed the lease, I don't mean I have a new play space. I mean, I have obligations to people who have invested in this company. I have staff to hire, product to produce, *clientele* to serve."

"I don't see—"

"Orders don't stop because Dad's sick and you're tired."

"I don't see how any of this is more important than Dad."

"Nothing is more important than Dad. That's not the point." Sid shed his coat; anxiety warmed him faster than the unseasonable evening. "Look, you're the one who insisted on moving him into your home against his wishes. Let's not *talk* about my and Andrew's—"

"No, let's *not* talk about your and Andrew's opinions, because you two have done nothing but voice them."

This wasn't altogether false. His sister's problems were her own, but his dad's weren't the kinds of problems anyone asks for. More importantly, Sid's ability to say no to her request was possible because their dad said yes when Sid wanted to leave home, follow his dreams, and "make Ma proud."

"I can't untangle immediately," Sid finally said. "Give me to the end of the week."

"Wednesday, Sid. I want an answer by Wednesday."

"Whatever I can offer, it's temporary. You understand that, right?"

"Wednesday."

He slept fitfully that night and the next. The perfect opportunity to tell Rue, "Hey, I know we just took the biggest risk of our lives, and you're depending on its success to pay rent and all, but I've got this… *thing*," didn't exist.

Wednesday night, he walked home from the train and went straight to his balcony. He flipped his studio key in his hand and looked up at the sky. "You understand Dad," his sister had said. He focused on the eastern sky and thought he spotted Altair, the brightest star in the constellation Aquila, but he couldn't bet on his accuracy.

His stargazing days with his father had gone by the wayside for more important happenings on earth. The few stars he could see through the light pollution meant little to him now; their names and constellations were gone from his memory, like long-forgotten answers to history exams. His evenings with Baba beneath those same stars had never been about passing tests or memorizing trivial facts; they were about time together, stories and quiet, laughter and occasional tears. They were about *family*.

Sid owed Rue the respect of letting her take part in his decision, and that needed time. He pulled out his phone to ask Anna for another twenty-four hours. A missed call from Dottie interrupted his plan; the timing was entirely too coincidental.

He called her back. "Dottie Mulligan, my sweet."

"Anna called," Dottie said before he was finished with his last word.

"Of course she did." Of course she did. After his retirement from Mordell, Lou Marneaux had volunteered in Claremont County's disaster management office long before Dottie became its director. With the lingering history of her friendship with Sid, once she came to run the office, Lou and Dottie became close. She depended on Lou; he appreciated the busyness of the office that filled his days and found joy in teaching community classes on safety, CPR and First Aid. Dottie had been keeping up on Lou's failing health since he left the position.

Still, Sid's skepticism around all-things-Anna spoke loudest. "How is she using you to reel me in?"

"No one uses me."

"Point taken," Sid said. "But between the three of you, I'm suspicious."

"You still CPR-certified?"

"What? What does that have to do—" It hit him. "Have you all lost your minds? I have a *business* to run here. I cannot help you *and* Anna—" Sid caught himself; neither Anna nor Dottie would ask for help if help wasn't needed. "How is he? Really?"

"He misses you. He seems unhappy."

"Shit."

"Look, Anna doesn't know I'm calling, okay? But she needs you. Your best friend needs you. I'll work on softening her up so you can still manage Bastra."

"How can I manage Bastra from Connelly, Dottie?"

"I don't know, but you were determined enough to make it happen. You'll figure out a way to keep it going."

Dottie knew "determined." She and Sid had met in sixth grade gym class and were put on the same in-class softball team. Dottie had already played for three years when Ryan Albridge stepped up to bat. Dottie eyed him from the pitcher's mound, and Ryan said, "I ain't taking no pitch from a girl." The teacher told him to shut up and "take it like a man." Dottie lofted three perfect pitches right over the plate. Ryan struck out. Dottie winked at the shit and wound up for her next victim.

After that day, Dottie and Sid remained inseparable until college. She was still an inspirational force for Bastra and Sid's dearest friend, even from over five hundred miles away. While she had been there from the start, history and determination were no longer enough. "Dottie, do you even *understand*—"

"I do, and you know I do. My question is, Sid… do *you?*"

The questions outnumbered the stars. The answers remained dimmed by the pollution of the unknown. Sid had faced innumerable questions and hidden answers most of his life, but his father's love had been the one constant that gave him courage to face it all. It was time to take hold of that love and walk into the unknown one more time—for Baba.

II.
UNDER THE STARS

"Did you grab my field glasses, Sid?"

"I got 'em, Dad." Sid turned the wicker rocker to face north and helped his dad into it. "Is this a good angle?"

Lou Marneaux settled into the cushions and focused on the night sky. "Looks great. It's a clear night."

Anna's call for help was not premature or par for her histrionic course. The dementia that riddled their father's mind made day-to-day activities a chore. It turned Sid's wise, quick-witted, active father into an occasionally mean and angry man who lived in a perpetual state of confusion.

Once he saw the truth of the situation, the frequency of Sid's presence in Connelly had increased from an occasional weekend in the winter to most weekends in the spring. Then most weekends had turned into one week a month. His niece was off to college, so he stayed in her bedroom during these trips, but his dad had become more confused by Sid's constant ins and outs. Sid's ability to run his business in the chaos of Anna's home had also become impossible.

"Ah, there's Aquila, Sid. To the east, can you see it? Do you need my glasses?"

Sid followed his dad's pointed finger, but the lights in the sky remained muddied in his mind. The stars to the east were unknown as the stars to the west. Sid considered fibbing and thought better of it. He wanted to remember, in honor of everything his dad forgot.

Now, as summer unfolded, Sid split his time between Chicago and Connelly as equally as possible: a week here, a week there, a quick weekend north, a ten-day jaunt south. Dottie had secured him a furnished sublet in a run-down apartment complex on the north end of town. C-DRT, as the community disaster response team was known, had an agreement with the landlord to keep it and another unit available for potential fire victims—a rare need. As such, it was low on the landlord's priority list for repairs. But it provided a roof, a bed, a shower, and a kitchen. In a blessed gift from the gods, a second bedroom allowed space for a sewing machine and worktable—a makeshift office that allowed Sid to sew, design, and communicate as well as possible.

All things considered, he made do.

At Sid's silence, Lou pressed. "Find the brightest star east of Polaris—what's it called?"

"Do *you* remember, Baba?"

Lou lowered his binoculars. "Do *I* remember? You insult me."

In Anna's need to control the chaos that surrounded her life with their dad, she had put strict limits on Lou's activities. Baba had always thrived in the outdoors, but Anna feared for his safety. "What if he wanders away?"

"You don't put him out like a dog. Go for a walk. Sit on the porch," Sid had tried to explain, but she wasn't to be swayed. So when Sid was home, he made it his priority to get Lou outside and under the stars, where he was more likely to be lucid.

"You forgot to put pants on this morning," Sid said. "It's a fair question." He shot his dad a smile.

"Mmm. Pants are a nuisance when all you do is sit in the house," Lou said, pointing further west. "Vega. Find Vega."

Vega was easy. Sid scanned further east and grinned. "Over there? Altair. At Aquila's neck?"

"Atta boy."

"What's Vega part of again?"

"Lyra, the harp. Twenty-six light-years away."

Conversation stopped as Lou scanned the sky with his binoculars and then his naked eyes. As they sat, his dad unwound. His brow, highlighted with thick gray hair, unfurrowed; his shoulders relaxed; his voice eased from the pinched, tense rasp it had become into the smooth baritone that had comforted Sid time and again when he was a boy.

Sid filed this night away to recall when a string of bad nights choked the man he knew.

"You go back tomorrow? Classes start again?" Lou asked as he tilted his head in a new direction.

Reality had a way of interrupting good moments lately.

"No, Baba. I already graduated."

"Yes. Of course. I remember now." Sid didn't believe him, but when his dad placed his hand on Sid's arm, he let it go. His dad's hands were veined and age-spotted now, a stark "Pennsylvania Pale," as Lou used to call it, compared to Sid's own tawny brown skin that mirrored his Bangladeshi mother's. "I think I'm ready to go in," Lou said. "Chai?"

"Iced?" Lou nodded and Sid took him into the house, to the couch with a permanent butt imprint in the leftmost cushion. Sid laid calendar pages on his dad's lap. Anna had kept them handy to help Lou orient in time. "Show me today," Sid said as he went into the kitchen.

"Today. June twenty-six. Out with the girls." Lou called into the pass-through, "Sid, we should go out with the girls. I miss girls."

Sid laughed as he gathered the cold spiced tea and milk. "They're talking about how horrible men are. I don't think we'd be invited."

"Then we should talk about how horrible girls are."

"You just said you miss girls."

"I miss a lot, Zico."

Sid smiled at the nickname. The story was that his mother had named him Zico during her pregnancy. He had kicked her ribs like the Brazilian soccer star, as if trying to create a new pathway out. Once he became a toddler, he'd kicked to express his anger until Baba put a soccer ball in front of him. "Kick that, Zico," Lou had said with an affectionate nod to Sid's independence and tendency to forge his own path. Once Sid had begun to play competitively, the name had stuck.

Sid missed hearing the name, but mostly he missed evenings like this with his father. He wasted so much time on reminders, on setting Lou straight, on repeating histories that should never have left the pulse of Lou's blood.

Lou shuffled through the pages of his calendar and sighed. "How long until you go back to school?" He patted his chest pocket to check for his protector filled with a protractor and pens, a reminder of who he once was.

"A while yet, Baba. It'll be a while."

MEANWHILE—WYLIE, PENNSYLVANIA

Sometimes, Eddie envied his son. He envied the latitude young children had in expressing their emotions. Happiness equaled ecstasy. Sadness equaled agony. Anger became fury, and fear blended them all together into the pile Eddie now held in his lap: a tiny five-year-old body convulsing in wailing cries. Tears practically shot from Adrian's eyes, and his sweaty, tiny limbs clung to Eddie as though letting go would result in a free fall from the top of the world's highest roller coaster.

And yet, society accepted the screams and pleas and gasping breaths from this boy. Adrian knew that the people he loved could not only leave, but also never return. No words existed to change Eddie's son's reality.

Maggie had been gone three months. The spells between Adrian's outbursts had extended. But now, as they faced Eddie being away for two weeks, grief and fear reignited. To a five-year old who had said a permanent goodbye to his mother just months before, two weeks might as well be another forever.

Eddie held him and rocked him on Maggie's mother's porch swing before leaving him here in Sharon's fine care. Adrian hiccupped and sniffled; his cries slowed for the first time in many long moments.

"Buddy," Eddie said, tugging at Adrian's arms to release them from his own neck. "C'mere, I want you to look at me."

Adrian relinquished his grip and sat back. His eyelashes clumped with tears, and his big loopy chestnut curls were matted damply on his head. When their eyes locked, Eddie had to catch his breath—Maggie stared at him from Adrian's blue-eyed, freckle-faced gaze, waiting to hear what he had to say.

"Can you listen now?" Eddie asked, scratching over Adrian's ears to loosen the curls.

Adrian nodded, sniffed, and licked at the snot glistening on his top lip. "You're coming back."

"I'm coming back. Our new house is less than an hour away. I'm going to get it all cleaned up and nice. Get your room set up—"

"But not *too* set up because I get to choose."

Eddie laughed more from relief than good humor; his boy was bent, not broken. "Yes. You get to choose. And I'm going to meet the new firefighters and find the best ice cream shop in town."

"You're coming back."

"I'm coming back," Eddie said. "Here, turn around. Let's see what the moon's doing tonight."

Adrian rested against his dad's chest and fell silent. A moment later he stood and peeked from under the porch roof. "Oh my goodness." With a furrowed brow, he held up a finger and ran to the back of Nana's house, while Eddie chuckled at Adrian's curiosity. After a few moments, Adrian ran back, breathless. "It's not *there*! It disappeared!"

Eddie patted his lap, and Adrian hopped up and faced the sky once again. "It's there, just hidden. By the time I pick you up, we'll be able to see the full moon again. And you know what else?"

"What?"

"While I'm gone, we're going to be under the same sky, so we can watch the moon reappear together."

Adrian patted his dad's arm and said, "Under the sky—not *in it*, like Mommy."

"Yes. I'm coming back."

"Nana has the calendar to count my sleeps," Adrian said, as his body relaxed with each spoken word.

"And our video dates."

"Can we find the Big Dipper on our video dates?"

"If you want to," Eddie said. "And I can show you the new house so you can start thinking about your room."

Adrian reached behind him to run his fingers along Eddie's shirt, a leftover habit from twisting his fingers in his mother's hair and later curling her scarf tails. "Nana's bed *is* soft."

"I bet it is. And she reads stories better than I do."

"She does great voices."

"Maybe I should take a couple books with me to practice."

Adrian giggled and spun around in Eddie's arms; his eyes shone brightly for the first time all evening. "I can draw another book to read."

"I can't wait to see it."

"Because you'll be back."

"I'll be back. We're going to be fine."

Adrian nodded and rested his head on Eddie's chest as his fingers worked the shoulder of Eddie's shirt. "We'll be fine. Because you'll be back."

III.
PERSEUS

"Claremont County C-DRT has arrived at the scene."

"Copy. Dispatch out."

Sid hooked the radio into its holder and looked at Mandy, his assistant for the fire run. "I'll find the fire chief," he said, "and you get the paperwork and comfort kits ready."

She glanced at the house, bit her lip, and smiled. "I won't forget anything?"

"You've assisted enough; you'll be fine. Everything is spelled out on the forms." He patted her leg and slipped between their seats to unlock the rear door of the ERV, the emergency response vehicle that doubled as a storage unit for necessary supplies and a miniature office in which to care for disaster clients.

When in town, Sid helped Dottie in the disaster office as much as possible. And while he would never have the same love for C-DRT that Baba did, Sid still enjoyed the rush of adrenaline and the feeling of satisfaction he had first experienced as a teen, accompanying Lou on an occasional run.

Sid swung himself out and lowered the wobbly steel stairs of the truck to the muddy ground, which was puddled with the gallons of water used to fight the fire. Small streams drained over the homeowner's yard and toward the street. The ground squished under his feet with each step he took toward Lieutenant Parker.

"Hey, Sid. You haven't met the new chief yet, have you?"

"Nope. Point me to him." Sid gave the house a quick assessment. "Minor fire?"

"Structurally, yeah. Emotionally—strap up. Chief entered looking for a dog. Came out emptyhanded. Family is next door. I think Chief's on the north side of the house."

Sid made his way across the yard and saw an unfamiliar firefighter sitting in the middle of the side yard. His turnout coat and white chief's helmet rested at his side; his head drooped between his bent knees.

"Hey, Chief. You okay?"

The man grunted, scrabbled his hands through his damp hair, and looked up. He was not much older than Sid, unusual for the chief of a fire department. The man's eyes barely opened; his skin was pale and blotchy. "Been better. Heat-sick."

"Let me get you some water. Stay put." Sid ran to the ERV, pointed Mandy to the family, and grabbed a couple bottles of water. When he returned, Sid saw that Chief had not only stayed put, he probably hadn't moved at all. Sid squatted and shoved an open bottle of water into Chief's line of vision. "Drink."

With another grunt, Chief poured the water over his face and head. "You need to *ingest*—"

Chief opened one eye, took the second bottle, and drank with long intentional pulls. He emptied the bottle. A lazy smile crinkled the corners of his eyes as his head tilted in question. "Are you some sort of angel?"

Sid laughed and sat down. Cold dampness seeped through his track pants. "Hardly." Chief's color remained peaked; his movements were lethargic, as if he was dragging his limbs through molasses. Sid took his pulse: slow, as expected. "Let's get you to the truck for some air conditioning, huh?"

"Nah, I'm fine."

"You're not. Where are your medics?"

"I'm going to need more than air conditioning to have this conversation." Sid helped Chief to stand and braced him more tightly when he wobbled. "Fuck. They are never going to let me live this down, are they?"

"Nearly passing out on your second day on the job? No. No, they are not."

ONCE IN THE ERV, SID placed a cold cloth on Chief's neck and shoved another open water bottle in front of him. Chief drank and grinned around the lip of the bottle like a drunken frat boy. "Hi."

"You're a mess." Sid grabbed the chief's name from his helmet and started filling out a client report. "Okay, Chief Garner. It's been a couple weeks since your announcement. I've forgotten your first name."

"Eddie." Eddie leaned against the wall and closed his eyes.

"Phone number?" Eddie didn't answer, but stared blankly at a cabinet across the truck. "Shit." Sid stood and knocked Eddie's boots with his foot. "I need to take off your pants."

"On the first date?"

"Mmm, you *are* in there," Sid said as he slipped the suspenders from Eddie's shoulders. Eddie grinned; his head hit the wall of the truck with a dull thud. Sid unclipped the sides of Eddie's pants, and, with a loud rip, pulled the front flap down to undo the Velcro strapping. "Can you help me out? Lift your ass."

With little cooperation, Sid got Eddie down to his station uniform and bare feet. Eddie sighed and wiggled his toes. "Oh, that's better."

Sid rearranged the cold cloth on Eddie's neck. When he sat, Eddie stared at him, chin in hand and a dopey grin on his face.

Regardless of the circumstances, Eddie was classically handsome: sandy blond wavy hair, blue eyes. He had a ruggedness about him that softened whenever he smiled. He would easily fulfill anyone's latent fireman fantasies, Sid's included—provided Sid had such fantasies, which he didn't. He hadn't the time.

"I didn't get your name," Eddie said with more clarity.

"That's because I didn't give it. Phone number?"

"9-1-1."

"For fu—" Sid grabbed his phone, found the phone number of the fire station and put it on the form. "And it's Sid, Sid Marneaux."

"Sid Marneaux, county disaster rescue worker and a hottie to boot. It's my lucky day."

The fireman fantasy faded into a pile of machismo idiocy. "Are you still out of it, or are you naturally a jackass?"

Eddie blinked and grunted as he sat up straight. "I'm sorry. I think my filter melted."

Sid found a box of granola bars. "Eat something. I hear edible tree bark improves brain function."

"Wiseass." But Eddie ate, took the cloth from his neck, and mellowed his drunken gaze into a friendly, professional smile. His cheeks tinged with a blush that looked much healthier than the blotched mess Sid had found earlier. "I'm sure you won't believe me, but I haven't done this before."

"What? Fought a fire or wimped out at one?"

Eddie opened his mouth to bite into the granola bar, but stopped. "You're lucky I have a sense of humor."

Sid cocked an eyebrow. "Probably luckier it didn't melt."

Chief dropped his wet cloth on top of Sid's hand and pencil. "I'll try not to wimp out next time we meet."

Sid grinned and met Eddie's eyes, which were now clear and steady. "I should hope not. My family's meager tax dollars don't pay for that."

* * *

"FAMILY OF FIVE. I PUT them up at the hotel on Station Street for two nights. Food, comfort kits, the dad had a few meds. We got those refilled." Sid pushed the folder of papers to Dottie for her perusal. "I'll call on them after lunch."

"Did you meet the new chief?" she asked, flipping through the paperwork.

"I did. We had to treat him for heat exhaustion." Sid grinned at the extra oomph he was about to put into the story. "Because he tried to rescue a stuffed dog."

She stopped flipping. "What?"

"Before we got there, the middle kid started freaking out about Harvey. He was in the house. Mom and Dad were talking to neighbors, I don't know all the specifics, but I guess Chief flew in. Spent too damned much time in there because he couldn't find Harvey and—"

"Because Harvey is a *toy*. Oh my god."

"Because Harvey *was* a toy. By the time we got there, Chief had almost passed out in the yard."

Her attempts at staid professionalism stopped at the word "toy." Between guffaws, she managed, "Where were the medics?"

"Taking another call. Manpower is down because of that damned failed levy."

"A stuffed dog."

"Named Harvey. I hope the station gives him shit for *months*."

"Did you document it?" Dottie asked between chuckles as she perused the folder of paperwork.

"Nah, I saved him the embarrassment. Just noted supplies and treatment. Mandy took the family into a neighbor's house."

"And you avoided dealing with the kids… how convenient," she teased and wiggled her mouse, clearly ready for her next task.

"It's not like I planned it. Hot fireman. Dead dog. I had other priorities."

She dismissed him with a flap of her hand. "Whatever. Thank you. I need to figure out how to convince that mechanic to fix our education van for half price."

If anyone could do it, Dottie could. Sid took his leave. A pile of recently used practice manikins needed cleaning in the workroom. He wanted to close the door and ignore them, but heard the words of his father, spoken years ago in this very office: "We clean them as soon as possible so bacteria doesn't grow, Zico." When he said he would help Dottie, this was part of the job, like it or not.

With a belligerent sigh, he grabbed sanitary wipes, a box of new lungs, bags of clean plastic faces, and his phone for music. Cleaning *could* lead to daydreaming. Daydreaming could lead to thoughts about a new blue-eyed, smart-assed fire chief who understood the value of a good stuffed animal.

EDDIE'S REASONS FOR VISITING THE C-DRT office the next day were purely professional—mostly. In light of yesterday's debacle, he needed to reintroduce himself. They had a right to know the chief was at least semi-competent.

It also wouldn't hurt to reintroduce himself to Sidney Marneaux.

The office was quiet when he stepped in. He peeked into empty offices until, in the back-most room, he saw the backside of a man bent over and grappling with an awkward nylon bag. The man wore a pale blue knee-length tunic and matching baggy pants and hummed along to soft music. Piles of faceless plastic infants rested on the table next to him.

"Ex—excuse me?" He knocked on the doorframe.

"Just… a second," the man said. He wedged a manikin in the stuffed bag, huffed, and zipped the bag before turning around. "Oh!" Sid's grin was wide and quick. "Hi, Chief."

"Hi. Is this a bad time?"

"No, no. You're fine. This is—" Sid looked at the faceless infants on the table and grimaced. "Creepy. It's creepy." He pointed across the hall. "Let's go to my office."

Eddie sat in the chair by the door. A whiteboard with handwritten class schedules hung next to Sid's desk. A floor-to-ceiling magnetic board held certificates from various training courses and sketches of what looked like menswear, all held in place with magnets from local businesses and high schools. The desk held an inbox of papers, a boxy CRT monitor, and a dish of wrapped chocolate candies.

"It's nice to see you with some color in your cheeks," Sid said.

Hard as it was to believe, Sid Marneaux was even more attractive now that Eddie could see and think clearly. Black shaggy hair framed his face and curled at the collar of his shirt. His eyes were an expressive deep brown, almost as dark as his hair, and his jawline had the slightest dusting of a black beard. Eddie blinked and focused on why he had come. "Yeah, let's... forget that ever happened."

"Except, it did," Sid said with a smirk. "I have the paperwork to back it up."

Eddie groaned. "I'm not sure I've ever been so embarrassed."

"Have they bought you a stuffed dog for your office yet?"

Eddie tried to level a stern gaze, but the flirtation in Sid's eyes unsteadied him. "If they do," he tried anyway, "I will donate it to the family."

"Aw, what a charmer," Sid said, sitting up and leaning on his crossed arms. "Barring that *impulsivity*... why didn't your PASS device activate to alert your crew you were in trouble?"

"I didn't stop until I hit the lawn and deactivated it."

"Not like you had a medic team to help anyway. This damned town loves its money more than its sense."

"Loves its *dollars*... more than its sense?" Eddie grinned. "That would have had more punch, don't you think?" Sid looked as if he wasn't sure whether to be amused or not. Eddie cracked the knuckles of his index finger and proceeded with the real reason he'd come.

"However you look at it, that was not good way to introduce myself. I want to apologize."

"It's fine. Except we're not equipped to help if something more serious had happened."

"You shouldn't be. Which leads to the second reason I came," Eddie said. "Are you the director here?"

"No, I just help out. You want Dottie Mulligan." Sid pulled a business card from his desk. "Here's her contact info. She's a hard one to pin down."

"Thank you." Eddie pocketed the card and grabbed a chocolate. "And you?"

Sid cocked his head, and a curtain of bangs fell over his eyes. "And me what?" He flicked his head to flip the hair out of his face.

Eddie cleared his throat. "Are you hard to pin—" *Jesus.* "Hard to find?"

The pleasant look on Sid's face broke into a huge grin as laughter bubbled out of him. Eddie couldn't stop staring and squeezing the chocolate in his hand. "Are you asking me for my number, Chief?"

"Eddie, please," he said, shoving the chocolate into his pocket. "I—yes. I am. I want to thank you. You were discreet and made an embarrassing situation somewhat enjoyable."

"Only somewhat?"

Eddie chuckled. "No offense, but I don't plan on doing that again."

"You mentioned that, yes."

Eddie rubbed his sweaty palms together; his body was a traitor. "Seriously, let me pay you back. I can cook lunch at the station. Dinner. Something."

"You don't need to—"

"I want to." He popped the knuckles on his middle and ring fingers. "You… intrigued me. We're going to be working together more. It might be nice to get to know you when I'm fully alert."

Sid grinned more smugly than made Eddie comfortable. "You any good?"

"Cooking?"

Sid scrunched his nose and smiled.

"Of course, cooking. Yeah, I won a bunch of community cook-off challenges in Wylie," he said. "Is that a prerequisite for accepting my invitation?"

"I don't want to embarrass you again."

Eddie searched for a quip. Stuck in the depth of Sid's eyes, his mind went blank. Maggie hadn't been wrong about Eddie's dating history: firemen, military men, gym rats—all of them noncommittal, uncommunicative, hairless, and as shallow as a baby's bathwater. But Sid looked him in the eye. He held playful conversations while showing genuine concern for Eddie's well-being and he was gorgeous while doing it.

Sid stood and leaned against the front of his desk. "Give me your phone." After punching in something, he handed it back. "Reply, and we're all set. And Dottie should be back within the hour. Or I can have her call you?"

Eddie looked at the message, at Sid, and at his phone again.

Sid: Woof. It's Harvey.

Eddie typed a reply and stood to go. "I'll give her a call," Eddie said. "And, uh—" he held up his phone and reached for the door. He missed. "I'll call you." On his second try, his hand landed on the knob. "For lunch. Or dinner."

"Something."

Eddie got to his truck without making a bigger ass of himself. He considered hightailing it out of there before Sid could come to his senses and ask him not to use the number. But when he grabbed his seatbelt, he remembered the promise he had made to Sid in the ERV: I'll try not to wimp out next time we meet.

"Fuck."

Back in the C-DRT office, Eddie found Sid cleaning manikins. He stood with a plastic lung in his hand and an open-chested infant manikin on the table. His phone was pinned between his ear and his shoulder.

"Yes. Tomorrow. You said the fabric would be in Chicago by—" Sid nodded to Eddie. "Yes, this is why we pay for expedited—I understand. Tomorrow. Thank you." The phone fell from his shoulder onto the pile of manikins. "Chief?"

"I broke a promise," Eddie said. Sid smiled, the asshole. "I said I wouldn't wimp out. I wimped out." Sid attached the lung to the manikin's "esophagus" and grinned again. *Ravishing* asshole. "Tonight," Eddie said. "It's my turn to cook tonight. I'd like for you to come."

"So soon? Afraid you'll wimp out again?"

"No." Unrelenting asshole. "Yes." Eddie popped a knuckle of his ring finger. "I'm afraid if I blink you'll be gone." Eddie closed his eyes as soon as the words left his lips. He balanced somewhere between "seize the moment," and "stick your foot in it." No doubt, if he kept talking he'd end up with his entire boot in his mouth.

"Mmm. That sounds loaded," Sid said. "We should discuss it over dinner."

Observant asshole. It *was* loaded, of course it was. Loaded with the fact that his life was currently spread between two cities and his heart was splayed across the sky. Nothing that could be discussed over dinner.

"We eat around five-thirty," Eddie said.

"I'll be sure to bring my halo."

"Halo? What?" Sid hooked the plastic lung into the cavity of the manikin's chest. When Sid smirked, Eddie remembered. It was a miracle this man was speaking to him at all. "It might be more fun if you left your halo at home."

Sid laughed and closed the plastic infant's chest flap. "I'll see you tonight, Chief."

IV.
ARIES

LATER THAT AFTERNOON, SID RECEIVED a text from Eddie.

Eddie: Any dietary restrictions? I'm not interested in dealing with an anaphylaxis patient tonight.

At least this one wasn't a pun. His reply to Sid's Harvey joke had read: Sorry, Harvey. Losing you was a doggone shame.

Sid: Thought you said you weren't going to wimp out on me anymore.

Eddie: Not wimping. Lazy.

Sid: Not a beef fan, but I can find my way around a meal.

Eddie: You're our guest; no beef.

Sid arrived at the station and was welcomed by a silent foyer and an empty watch desk. He pushed the buzzer and heard a crash followed by Eddie's voice.

"Someone go out there and let him in. Christ. Who's on desk duty?"

Josh Tremont, an old high school acquaintance, came barreling out of the residential area and wrapped Sid in a tight hug. "Zico! How the hell are you? I can't believe we haven't worked together since you got back!" Josh was a short, stocky man and, other than a thickening in the middle, hadn't changed much since school—overzealousness included.

"I'm not back; I'm visiting," Sid said as he peeled himself out of Josh's back-pounding hug. He followed Josh to the kitchen, which smelled of oregano and garlic. Sid was more taken with the welcoming sight of Eddie's ass bent over the oven door. When Eddie stood, he held two steaming hot baking pans; cheese hissed and bubbled over their edges.

Sid sidled up next to him. "You did *not* need to do this."

"I did. Have you *seen* unfed firemen?"

"Can't say as I have," Sid said. "Nice welcoming committee, by the way."

"Yeah, sorry. Josh—he's not wrapped too tight."

Sid laughed. "No, he never has been."

Eddie quickly tossed a salad, then whistled between his fingers to call the rest of the crew. He grinned at Sid with a toothy and ridiculous smile. "I thought we could eat in my office."

He and Eddie filled their plates and slipped away. Retiring Chief Weston had been gone only a few weeks. Other than old citations crookedly hung on the office's concrete walls and trophies from various charity sporting events covered in dust on top of a large filing cabinet, the room was unlived-in-tidy and lacked any sort of personality, except for the personality Eddie exuded whenever he opened his mouth.

"So, *Zico*—" Eddie said as they sat at a small conference table. "Josh tells me you were both on the Division II Soccer Team. State Champs? Pretty impressive."

"Why do I feel like he's told you my entire history?"

"Let's test." Eddie leaned in, bright-eyed, as though he had been waiting to show off his knowledge. "You're 'Zico' because you're, and I quote, 'The best soccer player the Connelly Miners have ever seen.'"

Sid groaned. "You did talk to Josh."

"It's hard to hear anyone else when he's around," Eddie said. "Although it seems your dad used to speak highly of you to the crew, too."

"He's my biggest fan."

"So, how many goals do you have to nail before you earn that nickname?"

"None. Ma was a huge soccer—excuse me—*football* fan. Said it was the one thing from home she didn't have to carry with her."

"And home was…"

"When she left, East Pakistan. Bangladesh now. She was a rabid fan and I guess when she was pregnant, I was a rabid rib-kicker."

"How in the *world* did she end up here?"

"She followed a handsome American grad student to avoid an arranged marriage."

"Your biggest fan?" Sid nodded. "That's… romantic as hell."

And it was, mostly. Sid tended to leave out the less romantic chapters. Like the chapter in which Ma never saw her parents again. Or the following one, in which they never *spoke* again, the possibility of forgiveness forever lost when her parents were early victims of the attacks on academics and minorities—Hindus in the mostly Muslim country—in the Liberation War. And the final chapter, in which she learned of their deaths while carrying her firstborn, their first grandson. Andrew.

Lost in grief and overcome with a sense of betrayal by her gods, Ma immersed herself in American life. She boxed up the clothes she had loved, the prayers she had prayed. She hadn't allowed her heart to reconnect with her faith and home until she carried Sid in her womb, much later in her life. "A sign," she had said. "A sign that it is time to heal and forgive."

Sid zoned out as he remembered the stories Ma and Baba would share every time the binding of an old photo album softly crackled open. The stories Baba continued to share, once Ma had passed, in a constant effort to keep her—and the few traditions she cherished—very much alive.

Sid felt Eddie's hand on his arm. Eddie was already mid-sentence.

"… here to help take care of him? How old is he?"

"Yeah. He's eighty," Sid said, flipping the lettuce in his bowl, ready to answer the next question about his much older father. "They, uh… thought they were done raising their family, but I had other ideas." He dared a shy grin, embarrassed that he had checked out mid-conversation.

"It's dementia?"

"And heart disease." Sid said.

"How is he doing?"

Sid began with a prepared answer, the one he used for old neighbors and family acquaintances. "He's doing okay. Day to day, you know," but when he stopped fidgeting with his food and looked into Eddie's eyes, his breath caught in his throat. Eddie wasn't making small talk, wasn't being generically kind. He was tuned in, with an understanding and patience at peeling away the complicated layers of caring for an elderly parent that went beyond what Sid had felt from anyone—even his closest friends.

And so, with Eddie's unrushed attention, Sid began to unpack the emotions and frustrations he hadn't yet allowed himself to express. He talked about Anna's overbearing control and her lack of understanding as to why that would make Lou lash out and became belligerent. He talked about Anna's calendars and charts and the daily schedule she kept Lou on. About her refusal to let their dad *do* much of anything. "It's like she's already put him in the ground," he finally said, feeling almost winded after exposing so much of himself, of his family.

"It's hard on the caretakers," Eddie said. "It completely takes over your life."

"It's hard on the patient too. Dad *lived*, you know? Just last year, he rode his bike five miles to the park and back almost every day. This is the man who threw on a backpack with a bunch of college buddies and hiked the fucking Hippie Trail. He didn't stop until he found what he was looking for. He *doesn't* stop. And now he has no choice."

"What was he looking for?"

Sid grinned with memories of his mom and dad and their great love. "He didn't know until he saw her."

Eddie met his smile, and a blush crept up his neck. "Sometimes we don't know what we're looking for until it's sitting across the table from us."

"No," Sid said, unable to pull his gaze away from Eddie. "We don't."

A longer pause rested between them. Eddie finally jolted and stabbed a bite of lasagna. "Then it's good you came back. Sounds like she needs you."

"Except I haven't really," Sid confessed. "I split my time."

"Chicago, right? What's in Chicago?"

As if on cue, Sid's phone vibrated on the table. Rue's face lit the screen. He declined the call.

"Everything," Sid said, stuffing his phone in his pocket. "Just about everything."

With that, Eddie went back to his food. Sid took his lead. They ate and laughed at the overheard shenanigans in the common room. Eddie, finished, sat back in his chair.

"You, um… you said 'everything.' You have someone in Chicago?"

"No," Sid said. "Some*thing*. Bastra." Eddie frowned in question, and Sid explained. "It means 'clothes' in Bangla. I make classic menswear for masculine-presenting women, transmen—people who fall into the cracks of traditional gender identity."

"Really?" Eddie sat up again, fully tuned in. "Did you sew as a kid?"

"Yeah. Ma taught me. I'd unwind from soccer games in the sewing room with her. Incense burning, the hum of the machine, the swish of fabric." At Eddie's visible interest, Sid let loose his passion, reignited anew after months of fighting to keep it lit while juggling his two worlds. "As I got older, I started noticing how clothes can transform people."

"Like when I put on my dress blues, I feel different."

"Yes! You probably carry yourself differently too. Like in school, my friends would drag through the halls, shoulders down, gossip on their tongues, but the moment they put on our soccer uniform, they could make quick tactical decisions and win games."

"My mom was a waitress at a crappy diner," Eddie said. "She'd put on her uniform for work and suddenly she cussed like a sailor."

Sid laughed. "My mom was kind of the reverse. She wore typical western clothes to work: slacks, blouses, low heels. Very classic and professional. But sometimes at home, she'd slip into a *kurta pajama*. They're loose and comfortable and reminded her of home. Librarian to Ma with a quick swap of fabric and fit."

Eddie's smile hadn't faltered as Sid spoke. "So, how does Sid Marneaux transform?"

"Ah. Well. I didn't figure that out until I got homesick in college. I had this massive project due. I was depressed and lonely. As I fussed with a set-in sleeve for this gawd-awful dress, I remembered Ma taught me how to set in sleeves using a *kurta* pattern of hers. So I took a break, researched, used my memory, and made my first *kurta pajama*. I'd never worn them as a kid, but as soon as I slipped it on and looked in the mirror, I was home again. I knew everything would be okay. And now, it's my work uniform."

"Is that what you were wearing—"

"Yesterday, yeah. They're super comfortable and they set me apart *just* enough. As a designer, I like that."

Eddie stared, a peaceful grin still lighting up his face. "So, now you transform your clients."

"We try. My goal is to make clothes work for people, not the other way around."

"How do you juggle all of that from here?"

"Not well, all the time. I have a great assistant who runs the show when I'm gone. We have a new hardworking staff, faithful clientele..."

"And a wish upon a star?"

"That doesn't hurt," Sid said. "I always feel like I'm in the wrong place, though. In Chicago, I should be here helping with Dad, and here..."

"I get it," Eddie said, gathering their plates. "You're not in Chicago. I don't see your dad… Where do you think you should be now?"

Sid's focus was far from his dad, far from Bastra. As they talked, he had sunk deeper and deeper into blue eyes and a chiseled jaw, into a place to breathe and be heard. He wanted more time. "Right now? The little ice cream place up the road sounds really good."

Eddie laughed. "Excellent. I need to find a proper scoop shop."

"I was right about you," Eddie said as he straddled the bench of a wobbly picnic table. Sid wasn't kidding. Connelly Creamery filled the bill: real ice cream shakes too thick for a straw and scoops so dense a triple cone looked like a full meal.

"How so?" Sid dipped into his peach milkshake with a spoon while Eddie unsuccessfully sucked his with a straw. It was the fire scene all over again: competence meets idiocy. This time, the edges of Eddie's brain weren't fuzzy, but he felt just as foolish. Sid's spooning technique, as his thick lips curled over the drippy cream, discombobulated him.

"Intriguing."

"You did *not* have enough brain capacity to even know that big a word at that fire."

"I did too," Eddie said, faking insult. "Why do you think I came to your office the next day?"

"To apologize for becoming a client over a stuffed dog."

Sid dragged his tongue along the curve of his spoon and curled the captured cream into his mouth. Eddie forgot the retort he had been so ready to spout off milliseconds ago.

"So, Chief," Sid said around a grin. "What's *your* story? Did your house burn down as a kid?"

Eddie cleared his throat and swirled his shake. "My, um—yeah." He grinned; there wasn't a graceful way to announce it. "My house burned down when I was eight."

"Oh. Shit."

Eddie laughed. "It's okay. I mean, Mom and I lost everything, but it led me here." Debating how much to tell, Eddie pumped his straw up and down into the thick cream. "Your affection for your dad is—enviable. I don't know who my father *is*. Could have been the old dude who made our shakes…"

"He skipped out?"

"No," Eddie met Sid's eyes again, safe despite the potential embarrassment. "She didn't *know* which guy she'd been with—"

"Oh."

"Yeah. Oh." Eddie tried to slurp some shake into his straw but a chunk of peach blocked his progress. Again. He pumped the straw. Again. "So, just me and Mom. Our house burned down; the station took us under their wing, one lieutenant in particular. I idolized him—he might as well have been Superman."

"Sounds like he was."

"No cape—fire hazard." Eddie took the spoonful of shake Sid presented.

"You're missing the best part with that damned straw," Sid said.

Eddie chewed and swallowed and mentally grappled for something to hang onto. He didn't talk about his childhood. Everyone in Wylie knew his story, and it wasn't the sort of picture to paint when trying to make a good impression. But here, in the dark of night splintered with blaring outdoor spotlights, Sid's quiet curiosity made Eddie's edges fuzz.

As if a beacon back to reality, Sid's phone buzzed. "Sorry—give me two." He took the call; it was obviously someone from Chicago. All Eddie gathered was something about suiting, a late order, not letting someone named Mitchell harass… he missed the name. Sid promised to call back tomorrow morning. He hung up, shoved his phone back into his jeans pocket, and donned a forced smile. "Sorry. So. You wanted to be a fireman because of your Superman."

"Do you need to—"

"No. I'm where I belong." This smile was genuine. "Superman."

"Right," Eddie said, clearing his throat to sound less like an awkward teenager. Sid's smile also discombobulated. "I practically lived at the station. They let me volunteer at sixteen, and I stuck around."

"And now *you're* Superman."

Eddie chuckled and accepted another spoonful of Sid's milkshake. "You of all people know better."

"Even Superman makes mistakes," Sid said easily as if it were true. "So, why did you leave?"

The answers were too complicated for peach milkshakes and deep brown eyes and seductive spoon skills—most of them. "Chief Conrad won't retire until he's dead. His son is next in line, and neither of them have a lick of drive. They work best sitting at a desk making schedules and cutting budgets."

"That's exactly what you replaced here. Connelly is lucky to have you."

"That remains to be seen," Eddie said. "Although I'm anxious to meet Dottie tomorrow."

Sid scraped up the last of his shake and relished the last drop. He handed the spoon to Eddie. "To get the chunks. They're the best part."

Sid held Eddie's gaze as he took the spoon. "Mmm. I'm not so sure about that."

* * *

"Here's what I'm proposing…" Eddie pointed with a French fry, and Dottie looked at him, eyes wide, as if he had the solution to world peace.

Dottie had insisted that Sid join her at lunch with Eddie and, though he should have been at his dad's going through the most recent batch of Bastra's online orders, he complied. It not only involved a free meal, but also an afternoon bumping hands with Eddie as they sat thigh to thigh in a tiny booth, sharing a basket of fries.

"We combine our volunteer forces," Eddie continued. "What happened the other day—disregarding the great pleasure of being disrobed by your lovely assistant—cannot happen again."

Dottie looked at Sid, and he grinned. He had conveniently left that detail out of the report. "No, it can't," she said. "If it were up to the district leadership—" Dottie smirked. "Screw 'em. I love sticking it to them now and again; it's all good."

"Let's make them happy instead," Eddie said. "Let's give your volunteers some more hands-on experience. Versions of this cooperative system exist all over the country. I tried getting it moving in Wylie, but…"

"If you're going where I think you are, Chief Weston didn't want to hear it from me either."

Eddie put down his drink before the straw met his mouth. "An on-scene support unit—"

"For major calls," Dottie continued for him, sitting up straighter. "Huge fires, hazmat, extreme weather." She wiped her hands and pushed her half-eaten burger aside. "So, like… body temp control with misters, heaters in the winter, nutritional support?"

"Exactly," Eddie said. "Your team cares for the clients as usual. We combine and share volunteers. I have retired firemen chomping at the bit to get out there in some fashion."

"And I have college students begging for something to do other than sitting with clients and filling out paperwork."

"And washing trucks," Sid added, before grabbing a handful of fries to shove in his mouth. While this whole exchange was endearing, lady-loving Dottie had yet to take her eyes off of Eddie. She blushed. She touched. She *giggled*.

"God, yes," she said. "Although they're not getting out of that either, the lazy-asses. Your dad would have—"

Sid's phone buzzed with a call from Anna. Sid excused himself and walked deeper into the almost empty restaurant.

"You're coming this afternoon?" Anna said, typically impatient.

"Yes… have I missed yet?"

"No. But you're later than planned—he's asking for you, and it's driving me nuts."

Sid looked back at Dottie and Eddie and rolled his eyes. Dottie's arms flailed as she talked. She never flailed her arms when she talked. "I told you I'd be late."

"You did, and Dad's rattled with the change. Please."

"Tell him I'll be there after *Deal or No Deal*." This satisfied Anna to the degree that Sid could smack a smile on his face and return to the table, right when Dottie patted Eddie's hands in excitement. She also didn't touch people.

"I have a truck," she said as Sid sat down. "Well, *you* have a truck. Starling County had an auction after buying new. I convinced Connelly to bid and we got it for practically nothing."

"The old jalopy at the back of our lot?" Eddie asked. Dottie nodded. "It's going to take some more cash. That thing is barely drivable."

"That's easy," Dottie said. "I raise funds like a badass."

"Something tells me you do everything like a badass," Eddie said. Dottie toyed with the short hair at the nape of her neck, looking about as coquettish as a broad with a penchant for warm beer and college football stats could.

"For fuck's sake…" Sid sucked down the last of his tea until it slurped and gurgled in his mug. He stared at Eddie as if he had unlocked a lesbian secret code.

Dottie excused herself to use the restroom.

"What?" Eddie, popped a French fry into his mouth.

"She is *flirting* with you!"

"What, like you were last night, seductively licking the fat end of a spoon?"

"I have no idea what you're talking about," Sid said. He pulled the straw from his tea and licked the drips from it.

"You. Are evil."

"And you are flirting with my boss." Eddie tried to argue again, but Sid powered on. "Dottie does not flirt. Not with men, not with women..."

"How do you know she doesn't flirt with women? Have you accompanied her in her dating rituals?"

"I have, and your smug face is disturbing."

"But you're smiling," Eddie teased. He looked at the phone still in Sid's hand. "Is your dad okay—"

"Have a chief who has ideas," Dottie said as she returned, in mid-conversation with herself. "And a willingness to follow through with them." She grabbed the bill and pulled her wallet out of her back pocket, snapping her fingers at Eddie as he reached for his own. "Nope. On me. Well, on District. They can spare our county a few paltry..." She headed to the door, leaving them to guess how her sentence might end.

Eddie looked at Sid as Dottie walked out the door.

"You get used to filling in the blanks with her."

They rode back to the office sardined in the front cab of Eddie's station pickup. Before anyone could get out, Dottie chucked Eddie on the shoulder. "We have a training next week. I'd love it if you came and introduced yourself, talked about this new venture."

"I'd be happy to. It's going to be a great program."

Sid unlatched his door, and Dottie grabbed his leg. "Not yet, mister. I have one more thing to say." Sid held his breath. "I never want to eat lunch while you two give each other google eyes over a basket of deep-fried potatoes again. Got it?"

Sid sighed and got out of the truck. Dottie followed and continued her lecture before Eddie joined them. "Seriously," she said, glaring at Sid. "He's hot. But do *not* let me be in the middle of that again. I need a bath or something."

"As long as I don't have to see *you* flirting again, we'll consider it a deal."

"I don't make deals." She tossed a glance at Eddie, who was stifling a laugh as he got out of the truck. "Don't fuck this up, Sid," Dottie said under her breath. "We need this relationship with the fire department."

"Am I crossing a line here?"

"No. No lines," she said. "Fuck who you want. Just not this organization."

"Yes, boss."

Once Dottie left, Eddie walked around his truck and hooked his pinky into Sid's. He stepped forward with his eyes trained directly on Sid's lips. "She caught me."

"She's good like that."

"So, I was wondering, in honor of not wimping out—"

"Can I take you to dinner?" Sid asked, in honor of not letting him. Eddie smiled and tilted his head. "That was my line."

"You fed me last night. We have a great Thai place north of town."

"Let me drive? I need to learn my way around here."

"Sure. Tomorrow?"

Eddie brought their hands to his lips and pressed a soft kiss to Sid's knuckles. "Tomorrow."

V.
SAGITTARIUS

"Hi, Daddy!" Adrian's face hadn't come into complete focus on Eddie's computer screen before he stepped out of the shot. "Look what I built! It's a dinosaur city!"

"Big enough for the T. Rex?"

"I—oh." Adrian darted to his tabletop Lincoln Log, Lego, and block creation and pulled a small tyrannosaurus figure from one of the streets. "This one fits. I might need to fix bridges for the seismosaurus, though. He's super tall."

"He's the tallest. Come here so I can see your face."

His eyes round with excitement, Adrian brought the dinosaur with him and started over. "Hi, Daddy!"

"Tell me about today."

"Nana took me to see the butterflies!"

"She did?"

Sharon peeked into the screen and waved. "We need new crayons," she said. "He worked them all down to the nub trying to draw every last one we saw."

"I have white. And that yellow no one can see," Adrian said as he danced the dinosaur across the desk in front of him. The loose, droopy curls around his face bounced with each motion, and, when he looked at the screen, one sagged over his right eye. Eddie reached out to fix it, stopped and laughed at himself. "Did you try to touch me? Daddy... it's a *computer!*"

"I know. I miss you."

"Do you have new friends yet? You won't miss me so much if you make new friends."

"I do. I had lunch with a couple yesterday and I'm going to dinner with one of them tonight." He slid a look over Adrian's shoulder to Sharon. She smiled and gave him a thumbs up.

"What do they look like? I'll draw a picture."

Eddie described Dottie and her rust-colored shirt, the faint freckles on her pink skin.

"Freckles like mine?" Adrian asked.

"Yes, except hers are more like dust on her skin."

"Mine are like polka dots," Adrian said. "What color is her hair?"

Eddie told him that she had short brown hair, and that the items in her pockets jangled when she walked. "She has bright blue eyes and a deep, fun laugh."

"How did you meet her?"

"She helps people after they have a fire."

"So, she's a good guy."

"She's a really good guy."

"Is the other friend a good guy?"

"He is, and... he's tall—taller than me!"

"Oh my goodness, no way—you're the tallest. Like a seismosaurus."

"Not anymore," Eddie said. He told Adrian about Sid's black hair and almost black eyes and brown skin— "Golden brown, like he was kissed by the sun," he added with a wispy sigh.

Adrian yawned and smacked his lips. A sappy daddy made for a dull daddy, apparently. "I'm gonna get a snack. I'll show you the picture tomorrow after we get more crayons."

"Get Nana—hi." Sharon's exhausted face filled the screen. The lift to her eyebrow seemed impatient as she waited for more information. "Yes, it's a date."

"I can tell. 'Kissed by the sun?' Really, Eddie?"

"Leave me alone; I normally date—"

"Dunderheads."

"Did Maggie keep *any* of my secrets from you?"

"Mmm, no. Probably not."

Eddie was grateful to have her looking out for him. For Adrian. "I'm not sure what to do with a guy who does more than grunt."

"It's good for you—your dating life has always given me stress."

"You're welcome. Is Ade sleeping okay?"

"No, he's waking a few times a night. Screaming." She pushed her long gray hair behind her ear. And when she looked at the screen with a tilt to her head, he saw Maggie's face—just as he did with Adrian—only gently aged and radiant. "He doesn't talk; he cries out, takes some hugs, and goes to sleep."

"Shit. I haven't slept this well since… it's been a while. I feel guilty as hell."

"Don't. Get him home with you, and you'll both settle in. If you're lucky, this *good guy* will be a kid whisperer or something."

"I haven't told him about Adrian. He's here temporarily, so I'm—" Adrian skipped behind Sharon with a box of Goldfish crackers. Eddie's thought derailed. "I don't know what the hell I'm doing. All I know is he makes me feel like I'm living instead of dying."

"Honey…"

"I'm being melodramatic." Mostly. "I met the guy three days ago and I—"

"You don't have to explain; it's wonderful." They shared a look, the "Maggie" look that reminded him she would be happy for him. She would have waited with a bottle of wine and a bag of barbecue potato chips and insisted on hearing every damned detail.

"Green shirt or blue?" Eddie asked.

"Dear god, you live in blue. Don't you have a nice buttery yellow or something?"

"Probably. I'll go with that. Give Ade a kiss for me. I didn't get to count sleeps with him before he ran off."

"Twelve sleeps 'til the full moon," she said. "Have a great evening, Eddie."

"You did not get me a flower." Sid sniffed, grinned over the top of the bloom and disappeared into his kitchen. His hair was ruffled, a tape measure was draped around his neck, and he had almost stabbed Eddie with the scissors in his hand when he'd reached for the flower.

On his way over, Eddie had ignored his GPS as she implored him to "Take a left onto Beckham Road." Instead, he'd stopped at a roadside stand. The purveyor had told him that orange roses meant desire and fascination. Eddie didn't know if the meaning was true, but the beautiful bloom and persistent man had convinced him to cough up some cash. Besides, Sid did have a way of stirring desire and fascination.

On the road, he'd engaged in a one-sided conversation about his concerns for the evening. Lady GPS's concern was to get him to his destination. "Continue on Crest Ridge for five hundred yards, then turn right onto North Canfield."

"He's a fashion designer, for god's sake," Eddie said, waving a car to change lanes in front of him. "Creative and smart and he's not even here when he's here because his dad's—his dad is sick. His dad is sick, and I asked him on a date. I'm an asshole."

"Turn right onto North Canfield."

"Except technically he asked me first. Maybe he needs a break. This is no big deal."

"Your destination is on the left." GPS voices were stupid. This was not a destination. It was a break—for both of them.

Sid had greeted Eddie not only with scissors in hand, but with a swath of navy suiting draped over one shoulder and another piece in his other hand. Eddie quickly decided that the faint scent of incense in the apartment was not a painful reminder of Maggie's absence, but a sign that she approved. It was clear: Tonight was about two distracted men in need of a better distraction.

Sid returned from the kitchen with the rose in a juice glass and set it on an end table. "No one's given me flowers before."

"I should start a new trend."

Sid grabbed his fabric and scissors. "I'm sorry. I lost track of time— give me five minutes?" He came back in four, furiously texting. "Sorry. Again," he finally said. "I'm almost tempted to leave this damned thing here."

"Is this a good time? Should we reschedule?"

"If I wait for a good time, I'll never *have* a good time." Sid pocketed his phone. "Dad's cared for, I skirted a potential disaster up home, I'm where I belong." He grabbed Eddie's hand on the way to the door. "You and me tonight, okay?"

Eddie mentally pocketed his own cares. For the moment, he too was right where he belonged.

"So, this is Connelly High," Sid said as he directed Eddie to the back of the campus. Stories of college and the fire academy had filled their dinner conversation. After Sid had won the glare-off as to who would pay the bill, Eddie had asked for a tour of the county. No tour would be complete without a trip to the favorite place of Sid's youth.

"And this… is where the magic happened." Small-scale stadium lights, still lit from an earlier match, shone onto the soccer field. The gate into the field was unlocked. They stepped inside.

"How many goals did you score on this field?" Eddie asked.

"No idea. I had a career record of a hundred seventy-two, but I knocked those in everywhere."

"Damn, you were a big deal."

"Nah, around here, *American* football is the big deal." Sid walked around the center circle and spun around. "It's smaller than I remember."

"You're bigger," Eddie said, grabbing Sid's hand. "Does it feel weird being here?"

They sat in the middle of the field. Its size seemed to stretch out, and perspective was restored. "It does. It's been a long time." Sid lay on his back and tugged Eddie to join him. "And in all the time I spent on this field," he said, "I never did this."

"Did you want to?"

"No offense to present company, but I dreamt it would have been after a winning game with Tyrone Lemmon. Built more for baseball than soccer. Lousy stamina on the field—great ass."

Eddie laughed. "Jon Marcum. Lousy basketball player. Got cut our senior year. Thighs… for days."

"Oh, what could have been."

"Eh, I dated too many exactly like him. We didn't miss anything."

Sid looked away from the lights to find Eddie staring at him. "Maybe it wasn't the right time."

"Maybe it wasn't the right guy."

With a loud pop and a whoosh, the field lights shut off. After laughing at their mutual squeaks of surprise, Sid wiggled closer. They fell silent and refocused on the night sky.

"Is that the North Star?" Eddie asked.

"Yep, Polaris. See? It's the tip of Little Dipper's handle. Big Dipper—Ursa Major, my dad would correct—is to the west of it."

Neither moved or spoke, letting the vastness of the sky rearrange perspective once again.

"I had a nice time tonight," Sid said.

Eddie reached for Sid's hand. "So did I."

The quiet they shared was new for Sid. Everyone had something to say: plans to be organized, money to be made, successes to be touted, or worse, failures to be shamed. As they lay there, the ground cooled on his back; Eddie's hand rested comfortably in his. Sometimes, silence sang the most beautiful of tunes.

"So," Sid finally said. "My place isn't much… but I have fresh peaches. Will you come?"

"I'd love to." Eddie sat and pulled them up to stand. His cheeks were flushed, his hair was ruffled, but his attention remained on the sky.

"Hey," Sid said, brushing his finger along Eddie's cheek. When Eddie turned, Sid caught a sadness in Eddie's eyes he'd not seen before. Sid knew the sky was for dreaming and melancholy, for longing and love. With his finger at the curve of Eddie's chin, Sid kissed him, lingering when Eddie's smile bent beneath his lips. "Thanks for being my first."

DISNEY WORLD MIGHT CLAIM TO be the best place on earth, but Eddie would argue that this place—reclining against Sid's chest while watching a mindless Seth Rogen movie, all cares, concerns, and worries tossed into the dark of night—beat out any amusement park's claim to fame.

When they returned from the high school, they had stood in Sid's kitchen and shared bowls of succulent peaches swimming in bourbon cream, Sid slipping slices of dripping peaches into Eddie's mouth, Eddie sucking juice and drops of cream from Sid's fingers. By the time they'd chosen the movie and fallen onto the couch, Eddie's limbs had loosened and his mind was free of any thought beyond the softness of the couch under his ass, the solidity of Sid's chest bracing his own back, and the warmth of Sid's arms tucked under his own. Even the occasional interruption of Sid's phone and his swift swipe to ignore the calls and texts couldn't have disrupted the evening.

Now the credits rolled. Neither of them moved except for Eddie checking the time on Sid's cable box: twelve forty-five. Eddie dared to adjust to relieve the numbness of his right butt cheek. He didn't want to invite the real world in yet, or to interrupt the soft rhythm of Sid's breathing.

The real world meant morning. Morning meant painting the kitchen in the new house, replacing light fixtures in the bathrooms, stripping wallpaper from what would be Adrian's bedroom walls. Eddie started negotiating his tasks. The kitchen could wait until after Adrian came home; he had all day Sunday for everything else, and, if push came to shove, those boards on the side porch could wait.

"You okay?" Sid's voice was raspy soft; his breath was warm in Eddie's ear.

"Yeah." He shifted again and sat up. "Sorry; I started tomorrow already."

Sid looked at the clock, sighed, and stretched. "It is tomorrow."

"It is." His eyes lingered on Sid's mouth, then moved up to his eyes. He could probably put off fooling with the light fixtures another day or two. "I should go."

"You have a lot going on tomorrow," Sid said as he stood. Eddie almost whimpered. "I'd offer to come help, but—"

"You're on dad duty, right?" Eddie stretched and groaned as he stood. He caught Sid staring at his stomach as it peeked out of the bottom of his shirt.

"I, uh—I am. Thought I'd bring him lunch, see if he can help make a batch of ginger—"

The kiss Eddie planted on Sid definitely ranked better than Disney World. Sid's lips gave in to Eddie's; a soft moan passed between them. Eddie held Sid's face, guided him so as not to miss one inch of his mouth: the full bottom lip, sweet as succulent peaches; the upper lip and its stubbled cupid's bow; the corners that slipped away as Sid smiled and chuckled at Eddie's unrelenting chase as he approached for his own taste. Eddie had been imagining kissing those lips since the moment he'd looked up from his heat-sick condition and seen Sid staring down at him.

"Ginger cookies," Sid said on a gasp. His hair tickled Eddie's nose as he worked his lips down Sid's neck and up to his earlobe. "Shit... Eddie?"

Sid's arms weighed on his shoulders. His fingers scratched at the nape of Sid's neck in a gentle invitation to stay put, kiss more, be near. "Mmm?" Eddie couldn't stop; Sid's skin was like silk under his lips and hinted of salt from the humid night air.

"C'mere… let me… *fuck*." Sid sucked Eddie's bottom lip and stepped back. His grin was wicked; his breath was uneven and shallow. "We should have been doing this instead of watching Seth Rogen."

"We'll plan better next time." Eddie was not quite ready to give up *this* time. Sid looked at Eddie's mouth and touched his tongue to his own bottom lip. "Kiss me to the door?"

"Don't forget your sandals." But Sid was on him before he could orient himself to where his sandals might be. He walked Eddie backward and stumbled from the carpet to the foyer until he had him against the door with frantic, perfect sweeps of his tongue into Eddie's mouth, nips on his lips, and a tug of his hair and his hips, urgent, pressing.

Eddie couldn't have caught his breath if he'd wanted to. He slid his hands down Sid's back to his ass and pulled him in hard and harder. Sid's fingers tightened on Eddie's waist until they both came up for air, laughing and kissing. A blush heated Eddie's face until all he could say was, "Fuck, that was not a smooth exit."

"That was not an *exit*." Sid kissed Eddie's temple and kept his lips there as their hips continued small undulations, press and release, yes and no and yes *please*. With one more shift, Eddie felt Sid's cock, hard against his hip.

"Sid."

Sid pulled away with a lazy smile and kissed Eddie's swollen lips once more. "Do you…" Sid started. Eddie rolled his hips without thinking, and Sid groaned, closed his eyes, then stared at the door next to Eddie's head as if re-centering himself. "Do you *have* to leave?"

"Tell me to stay, and I won't have to leave."

Sid took Eddie's wrists, kept his eyes unwavering on Eddie's, and brought his hands against the door so they trapped either side of Eddie's head. His dark eyes were commanding and sure. "Stay." Eddie wished to make an equally sexy reply, but now Sid's tongue was doing amazing tricks at the curve of his neck. He nipped Eddie's earlobe and trailed his tongue along its shell to whisper, "Kiss me to the *bedroom*, Eddie."

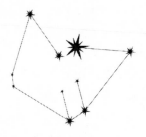

VI.
LYRA

"Kiss me to the bedroom," sounded good—in theory. On the way past an end table, they almost knocked over a lamp when Sid flung Eddie's shirt off. Sid's shirt had too many buttons for Eddie's patience. His failed attempts were interrupted by his broken chants of *"Skin, your skin, you taste like... like..."*

Sid wouldn't find out what Eddie thought he tasted like. And as buttons sprinkled the hallway, he couldn't imagine he would ever care— not as long as Eddie continued to mouth at his shoulders. As long as Eddie kept dragging his tongue along every valley of Sid's clavicle and neck, Sid couldn't imagine he would ever care about much of anything again.

They stopped with a solid thump along the wall between Sid's workroom and linen closet. Eddie kissed and stared and ran his hands over Sid's shoulders and chest as if he had never seen a man before, as if Sid were an anomaly to be revered. He unbuttoned Sid's shorts, and his knuckles brushed against the underside of Sid's cock. Sid groaned and stopped him.

"Wait. Shit." He laughed and pointed to his bedroom. "I need to find—" He swiped his hand down his face. Eddie was undeterred, and continued to massage the bulge in Sid's shorts. "Go in and wait for me. I'm not sure if I packed condoms."

Eddie snorted, stopped his delicious motions, and stepped away with a kiss. "I have some in my car, if you come up empty-handed."

Sid pointed to the room. "I'll be right in."

Sid mumbled and cursed as he shuffled through a box filled with cold medicine and extra toothbrushes. The sexiest man with the most magical lips waited for him in his bedroom, and he hadn't had the foresight to—his hand landed on a promising shape. He shook the box and peeked in. Three. With a gentle squeeze to his still-very-clothed cock—as if to say, "Hang tight, buddy; relief is on the way"—Sid shut the closet door and took a couple of deep breaths.

"So sorry," he said on the way to his room. "Nothing like breaking the—"

Eddie had dimmed a bedside lamp to its lowest setting, turned down the bed, and now sat propped up against the headboard. His pants were undone. He stroked his dick over the thin fabric of his underwear.

"Well, aren't you a welcome sight," Sid said.

"I'm getting lonely," Eddie said, trying on a pout.

Sid leaned against the doorframe and walked a condom packet between and across his fingers. "Looks like you're doing fine on your own."

"I bet you could do better." Eddie's hand kept stroking steadily; his eyes were unwavering. Sid flung the condom across the room like a Frisbee. "One?"

"Eager." He flung another, and, arriving at the foot of his bed, crawled on. He pulled Eddie's hand from his cock and placed the third condom in his palm. "Three's the limit tonight, I'm afraid."

"Mmm, I think we'll manage." Eddie raked his fingers through Sid's hair, pushing it over his ear. With a gentle tug, he pulled Sid on top of himself, leaving all pretense of "I should go," and "It's getting late," and "Maybe next time," in the living room where it belonged.

Eddie rolled them over and settled between Sid's legs, picking up right where they'd left off in the hall. Suckling and biting with wet kisses, he covered Sid's neck and shoulders, stopping long enough to refuel at Sid's mouth. Sid's focus splintered between Eddie's lavishing mouth and the muscles that flexed and moved under Sid's hands. It had been so long, too long since he had cared, taken the time, allowed a goddamned moment to enjoy the body of another.

Eddie worked his mouth down Sid's chest, nipples, and the slight ripple of muscle along his stomach. From right to left flank, he slid up for another kiss and disappeared again to mouth along the waistband of Sid's shorts. He popped Sid's shorts open and lowered the zipper so slowly Sid could have sworn he felt each tooth release.

"You're a tease," Sid said, lifting his hips in search of Eddie's hand or his mouth—the solid pressure of his chin would do—as Eddie eye-fucked him over his clothes.

"You're gorgeous."

Eddie kissed the damp spot on Sid's boxer briefs and stopped. His eyes landed on the boxer's waistband. Sid's heart stopped. If further proof was needed that he hadn't planned to end up naked tonight…

"You have your last name on your underwear?"

"I… there's a good reason—"

Eddie chuckled and bent to kiss the M hovering at Sid's left hip bone. He kissed across the band, A-R-N—"There has to be a story here"—puffs of warm air sent gooseflesh across Sid's stomach and made his dick twitch with each faint brush of Eddie's cheek on his shaft—E-A-U—"I'm not sure we should continue until I hear it"—X. With a satisfied smirk, he sat back on his own feet. "I know you're not this vain."

"I'm not, it was a—" Sid reached for Eddie's hand to pull him down, but Eddie stayed firm. "Can we… I mean, your lips, and you were—" He sighed at the stupid look on Eddie's face. "Nothing is happening until you hear this, is it?"

"Nope."

"You have this, as you say—*gorgeous*—man underneath you, and you'd rather hear about his staff's stupid sense of humor."

"Yes. I can kiss you while you talk. Does that work?" Eddie bent down and placed a tongue-led kiss right under Sid's navel.

"No. Fuck me, no. It does not because—" Sid pushed him back, shrugged himself all the way out of his shorts so the whole ridiculousness was exposed. He lay back down and Eddie straddled him again. "One. I don't normally wear them." Sid huffed. "I need to do laundry, okay? Two." Sid hissed as Eddie traced his tongue around Sid's nipples. "Some of my girls wanted branded boxer briefs. We were trying out a bunch of—" He hiked up on his elbows, hoping that when he was finished, they could *get to it*. "Fonts. Why do you *care*?"

Eddie brushed his lips down the center of Sid's abdomen. "Shall I stop?"

"Three, my assistant is a smartass and ordered these during our trial run, and—" Eddie swirled his tongue around the rim of Sid's navel. "Fuck. Me. They fit. They're comfortable, okay?"

Eddie smiled. His shorts hung off his hips, and Sid was about to explode with a need to touch, to lick at the lines of muscle peeking out, taunting him. "I think it's cute," Eddie said, unmoving.

"What are *you* sporting there, Versace?" Sid asked. He yanked Eddie down and hooked his leg around his hips. He wasn't letting him disappear again. "Wylie City-embossed Fruit of the Loom?"

Eddie wiggled down. His lips were a constant dance all over Sid's skin. "You wish." He curled down the elastic band and tongued the tip of Sid's cock. Sid stopped trying to talk; his bones went limp as Eddie stripped him naked.

Eddie stood to slip off his own shorts and briefs and returned to press slow kisses up Sid's legs before Sid could whimper at his absence. He settled between Sid's thighs. "*My* briefs—" Eddie kissed and nipped at the skin *around* Sid's crotch. Sid squirmed beneath him as he chuckled, "Are big baggy boxers. With a fireman on the hip."

"Eddie, fuck…" He wanted to sound commanding. All that came out was a breathy giggle and a gasp of those two barely coherent words.

"His hose snakes up the fly." Eddie licked the valley between Sid's thigh and crotch and spread his legs farther apart. He nipped at the tendon as it pulled taut, then sucked the tender skin around it. "They're incredibly sexy."

Sid moaned and laughed. "Blow me, Eddie." His cock ached for touch.

"I'm working on it, babe." Eddie hiked up from between Sid's legs and lingered over Sid's body as if he wanted to devour him.

"Eddie, please." He wrapped his hand around himself, capturing the moisture from the tip. Finding Eddie's eyes on his, he brought his finger to his mouth and licked off the pre-come. "Put your mouth on me."

"Oh, fuck."

With a swirl of tongue around the tip of Sid's dick, Eddie stopped teasing. Sid sank his fingers into Eddie's hair as Eddie encased him in the perfect suctioned heat of his mouth—a glorious drag of pressure as he pulled up and bounced over the head, licked the frenulum, gathered every drop from the slit. If Sid had thought Eddie's mouth and lips were masterful before…

Sid held on, wanting to feel Eddie's full body on his, but having no desire to stop the long strokes of Eddie's tongue up the underside of his dick; to release the heat of Eddie's hands, firm on his hips; or to still Eddie as his hand slipped between Sid's legs to cup his balls and roll them in his fingers. His entire body on fire with need, Sid squirmed and whined and batted his hand around on his bedside table.

Eddie popped off and licked his lips; his fingers kept stroking over and under Sid's balls. "Looking for something?"

"Lube."

Eddie pressed Sid's puckered hole with the tip of his finger, kissed his hip, and stood. His dick stood straight, long, and pink-tipped. A light brown patch of hair matched the trail from his navel and the soft dusting that covered his thighs. Sid's fingers brushed along his thigh, then hooked into his hand. Eddie bent to the drawer and brought Sid's fingers to his lips. "You'll tell me what you like?"

Sid felt drunk. His bones were fluid and weighed down. "I like *you*. Please come back."

With a smile, Eddie pulled the lube from the drawer, tossed it onto the bed, and took Sid in his arms, skin on skin. Soft friction built as their dicks slotted together, pressing and retreating with each shift, with each kiss. Sid rubbed his calf up and down Eddie's leg, until, locking eyes, he bent his knee, open, ready. "Want you."

Eddie gathered lube on his fingers and slipped them past Sid's balls to his rim. Pressing slowly, he slid in a finger; his eyes stayed on Sid's to kiss him, to tell him how beautiful he was. "Want to be good for you."

Sid held Eddie's wrist. "You're good for me." Sid fucked himself on Eddie's fingers. "Be in me."

As soon as the words left his mouth, Sid grabbed a condom and rolled it on Eddie. Whispers of "hurry" and "come on" and "so impatient" ghosted between them until Sid fell onto his back and slipped a pillow under his hip.

Eddie stared and stroked himself. He looked awestruck. "Sid, my god." And Sid, overwhelmed by both an electric physical *need* and the buzz of emotional connection that hummed every time their eyes met, understood. To be heard, to be teased, to be *wanted* like this... Sid had forgotten.

Frozen in each other's gaze, they found a steady, easy pace. The world stilled around them, save for the pat of skin on skin and breathy huffs and soft groans when Eddie pulled away to watch Sid move and beg to get *on* with it.

"Kiss me... your mouth," Sid said. Eddie's blue eyes were dark with focus; a sheen of sweat covered his chest and neck. He folded Sid's thighs to his chest and did as asked, giving him a dirty kiss, sucking Sid's tongue into his mouth as he sank deeper and sent rolls of sweet pleasure through him with every thrust. He tucked his face into Sid's neck, his hot breath on Sid's skin, pushing and filling.

"Want to see you," Eddie said as he unfurled, released Sid's legs, and pulled Sid up onto his thighs. "Touch yourself, let me watch you." When Sid wrapped his hand around his cock, Eddie stared at Sid's face. His hips gently rolled in and in as Sid's motions sped. Eddie kept with him, deeper, faster; his fingers, holding on tight, pressed into Sid's thighs.

Sounds of heady, masculine sex filled the room and Sid's senses. He was close, too close, not wishing for an end, but needing the release. His body was tight and coiled, ready to unravel, but Eddie kept the pace; his eyes were on Sid's cock peeking in and out of Sid's fist. "There you go. Come on, sweetheart," and with Eddie's ragged words, Sid came with a shout. White ropes of come shot up onto his stomach and chest with each pulse.

"Oh god, yes…" Eddie grabbed Sid's thigh and thrusted harder, lost to his own pleasure until he toppled over the edge, bucking and sinking into Sid with each orgasmic wave.

Sid curled Eddie, winded and ruined, to him. After long moments, after untangling from one another, Eddie ran his finger through the wetness on Sid's chest and chuckled as Sid's breath hitched at his touch. "Washcloth?"

Sid brought Eddie's finger to his mouth and licked it clean. "Closet in the hall."

"You are too much." Eddie kissed him, sweeping his tongue into his mouth for a taste before leaving the bed. When he returned, they cleaned themselves and sank into the sheets.

"Will you stay until morning?" Sid asked, unable to imagine sleeping alone.

"Show me around your kitchen, and I'll even cook you breakfast."

* * *

SID HANDED EDDIE A TOOTHBRUSH, talking around his own. "Here."

"Are you saying I have morning breath?"

Sid pushed the toothpaste in front of Eddie and grinned in the mirror. The fact that he could function at all was a miracle. He wouldn't be out of bed had they not run out of condoms.

Sid's skin tingled, his dick felt as if it wouldn't work right, and the hickey on his left flank made him realize that no, his dick worked fine. It jumped every time Sid caught the sight of the discoloration in the mirror.

The last place he wanted to be was his father's, and yet the reality of his day lingered in the background of every move they made.

"I have track pants in that bottom drawer. T-shirts are in the drawer above. I don't know where our shirts *are* from last night."

"Ah, no sense doing the walk of shame to my car."

"Hey now. We've had…" Sid calculated as he dried his mouth. "We've had four dates already. No shame."

"Four?" Eddie asked around his toothbrush.

"The blind date at the fire, which you were half conscious for. You still owe me."

"For what?" Eddie spit and rinsed and stared at his toothbrush. "Illicit use of nonprofit water? It wasn't even cold."

Sid grabbed Eddie's toothbrush and stuck it in the holder with his. "It was wet, and you were an idiot."

"You also took off my pants, so I call that even."

"I call it a date." Sid hip-checked Eddie and turned to lean against the sink. "Then, a two-fer. You cooked me dinner, followed by milkshakes where you failed at Sucking 101."

"Milkshakes should be sucked, not spooned. The peaches were too big."

"After last night, I'd say you have the power to suck a bowling ball through a straw. I don't want to hear it."

"You're welcome."

"Our *fourth* date was last night. Therefore, no shame." Sid sucked in a breath as Eddie stepped closer. His darkened eyes and parted lips looked predatory; his hand landed on the knot of the towel wrapping Sid's waist. "We're out of condoms," Sid reasoned.

"I have some in my car."

"You're naked. Ish."

"You told me where I can find some clothes."

Sid cleaned a smudge of toothpaste from the corner of Eddie's lip with the tip of his tongue. "At least find pants, so I can take them off when you come back in."

*   *   *

IN TWO DAYS AND NIGHTS, Sid and Eddie had fallen into a pattern. No matter what demands the days might put on them—from the station or Chicago, from Sid's dad or Eddie's home repairs—nighttime was reserved for them. Sid ignored his calls from Chicago and tended to them in the morning, and Anna always had bedtime duty with their father. Lower-ranking officers rotated the night shift at the station.

Sid spent this day bent over his worktable, cutting sample shirt patterns for a meeting in Chicago. The ginger-colored pincord cotton he tested was light, airy, and easier to work with than he had anticipated. By dusk, when Eddie sent a text from the premiere C-DRT and auxiliary team meeting, Sid's back ached, his head pounded, and he yearned for the nightly comfort he found in Eddie.

Eddie: You know I love Dottie, but this meeting is dull.

Sid: If you're looking for entertainment, I'm not your man. I'm decrepit and cranky.

Eddie: Fair enough. I'll start the show: why is our speaker dressed like Popeye?

Sid took that as a cue to take a break. He closed his workroom door on the unfinished shirt and made himself comfortable on the couch.

Sid: Your speaker is wearing a sailor collar and neckerchief? Carting around a can of spinach?

Eddie: Sadly, no spinach. Didn't Popeye wear a blue and white striped shirt sometimes? High-waisted navy pants? This guy even has freaky thick, hairy forearms.

Sid: Oh! Jerry! He used the scare the shit out of me when I was a kid. Does he still have bad breath?

Eddie: I don't want to know how you know he has bad breath.

Sid: Corncob pipe. Smelly breath.

Eddie: Of course. I'm wondering if he brought Olive Oyl—that would make this more interesting.

Sid: She's cheating with Bluto.

Fifteen minutes later, break over, Sid threaded his machine to begin stitching shirt pieces together.

Eddie: What happened to the Pope when he went to Mount Olive?

Sid: What? The Pope, Mount... what?

Eddie: Popeye almost killed him.

For fuck's sake.

By the time Eddie arrived that night, Sid had finished the shirt and found time to eat dinner. He handed Eddie a beer, watched his Adam's apple bob as he gratefully took a couple pulls, and took the bottle back.

"Did you eat?"

"Yeah," Eddie said, kicking off his shoes. "We need to get Josh off the cooking schedule. He'd burn water—"

Sid was on him before he finished; he was uninterested in one more second wasted on Josh, on Bastra. In a week, Sid would be in Chicago without this treasured, glorious unwinding at the end of the day. Without this man. Without his stupid humor, his mischievous smile, and his wicked tongue doing delightfully obscene things.

Tomorrow he would juggle the demands of his father, of C-DRT, and of Bastra all over again. But the night belonged to them.

* * *

TWO DAYS LATER, WHILE SID was half awake and fumbling in his fridge for milk, Rue called.

"Hey, baby. How's it going?"

Rue called Sid "baby" on only two occasions: when she was proud of him and when she had to tell him something he wouldn't want to hear. Sid couldn't think of any reason for pride. He groaned and took a seat at his kitchen table. It was only 7:30 a.m., and he was already in trouble.

"What'd I do?"

"It's nothing, you know?" she said, taking a long, loud drag from her cigarette. "You've just been—"

"Hard to reach."

"Hard to—yes. At night. And I know you've got your dad, and we're all so on board with that shit, but Sid…"

"Trial Line's going into production," Sid said. "I was there last quarter and now I'm here."

Bastra had begun as a custom-only company offering classic shirts, suits, trousers, and jackets. The prices were high, the production was slow, and the clients were loyal because they knew they were getting true bespoke clothing. To broaden the client base and make pieces more affordable, they'd added a quarterly campaign: the Trial Line. Taking into account suggestions and requests from clients—"I'd love a heavier-weight dress shirt for the winter," or "I love the leg cut of these, but the low waist hits my gut funny"—and Rue and Sid's professional feel for the market, they now designed four small, limited-run ready-to-wear lines every year.

Sid had been working on the creation of the winter line while in Connelly. Unlike seasons past, the fall line was in production now in Sid's absence. The summer line had been shipped before he left. Sid had always been in Chicago to juggle the transition. They'd planned his visit to Connelly poorly this time.

"You were here," Rue said. "I can put out fires like the best of them, but—"

Ha. Ha. Put out fires. Like Eddie—his delinquency-encouraging…
boyfriend? No. Yes? Lover? Eww, that made them sound like creepy
aging hippies.

"But I've been unfocused," Sid confessed. "I'm sorry. Do I need to
fly back early?"

"No. But, maybe a conference call this afternoon? No one's angry,
but it might be a sign of goodwill."

"Yes. Sure. I'll—" Sid stopped. Rue wouldn't have made this call
on her own. She'd have kicked him in the ass in person the next time
he landed in town. "Mitchell put you up to this, didn't he?"

Rue answered with a crackle of her lit cigarette.

"Okay, I hear you. I'll call at two your time. Make sure he's there."

"How's your dad?"

"Forgetful. Moody. In fact, I have morning duty today, so I need
to fly. Thanks for running interference with Mitchell."

"See you in a few days."

As promised, Sid made a conference call to apologize to his staff for
his recent scattered attention. He listened as they complained about
things like the brand new serger that had jammed for the fifth time
in two days, "goddammit, how much did we *pay* for that?" When he
hung up, he arranged for a service call.

Jammed sergers weren't crises in Connelly. Delayed orders held low
value. Fading memories, difficult sisters, filling holes that his father
had left in the community carried more weight here. And admittedly,
a budding relationship had given Sid a soft place to land when it all
piled on.

Before his rendezvous that night with Eddie, he finished another
sample pincord shirt—in aqua—and worked on sketches of layout
ideas for their website redesign.

The next day, he listened as the web designer told him that much
of his design would cost twice what he'd budgeted.

That evening, his dad dropped a bowl of mint chocolate chip ice
cream—the good, *green* kind with real sugar and mysterious ingredients

59

that Anna always groused about letting him have—and bitched and griped and complained about how inadequately Sid cleaned it up. About the inappropriately small scoops when Sid refilled his bowl. About how mad Ma would be when she came home and found that her favorite dish had broken because—there was no because. Because Lou was mad and embarrassed and confused.

Sid was at the end of his give-a-damn.

Whatever happened during a given day, Sid couldn't wait for his night with Eddie. They might talk about their days over a beer at Sid's rickety kitchen table, or strip each other naked and forget their days until sweat clung to their skin and daily trials became mere anecdotes to be shared as they slipped into sleep.

Tonight, just as Sid poured himself a glass of cheap wine, Eddie walked in and kicked off his shoes. Without a word, Sid poured another glass and handed it to Eddie.

"Go change," Sid said as Eddie took the wine. "It's been a day. Tomorrow is going to be a day and the next and… I just want to drink wine and watch mindless television."

"Meet me in the bedroom?" Eddie said before kissing Sid's cheek.

"You're a prince."

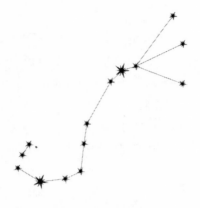

VII.
SCORPIUS

"You're tense," Eddie said. He straddled Sid's thighs to massage his shoulders and back. "You're not normally strung this tight. What's up?"

"You've known me a week and a half. How do you know what's normal?" Sid groaned on the last word as Eddie hit a knot over his left shoulder blade. Mindless television hadn't happened; Sid had face-planted on the bed as soon as his thighs hit the end of the mattress.

"Am I wrong?" Eddie asked.

"No. I'm sorry it's visible."

"Don't be." Eliciting another moan, Eddie ran firm fingers down Sid's neck and across his shoulders. He was a master. "Would talking about it help?"

"It's boring work shit. I can't imagine you'd—"

"I'm fascinated by your work shit."

Sid lifted his head and looked at Eddie and found, as always, soft concern, bright curiosity, alert, patient listening. Besides, if he kept going with the back massage, Sid would be asleep in a matter of minutes. The night was too young for sleep.

"Okay, yeah. We need more wine, though." When Eddie returned with refilled glasses, the rest of the bottle, and a plate of fruit and cheese, Sid kissed him and dove right in. "I'm in the doghouse at work."

"You're—the dog owner. How does that work?"

"My assistant called. They've noticed I'm not responding to work calls at night. Rue doesn't care, but it's not going over well with Mitchell."

"And Mitchell is…"

"Mitchell is—" Sid sighed. "He's an investor—our biggest individual contributor, and not much of a people person."

"Ah, someone you don't want to piss off."

"No, but while he has a great business mind, he doesn't have a grasp on the fashion industry and, more importantly, *our* corner of it. He still thinks we'll be the next Michael Kors or something…"

"Is that something you want?"

"Maybe in the future, sure. Walking into Macy's and seeing a huge Bastra line wouldn't make me mad. But that's out of reach right now. He's not concerned with what's going on in anyone's life. He only sees the bottom line."

"I don't know much about business, but don't you need a bottom-line guy?"

"We do. I need reminding that a line of fifteen experimental pieces, while cool as hell, will not sell. Not selling means I go back to tailoring old white men's suits."

Eddie grimaced. "So, what can I do to help?"

"You have been." Sid sat on Eddie's lap, cupped his face in his hand, and pressed his lips to Eddie's once and again as the tension of his imbalanced life slipped away. "You take me apart, so I can be whole again for another day."

"Sid…"

"You know this wasn't supposed to happen, right?"

"Us?" Eddie tipped Sid onto his back and sucked sweet kisses on his neck as Sid moaned. "I'm so glad you saved me."

Sid fell freely into his arms, into his touch, into another night when he knew he was right where he belonged. "I'm so glad you're an idiot."

*　*　*

THE TEXT ARRIVED THE NEXT day as Sid sat down with his dad for lunch.

Eddie: So, I came up with a name for the auxiliary team.

Sid: We were looking for a name?

Eddie: Everything needs a name. You guys are C-DRT, which, I've been meaning to tell you, sounds like a first-grade reader. "See dirt. See flower. See rain water flower."

Sid: For fuck's sake—are you bored?

Eddie: Not bored. Genius. So, if you're C-DRT—county disaster, the aux team should be C-AUX—county auxiliary.

Sid: You do realize…

Eddie: YES! Tell me I'm brilliant.

Sid: We are not naming the auxiliary team "cocks."

Eddie: I thought you were a fan of cocks. C-AUX.

Sid: Only of yours, my dear. Only yours.

THOUGH SID HAD SIBLINGS, HE'D grown up as an only child; Anna and Andrew were fifteen and seventeen years older than him, respectively. Because of that, he'd never had to share his dad's attention. And now that Lou's attention was scattered, fractured, and less than his own, Sid protected his time alone with his father.

That evening, after a long morning meeting with Bastra's web designer and a longer day with both his sister and his father, he finagled Baba from Anna's grasp and outside for some stargazing. The afternoon's humidity had broken. The trees that edged the back of Anna's yard and housed the last of the season's cicadas, desperately singing for a mate, stood still. Light cloud cover fled with the humidity. A perfect night.

Lou sighed as he settled into the cushioned chair with iced chai at the ready and binoculars standing by. Sid left his phone in the house—promises to be more attentive to work did not include evenings with his father. After a few moments enjoying the quiet of the evening, Lou patted Sid's hand.

"How's soccer practice going this season? Are the new kids any good?"

"Baba, I don't play anymore," Sid said. "I haven't played since college."

"Mmm. Right." Lou fell silent and reached for his binoculars. "Have you thought more about coaching the kids over the summer?"

Sid started to correct the long-outdated question, but stopped himself. Lou's doctor had suggested that gentle correction was best, but the futility and constancy of that wore thin. Sometimes Sid simply wanted to *be* with his dad. The details didn't need to be right.

Sid debated his answer long enough that his dad forgot his question and moved on. He lifted his binoculars and said, "We need to get the telescope out. Delta Aquarid shower starts soon." Sid froze; Anna had given Lou's telescope away—along with Lou's favorite chair—when she moved him into her home. "Where did Ma put that anyway?" Lou asked, switching timeframes all over again. "She always says it's in the way."

That much was true. After Ma passed, the scope had lived in the corner of Lou's living room—angular, black, and not as out of place as Ma would have liked to think. "Maybe she put it in the basement, Baba. We'll get it in time for the meteors."

Sid didn't know what was worse—constantly correcting the man who had always been a source of knowledge and wisdom, strength, and constancy—or lying, telling unflinching, flat-out untruths for the sole purpose of saving the serenity of the moment. He searched for middle ground.

"Did Ma ever watch the stars with you?"

"She did at first. On the way through Europe, we were always the last ones to turn in." Lou rested the field glasses on the small table next to him and tilted his head back to look overhead. "We had the best views then; some nights we'd see the Milky Way."

"We should get out your albums. I haven't looked at your pictures in years."

"That would be nice." Lou sighed and closed his eyes as if replaying the memories. Sid hoped they had remained bright and true, unlike so much else. "After her parents were killed," Lou said, wistful and quiet, "we'd spend every night outside. Even if it was cloudy, and there was nothing to see, she'd come out to make sure the stars were still there. 'If there are no gods to hear my prayers, maybe the stars will listen.'"

"When did she stop? She never came out with us."

"Once Andrew came. Life changes with a child. Your time isn't your own anymore." With the glasses back up to his face, Lou's brief lucidity slipped. "She still doesn't come out. Says she's too tired."

That had been, and always was, Anna's answer to their invitation to join them. "That's okay. It's nice just the two of us."

"Yes. Yes it is." After a few moments, Lou patted Sid's hand. "Let's turn this party around. Saturn and Mars should be crystal clear to the south." He stood on his own, slow and wobbly, but independent and proud. "Yes! Sid! Look!" He handed Sid the binoculars. "Look. You can't see the rings, but they make Saturn look oval-shaped."

"What am I looking for?" Sid had forgotten. He hated it: relying on a man who no longer remembered to brush his teeth every morning to remind him of the details of the night sky.

"See that reddish star straight out? That's—"

"Antares!"

"Atta boy. Saturn is the next brightest to the west there."

Sid scanned west and gasped. "Oh, Baba, we do need a telescope. I remember seeing the rings years ago."

"Mars is over to the east there. Brighter still."

As he followed his dad's direction, Sid's mind zipped to Eddie like a shooting star: to the night they went to the soccer field and looked at the night sky with elementary knowledge of what they were seeing—the

North Star, the Big Dipper; to Eddie's soft lips that soothed at first touch; to a week of nights when the comfort of the night sky blanketed their time, a few hours of grace in the midst of his crazy life.

Sid surged with a desire to call Eddie now, to tell him to bring an extra blanket. After Baba was in bed, somewhere between, "I'm home" and "Goodnight," Sid would take Eddie outside and show him Mars, Saturn, Antares—the red star that was 833 times bigger than the sun—because Eddie made Sid feel bigger than the sun.

"I met a boy," Sid blurted out. "A man, of course. I—I met someone."

Lou gently pulled the binoculars from Sid's eyes and studied him. "You like him." It wasn't a question. It didn't need to be.

"I do. He's the new fire chief. You should see him with Dottie… they're so funny together."

"I should check my calendar when we go inside—see when she needs me in the office again." Sid didn't correct. He took his dad's hand and missed the firm grip they used to share. "You wearing condoms?" his dad asked.

"What?" Sid stepped away as if slapped and began to gather their things. "Baba—I don't think—"

"Sidney Pravit." Even at almost thirty, his full name on this man's tongue sent a rush of heat through his body, the result of memories of chastisement for poor choices. "This is not a game, young man."

Sid's heart sank. The rush of heat chilled; his skin felt clammy. Sid thought he had him—the right time, the right place. But in the blink of his dad's eye, Sid was seventeen again. "Yes, Baba. I'm being safe."

"Good man. Bring him to your next soccer game. I have to give him a hard time—see if he can pass muster."

* * *

THAT NIGHT, WHEN EDDIE WENT to Sid's, he took Eddie out to see Saturn, to see Mars and a star called Antares. The moon, to anyone not looking at a calendar as Eddie had for the last two weeks, seemed full. But, as Adrian had reminded him the previous afternoon, there were three more sleeps until the full moon. And now, only two. Everything would change on the night of the full moon, the night Sid left for Chicago. The night Adrian came home to Connelly.

In the morning, Eddie had an early call. Before leaving, he bent to kiss Sid's temple. "I'm heading out." Sid stirred, reached out a sleep-heavy hand, and almost poked Eddie in the eye. Eddie kissed him again and ran his fingers through Sid's hair, which was splayed over the pillow. Tousled tendrils tickled Eddie's nose as he kissed Sid a third time.

"Mmm... have a good day." Sid rolled onto his back. He blinked his eyes open as he caught Eddie's hand. "I forgot you were wearing your blues today."

Sid sat up. His eyes drooped. He smacked his lips. He was stunning. Eddie had come to appreciate the new life they'd started in such a short time. The lingering heat of their nights together filled his days as he balanced his new job, his new community, and getting his own home ready for Adrian's arrival, an arrival he had not yet mentioned to Sid. He would. Tonight. Eddie would finish the light fixtures at the house after his shift, and after dinner they'd meet here. He would tell Sid about Adrian, about his love for Maggie, and about the great kid Adrian truly was.

"Eddie? You okay?" Sid took his hand. "You're looking peaked."

Eddie stretched his neck and feigned discomfort from his shirt collar. "I'm good. Nervous. The paper will be there today. I have to hand out some citations." He wiggled the knot on his tie. "Is my tie okay?"

Sid, now on his knees, straightened and smoothed the silk down Eddie's chest. "Where's your hat and jacket? I want to see the full picture."

Eddie brushed Sid's cheek with his thumb and kissed him. "In the living room. Lie down. You're not supposed to be awake yet."

"I'll go back to sleep. Let me see."

Eddie complied, and was flooded with memories of Maggie's phone loaded with picture upon picture of Eddie in his dress blues. She'd be so pleased to see him now, with his white chief's hat and his jacket sleeves decorated, not with three gold stripes as he'd had in Wylie, but five. She'd also be angry, knowing he hadn't told Sid, the man who was quickly weaving his way into his soul, about the greatest treasure in their lives.

When he walked back into the bedroom, Sid stood. The sheet slipped from his naked body, and he took Eddie in his arms. As they swayed to unheard music, Eddie's heart filled to bursting—it would all work out, of that he was sure.

"What's up?" Sid said, stepping back, tracing the lines of Eddie's jacket's placket. "You're melancholy." Sid took Eddie's hat off and plopped it on his own head.

Eddie laughed and fluffed the waves of Sid's hair that stuck out from under the band of his hat. "And you're sexy." He bumped a finger under the small bill to catch Sid's eyes. "Just thinking about you leaving. And how I'm going to miss you."

"We have two more nights. Don't push me out yet."

"No, I won't." Eddie pointed to the bed. "Come on. Lie down and get another nap before your day starts."

"Okay…" Sid said, sinking back into the pillows. "You sure you're—"

"I'm fine. I'm happy—ridiculously happy." Eddie kissed his way up Sid's body as he covered him with the sheet. He brushed rogue bangs from Sid's forehead and kissed his temple. "We'll talk tonight, okay?"

Sid flicked his eyes open. "Will you still be in full dress?"

"Would you like that?"

Sid grinned. "Yes. I need to assist you in removing it. That would make *me* ridiculously happy."

* * *

"Dot, I'm going to take off." Sid had spent his day at C-DRT. He had taught a CPR class, turned in his paperwork, and packed to go. More work awaited him at home.

"Don't forget those comfort kits for the truck."

"Oh, shit. Yeah." When not in use, the ERV lived at the fire station. Wanting to be sure to catch Eddie there, Sid called ahead.

"Connelly City Fire Department. This is Lieutenant Parker."

"Hey, Parker. Is Chief in?"

"No, he ran to Wylie to pick up his kid. He should be back in about half an hour."

Sid dropped the box of kits onto his desk. "Pardon me?"

"His son?" Lt. Parker explained. "His mother-in-law had some scheduling problem, so he went early—" The lieutenant took in an audible breath. "Is this Sid?"

"Yes."

"Shit. I thought you knew…" While the lieutenant fumbled, Sid sank into his chair. His skin burned from the inside out. "I'll tell him you called, and uh… he can call you back. Soon. Like in half an hour."

"No. Don't—don't tell him I called."

Sid put the phone in its cradle and pulled out his cell phone. A fog settled over him as he walked to his car.

Picking up his kid. He has a *mother-in-law?*

Sid's limbs weighed him down as though he had entered another dimension, as though the last two weeks had been a dream, a dream in which the man he was falling in love with was a stranger all over again. The time he'd sacrificed with his dad, *with his job*, had all washed away with the utterance of one phrase.

A child… a *child*… possibly a wife, stood in the corner of Sid's life, waiting to step in and unbalance him all over again.

He dialed Rue. "Change in plans. I'm coming early. Can you still stock my kitchen?"

"Yeah. How soon?"

"Tonight, if I can. I need to get out of here."
"Should I invite Captain Morgan?"
"You're my favorite. I'll call later."

VIII.
LEO

"Nine-oh-one West Rainier," Sid said as he slid into the cab. Fell in. He landed in the cab. Somehow.

He had aimed for a fuck-I-can't-feel-anything sentiment, and the alcohol was doing its job; the bourbon-and-gingers he had downed on the flight had hit him like a speeding train once the plane landed.

"Uptown?"

"Mmm? Yeah."

Unfortunately, the ache remained. The anger, the confusion, the sense of betrayal survived under the liquid weight of the booze.

He must have dozed; it seemed like mere moments before the cab pulled up to his apartment. He remained hazy as he fished through his wallet for the right credit card. "Is that American Express?"

"Yep," the cabbie said without looking. Sid swiped the card and unlatched his door. "Have a good night, sir."

"Too late."

Sid stood in front of his apartment building, a brick block that looked like the one next door and the one across the street and the one two buildings down. When he'd first moved in, he accepted its blandness. The neighborhood's diversity brought it to life with beautiful people, beautiful food, and great nightlife—a life he had to admit he hadn't taken the time to enjoy in entirely too long.

He was thinking too clearly, having wasted his drunk in the cab. That would not do.

In his apartment, he kicked off his shoes and headed straight to his kitchen. Bright colors, huge windows, and overstuffed furniture normally welcomed him home, but tonight, the sharp contrast to his run-down place in Connelly—and the memories he'd most recently made there—lured him straight to the bottle of Captain Morgan Rue had left on the counter. She had stocked his fridge and left a note: *You sounded upset. Go easy.* He poured a glass of rum with a dribble of Coke.

He'd intended to go to the studio, jump into work, and busy his mind, but his mind was far from mindful. His bed invited. It was tall, and lush with his favorite pillows and four hundred kabillion thread-count sheets and everything he loved—nothing like that soft, creaky piece of shit in Connelly.

He stood in the middle of his bedroom clad in underwear and held a glass of rum-flavored ice as his mind rewound to last night, to when he had taken Eddie to find the stars and planets. Afterward, they had stripped down to their underwear, and before they had crawled into bed, an old Beyoncé number had come on the radio. Without a word they began what would be their first and—now, Sid was sure—last underwear party.

They'd danced for close to an hour. They didn't sleep for another two.

Sid refilled his drink and checked his phone: fifteen voice messages and thirty-one texts.

"Fuck me." He shot a text to his sister: In Chicago a day early. Call me for any emergencies.

She'd be ticked, but he wasn't missing any scheduled time with his dad.

He poured himself another drink and made a call.

"I thought Pennsylvanians were in bed by ten o'clock."

"I'm not Pennsylvanian. I'm Pennsyl-cago-deshi... an. And there is no curfew in Chicago," Sid said, falling onto his couch.

"You're here. Is this call to report your location or to beckon me like I had nothing better to do with my night?"

Mitchell Campanello might be an old college friend and Bastra's biggest individual investor, but that did not mean Sid liked the man. His support for Sid's travels back home had been less than generous. As Mitchell's voice whined in Sid's ear, Sid couldn't remember why he'd called, other than to relive a drunken college night or two.

"I'm sure as shit not begging you, Mitchell. Do what you want."

"Are you here early to tell me you're staying? That you've had an attitude adjustment? I mean, Rue is adequate, but—"

"She's more than adequate, and you know it. Dad's still—" Sid took another swallow of his drink. "I am not staying. Yet."

"Are you drunk?"

"Still drinking. Don't make me drink alone. Bring takeout."

"Fine. Give me twenty."

Sid ignored all the other messages, sprawled on the couch, and stared at the ceiling. The room spun. His phone buzzed; he grabbed it.

Eddie: Again, I'm sorry. I couldn't end the day without saying goodnight.

* * *

SID CURLED DOWN THE EDGE of the duvet. The pain of a thousand knives sliced through his head; a crashing wave of nausea coursed through his gut. He swallowed and tried opening an eye. An empty bottle of Captain Morgan sat on his bedside table along with a glass of rust-colored water. A bucket sat by his bed; his clothes lay in a pile by his chair.

He hiked himself up on his elbows and fell back to keep himself from vomiting. A note caught his eye. As he grabbed for it, he knocked the empty bottle off his table.

Next time you have boy troubles, call Rue. I left an egg sandwich in your fridge. —M

The thought of food sent him over the edge. Making a beeline for the toilet, he barely missed stepping in the bucket.

"Sid? Are you… fuck." As Sid sat after his final wave of sick, Mitchell dug in the linen closet for a washcloth. He wet it and handed it over.

"I thought you left." Sid wiped his mouth and avoided Mitchell's eyes.

"I was on my way out." He wiped Sid's brow and neck and flushed the toilet. "What the hell is going on with you?" he said, joining him on the floor. "You don't do this kind of shit."

"Don't you have someone to terrorize over brunch?"

"No, but since you're here, I moved our meeting. Today at two."

No one understood why Sid kept Mitchell around. He was The Rich Kid in school—an entitled, impatient, malevolent prick. He provided booze for group gatherings, drove the sexy car for road trips along the lake to Grand Beach in Michigan, and, on occasion, footed the bill for whatever lakefront property housed them. Then, his usefulness, while shallow, was obvious.

Sid could never figure out Mitchell's unwavering interest in Sid's company until one day, when he brought a man for Sid to see.

Nico resembled Mitchell: slight, dark hair, pale complexion. Once Sid had heard the rhythm of Nico's speech, he understood.

"You're Mitchell's brother."

Nico smiled at him. "You've heard of his sister, Monica, I'd assume."

Sid draped a tape measure around his neck. "I have." He smiled and got straight to work. "So, what kind of job are you interviewing for? And do you mind if I take some measurements?"

"I don't mind—it's my hips that give me grief."

"Your hips are beautiful. It's the clothes that give you grief."

As far as Sid knew, he and Rue were the only people who knew about Mitchell's trans brother. Nico lived in South Bend, and Mitchell wasn't one to talk about his personal life. But, when Mitchell was having sixteen kittens about losing money because of this delay or that, Sid tried to remember that Mitchell's passions, while often misspoken, came from a place of caring.

At the moment, Sid was too nauseated and humiliated to give a damn.

"How much did I drink?"

"You were drunk when I got here. It doesn't suit you."

Sid grunted.

"And who the hell is this Freddie dude that after a couple weeks you'd completely fall apart?"

"His name is *Eddie*. And you wouldn't understand. You don't sacrifice for anybody."

"Excuse me? Who has given you so much mon—"

"Oh, shut up. You know what I mean. You don't sacrifice for *people*. For—" Sid burped. "For love."

"For lo—Jesus Christ, no. Because I'm not into vomiting my feelings and sitting naked on cold tile floors."

Sid looked at his crotch, exposed from a gap in the fly of his boxers. "I am not naked."

"You might as well be. Why don't you call him and get the story?"

"Because no story fixes it, Mitchell."

"And smelling of vomit does?"

"Don't you have a meeting to prepare for?" Sid's head throbbed. Mitchell's presence suffocated.

"Are you done retching?"

"Undecided."

"How long are you in town?"

"At least a week," Sid said.

"I sort of like this Freddie guy. Good to see your priorities in line."

"Thank you for the sandwich." Sid looked at the bathroom door and hoped his message was clear.

"Fine. Two o'clock. It's important."

When Sid heard his apartment door close, he mumbled something about throwing Mitchell and Anna into a room to fight it out and see whose self-importance would win out. He stood, ignored his phone buzzing somewhere in his room, and relieved himself. He stumbled to bed—the faithful bed that didn't care that he was a vomit-smelling asshole—and fell asleep.

WHAT SID HOPED WAS HOURS later, he awoke to his phone, muffled by fabric, buzzing, buzzing, relentlessly buzzing somewhere in the distance. He had a moment of gratitude—he was awake and pain-free enough to hear the muffled buzz, but not be annoyed by it. The nausea had disappeared.

Dottie: You were on call last night. We had a fire and you were nowhere to be found. Answer me or I swear I'm calling the cops.

For fuck's sake.

Sid: Do not call the cops. In Chicago. Left without thinking. Sorry.

Dottie: I'm calling you in thirty. Be available.

Sid: I will not be available; I have a meeting. I'm fine. We'll talk when I get back.

Dottie: You're in the doghouse, mister.

What else is new?

Sid showered and showered. He thanked the gods that he didn't have to pay a water bill and showered some more. He had hung a *kurta* in the bathroom to steam smooth; he finger-pressed the tunic's collar as best he could before putting it on.

Sid heated the sandwich Mitchell had left him and plopped into the chair in his reading nook. Until the purchase of the studio in Lincoln Park, the area had been used, along with his second bedroom, for studio space. Clients had come to his home for fittings; Rue had often slept on his couch when hours went long. But now, the nook, with its wall-to-wall window, completed the transformation from part-studio to home. In the corner opposite the chair sat his mother's *mandir*, a dark brown floor cabinet that, once-upon-a-time, served as a small worship shrine.

Even with Ma's slow rebirth of faith during his childhood, it sat in the living room—a simple piece of furniture. But from time to time, Ma had opened its doors and prayed. After performing *puja*, she'd close the cabinet doors and determination would flash bright in her eyes. She would stand and smooth her hands down the front of her *kurta*, as if wiping away the last of her stress. At these times, her patience would lengthen; her words would come freely and without the day-to-day tension that easily accumulated while raising a boy years after she thought she was through raising children.

He could use his mother's calm, her wisdom, maybe even her gods, but on this day, shame at his own behavior kept Sid from approaching the beautiful piece. Besides, his head throbbed, the sandwich offered limited energy, and he had a business to tend to.

The meeting was worse than a hangover. Mitchell regularly pushed to get Bastra into local boutiques, but individual customer connection had given Bastra its start; it formed their mission. Sid wasn't prepared to pull away from that focus. Mitchell also had financial clout they couldn't ignore. So Sid, Rue, and their lead seamstress patiently abided him. He not only repeated his lecture about the importance of brick and mortar presence, but pulled out financial reports to prove it. And, with great confidence, he announced that Out & About, a new boutique, would be opening soon in Andersonville—a prime neighborhood for Bastra's clientele.

"That sounds—" Sid stopped himself. It sounded fantastic. Promising. But also— "I'm not sure how we can set our sights on them right now. Between my situation and the Trial Line campaign going into production, it's a miracle we're even keeping up with the custom orders."

"Actually," Rue started, "We're behind."

"Why didn't you—"

"I wanted to talk to you in person," she said. "Just two weeks. Everyone's been very patient, but—"

"Those clients need to be our focus," Sid said. "It's why we're here."

"But that's not where the money is." Mitchell pounded his financial reports as if the force of his finger would make Sid see things his way.

"It's gotten us this far," Sid said, unwilling to budge.

"*I've* gotten you—"

"Okay, who wants a brownie?" Rue pulled what seemed to be a magic plate from her desk, loaded with her infamous dark chocolate brownies. She slid it and a platter of cheeseball and crackers across the conference table. After everyone—except Mitchell—filled their bellies, the meeting adjourned.

Sid and Rue were the last to leave. "The fuck is your problem?"

Rue Slovitz was not someone to be pedantic with, or to generally fuck with. Her life had been a series of abuses, neglects, fights, and alienations that had left her alone on the streets of Chicago for a good portion of her childhood. When they'd met during Sid's senior year of college, she had emerged from her circumstances as a strong, no-flash, no-flare woman who could create a new nation by will alone. Bastra wouldn't exist without her, especially since Sid's travels to Pennsylvania. She lived and breathed the mission of Bastra, the look of Bastra, the entire essence of Bastra. It was Sid's baby, but Rue nursed it to good health.

"Wait. *You* think this Out & About boutique is a good idea?"

"Fuck no. We don't have the time. They haven't even opened. They could just be a consignment store or something." Rue swiped a cracker into the half-eaten cheeseball. "I'm talking about your drunken snivel-fest over... a boy?"

"I see Snitchell got to you first," Sid said, licking the last crumbs of brownie off of his fingers.

"And another thing—I can't decide if I'm relieved or insulted you called him to cry to."

"One, I did not cry."

"You cried. Stop before you make a bigger ass of yourself."

"Two, I called him because he would drink first and lecture later. You usually skip the drinking. Three, I cry when I drink."

"Also bullshit. You knew I'd be pissed you were blowing us off so you could blow someone else...*and* letting me think the problem was your dad."

"I never said I was blowing you off for my dad. You did."

Rue took the plate of brownies away when Sid reached for his fourth. "What's his name?"

"Eddie Garner. New Chief of Fire in Connelly. Apparently, he's also a dad."

"Yeah?"

"Potentially married."

"What?" Rue sat back and pulled out a pack of cigarettes.

"Do not light up in this studio." Sid sat up and glared at her. "Have you been smoking in here with the fabric and—"

"My god, you are wound tighter than a tourniquet."

"Exactly my point. Even if he's not married—" Sid flipped his hand in the air, as if that could make everything disappear. "I have enough childish behavior in my life between Mitchell, my father, and my brother."

"Not sister?"

"She's not childish; she's mean and scared." Sid thought, then added, "And bitchy." He rubbed his temples; this scenario felt worse by the minute. "My point is, I have no control over my life right now and the last thing I need is another—"

"What's so good about him that you had a temper tantrum and cried in Mitchell's vodka?"

"We had rum."

"*You* had rum. You wouldn't share. Mitchell had vodka."

"He listens to me. Hears me."

"Mitchell listens?"

"No. Eddie," Sid said. "Pay attention."

"Eddie listens. Okay…"

"He gets the shit with Dad. He asks about him every day. He's fascinated with my work. He's… strong." Sid's anger slipped from his grasp. "And silly. And an amazing lover, and I feel like I'm important to someone because I exist. Not because I can do something for him."

"Oh hell… you've got it *bad.*"

This is why he didn't call Rue last night. "It's obviously one-sided anyway."

"How the hell do you figure that? He spent all this time with you instead of with his kid."

"If his kid isn't a priority, that's shitty. But if that boy *is* a priority and he couldn't bother to tell me, then I'm obviously not a priority."

Rue blinked, looked longingly at her cigarette case and sighed. "He must have a reasonable explanation."

"I don't even care if he does. I had no business getting into a relationship anyway. My dad is—he's disappearing, Rue."

"I'm sorry." She pushed the plate of brownies closer.

"He thinks I'm seventeen years old. All the shit I've worked for all my life—all of this to 'make Ma proud' doesn't even exist to him. Every time I leave there, I feel like—" Sid considered grabbing one of Rue's cigarettes for himself. "This company is mine, I do this for me, you know that, but I feel like I'm working my ass off for nothing. And Eddie… I didn't have to prove anything. I didn't have to *be* anything."

"Adding a kid does complicate things," Rue admitted.

"It's my line in the sand," Sid said. "I have to draw one somewhere or I'll go nuts."

"Minus the kid detail, he sounds like a great guy." She gathered up her belongings and stood. The bleached-blonde tuft of hair she kept sprayed straight out in front of her flopped over her eyes. "You need to find an eraser for your line and listen to his story."

Sid didn't want an eraser, unless it could erase the last two weeks of his life. He grabbed another brownie and decided to look forward instead. "Will you be honest with me, Rue?"

"I always am."

"Are we doing okay? This boutique, I mean, we talked about that— for the future."

"We did. But the present says we have a Trial Line to complete and the next campaign to prepare. Maybe you can help us catch up with custom?"

"Yes, of course. But financially—I know you don't like to talk money," Sid said, "but are you making it? You good?"

"I'm good. But maybe we shouldn't put this boutique idea too far on the back burner, huh? If they take off, it might be attainable."

"I have a fitting with Shi in the morning. She's an early adopter. I'll talk to her about it, if that's okay."

"It's more than okay. Tell her about Eddie, too. You know how she's got that third eye, or whatever it is."

"She does not have a third—" Sid laughed. "She's wise, Rue. Insightful. You, however… need a nap."

*   *   *

AFTER TWO DAYS OF SILENCE from Sid, Eddie gave up trying to reach him. After five days, his regret morphed into anger. People left him; he had learned that early on. If Sid contacted him, fine. If not, he would chalk up their time together as a weak moment and a fucking great time.

"Daddy?"

Adrian's first few days in Connelly had been rocky at best. Eddie had expected problems, but he had also remained hopeful that the universe might take pity and make it easy on them. Adrian still didn't sleep well. He hated where Eddie had put his bed, and tonight he'd had a fifteen-minute meltdown at dinner because his green beans had touched his macaroni.

Now bedtime loomed, and Eddie made no move to get Adrian ready. He sat at the kitchen table and spun a bottle of root beer in his hands—spinning, sighing and spinning.

Adrian tapped Eddie's hand. "Daddy. I'm waiting for you to answer me."

"What?" The bottle wobbled. Eddie saved the impending mess. "I'm sorry, buddy. What do you need?"

"Nothing. You look sad."

It was possible his regret had landed more in the realm of sadness than anger. They were emotional neighbors anyway. "I am sad. And angry."

"Are you sad and angry at me? I ate my macaroni."

"You did, buddy. No, I'm sad and angry at myself."

"Why?" Adrian popped open his brand-new box of crayons and tapped a green crayon on his chin. He drew a circle and two smaller circles inside of it.

"Remember my new friend, Sid?"

"The one I drew a picture of?" Adrian flipped through his papers, pulled out the drawing, and handed it to Eddie.

"Yes, that's the one. I—" Eddie needed new friends. He missed Sid in a ridiculous way, and he was confiding in a five-year-old. "I was trying to do the right thing and I sort of messed up and did the wrong thing."

"You should 'pologize. Everybody does the wrong thing sometimes." Adrian's green circle now had one blue eye and one purple eye. Adrian added curly orange hair.

"I've tried. He's…"

"Oh, he's *mad*." Adrian added eyebrows, slanting inward. Angry.

"He's mad. And I'm sad because I like him a lot."

Adrian added arms and a fat body to his creature. He stopped drawing and looked at Eddie with a huge grin. "Like him… like a boyfriend?"

As angry and sad and regretful as Eddie felt, he couldn't stop himself from laughing and admitting the truth. "Yes. Like a boyfriend. But I think I messed it up before it got all the way there."

Adrian started adding grass and flowers to his picture. In the top right corner, he put a cloud and rain. "Rain to water the flowers," he said. "You have to 'pologize. He'll listen. You said he was a good guy."

"He's the best of the good guys. And you... are the latest of the bedtime guys."

"No. I'm drawing."

"You can finish in the morning."

"I'm drawing the grass. It's not done. And I have to add two trees."

"I'll cut you a deal," Eddie said, standing to turn off the living room lights and start the dishwasher. "Finish the grass. The tree happens in the morning."

The evening careened downhill from there. Two crayons landed in pieces against the back wall of the kitchen; Adrian scribbled all over his picture that was "supposed to be for *you*, but now I'm angry at you too." And, as Eddie closed Adrian's door, in his final fit of pique, Adrian told him he was glad his new friend was mad at him. Eddie was, after all, the worst of the dad guys.

He should have stayed in Wylie. The kid didn't need more daddy time, because it was clear Eddie hadn't a clue how in the hell to be a daddy, or a boyfriend, or, in light of the stuffed dog that now manned his desk at work, a fire chief.

He traded his root beer for a real beer and sat on his back porch. The full moon of nights before had waned. A storm front blew in from the northwest. The air smelled wet and wormy.

You have to 'pologize. He'll listen.

When people left Eddie, they left of their own volition, like his father and later his mother. Or they left because Eddie had pushed them away, like the dunderheads he used to date. Or they left because the universe had deemed it must be so—like Maggie. But Sid was different. He led a full, crazy life, but even in the midst of it all, he *chose* Eddie. And Eddie had blown it anyway.

He had to *'pologize.*

Eddie: The moon is beautiful tonight, but a storm is rolling in. Still thinking of you. Goodnight, Sid.

He put his phone on the side table and closed his eyes. Minutes later, he heard back.

Sid: Goodnight, Eddie.

Eddie: Sid? You there?

Sid: The moon is nice tonight, isn't it? So clear it almost looks painted in.

Eddie: You in Chicago?

Sid: Yep, looking at the same sky as you. I'll be back next week. 'Night.

"Goodnight, Sid." Eddie looked to the sky and wished for extra patience for tomorrow. "Goodnight, Maggie."

IX.
CASSIOPEIA

AFTER A FULL WEEK IN Chicago, Sid left confident that he could manage the demands on his time with a semblance of grace. The Trial Line production was on its feet, his first few samples for the next campaign had been approved, and custom orders were almost caught up.

As far as his heart was concerned, it would heal. Time and reprioritizing would mend it. Eddie had always reminded him to take time for himself. He didn't need Eddie to heed that advice.

On his way home from the airport, Sid stopped to see his dad. Before Lou had moved in with Anna, her home had been a pleasant place to visit. As Sid had with sewing, Anna had inherited their mother's penchant for gardening. She kept a colorful landscape year 'round, had a beautiful vegetable and herb garden in back, and put together overflowing pots so astounding that Sid regularly drove nine hours to and from Chicago to cart a few to his balcony. As a single mom who worked more than full-time, Anna was an immaculate housekeeper, had classy yet comfortable furnishings and, while not the best cook, offered her best whenever family gathered.

But when Sid had first arrived to help her that spring, he'd been surprised to find her front landscaping held its shape only because of a neighbor's semiregular offer of assistance. Her herb garden still gasped life with sturdy rosemary and thyme, but they had flowered and grown twiggy. Inside, the house swirled in turmoil. The once beautiful furnishings were now hidden beneath blankets and flotsam from the daily care of a man who sapped all of Anna's energy. The kitchen table was perpetually cluttered, and the counter by the telephone was loaded with scraps: notes, phone numbers, directions for medicines, and pamphlets. She rarely had visitors anymore, but when she did, she fussed and straightened and insisted the mess was unusual that day.

"Well, there's my son!" Lou said as he turned off the television. "What's a dad have to do to get a visit, huh? It's been *weeks*."

Sid bent down for a hug. Anna grabbed Lou's calendar.

"Now, Dad… look." She laid the dog-eared pages on Lou's lap. "Here's today."

"And here's Sid's name," Lou said. "So, it's been… one week. What did I say?"

"Too long, either way," Anna muttered as she disappeared into the kitchen.

"It doesn't matter, Baba." Sid said, as he sat on an ottoman shared with Lou's feet. "I'm here now."

"That you are. How's Chicago? Did you win your soccer tournament?"

"I work in Chicago, Baba. No soccer this time." Lou's eyes appeared dull. He looked more tired than usual. "How are you feeling?"

"Anna said she won't take me to the math department again."

"What?" Sid shot a look toward the kitchen. "Anna?"

Anna, slammed a stack of papers onto the counter and spoke through the pass-through. "You keep telling me to get him out of the house, and I tried. Never again."

"The hell happened? Baba…"

Lou pursed his lips and crossed his arms over his chest. He patted his pocket for his protractors and pens and grunted when he landed on the plastic protector.

"He got lippy with Professor Phelps the other day."

"Tom Phelps is a jackass, and it's about time someone told him."

"Maybe he likes being a jackass," Sid said. "He has been ever since we've known him." Lou took a labored breath and coughed, wet and loud. The congestion was new. Sid looked at his dad's ankles and pressed his thumb against the flesh, leaving a clear indent. "Anna, when did this cough start? What's his blood pressure been?"

She brought glasses of lemonade into the room and glanced down at her dad's legs. "A little high—one-fifties over low hundreds."

"Okay, look. He's pitting."

"Do you *mind?*" Lou yanked his leg back. "I can hear, you know. Don't talk over me like I'm not here and don't understand."

"Sorry, Baba. I'm worried about your breathing and swelling, okay? I want Anna to call the cardiologist tomorrow."

"The cardiologist is an asshat," Lou said.

"You don't like many people, do you?" It never stopped hurting, this personality change in his father.

Lou looked at his son and smiled meekly. "I like *you.*"

"I like you too, but I don't like it when you're cranky like this."

"I'm sick of being in this house," Lou said. "But I get too tired when I'm out and about."

"Would it be easier if we got you a wheelchair?"

"I don't think that is remotely necessary," Anna snapped. If Sid could win five dollars every time he not only predicted what Anna would say, but even its precise timing, he wouldn't have to worry about Mitchell Campanello ever again.

"Like some sort of invalid?" Lou asked.

Anna huffed and busied herself in the kitchen.

"No, like a man whose body is slowing down, but wants to get around." Sid checked to make sure Anna was out of earshot, leaned close to his dad and whispered, "You could get away from your grumpy daughter now and then."

"Will you take me to the park?"

"I will take you to the park."

Lou took a long drink of lemonade. "I might consider a wheelchair."

After an awkward hour in which Lou flipped between two old movies neither Anna nor Sid recalled seeing, Sid took his leave.

"I'll walk you out, Sid. Dad," Anna looked at Lou as if he was the class troublemaker. "I'll be five minutes. Don't. Move." Lou grunted as she closed the door.

"Why do you *do* that? No wonder he feels like an invalid."

"This is exactly what I want to talk to you about. I've about had it with you coming and going as you please, and spending every minute telling me how I'm not taking proper care of him."

"Hold on, what? When did I say—"

"His blood pressure's high," she began, counting each infraction on her fingers. "He needs to see the cardiologist. He's not an invalid, *Anna*. He needs to get out of the house. You have no goddamned idea—"

"Stop. I know full well what you're going through, but I am not going to apologize for seeing the things you refuse to see."

"Are you going to apologize for taking off early?"

"I already have, and, as I recall, it didn't affect our schedule here at all." Anna glared at him until suddenly her attentions shifted to somewhere over Sid's shoulder. Sid followed her gaze. The curtains moved and Lou slipped out of sight. "I'll take care of Doctor Asshat."

"No. You'll—I won't know what he says. I have a folder. I can't keep track if you're taking over like that."

Sid closed his eyes, pinched his brow, and remembered why he'd not been able to live with her, even for the weekend. "So you want complete control, but you need my help. I'm not sure I understand—"

"I hear your phone buzzing in your pocket all the time. You're distracted. You're never here when you're here and then you come over and act like you have all the answers."

Sid gave up trying to reason with her. "Fine. Just get him to the doctor. That cough wasn't there before I left. I shouldn't have to point that out to you."

"Fine."

He stared at her for a few long moments and considered suggesting that her kids were old enough to pitch in and help, but knew that would be yet another argument.

An argument was one more thing he did not need; another one waited for him in the C-DRT office. Dottie might kill him.

DOTTIE DIDN'T KILL HIM, BUT she wasn't happy with him either. He'd fucked up; he'd earned it.

After their talk, Sid worked on backed-up correspondence. She came into his office mid-sentence. "…was completely screwed up on this fire Saturday. We're doing another training. I need copies of all the forms—ten of each. Can you manage that without getting your feelings hurt?"

Sid looked up from his computer. "Can I suck my thumb between sets?"

"You know, I'm sorry it ended up this way, Sid. But if you ask me—"

"Which I didn't."

"He's a good man—there has to be a reasonable explanation." Sid rolled his eyes—he'd heard that quite often enough. "And frankly, your attitude is concerning me. If we have a fire—"

"It will not affect my work. I plan on talking to him." Sid found the necessary files quickly; everything in his office had remained as organized as his dad had left it. "Not today. My sister—I can only jump one hurdle at a time." He tossed the documents on his desk. Dottie's expression softened. "He might have screwed up gloriously, but I left town and wouldn't talk to him. It's possible we're too stupid for each other anyway."

"You're both pretty dumb," she said, turning to leave. "Oh, did I tell you?" She sat in his chair instead. "I met his son. He's darling—"

"Stop. I don't want any editorials on this child. I need to talk to Eddie first before I get my emotions all wrapped up in it."

"Oh, it's too late for that." She wasn't wrong.

"Do I need to schedule meeting space for this training?"

"Yeah, the firehouse was perfect last time."

Sid chuffed. "Of course it was."

EDDIE TRIED THE C-DRT OFFICE with no success. He drove past Sid's apartment, and, not seeing his car, continued north to the high school. The setting sun cast a swath of pink and purple across the sky; the day's humidity had halved. If he hadn't had this errand, he would be straddling a rickety picnic bench eating peach milkshakes at Connelly Creamery with his son.

Instead, Parker's wife watched Adrian so Eddie could clean up his mess. He pulled into the gravel lot outside the soccer field where Sid knocked ball after ball into the goal, oblivious to the world around him.

Eddie approached, cleared his throat, and took a breath to vault his voice across the field.

"Good even—" Sid stopped mid-kick and spun around. Eddie continued, "Good evening. Sorry. I didn't mean to startle you."

Sid turned and sailed a side shot right into the corner of the goal. Eddie walked toward Sid as he knocked two more balls into the goal. "I understand why you're upset with me." Sid ran to retrieve his shots, piled three balls into his arms, and, without looking at Eddie, lined them up at the penalty arc.

Before Sid could run off to grab any more, Eddie took two himself and stood between Sid and the net. "I'm trying to talk to you like an adult."

"Oh, you mean like you *weren't* for the past few weeks? Like that?"

"How could I have missed that you're a petulant child?"

"Because you were too busy making sure I didn't know you *have one?*"

Sid took the balls from Eddie's hands. He lined them up and looked through Eddie to the goal.

"Sid, I am sorry. I fucked up… in a huge way. But I think—" Sid knocked a ball toward the goal. It hit a post and missed. Eddie charged on. "I think I proved that I—can you at least *look* at me?"

Sid stared at him and kicked another ball. Eddie wondered if Sid would listen better if he fought back and played goalie.

"You know, I sat with you and listened to the load you carry," Eddie said. "I empathized. I genuinely cared. The least you can do is return the favor."

Finally, Sid stopped beating the hell out of the balls and stared at Eddie. "Maybe I can't be burdened with one more thing."

"I'm not asking to be unburdened. I'm asking that you *listen*. Then you can go on your way, and I'll be grateful for the time we had."

Sid's gaze wasn't kind. "When were you planning on telling me, Eddie? Or was I just a plaything who didn't earn the right to the important details of your life?"

"Sid!" Eddie approached, but Sid knocked another ball into the goal. "How can you even think that?"

"I don't know what to think." Sid rolled the next ball under his foot. Damp from the grass, it slipped and hit Eddie's shoe. "I mean, a kid is bad enough, but a mother-in-law? You're *married*?"

"Mother-in—" Eddie sighed. He was such an idiot. "I'm not married. She's not really—" Eddie took Sid's lead and lined up the ball that had hit his foot. He pulled back and sailed it into the goal. "This is why I want to talk to you." Sid's next attempt sailed up and over the net. Eddie took a step closer. "My feelings for you don't change—nothing between us changes because I have a son."

Sid eyed his next ball, sighed, and looked at Eddie. His eyes softened, but the pain was unmistakable. "Maybe it does for me."

It was a hit Eddie had hoped he wouldn't have to hear. "I never meant to hurt you."

"And yet…" Sid reared back and knocked his last ball directly into the center of the goal.

"I've arranged a sitter tomorrow," Eddie said with one last flicker of hope. "I'm going to be at that Thai place at six o'clock. I'd like it if you joined me."

"No."

It had all happened too fast: the romance, the infatuation, the connection. Eddie knew it, had felt the grip of reality slipping away every time his fingers caressed Sid's body, every time his lips grazed his skin, every time their smiles met in utter joy. None of this should be a shock, but as he stepped away from Sid's one-man firing squad—with soccer ball bullets—the loss sped through him like a raging fire.

"Wait!" Eddie stopped at Sid's call. Sid passed a ball to Eddie with the side of his foot. "Let's go somewhere we haven't been before. There's that little bar on Mound. It can be loud, but they have a couple quiet booths."

"Loud? You planning on yelling at me?" A smile curled at the corners of Eddie's mouth, the first one since the day Sid left town.

"Maybe."

Even with the hurt and anger in Sid's eyes, he was the most desirable man Eddie had ever seen. "Well, at least you'll have to look at me to yell."

Now that Sid looked Eddie straight in the eye, the exhaustion that hovered over him became clear. Dark circles underlined his eyes; his stance slumped slightly. His week in Chicago hadn't been easy.

"That's half the problem," Sid said. "I can't *not* look at you."

"Good." Eddie nodded and lined up a shot from the passed ball. He skirted it right inside the left goalpost. "I'll see you tomorrow at six."

X.
URSA MINOR

EDDIE ARRIVED EARLY. THE PUB was empty but for a few patrons at the bar who looked as if they had spent most of their day there.

When Sid came in, Eddie approached him for a hug and kiss before thinking about it. It became an awkward two-step with hasty pecks on the cheek and Eddie stupidly announcing, "I ordered crab dip."

"Sorry I'm late," Sid said. "Dad's doctor appointment ran late."

"How is he?"

"He had some congestion. Doc's going to try some new blood pressure meds."

"It might take them some time to get it right," Eddie said as they took their seats at a back booth. They talked about the oppressive humidity, about the progress of the auxiliary team, and about how impressed Eddie was that the businesses in town were ready to jump in with money to help make that happen. They ate crab dip and drank beer and behaved like two men who were meeting to make the boss happy after an unfortunate work-related confrontation.

The dip landed in Eddie's stomach like a brick. His stories lacked passion. Sid's attention wavered to the televisions overhead and to the stray drips of dip on his small plate. Eddie considered screaming or planting a big wet one on Sid to jolt the conversation into something more interesting. They ordered dinner and fidgeted with their cardboard coasters.

As Sid took the last swig of his beer, Eddie broke the impasse. "Thank you for coming tonight. I know you're busy and... I know I royally fucked up." Sid listened, but his eyes reflected caution—a warning that if he didn't get this right, there were no third chances. "I fucked up an amazing thing." Sid didn't say anything, but a smile teased the corners of his mouth. "So this is the short story: I have a kid. Full-time," Eddie said, his voice pinched with nerves. "He was at his grandmother's while I got the house ready."

"Your mother-in-law..."

"No. She's not—" Eddie sighed. "She's part of the longer story—if you want to hear it."

"This is why we never went to your house. I'd have seen a child's bedroom."

"Yes." As soon as he admitted it, Sid looked away.

"Why didn't you just *tell* me?"

"I'm so sorry, Sid. You said—a few nights before you left—you said that we weren't supposed to happen. And, it's true. I didn't plan on you... on what I *feel* for you. I didn't want to break the spell and I ended up lying."

"You *omitted*. A huge damned thing."

"Actually," Eddie's eyes flickered with hope. "He's sort of tiny."

Sid grinned. "And I behaved... like a child." Their mirrored smirks acknowledged the irony. "I also learned that doing so tastes like vomit and shame."

Eddie grimaced. "Did you get drunk?" Sid didn't need to answer; his attention was focused on the curve of his beer mug. "I'm oddly touched."

"Oh, don't be. I can be an idiot, too," Sid said. "So. Tell me about your son."

As their dinner arrived, Eddie pulled out his phone. "Can I show you his picture first?"

Sid smiled, but shook his head. "Not yet? I believe Dottie's word for him was... *darling*. I probably should go into this without bias."

"He is darling," Eddie admitted. "He's also a little shit."

"Well, he is yours."

A quick draft of cool air brushed Eddie's right shoulder. It brought a sense of a comforting touch from Maggie. It all began with her. "I met Maggie James in third grade."

"This *is* a long story." Sid winked over his sandwich before taking a huge bite.

Eddie hadn't told their story before; everyone knew it. His heart raced; his hunger evaporated. Sid waited patiently. "We were best friends from the start. She stood with me and watched our house burn down. Her mom let us stay with them until we found a new place. I think Maggie's love of thrift stores and vintage clothing came from trying to restock our closets. She helped me with math, and I helped her with history. Once we were on our career paths, nothing changed. Maggie and Eddie."

"You love her."

"Not romantically, but—I've never loved anyone more." Eddie finally took a bite of food. It clung to the sides and roof of his dry mouth. He pushed his plate aside. "She wanted nothing more in life than to be a mother. So, after getting a good freelance business going with her pottery and paintings, she set out to do just that. And I sat on the sidelines wondering what in great hell she was thinking. She didn't want a husband. She didn't want a dad for this child-to-be. She wanted a donor."

"I bet that went well."

"It was ugly. Men treated her like shit over and over again. I wanted it to end."

"Superman to the rescue." Sid was hardly eating. His tense posture had already softened. He wasn't stupid; even with only this much information, it was easy to start putting the pieces together.

"Well, a vain attempt at Superman, yes. We fought. We cried, but I knew that she would be the best mother to ever grace this godforsaken planet."

"Did you want to be a father?"

"No. So we fought more. We went back and forth for weeks until we came to an agreement." Eddie pointed to himself. "Donor. Period. I'd be on the birth certificate, but this was her child. Her last name. Her responsibility. It's what she wanted."

Sid cocked his head; he'd already figured out the finale.

"When Adrian—that's his name. Adrian. He's—" Eddie took a shaky breath. "When he turned two, she was diagnosed with cervical cancer." Sid muttered, "Oh god." Eddie plowed through the rest. "She beat it. Like a demon she beat the fuck out of it."

"Eddie… fuck."

"Last summer we found out it had metastasized. She, um… she left us in March."

Nausea washed over Eddie. Silence draped them as the story seeped into Sid's understanding.

"I'm so—Eddie, I'm so fucking sorry." Sid reached across the table with both hands. Eddie grabbed on and clutched his fingers. "How old is he?"

"He turned five not long after she passed."

"Five years old…" Sid shook his head; his thumbs brushed across Eddie's knuckles. "So fucking unfair."

"I'm sorry I didn't tell—"

"No. Stop. I wish you would have told me, but—" Sid's eyes teared. "The timing suddenly seems unimportant."

"Adrian's why I moved here." A floodgate opened, and Eddie spilled rambling words. He was comforted by Sid's presence, an anchor reminding him that he wasn't alone. "I mean, the lack of upward mobility contributed, but the schedule was rough. Chief wouldn't give anyone leniency. A buddy told me about the Connelly opening, and I jumped. The hours can be nuts, but I'm more in control. I can keep day shifts and—" Eddie stopped. Sid listened, but seemed distracted; his focus was off in the distance. "Sid?"

"I'm just—I'm struggling," Sid said. "If you'd have just *told* me, I might have been able to help."

"You did." Eddie grasped Sid's hands more tightly. "You stitched me together without knowing it. I was afraid to break the spell, and you already had so much to deal with."

"No, I mean… Eddie, I haven't told you all of my story either."

THEY NEVER WENT BACK TO their food. Sid's mind raced with guilt over his anger, with grief for a woman he'd never meet, with amazement at how connected their lives really were. He invited Eddie to follow him to a park in Waterson Township.

They walked along a tree-lined path that led them to a pond covered in lily pads. A chorus of frogs and crickets made a quiet backdrop. They sat on a bench to watch the sun set beyond the surrounding trees.

"When I was about nine… maybe ten," Sid started, "I'd had a fight with a friend at school. I don't remember him now, but I remember being afraid we weren't going to be friends anymore. Ma told me that people come into our lives for a specific reason—to teach us something, for us to teach them." Sid smiled at the faint memory. She had just come home from work; her eyes were tired. A small painting of the god Vishnu hung on the wall behind her and appeared to look over her shoulder right into Sid's eyes. "I'm not sure I completely believe that, but while I was in Chicago, I wondered what the point was… of meeting you, of giving up that time that should have been devoted to my dad, to my job."

"Sid, I didn't mean to—"

"Wait." Sid looked at Eddie and shook his head in disbelief at the pain this man had gone through so recently. His mother's belief in karma must have been bogus; it made no sense here. "Ma said timing is always as it's meant to be…" A bullfrog let out a string of rumbling moans. His mom probably would have found meaning in the timing of that as well. "You know that picture of my folks in my living room? The *old* picture?"

"Yeah. I understood why you're so—" Eddie blushed and squeezed Sid's hand. "Beautiful. They're a gorgeous couple."

"I brought it with me because it's the *last* picture they took together, Eddie. My mom died when I was ten," Sid tumbled into his confession; it had been years since it felt like a burden that needed to be lifted. "I don't talk about it because after a while it becomes this thing that happened and not a traumatic marker… which is probably the last thing you want to hear—"

"You *know*." Eddie pulled his hand from Sid's. "You know what Adrian's feeling and thinking and, oh—" He stood to pace on the dock, spinning around to Sid as if he might have the answers to the universe. "When you said your mom was gone, since your dad's older, I guessed—" Eddie sat down and scooped Sid's hand into his. "Was it like Maggie?"

"No. It was sudden. She had a cold, then bronchitis, then we were visiting her in the hospital. We played *bhabhi* one night—it's a card game—and we laughed so hard she had a coughing fit. Scared the charge nurse half to death." Sid chuckled at the memory of the poor woman flying in thinking Rimi was on her last leg and finding them buckled over in hysterical laughter. "Dad put me on the school bus the next morning, and she was supposed to be home waiting for me that afternoon." Sid gasped as the pain hit him afresh, as if he was seeing the movie reel for the first time.

"You never saw her again." Sid shook his head. "What a beautiful last memory, though," Eddie said wistfully. "I hope I go out laughing."

"Don't go out early, okay?" Sid sat back and blinked the film from his memory. That moment at 3:43 p.m. on May 19, 1998 wasn't what he wanted to talk about. "I guess I'm just confused though, Eddie—I mean, we spent a lot of time together and not once did I see a moment of grief. Forget Adrian—*you* lost so much."

"I know. I've become an amazing actor—trying to keep it together for Adrian, you know?"

"How's that going for you?" Sid guessed the answer. When he and his dad fell apart in a Sears dressing room over a pair of jeans that didn't fit, everything had started falling back into place for them. The connection he had with his father remained unmatched by Sid's siblings.

"Not well. I thought the change in scenery would help, but... it's been rough."

"Can I make a suggestion? I mean, if Ma's to be believed, we've been pushed together for some reason, and this seems—"

"God, yes. Tell me. You *know*."

"Grieve with him. It's been what? Three months?"

"Almost four, yeah."

"He's going to try to be brave because you're being brave, and Eddie... this is not the time for bravery. Save that shit for stuffed dogs." Eddie was so focused on Sid's words, he didn't flinch at the joke. It wouldn't be easy, Sid was sure, but he *did* know.

"I'm afraid I'll scare him," Eddie said.

"He has to know it's okay to be sad. It's okay to be mad as hell. He needs a safe place to be as ugly as he needs to be. And you do, too."

"I can't dump that on him."

"No, but you can share it with him. Look, I'm no expert, but he understands more about death than any kid should. None of his friends are going to understand; it's you and him."

Eddie nodded and kept Sid's hand in his. Nature took the conversation for a spin: a welcome breeze rustled the leaves; turtles gurgled water; two red-tailed hawks circled the pond.

"I miss her so much," Eddie said. He brightened as he reached into his pocket for his phone. "Can I show you their pictures now?"

"Yes. Please."

A tear slipped from Eddie's eye and landed on his hand. He ignored it and scanned through his phone. He stopped, stared, smiled sadly, and handed over the phone. "My Maggie."

Sid took the phone as tenderly as if he was holding her. "She's beautiful. The true girl next door."

"Yes. Her hair was always that long, that thick and red and wavy. When we were kids, I thought it had magic."

"Did she lose it?"

"Yeah. She didn't lose her magic, though." Eddie scanned through his phone. The smile that spread across his face when he landed on a picture of a little boy with large, floppy, chestnut curls could have raised the sun at dusk. "This is my son. Adrian James Garner."

"He has your name now."

"He's mine now. Maggie's orders."

Sid took the phone to get a clear view. Dottie was right. The kid was darling.

AFTER THE SUN SET, THEY drove to a spot on the north edge of Claremont County that overlooked Tomlin Valley. Sid and his dad had spent many an hour here on the hood of the car—just as he and Eddie were now—stargazing, talking about school and his sports teams. Here he had told his dad he was gay, and here his dad had cocked his head and said, "Huh." The conversation had returned to Coach Samson and his proclivity for putting Sid in goalie position instead of forward, where he excelled.

"So, what does Adrian like to do?" Sid asked. The anger and hurt that had propelled Sid through his week in Chicago was already a lost memory. Listening as Eddie lit up and talked about his son could only help heal the cracks that remained between them.

"He loves to draw. And build. He creates cities on paper and with blocks. He loves dinosaurs… is really into the concept of good guys and bad guys… wants to label everyone."

"The world makes more sense that way, I guess."

"It does. Oh! And he plays soccer. Practice for fall season starts in a few weeks."

"Oh, god, he's in the herding league?"

Eddie laughed. "Yes. Little moving piles of kids roaming the field until—*whoosh*—a soccer ball comes flying out of the horde."

"I love watching kids that age play. I used to coach a couple summers during college—nine and ten-year-olds. Much more organization, but every once in a while, even they would pile up and just beat hell out of each other's shins."

"You should come to a game."

"I'd like that. Make sure they're teaching them right." Sid knocked Eddie's shoulder with his own. They fell silent. Fireflies lit the brush in front of them with twinkles of light; the stars overhead shone clear.

Out of the silence, Eddie said, "I hope he makes new friends. No one here knows what happened. I can't tell if that's going to be a good or bad thing."

"Ignorance might be in your favor. I had friends who stopped talking to me, like dead moms were contagious or something."

"Sid."

"Sorry. That was crass. Just keep an eye out. Kids can be mean."

"Yeah, he's had his share already—he's little. He gets picked on sometimes."

"Does he tell them his dad's the fire chief and they better be careful?"

"He damned well better not. Dad's just dad. Not Superman."

Sid spotted a constellation west of Vega: foot, knee, hip, waist, shoulder, arm. *Hercules.* He smiled, hearing his dad's, "Atta boy," and asked, "What do you love about being a dad?"

"Giggles are pretty awesome," Eddie said without a second thought. He tilted his head up and closed his eyes, as if gathering all the good of his circumstance. "But mostly, I love that Maggie's story isn't over. And it's better now because it includes plastic dinosaurs and block cities, and… soccer herds."

A comfortable silence enveloped them, but after a long resigned sigh, Eddie said, "I should probably head home." He hopped off the car and offered his hand for Sid to join him. "I don't want to take advantage of sitters—they're my lifeline."

"Sure. I understand." Sid retrieved his keys from his pocket, but couldn't make a move to his car.

"Sid," Eddie said. He looked younger, like a boy hoping his prom proposal would result in a yes. "Where are we now?"

Sid smiled and hooked his pinky in Eddie's. "I lost my focus… with you. I don't regret it, but I need to concentrate on my dad and my company and get my head screwed on. As much as you say Adrian won't change anything…"

"He will. He's changed my entire life." Eddie gathered Sid's hand in his. "So, it's probably pushing it, but I'd kick myself if I didn't ask." He looked at Sid with bright blue eyes, expectant but so sweetly tentative. "This is where I want to kiss you."

Sid closed his eyes and squeezed Eddie's hand, because yes. *Please yes. Kiss me like you did the first night. And the fourth morning. And the last night.* But "this is where I have to say no" was the right answer, and the one he said aloud.

"Of course. I understand." Eddie swung their hands together. "Can I call you?"

"Yes. Ma was right; we met for a reason. I don't want to lose that."

Sid did kiss Eddie's hand before they parted and went to their own cars. He motioned for Eddie to roll down his window. "Can you do me one favor tonight?"

"Anything."

"When you peek in on Adrian? Give him a kiss for me."

"I'd be happy to. Goodnight, Sid."

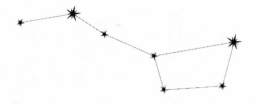

XI.
URSA MAJOR

EDDIE: WHY DOESN'T A FIRE chief look out the window in the morning?

Sid was back in Chicago. Eddie had respected Sid's request for space in the two weeks since they talked. His only point of contact had been texts like these: corny, ridiculous, and perfectly timed. Today's arrived after another meeting with the web designer. While the new design would go live in a matter of days, getting there had been grueling.

Sid: I have no idea. Why doesn't a fire chief look out the window in the morning?

Eddie: Because then he wouldn't have anything to do in the afternoon.

Sid: Do you need something to do? I think Mandy has a CPR class this afternoon. I bet you know a thing or two…

Eddie: I'd much rather be your manikin.

The next day, his phone interrupted a meeting with Mitchell.

Eddie: What does Popeye do to keep his favorite tool from rusting?

Sid bit back a laugh, shoved his phone in his pocket, and tried to pay attention to Mitchell as he rambled on about "spreading our wings," and "once Sid gets back here full-time." Sid gave up and answered Eddie's text.

Sid: Why do I fear this is a double-edged tool?

Eddie: Because you have a dirty mind.

Sid: I didn't say double-ended.

Eddie: Hmm. Maybe I'm the one with the dirty mind.

Sid: I think you're making this up as you go.

Eddie: He keeps it from rusting… by sticking it in Olive Oyl.

It would be easy to call Eddie, to act as though a huge *thing* wasn't taking over his brain. On the surface, their friendship remained. But the attraction kept him up at night—in numerous ways. Still, no matter from what angle Sid looked at the situation, a romance—with a little boy standing in the corner—was not going to work.

To shut Mitchell up, he and Rue agreed on an incognito visit to Out & About on his next visit, which ended the meeting. As he walked to the train station, the stars hid behind an incoming storm front. He heard from Eddie again.

Eddie: Adrian was ticked off I sent the last joke after he left for the sitter's. This one is from him. Ready?

Sid: You're training your son to have this cornball humor?

Eddie: I'm a good father.

Sid: Of course. Hit me.

Eddie: Some people's noses and feet are built backward—their feet smell and their noses run.

Sid: Tell him if he leaves now, he might catch his nose before it runs away.

Eddie: Nice. He did an apple juice spit take. On my face.

Sid: Does Adrian know about me?

Eddie: He knows you're my friend. He drew a picture of you and Dottie that I need to give you next time you're home.

Though Sid appeared to be holding it together, in the past week he'd had to redo directions for two of the four Trial Line pieces because he'd missed important steps. He'd sent Rue to a local entrepreneurs' meeting that didn't happen until the following month. He had missed his train station twice... *twice* he'd had to get out at the Argyle station, casually cross the platform, and get back on to exit at Wilson.

His brain was a shambles. He wasn't ready to see Eddie. He didn't respond.

Eddie didn't text for two days. Sid considered digging for puns online so he would have something to say.

*   *   *

"Adrian, get over here now. I'm not telling you again."

In their month in Connelly, Adrian and Eddie had begun to make themselves at home. They found a compromise for Adrian's wishes for his room. Dinner planning became a team task. This weekend's big chore was to purchase a long list of kindergarten supplies—including, but not limited to, many boxes of crayons.

Their last stop was the farmer's market. Eddie's patience had run out two errands earlier.

"But it's a *tractor!*" Adrian stomped his foot.

"And it's crowded. I want you next to me."

"I'm mad at you."

"Then we're even." Eddie walked to Adrian, took his hand, and directed him to the enormous bin of peaches inside the barn. Farther back, safely tucked behind more quarter crates filled with ears of corn, stood Sid. *Oh, god.* As he grappled with how to say, "Hi! Here's my son. You know, that dude that sort of made me a crazy person?" he distracted Adrian with the fruit.

"Help me pick some peaches. We can check out the tractor when we're done."

"Last time the peaches were all too hard," Adrian said.

"They were from the grocery." He glanced in Sid's direction, unsure what to do. He had an elaborate plan to introduce them to one another. It did not involve produce, a public place, or a cranky errand-running partner. "They'll be better here, don't you think?"

"I hope so." Adrian counted the peaches Eddie picked out and gingerly placed them in their bag.

"You know, if you do the sniff test, you'll get perfect peaches every time." Sid said.

Eddie knocked the display with his bag. It wobbled and unseated the topmost peaches. "Hi! Sid!" Eddie managed. He caught a rolling peach and shot a look to Adrian, who had unhelpfully melted into a giggle fit. "Wow. Hi. I, um… wasn't expecting you."

"I can see that." Sid smiled at Adrian and pointed to Eddie. "Is he usually this silly?"

"Yes. Who are you?"

"I'm Sid. Is your nose still running?"

"Oh! Hi! I'm Adrian! We're trying to pick peaches, but—" Adrian caught one more rolling peach and plopped it onto the pile. "It's not going so good."

"Can I show you a trick?" Without waiting for an answer, Sid sifted through the peaches. He picked one with good color and gave it a gentle squeeze and a sniff. "Okay, Adrian, smell this one."

Eddie couldn't speak. Sid was a natural. He had Adrian in the palm of his hand.

Adrian sniffed and lifted the peach to Eddie. "It smells like a peach, Daddy."

Sid told him to put that one in their bag. "Now, let's try—" Sid skimmed through the pile, found another peach, and passed it to Adrian. "This one."

Adrian sniffed and grimaced, lifting the peach to Eddie. "Doesn't smell like anything."

"Which one do you think will taste better?"

"The peachy one!"

Eddie dug out the peaches he and Adrian had lazily picked. Adrian did the sniff test while Eddie stared. "Is that why the peaches at your place are always so good?"

"Probably. Bourbon cream doesn't hurt either." Sid's gaze lingered on Eddie's eyes until Eddie took a breath to speak. Sid tore himself away and picked his own peaches. "Peaches that smell peachy are the peachiest." Sid plopped fruit into his bag after a quick whiff of each one.

"Hey, Sid." Adrian had escaped Eddie's side. He tugged on Sid's tunic. "Why are you wearing a dress?"

"Adrian! That's not—"

"It's fine. It's a fair question," Sid said, squatting to Adrian's level. "Why are you wearing a blue striped shirt?"

"Because… I like blue. And it was clean. And it's a play shirt, not a school shirt."

Sid nodded and made his own list. "This is a *kurta*. It's a shirt too."

"Oh."

"And I'm wearing it because it's comfortable when I teach, which I did this morning." He leaned in closer, as if sharing a secret. "Know what these baggy pants are called?"

"No…"

"Pajamas."

Adrian gasped. "Oh my goodness. You're wearing your pajamas? I'm not allowed to wear mine outside!"

Sid laughed. "They're not pajamas like you wear to sleep. I teach in them." Sid hiked his shirt to give Adrian a peek at the drawstring waistband. "When I bend and stretch and squat they move right along with me."

Adrian touched the sleeve of Sid's pale orange shirt. "You match the peaches."

Sid looked at Eddie. His smile spread clear across his face; his eyes danced with joy at Adrian. "I guess I do, huh?" Eddie could barely breathe.

"Yep." Adrian turned to Eddie and grinned. "Can I climb on the tractor now?"

"Yes. Go." He cleared his throat, wanting to sound more authoritative than breathless. "Walk and do not push!"

Adrian flapped his hand at Eddie. He waited his turn and climbed into the seat. Eddie jumped when Sid stood beside him.

"You're jittery."

"I know. I guess I had something…" Eddie kept an eye on Adrian awhile pulling Sid away from the crowd. "I didn't know if you were… if we were ready. To meet."

"Doesn't matter. We're here." They looked over to the tractor in time to see Adrian—now in the driver's seat—lean down and offer a hand to another little boy who needed a lift. "He's a good guy. Like his daddy."

Once everyone paid, they headed to their cars. Adrian hopped into his car seat and playfully pulled Eddie's hair when he buckled him in—as he always did, as though the earth hadn't inexplicably shifted when Adrian met Sid. Eddie left the door open and leaned against his car.

"I'm sorry I made this weird."

"It's fine."

"I miss you." He remembered Adrian's drawing peeking out of his school bag. "Don't move." He retrieved the artwork and handed it over. "My Michelangelo."

"My name is *Adrian*, Dad."

Sid took the drawing and bent to talk to Adrian. "Tell me about this. I like it."

"It's you and, um, Dad's other friend."

"Dottie."

"Yes. You're helping people at a fire." He pointed to a house with flames coming out of its windows. "You're a good guy."

"Can I hang it up in our office?"

Adrian nodded, and Sid stood. Eddie couldn't read his expression, but Sid said, "I miss you too."

"Dad! Hot! Come on!"

Eddie rolled his eyes. "We'll talk? Later?"

Sid kissed his own fingers, waved, and ducked into his car. Eddie started the engine and, before putting the car in reverse, sent a text.

Eddie: The fruit magnate was a crook. He was impeached.

Sid's grin as he drove away would fuel Eddie through the next week.

* * *

SID: HOW DO YOU TICKLE a rich girl?

Sid sat in his studio in Chicago. He was grateful for the air conditioning. The mid-August heat had been oppressive. He couldn't find a good-tasting peach at his neighborhood market to save his life. He missed Eddie. Curly-headed animals, fruit, buildings, and sewing machines invaded his dreams.

Eddie: Why would I want to tickle a rich girl?

Sid: Play nice now. I finally have a joke, and you're changing the script.

Eddie: Fine. How do you tickle a rich girl?

Sid: Say "Gucci Gucci Gucci!"

Eddie: I'm impressed. Career-centered and everything!

Sid: Have a good day, Eddie.

Eddie: Ade says you need to work on it. He didn't get it.

* * *

BACK IN CONNELLY, SID PUT in a few hours at C-DRT. Adrian's picture hung on his magnetic board alongside some of his own sketches he'd left behind. Before his bag left his shoulder, Dottie called from the depths of her office. "You have a delivery, Sid."

The shit-eating grin she wore when she surfaced could frighten children. She flipped on the conference room light, and in the middle of the table sat a vase with a single yellow rose.

"When did this come?"

"About half an hour ago. Open the damned envelope. It's making me all itchy."

Sid grabbed it and held it up to the light. "You mean nosy. Don't confuse your physiology with your personality."

"Open the damned thing or I'm making you take the midnight-to-six on-call shift while you're in town."

Sid lowered the card and glared. "I will take the seams of those pants I'm making you in by half an inch."

"Open the card. You know it's from Chief Garner."

"I know no such thing. I could have admirers all over Pennsylvania *and* Chicago." Sid shoved the card in his bag and sauntered into his office. He closed the door. Dottie's steel-toed shoe stopped it before it latched. "Sidney Pravit Marneaux?"

"Yes?"

"I hate you." He yanked the door open, and Dottie fell in. She plopped into the seat across from his desk. "I'll sit here all day then. Not like the computers are working anyway."

They stared each other down. Sid broke before she did. He opened the envelope and read it to himself.

A yellow rose for friendship… and joy. Eddie & Adrian

He handed the card to Dottie. "I forgot to tell you. I met Adrian." "And?"

"You're right; he's darling." Sid sighed, leaned back in his chair, and inspected the pocks in the ceiling panels. "I don't have time for this, Dottie, darling or not. My plate is already too full."

"Come on, Zico. Everyone needs to leave room for dessert."

And that highlighted the problem perfectly: Eddie was so much more than dessert.

XII.
AURIGA

By the end of summer, Sid planned a longer-than-usual stay in Connelly. After Bastra's visit to Out & About, they decided to use the spring campaign of the Trial Line to test a more casual line of clothing: brightly printed dress shirts; informal jackets and vests; pants cut looser at the crotch, tighter down the leg. Out & About was doing well, and it would serve Bastra well to play with the styles that were walking out the boutique's doors. Ultimately, they shared similar clientele.

Sid had driven his car to Chicago to bring back bolts of fabric he could use to start experimenting with the new spring line. While seeing clothes transform his clients drove his passion for this business, creating new designs most fulfilled him. Moving a vision from his mind onto paper, tearing that vision apart to make pattern pieces, and finally fashioning a pile of fabric into something that would transform the client lit a fire in him.

Between days with his dad, he looked forward to welcoming fall to Pennsylvania by drinking hot mugs of chai, burning incense, and churning out ideas he had long ago blocked. He loved Bastra's classic wear. But sometimes, "classic" stifled his creativity.

It was Community Day in Connelly, the Sunday before Mordell College's freshman orientation. Every year, festivities began with a parade from the center of town to the campus, where carnival rides, a local talent show, and, of course, a beauty pageant, entertained the masses. Every year, the Marneaux family enjoyed the parade together. Sid met Anna and Baba there.

"Can I ride, Mr. Marneaux?"

As they found their seats, a little blonde girl ran in front of Lou's wheelchair. Sid stopped pushing as she tried to climb up on Lou's lap. She was a pretty little girl with a button nose and apple cheeks. Her hair trailed down her back to the waistband of her shorts.

"Hey, hey," Sid said, as she tried again. "That's not a good idea."

"Oh, she's fine," Lou said, patting his lap. "Hop up here, sweetie." Sid shot a look at his sister.

"Neighbor kid. Olivia. In love with Dad."

"Parents?"

"Taking care of newborn brother. She's ours today."

Olivia leaned backward to look upside down at Sid. "What's your name?"

"Sid." He pointed to his dad's head. "He's my dad."

"I've seen your picture in the house."

He asked Anna, "How come I haven't seen this child before?"

"She moved in last week when you were gone." Anna shrugged. "Dad perks up when she's around."

When they got to their spot, Olivia hopped off Lou's lap and danced around the chair. She made up songs about parades and candy and her candy bag. Sid shot another look at his sister. "By 'today' do you mean all day?" If Sid looked closely enough, he might have detected a slight smile on her lips, but it had been so long since he'd seen one, he couldn't be sure.

"You're going to sit with me on the curb, Sid," Olivia announced. She pulled his arm, sat on the curb, and yanked. Sid sat.

A gunshot sounded, and Olivia's attention left Sid for the road. It would be minutes before the parade arrived at their seats, but it could already be heard.

"They're coming!" Olivia clapped.

"They're coming!" Lou nudged Sid's back with his knee. "Get a Tootsie Roll for me."

"It'll pull your teeth out."

Every township in Claremont County participated in the parade. Police cars, paddy wagons, squads, engines, township chiefs' trucks all blared their sirens and honked their horns. The word *cacophony* didn't begin to describe the noise. Connelly City led the parade with the police department seconded by the medics. Engine Number One brought up the rear.

Connelly's new chief held onto the grab rail and rode outside the passenger door of the huge truck. He wore his chief's helmet with his station uniform and waved and smiled like a practiced politician. For his first public appearance, the department had hung a sign on the side of the truck to introduce Eddie to the community.

The parade came to a standstill. Eddie took off his helmet and tossed it into the cab. He walked up and down the curb and tossed out goodies. Sid couldn't take his eyes off of him.

Eddie spotted Sid, grinned, and motioned for Sid to cover his eyes.

"Is this your boy?" Anna asked.

Sid couldn't look away. "That's the chief, yes…"

"Damn. You know how to pick 'em!"

"Stop. Now."

Olivia stopped dancing and attached herself to Sid's arm. She hid her face behind his back. "Olivia… they have candy."

"You get it."

"I am not running out into the street to get candy. Come on, now." He tried to maneuver her so she could see. She wasn't having it.

When he looked up, he faced an oversized, rainbow-swirled lollipop… right within licking range. Gorgeous and quite bratty, Eddie smiled behind it.

"Hi," was all Sid could manage.

"Hi." Eddie wiggled the lollipop.

"This has to be the gayest thing I've ever seen you do," Sid said as he took it. "And that's saying something."

Eddie squatted at Sid's eye level. His blue eyes pierced Sid's sad attempt at acting as if this wasn't affecting him. "I don't care. I still miss you."

Before Sid could find a breath, Eddie turned to Olivia, who had wiggled her head between Sid's body and his arm. "And who do we have here?"

"O…" She pulled free, but stood close to Sid. "My name's Olivia. Your trucks are *too loud*."

"They are super loud. How old are you, Olivia?"

"I'm four. Four and one half."

"Well, Olivia who's four and one half… let me see if I have something special for you." Eddie stood and turned to the truck. "Adrian! I need your help, buddy." Eddie hiked himself onto the truck and opened the side door. Sid was so busy gripping the stick of the damned sucker, trying to remember why he hadn't spent every night of his life with this man, that he almost looked right through Adrian hopping out of his dad's arms. Adrian was dressed in full firefighter turnout gear: a red captain's helmet, a "Kevlar" coat and trousers decorated with reflective striping, and the most important piece—the swagger.

"Oh, for fu—"

Eddie handed Adrian a bag and pointed to Olivia. She stepped away from Sid's protective arm and watched Adrian approach as if he was the King of the Fireman's Ball.

"Hi. I'm Adrian." Ade pulled out a plastic fireman's hat from his bag and handed it to Olivia. "Want a hat?"

"Yes!" She put it on with the bill in front.

"No, silly," Adrian said. "That goes in back so the water can pour off." He flipped the hat on her head and bopped the top of it for good measure. "There." He handed her his bag. "Here's some candy, too. My dad's the chief, you know."

"All right, buddy. That'll do for now," Eddie said as he scooped Adrian around the waist. "Back into the truck with you."

"*Bye, Sid!*" Adrian called. Eddie jogged to catch up with his vehicle, jumped onto the runner, and maneuvered Adrian into the passenger seat through the open window.

As the truck slowly pulled away, Eddie jogged back to Sid and squatted, looking him square in the eye. Sid leaned in quickly, so as to not second-guess himself, and kissed Eddie on the lips. He missed him too. Desperately. "I'm still here."

"I'll be waiting."

A whistle from Lou brought them back to reality. Eddie winked and caught up to his crew.

"Look at how big that lollipop is, Sid!" Olivia said. "You're lucky!" She virtually drooled over it; her eyes were as big as the confection.

"Yeah, but you got a hat."

"Yes, I did." She wiggled herself taller and patted the top of her hatted head. "But you... you got a *kiss!*"

"Yes, I did. Looks like I win."

EDDIE: OKAY, GIVE ME THE 4-1-1 on that little blonde Miss Thang you had at the parade. My son is out of his brain.

Sid walked from the parade to a cookout at his sister's. All he *wanted* to do was ditch the family, run to Eddie, and forget his inflated sense of responsibility. Getting away from Olivia would be a bonus. If she tugged on his wrist one more time to tell him what piece of candy she ate...

Sid: Miss Thang?? Who is that baby rock star you paraded around? Breaking little girl's hearts and offering them candy.

Eddie: Some little shit I found on the street. He's in love, Sid. I'm not ready for this. He will not shut up about OH-livia and her long yellow hair.

Sid: If I could, I'd dump her off on you.

Eddie: No thanks. We're off to ride the Ferris wheel or life as we know it will end.

Sid: Have a good time. And… thanks for the lollipop.

Eddie: Thanks for the kiss.

"YOUR GUY'S LITTLE BOY IS awfully cute," Anna said, avoiding eye contact by fussing with chicken on the grill.

"He's not my guy, Anna." After his most recent trip to Chicago, Anna had caught him in a weak moment and, against his better judgment, he'd told her everything.

"I guess I wonder why not?"

Sid took the tongs and rearranged the chicken. "I'm confused, okay? And—" He hung up the tongs and looked at her for the first time in what might have been weeks. She had aged so much in the past year. Still stunning, she was a pleasant blend of their parents but looked mostly like their mom. Her eyes were huge brown orbs, and her hair, now colored auburn, was long and silken, curlier than Ma's, so luscious the urge to touch it was as strong now as when Sid was a boy.

Anna's love was hard at the edges, geometric and exact, where Ma's had been soft, fluid, and gentle. Both were unwavering. Both were true. "Anna, look. I'm scared. I'm confused. You *know* I have too much shit to be juggling, and I don't think any of my shit is helpful in building a relationship with a man who's raising a child."

She glanced at their father before sitting down. Her son, Tyler, had him engaged in a story. Olivia sat nearby, putting clover into small bundles for whomever walked by. "I'm the last person to tell you how to run your love life."

"It hasn't stopped you before."

Anna ignored him. "Every parent worries about having enough time."

"I am not that boy's parent."

"But you love his father," she said as if she had cracked the biggest mystery in the universe.

"Love is an awfully strong word, Anna."

"You kissed him like you love him."

Sid needed to get back to Chicago where he could kiss and fuck and flirt with anyone he desired—sans peanut gallery. As if… he would actually take the time to do those things. It had been too long since he'd bothered.

"I'm just saying," Anna said, "it seems to me you have *two* reasons to be home more."

"Anna…" The truth was, on his road trip from Chicago, he had not only brought back numerous bolts of fabric; he had also grabbed pictures to make the sublet more like home and, for inspiration, an oversized chest full of fabric scraps. The lines of "home" and "away" continued to blur. But Anna didn't need to know that. "Really, this isn't any of your damned business."

"Zico! Come over here!" Lou's voice rang remarkably strong. And, with Tyler at his wheelchair's helm, he was suddenly close by.

Sid handed Anna the tongs. "More sauce and they should be ready." He pulled up a lawn chair to sit with his dad. "Sorry, Baba."

"You know I don't like you speaking to your mother that way." As Anna walked by with the platter of chicken, Lou smacked her ass.

"Dad. Look at me."

"What?"

"Who is that?" He pointed at Anna who had stopped and, with a silent plea, implored Sid to let it go.

"Well, that's your mother—" Lou looked at his daughter and grandson. "Where's Rimi?"

"She's not here, Baba."

"Hmm, well, I don't like you talking to my daughter that way, either."

"I know," Sid said. "I'm tired. Sometimes I want to go back to Chicago and pretend these last few months never happened."

"What, with that young man? So, go. No one asked you to come."

"Actually…"

"I'm not enough for you to come visit?" A teasing spark lit in Lou's eye. It shone brighter than the stars.

"You are exactly why I came to visit."

"And that handsome young man can't be hurting anything."

"He's complicated things," Sid said.

"I know you, Zico. Something tells me you've complicated things more."

Anna came by with glasses of lemonade and a kiss for each of the crowns of their heads. Of course she would kiss Sid now—she had Dad on her side. "He sends me flowers and corny puns," Sid told them. "Did I tell you that?"

"I forgot which room was my bedroom last night, Sid. You might have." Lou patted Sid's knee. "He's kind?"

"The most kind."

"Responsible?"

"Obviously."

"Does he make you laugh?"

"Yes…" Sid took his dad's hand. "I miss you, Baba…" He missed this version of his dad and the solid belief that he would always be here, like this.

"I miss me, too." With a squeeze of his hand, Lou shifted in his wheelchair to get closer. "Here's how I see it, Sid. You need to forget *all* the reasons why you think you shouldn't be with this man and start looking at all the reasons you should."

"That sounds like something Ma would say."

"How do you think she got all the way from Dhaka to here without turning back?"

Sid took a long drink of his lemonade and studied the pulp floating in the glass. "He does have a lot going for him."

"And, Zico, I think you have a lot to offer that little boy. If nothing else, you'd make his dad a happy man. And a happy dad makes for a happy kid. You of all people should know that."

EDDIE: IF THERE WAS A bisexual pride parade, would it go both ways?

The real question might have nothing to do with Eddie's character or his son. It might have to do with living with the man's humor. Sid turned off the last light and headed to bed. Ever since the parade, Sid had fought to focus on the new design ideas spinning in his head. At the first lull in forward progression, his mind had clouded with images from the day of the parade: Eddie's lips on his, that damned lollipop and the smile the glowed behind it, the lucidity and clarity in his dad's advice. He hadn't liked one piece he'd made in the last two days.

Sid: Seriously? That's the best you have?

Eddie: Okay, how about this one? What do you get when you cross a rooster and peanut butter?

Sid: Well, we know there's a cock in the answer.

Eddie: *sings the Jeopardy theme*

Sid: You are an ass.

Eddie: A cock… you were on the right track… that sticks to the roof of your mouth.

Sid: You're making me think obscene thoughts.

Eddie: You shouldn't have kissed me. It obviously gives you a dirty mind.

Sid: I probably shouldn't have.

Eddie: Oh.

Sid: I'm cloudy is all.

Eddie: I hope I can bring you some sunshine.

Sid: You do, Eddie. Every damned day.

And that was exactly Sid's problem.

*   *   *

CLAREMONT COUNTY DISPATCH TO CONNELLY City Fire. 552 Linden Street.
Five-five-two Linden Street. Residential fire. Time of dispatch 14:32.
Connelly City Fire. 552 Linden Street. Residential Fire. Clear.

"Oh, hell. Dottie, I'll stay… you go on."

"Are you sure? You might be waiting for nothing."

"Yep. Go. Turn your phone off—I'll hear if we get dispatched."

"You just want to see the chieeefff," Dottie sang.

"Get the fuck out of here before I change my mind."

Dottie left. Eddie had sent another rose—lavender-colored—with a tag that simply read, "Enchanted." Sid pulled the bud vase closer and fingered its delicate petals. Spinning the vase, he watched the overhead lights pick up highlights and shadows of the folded bloom. The radio beeped and buzzed in the background. Dispatch discussed school bus runs, squad runs in other townships, and the fire that burned on the east side of Connelly.

Before long, county dispatched him to the scene. He touched his nose to the flower and inhaled deeply before taking off to pick up his volunteer.

When they arrived, emergency vehicles blocked the street so that Sid and his rookie volunteer, Jake, couldn't see the affected house. Even half a block away where they parked, the heat of the fire smacked their skin. The sting of smoke bit their lungs as they approached on foot.

"This is your first fire?" Sid asked, holding Jake back. Jake nodded and stared without a word. Sid remembered his first run with his dad and the wisdom his dad had offered that day. "We are here to provide shelter and basic needs for the family," Lou had said. "We don't judge who they are, why the house might be burning down, or how they're behaving. Understand?"

"I'll be fine, man," Jake said with a cockiness that screamed naiveté. He was a star punter on the Mordell football team and carried himself as if nothing could ruffle him. "You said it should be straightforward, right?"

"I don't believe I did. This is the worst day of this homeowner's life. Nothing is straightforward." Jake grunted. "Let's go find the chief and see what we've got."

Not seeing the white helmet anywhere, Sid approached the captain.

"Hey, Captain. Where'd Chief escape to?"

"I'm your man for now. Chief's inside."

"He's inside?" Eddie had done it again. "Why isn't he out here super—" It wasn't any of his business. And the fire was too big for the captain to chit-chat with a damned volunteer worker.

Flames engulfed the back half of the two-story house. Yellow-brown smoke billowed out of windows and between the siding and the roof, where firefighters stood and created holes in shingles and flashing to allow heat to escape.

An engine from Waterson Township arrived, and more firefighters emptied onto the scene. They unraveled hose, shouted orders, and got straight to work as smoke and flames billowed from the house.

Sid swallowed hard and tried to find a brave face to plaster over his petrified one. "What do we—" From the house, a hiss, a *whoosh*, and deep muddled *boom* cut through the air.

"Shit. Step back, boys!"

Before Sid could move, a fireball shot from under the roof. The left side of the house collapsed; half of the roof caved with it. Dust and debris clouded the air until smoke and walls of bright orange flames took over.

Eddie was still inside.

XIII.
DRACO

THE MOMENT THE BACKDRAFT HIT, Captain Harris turned to the engines and spun his forearm round and round. "Get them *out* of there!" Firemen rushed to their trucks; others moved their hoses closer. Horns sounded three times. Two firemen spilled out of the house as smoke billowed from their bodies. They flagged down the medics and pointed to the burning house.

"Garner, do you copy?" Captain Harris barked into his radio. "Chief! Do you copy?"

Sid stood frozen, willing Eddie to come through the front door or to saunter from the back, as if he'd taken an afternoon stroll and was completely unfazed, saying, "Damn! That's a hot one!"

Instead, flames billowed from the east side of the house; black smoke filled the sky. Sid sat with Jake in the auxiliary tent. An older gentleman stood watching at the edge of the tent, evaluating the scene, and reporting to other volunteers.

"Sid, he's on the move," the man said. "His PASS hasn't activated."

"What if it malfunctioned? What if—" It didn't matter. No technology would help him believe in Eddie's safety until he saw him moving, breathing, smiling—*anything* beyond the flames and water and thick, black smoke.

Captain Harris counted his crew and grabbed his radio. The volunteer stepped out of the tent and approached him, but before he was more than two steps out, the captain put up a hand, smiled, and gave him a thumbs-up.

Sid stood, brushing off an offer of water. "Eddie?"

"Yeah," the man said with a crooked smile. "He's okay." He sat Sid down and put the bottle of water into his hand. "Walt Burgess. Retired from the department in oh-seven. Worked a few of these with your dad. How is he?"

"What?" Sid's mind was centered on one man and it was not his father. "He's—fine? Where's Eddie?"

"Making his way out," Walt said. With a smile, he added, "Is Chief your boy?"

Sid nodded. He nodded as naturally as if they hadn't spent the summer dancing around each other, testing and retreating from the intimacy that had at first been so easy for them. All cloudy thoughts parted; he believed Chief was his boy as assuredly as the flames snaked outside of the home and up into the sky.

If only Eddie would come out of the fire.

"He's my boy." Sid stood and peeked around Walt. "Where is he?"

Movement from the front door caught Sid's attention. He moved Walt aside. "Eddie…" Eddie stumbled down the porch. A woman's bloodcurdling screams cut through the cacophony.

Eddie carried a limp and seemingly lifeless, barefoot child over his shoulder.

"Jake, back to the truck," Sid said, frozen in place.

"But…"

Eddie handed the child to a medic. He ripped off his helmet and mask, opened his coat, and bent over, gasping for breath.

Sid inched closer, fighting the urge to go to him as if he, too, was on fire.

"He'll be all right," Walt said. "Let him be."

Jake joined Sid at the edge of the tent with his phone up, ready to take a picture of the burning house.

Sid smacked his arm. "Put your *fucking* phone away."

"But this is *awesome!*"

"Get in the truck. And if anyone asks you any questions on the way, you send them to me, do you understand?"

"Yeah, man... Jesus. Chill out. I'm going." Jake backed away toward the ERV.

"I am so sorry," Sid said. "We train them—*Dad* did, anyway..."

"You can't train empathy, son." Wade looked at the house with the calm of years' experience. The companies' efforts were working. Flames abated and smoke dissipated, but a long day loomed ahead.

"That boy didn't make it, did he?" Sid asked, fearing the answer.

"It didn't look good."

Walt called across the lawn. "Chief, come on. Sit. Rest. Rehydrate." He shook his head as Eddie conceded and trudged to the tent. "The parents said the boy wasn't home, but Chief had a feeling."

"Sometimes you have to go with your gut," Sid said. Eddie carried his helmet as if it weighed as much as an anvil. He hadn't glanced more than a foot in front of himself, as though he was still mentally fighting the battle inside the house.

Volunteers on the auxiliary team replenished oxygen tanks and checked firefighters' vitals. On scorching summer days, the team provided misting stations to help regulate body heat; controlled heaters would bring relief in the bitter winter months. While his attentions had been scattered in Chicago and with his dad, Eddie and Dottie had made this happen. The benefits on a fire as large as today's were immeasurable.

Eddie dropped his coat and flopped into a chair before catching Sid's eye. "C'mere."

Sid went to him. "Are you okay?"

"I'm fine," Eddie said, accepting bottled water from a volunteer. "I thought we had that fucking roof opened up enough in back."

"There must have been a pocket somewhere."

Eddie looked at the house, which now presented a much calmer scene. He downed the bottle of water and waved off the offer of another. "I need to get back," he said and took Sid's hand as he stood. "Come by the station when you're done?"

Sid wiped a smudge of ash from Eddie's face. "We're all going to be here a long time."

Eddie took off a glove and grabbed the edge of Sid's C-DRT vest. "I know, but…" He ran a thumb over the reflective trim as his eyes met Sid's. "Please come find me."

"I'll find you. Be careful."

EDDIE STARED AT AN OPEN folder on his desk. The words blurred. The lines of the forms bent into waves. The pen in his hand weighed heavily, as if filled with iron. They'd been back from the scene barely an hour: enough time to shower, guzzle a couple mugs of coffee, and call Adrian. He had needed to hear his son's voice.

Lifting his head to greet Sid when he arrived took effort. "Hey," he said, his voice as weak as every muscle in his body.

Sid closed the door behind him and put a paper bag on Eddie's desk. "I didn't see you eat on-scene."

"I didn't. Thank you." Eddie opened an unappealing sub sandwich: an indistinguishable sauce had seeped into the bread; the green peppers lay limp; the meat and colorless cheese slopped out of the sides. He ate with a ravenous vigor.

"Don't forget to chew."

"Mmpf." Eddie worked a rogue green pepper into his mouth. It tasted as horrible as it looked. Sid sat quietly, expectant. "I heard you were worried about me," Eddie finally managed.

"I'm still rattled."

"We're trained for these types of events, Sid."

"I don't care *how* trained you are, Eddie. Men die in backdrafts."

"They do." Eddie focused on his sandwich. He needed to meet with his crew, finalize paperwork, be the administrator. All he wanted was to take Sid home—

"Eddie, have I done something wrong?"

"No, I'm not mad at you." He put his sandwich down, wiped his mouth clean, and sighed. "I'm mad at me and I don't—"

"Why?"

"Can you come to my house after I get Adrian to bed? I need my son first, but I—" The thought of being alone tightened his chest. "Just come sit with me?"

Adrian cooperated at bedtime as if he knew his dad was balancing on a loose tightrope. He talked from pick-up to lights out, but now he slept. Eddie hand-washed the day's dishes just for something to do. He stared at the pages of whatever novel he had blindly grabbed from his bookshelf. He gave up on patience and sat on the front porch to await Sid's arrival.

He didn't greet Sid with a hug. He didn't kiss him hard on the mouth for bringing ice cold beer and piping hot pizza. He didn't drag Sid up to his bedroom to bury himself in life, in soft heat, in ecstasy and animalistic, carnal lust—with a side of deep affection—but, oh, *god*, he wanted to.

Instead, Eddie took Sid to his back patio. When he'd moved in, the small yard had been overrun by old, dying trees that obscured sunlight, moonlight—life outside of their fenced-in yard. He had coughed up a pretty penny to get the trees cleared out, but now the yard was a haven, a place of peace in which to reconnect the shattered shards of his life.

"It's nice back here," Sid said. "More quiet than I'd expect in town."

"I guess I'm far enough from campus."

They quietly ate, sipped beer, and listened as the crickets chorused their nightly serenade. Even in this perfect setting, the unanswered questions of the day took over Eddie's mind.

"Did the family say what the hell happened?" he asked. "I know the boy started it in their bedroom."

Sid sat up in his chaise. "*Conner* started it?"

"Yeah, a bobby pin in a socket in their bedroom."

"Oh, my god." Sid sat back and stared into the sky. "He was at a friend's house," Sid said. "They had a fight and he walked home. Mom and Dad were out in the shed cleaning, so I guess he occupied himself."

"He ran clear across the house and hid. We go to preschools and elementary schools to teach kids about this shit."

"He had to have been terrified, Eddie."

"I know. I'm angry. That backdraft shouldn't have happened. Had I stayed out there and been in charge, it wouldn't have."

"You don't know that. Did the captain do anything differently than you would have?"

Eddie sighed, resigned. "No. Probably not. I might have spent more time over that second-floor bathroom." He took a swallow of beer. "Either way, a kid's dead, and I'm responsible."

"Eddie, you can't—"

"I can. I am. It's my *job*."

Sid fell quiet. Eddie stewed, replaying the afternoon in his head on infinite loop. He measured every move he'd made to see if he could have done something differently.

"Eddie, I can *feel* you winding up. You cannot blame—" Eddie shot him a look. "Is it possible he was already gone?"

"Yes. Likely. I just grabbed him and moved." A valve released, and Eddie let the moments before and after the explosion pour out of him. "He was like liquid lead in my arms. I was three steps from the first floor when the backdraft hit. Blew us down. I had to climb over debris from upstairs. It kept slipping and breaking. I couldn't get momentum. I couldn't see. Even with my helmet light, it was so fucking *dark*. I just wanted to get him out."

Had he not gone in, the boy would have been ash. That had to amount to something.

"Do you ever get scared?" Sid asked.

"Afterward. This is the first time I've lost someone—I don't know what I'm feeling."

"I'm so sorry, Eddie."

The opening of the back door didn't stir him but, "Daddy?" did.

"Hmm?" Eddie jerked and blinked at his groggy son standing beside his chair. He carried a well-loved blanket wadded in his arms; his hair flew everywhere.

"Ade… what are you doing up?"

"I had to potty. The light confused me." He rubbed his knuckles around his eyes and looked at Sid. "Why's Sid here?"

Sid smiled and stood to collect their beer bottles and pizza trash. "Hey, Adrian."

"Too late for questions. Let's get you to bed, huh?"

"Eddie, I'm going to go. Why don't you go up with him? You're exhausted."

Eddie scooped up Adrian and nodded. "That sounds like a good idea. Ade, you wanna sleep with Daddy tonight?"

"In your big bed?"

"Yep. Bring your music too."

Adrian took off upstairs, and Eddie sighed. "He's entirely too awake for midnight."

Sid dumped the trash, stopped at the front door, and pulled Eddie into his arms. "I'm glad you're okay." Eddie fell limp and almost whimpered with relief at having someone else hold him up.

When they broke apart, Eddie snuck a kiss to Sid's cheek. "You're still here. Thank you."

"We'll talk soon."

"Daddy! Where *are* you?" Adrian's voice hit like ice chilling Eddie's veins.

But before the chill set in, Sid took Eddie's hands and reminded him of the blessing amidst his pain. "Hold him tight tonight."

ELEVEN STEPS SEPARATED THE FIRST from the second floor. As Eddie trudged up each one, he would have sworn there were forty. Fifty. A-billionty, as Adrian would say. Guilt shamed him for feeling so burdened with his son when, not a mile away, a family faced a lifetime without theirs.

Sid's visit had breathed new life into him and supplied a strength he hadn't known he needed until it propped him up and held him close. While he had come to realize that the separation between them had been wise—it had allowed Eddie to get more settled and Sid to find a balance between his work and home battles—he'd missed their friendship. He'd missed Sid's mind, the creative way he saw the world and put himself in it.

Eddie took an extra moment before opening his bedroom door. Now was the time to sleep, to take a few moments and smile with his son. When he opened his door, however, it took everything he had not to bolt outside, chase Sid's car, and forget he ever had a son.

"Hi! I'm ready, Daddy!" Adrian looked at him with the glow of a boy who had slept for eight hours every night of his life. He had brought not only his music, but also hours' worth of activities: a box of crayons, a stack of blank paper, a small box of blocks, a large army of plastic dinosaurs, and his ratty blanket. All they needed was a sprawling Labrador retriever and Eddie wouldn't have an inch of mattress for himself.

"Adrian, it's after midnight. Not playtime."

"I'm not sleepy."

"I am. If you want to stay with me tonight—"

"I'm not sleepy." Adrian grabbed a crayon and began to draw. Eddie seethed as he got ready for bed. Ugliness and impatience ran through his mind like a speeding train, careening toward a concrete wall and ready to explode:

Don't you understand *what happened today?*

Don't you understand *that I miss her too?*

Don't you understand... anything?

As if overseeing Eddie's thoughts, the queen of hearts card Maggie had carted around in her wheelchair pocket stared at him from its new home, tucked into the mirror frame on his dresser. And it was as if Eddie could hear her voice: "He's five. Adrian understands none of those things."

Eddie took a deep breath, as if to soak in the warm scent of incense and her patient smile. At thirty-three, Eddie wasn't sure he understood those things either.

"Why was Sid here, Daddy?"

"Did that upset you?"

"No." Eddie looked at Adrian's new picture of Sid. He carried a peach. "I saw him hug you. You're sad."

"We had a sad fire today. I needed a friend to talk to."

"Did you save the house?" Adrian cocked his head, blindly picked a new crayon, and drew the first lines of a building.

"No."

"Did someone get hurt?"

"Yes. A boy your age."

Adrian looked at Eddie, fear flashing in his eyes. "Will he get better?"

"No."

The brush of Adrian's crayon over the paper stopped. He put his crayon in his box, shut it, and dropped his stack of paper onto the floor. "What if…" Adrian curled himself under Eddie's arm. His breath was uneven and he traced slow designs all over Eddie's chest. He started to speak and stopped, whined, and fell quiet.

"Adrian, you can say anything. Anything at all."

"What if—" Adrian's voice wobbled. His sniffed and wiped his nose and tapped Eddie's chest as if trying to slot his voice into the rhythm. "What if Mommy found him."

Eddie grabbed Adrian's hand and pulled Adrian onto his lap. "Ade… buddy."

"What if she found him. She knew he was coming, and that's why—" Adrian sniffed and hiccupped; a new spring of tears bubbled under the surface. "That's why she doesn't talk to me when I see her. She—she's—" He stopped, looked at Eddie, and finished his sentence in a wail. "She's waiting for another boy!"

Overcome with tears and grief and emotions he couldn't possibly understand, Adrian melted into Eddie. Eddie held his son and rocked them together; he patted his hair. He said nothing. Nothing would help. Nothing would take it away.

Adrian's body stopped shaking, and he tried to talk. "Is that why, Daddy? Is that why she doesn't talk to me?"

"I don't know what you mean."

"At night. I see her. The movies when I sleep and—"

"In your dreams? You dream about Mommy?"

"Yes! She won't talk to me. She smiles and she wears that blue dress that matched my sky crayon and—" Adrian sat up and frantically wiped his eyes. "She has her *hair*! She's at a party and I go to talk to her and—"

"Does she stand in line?"

Adrian sat back and stared at his dad as though he had the answers to every little boy's questions. "You see her too?"

Tears stung Eddie's eyes. Anger at the day bit like a rabid dog. Anger at the unfairness of it all, at the sickness of a world that allowed five-year-old boys to miss their mothers and mothers to miss their five-year-old boys. Anger at a world that created Margaret James and promptly took her away. Anger that people left him, left this world, even when he was supposed to have saved them.

And, as a soothing rain, Sid's simple plea washed over him: *Grieve with him.*

Eddie looked at the queen of hearts card on his mirror, and, for the first time in months, he didn't fight the tears; he talked through them. "When I see her, she's in a line. She's wearing those ratty jean shorts—do you remember those?"

"I could put my thumb in the hole near her belly and tickle her."

"Yes!" They laughed through their tears. Adrian soothed Eddie now. His tiny hands were soft on Eddie's cheeks; his big blue eyes were bright and encouraging. "She has her hair in my dreams too, but when I go to her—"

Eddie couldn't talk anymore. He folded Adrian in his arms as they cried and reasoned the unreasonable. Time lost meaning. Sleep lost importance. Nothing mattered beyond Adrian's caring reflection of Maggie, of love, of life right here in his arms.

Muffled in Eddie's chest, Adrian confessed, "I hate going to sleep. Because *then*—"

"Waking up means she leaves again."

Adrian nodded. "I want her to come back."

"I do too, buddy. But we're doing okay, huh?"

Adrian scratched his fingers along the nape of Eddie's neck. "Do we have peaches?"

Eddie looked at the clock. Time still didn't matter. "Last of the season. Wanna share one?"

"In bed?"

"In bed," Eddie said. "I bet they taste better here."

* * *

THE FOLLOWING NIGHT, EDDIE STOOD in front of the television next to Adrian and sifted through the list of potential movies to stream. Adrian's pajama pants clung to his bottom and thighs because he hadn't dried himself properly after his bath. Every time Adrian gently shook his head "no" to one of Eddie's suggestions, a drop of water from his incompletely dried hair would fall on Eddie's foot. One minute before Eddie's two-minute warning—"If you don't pick something in two minutes, we're watching *Bride of Chucky*"—the doorbell rang.

Eddie handed the remote to Adrian. "Pick something before I come back, or we're skipping movie night." Anticipating the third high schooler of the week fundraising for the marching band, he scowled as he swung the door open.

Sid stood on the porch with a flat white box in his arms. "I took a break and went to that bakery up on Stephens Road," he said. "It was the last-hour special. I got carried away." Sid lifted the lid of the box. "Strudel?"

"Stru—" Eddie looked in the box where a dozen oozing, crusty pastries looked back. "Yum. Come in. We're just getting ready for movie night."

"Hi, Sid! What about *Monsters, Inc.*, Daddy?"

"I'm sorry." Sid tried to hand over the box of goodies. "I should have called—"

"No, you shouldn't have. You should join us." They shared a look. Eddie knew he was pleading. Sid contemplated, glanced at Adrian who had set up the movie and was now doing somersaults across the living room floor. "He settles once the movie starts. Promise." To tie a bow on his proposition, he pointed to the box of strudel. "I have ice cream."

"How are you holding up?" Sid asked as Eddie pulled out plates and dug for his ice cream scoop.

"Good. Fine. Vanilla or cookies and cream?"

Sid rested his hand on Eddie's arm and stilled his almost frantic movements. "Hey. Look at me."

Eddie dropped the scoop in the ice cream and turned to Sid. "I'm sorry. I'm a little wound up. You—I didn't expect you." *And I'm so tired I want to throw myself in your arms and bawl.*

"I know. I should have called. I just spent most of the day worrying about you. Yesterday was *not* a typical day."

"No. And I've spent the day pretending it was."

"You don't have to anymore," Sid said taking over the scooping job. "Go on and start the movie. I'll bring these out."

Eddie and Adrian curled up together in the recliner while Sid stretched out on the couch. The only parts of the movie Eddie caught were when Sid and Adrian's laughter blended in an audible joy that healed his weary heart. He invited Sid to stay after he put Adrian to bed.

"Because tonight's been very nice and we're not going to ruin it, are we?" Eddie said to Adrian, nodding as he spoke.

"No. We're not. Thanks for dessert, Sid!"

As if Maggie had descended and placed her hands of peace and calm on him, Adrian snuggled right into bed. In a long line of long nights, the small favor soothed.

When he came downstairs, Sid had his coat on. "So soon?"

"Yeah, I have more work to do tonight. I just wanted to check on you."

"Thank you." Eddie said, gratefully stepping into Sid's open arms.

"After Ma died," Sid said, still holding him close, "any death hit hard. Harder than it normally would have."

Tears stung Eddie's eyes. Of course that factored in. It's what had spilled into his bedroom last night when Adrian confessed his deepest fears, his nightmares. Eddie stepped back and took Sid's hands in his. "They said Conner was going to start kindergarten in the fall. He and Adrian might have been friends."

"I know. It's unfair."

Eddie nodded and stared at Sid's long fingers, grateful to have him to hang on to. "I save people, you know? They're not supposed to *leave*."

"Sometimes they do," Sid said. "It's not the same thing, but—I'm still here."

"No. It's—it's everything right now."

With the warmth of Sid's kiss on his cheek, Eddie turned in early. Adrian would wake him again, but until then, he slept.

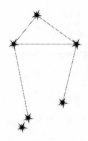

XIV.
LIBRA

If dictionaries had live updating capabilities, a photograph of Eddie's current situation would be found next to the word *catastrophe*.

Eddie enjoyed his Sundays off. But today, two days after Sid's visit, Lisbon Township had a multi-unit. Something had crumbled in their chain of command; they were shorthanded. They called a third alarm to Connelly City. "Day off" now meant as much as "free beach vacation." Neither was happening.

In Wylie, Eddie had had reliable emergency childcare. Sharon was dependable; fellow firefighters' families or a neighbor friend filled the gaps. In the new community, his options were less established. His next-door neighbor had a previous engagement. A funeral kept the daycare teacher who had offered emergency assistance unavailable. The station wives sent their regrets.

He could think of one other person to call: the person he had promised himself he would never, ever, at any time, *ever* call for babysitting duties. Eddie had danced on a cloud of hopefulness since Sid's last visit. His concern reached beyond friendship and understanding. But now, Eddie needed help.

Catastrophe.

While Eddie paced his office floor, cracked his knuckles, and tried to pull other options out of the depths of his ass, Adrian drew new, imaginary worlds. The fire continued to burn without an incident commander.

Cat-as-tro-phe. "I'm going to regret this."

"What?" Adrian missed nothing—unless it was a reminder to make his damned bed.

"Nothing. I, um—what do you think about Sid?"

"He's nice. I liked his dessert," Adrian said as he drew another building. "He kisses and hugs you a lot."

Eddie closed his eyes and pinched the bridge of his nose. "Yes. Yes, he does. Would you like to play with him today?"

Adrian shrugged. "Sure."

If he's willing. If he doesn't shove that rainbow lollipop with an apple strudel chaser up my ass and never again say, "I'm still here."

Catastrophe.

Eddie dialed Sid's number.

"Yeah, hello?"

"Sid? Hey." He paused, waiting for joyous recognition; he got silence. Adrian drew a raincloud. "I know you're working. I wouldn't be calling if it wasn't important and desperate and a complete fucking—"

"*Daddy!*"

"Sorry, buddy. A complete *freaking* catastrophe, but I need—I swore I wouldn't do this, I did, and I've tried everything else first, but there's a—" Eddie stopped, remembering the obvious. "Shit. Are you on call today?"

"With C-DRT?"

"Yes."

"No. I'm working on some new designs. What's up?"

"Never mind… I'll figure something out."

"Eddie, what do you need? You wouldn't have called me—"

"A multi-unit in Lisbon. I'm completely and totally out of options and I have to get there in negative time."

Sid sighed. In Eddie Catastrophe Time, the silence lasted at least twenty-five minutes. Finally, "You need someone to watch Adrian."

"I do."

Longer sighs bookended another silence. "Where is he?"

"With me at the station."

"Will he occupy himself? I'm seriously under the gun here."

"Yes! Yes, yes, yes. He has his bag of activities. Parker is here and will give you the security code to get more crap from the house—which is probably a good idea. Take—take him anywhere." Eddie moved quickly out of his office. He jogged downstairs and slipped into his turnout gear. "He's... sort of used to adapting wherever he is."

"He's okay at the station until I can get there?"

"Yes. Parker's here. Thank you. You have no ide—"

"Just... go, Eddie."

"Right. Thank you."

Sid disconnected. With no more time to spare, Eddie whistled for Adrian to come to the garage.

"I need you to sit at the watch desk with Lieutenant Parker. Sid will be here soon."

"Okay. Be safe, Daddy."

"I will." Eddie stopped before getting in the station pickup. "You behave with him."

Adrian rolled his eyes and waved. "I *know*."

He knows. He's a good kid. He spent the last year and a half of his life being shifted from caregiver to caregiver and he was fine. Every time.

Eddie got in the truck and backed out. "Sid is going to kill me."

"I'm going to *kill* him."

Sid tossed his phone on his table. He growled at the pattern tissue that flipped onto the floor.

After the day at the fire, Sid's creative block had broken. He had two more pieces to finish before returning to Chicago for fittings and a photo shoot for advertising, press kits, and the website.

He also knew that Eddie wouldn't have called if he hadn't been backed up against a wall. Sid snuffed out his incense, secured his stacked pattern tissues with weights, and went to the fire station.

"So then… the monster comes in!" Adrian's monologue had started the minute he climbed into the car seat Lieutenant Parker had graciously installed in Sid's car. "His claws are out and his teeth are sharp and he's roaring." Adrian clawed and fanged and roared. "And somehow… *somehow*, Sid!" Adrian took what seemed like his first breath in at least ten paragraphs. "Are you listening to my story?"

"I am listening." Sid looked at Adrian and couldn't help but smile. This kid's enthusiasm for every word out of his own mouth was pretty spectacular. "Your monster is roaring and baring his teeth… then what?"

"*Then*! Oh my goodness! Then, he starts taking people out. But only the bad guys! How does he know who the bad guys are and who the good guys are?"

"I don't know. Do you?"

"*No*! But *he* knows. He looks at one guy, and you can see—it's so cool! You can see his… his… skin? Scales? You can see it, like, soften. And he lets him go. And he lets a lady go and *then* he sees one of the bad guys and—*bam*. Takes him out!"

"Takes him out? How?" Traffic came to a standstill; Adrian's story surged on.

"He has like these huge spiky mallet… things on his hands. They show up when he swings his arms, and *wham*."

"Ouch."

"Yes. Ouch." Adrian sighed and flopped against his seat. "I want a monster."

"You have people you need to take out?"

"No. Well. Not *really*. A kid at my old house that was kind of mean. But I got a grownup when he said stuff."

"That's a good idea," Sid said as he pulled into his complex. "So do you need a monster?"

"No, but it would be fun to scare people. I'd be the only one who'd know that the monster was nice." Adrian wiggled himself higher in his car seat and surveyed the new scenery. "But monsters aren't real."

"No, but I might know a way to get you one."

"How?"

Sid got out, grabbed a bag of Adrian's belongings, and opened Adrian's door. Adrian stared at him. Sid stared at Adrian.

"You need to—" Adrian pointed between his legs at his car seat's buckle. "Undo me. They make it so kids can't escape."

"Of course." Sid squatted and unbuckled Adrian as he handed him his bag. "I should probably apologize right up front."

"What for?"

"I don't spend a lot of time in charge of kids your age." Sid pulled out Adrian's second bag and pointed toward his front door. "So if it seems like I don't know what I'm doing, it's because I don't."

"That's okay," Adrian said. "I'm five. I never know what I'm doing."

Once inside, Adrian put down his bag. He sniffed, stilled, and sniffed again. His eyes grew bigger as he looked around from his frozen spot in Sid's small foyer.

"Ade? You okay?"

"It smells like—"

Sid mentally kicked himself. "Your old house." The incense discussion with Eddie had been brief on his and Eddie's first morning together. Eddie confessed that the scent brought bittersweet memories, but said nothing more. Sid saw pain in his eyes then, a longing that he didn't understand at the time.

"Yes. Like Mommy." He took another deep breath and closed his eyes. He smiled and stepped in. "You burn skinny sticks too?"

"I do. My mom and I would burn them when we sewed... and I still do."

"Can we burn one today?"

"If you'd like."

In the studio, armed with a bowl of peaches, Adrian looked at a plastic glass filled with peach and cream roses and asked, "Are those from Daddy?" which was followed by, "Is he your boyfriend?"

"What would you think about that?"

Adrian's answer was quick, without thought. "I think that'd be pretty okay." Adrian stuffed his nose into the tiny bouquet of flowers. "When he buys them, Daddy says all the colors mean something different. What do these mean?"

"I think they mean your dad thinks I'm pretty spectacular."

"I don't know what *that* word means, but Dad usually isn't wrong." Once Adrian had his paper, crayons, and colored pencils and had been convinced that the gauges and measures littering Sid's workspace wouldn't be helpful in his own creations, he asked the most important question of all: "So, how do I get a monster?"

"We can make one," Sid said.

"How?"

"You draw amazing pictures. I make things with fabric. Together, we can make a monster—like a doll."

Adrian gasped. "You can *do* that?"

"I can." Sid swiped a peach slice out of the bowl and slurped it into his mouth.

"I want to make a hundred monsters!"

"Let's start with one, huh? Why don't you draw the story you told me in the car?"

"Yes!" Adrian took a peach and licked his fingers before grabbing a blue crayon. "Peaches that smell peachy are the peachiest. Daddy says that every time we go to the store."

Maybe Sid wouldn't *kill* Eddie. A kiss sounded much better. The difference was so minute, it seemed silly to mince letters for accuracy's sake.

As Sid finished the last seam of a new vest design, Adrian hopped off his chair and brought his picture for inspection. He checked out Sid's work first. "What's that?"

"It's a vest." Sid draped the knit, rust-colored waistcoat over Adrian's shoulders. "A casual vest." He buttoned the one button that hit Adrian's kneecap. "It's also for someone much taller than you."

"One day you could make me one that fits." Adrian wiggled his bottom. "I like it."

"It would be cute; nice shirt, blue jeans. You'd be stylin' up kindergarten."

Adrian scrunched his nose and handed over his picture. "I sorta drew a hundred monsters anyway."

"That's okay." Adrian had created an entire cityscape: cars, buildings, a small park with kids playing, and pedestrians lining the streets. "You have a great imagination, Ade."

Adrian shrugged. "I just see pictures in my head and put 'em on the paper."

Sid pointed to a person in a bright red coat. "Tell me about this person here."

"She's about to get splashed by that bus. But, the monster—" He pointed to an orange creature barely visible from behind a building. "He's going to jump between the bus and the curb so she won't have to go home and change clothes."

"He's a gentlemanly monster."

"He's still learning. He does the little jobs. But *this* guy—" Adrian pointed to a large blue monster that towered over the buildings and had, for its size, a surprisingly happy smile on its face. "He's the boss. He's the one I want."

"Okay, so here's your next assignment." Sid pulled out one of his design sheets. "I want you to get a clean sheet of paper and draw that monster, like this. Head to toe. We're going to take your design and make a pattern, like I'm doing with this outfit."

"What are we going to make it out of?"

"That's the best part." Sid stepped into his closet and pulled out the chest of fabric he had brought from Chicago. After lugging it down the three flights of stairs and hiking it into the trunk of his car, he had questioned his wisdom.

Adrian's eyes grew with each inch it traveled across the floor. Sid had made the right choice. One needs a box of sentimental, bright fabric to create a proper monster, after all.

Sid lifted the lid, and Adrian's mouth dropped. "It's a treasure chest!"

Under scraps of gabardine and shirting, satin lining, and T-shirt knits, were piles of linen and cotton muslin, chiffon, silks, and brocades—scraps from his mother's days of sewing saris, dresses, and *kurtas*. The colors were bright and bold; the fabrics were rich with texture and—to Sid—history.

"You can use anything in here, okay?" Sid said. "I'd pick some out before you color your guy."

"Oh my goodness." Adrian sank his arms deep to the bottom of the chest to pull out the most luscious of treasures. He smelled the fabric and ran it over his cheek; he draped long swaths over his shoulders and made noises of awe and discovery. Sid tried to work, but Adrian's joy dragged him away. He got on the floor and sifted through memories and tossed pieces of silk on Adrian's head. He imagined a special belly patch for the monster with this fabric, a pair of pants with that.

Before long, Adrian had a pile big enough for the one hundred monsters he had originally drawn. He began to draw his single monster, chattering and mumbling as he worked. He sat up on his haunches and then stood at the table. He tapped crayons on his chin as he thought: a miniature genius at work. As they fell into a good groove—"Sid! We didn't light the sticks!"

Sid lifted his foot from the sewing machine pedal. A forgotten green and gold brocade from their treasure hunt was draped over his shoulder. "We didn't." He pulled a basket from a shelf filled with boxes and loose incense sticks. "You choose."

"Can I tell you a secret?" Adrian asked as he made his way over. "I think they all smell the same. I picked the purple ones with Mommy because that was her favorite." He pulled out a bland, tan stick. "We can do purple next time."

"Help me light it." Sid grabbed the burning dish from the shelf and brought it down to their worktable.

"I'm not allowed to play with matches."

"I'll do the match; you blow the flame away." Sid struck a match and held it to the tip of the incense, where it ignited a small flame. "Okay, buddy. Softly now."

Adrian closed his eyes and puckered his lips, emitting the softest breath to extinguish the flame, but maintain an ember of heat at the tip of the incense stick. He was a pro. "I like the way the smoke swirls up and up to the ceiling."

"It is pretty, isn't it?" Sid put the stick in the dish and set it on the worktable as the sweet woodsy scent filled the room.

He had shared the same moment many times with his mother before she prayed or before they sat down to sew. Kneeling in front of her *mandir*, she would ring a small bell, and Sid would help her light the incense. She cleaned framed images of Vishnu and Shiva, two of the three gods of the Hindu Trinity—the gods of protection and transformation. They were gods who knew that young children died, mothers of young children died, but balance would be restored. Transformation would renew in twists and turns that mortals rarely saw.

Adrian traced the air in the pattern of the smoke until his arm couldn't reach. He started again, "Up to the sky," and again, "up, up, and up to the—" His eyes left the stream of smoke and focused on the wall behind Sid. "Sid. Where did you get that picture?"

Sid turned and smiled at the sentimental piece he had brought from Chicago. His workroom—whether here or in Chicago—existed because his mother showed him how to move fabric through the sewing machine. Her foot guided the pressure of the pedal while his rested on top; she taught patience and accuracy when cutting and measuring.

He sewed because of her, for her, with her. She belonged in the room with him.

"That's from my aunt," Sid said, standing to pull the picture from its nail. He sat at the worktable and patted his lap to have Adrian join him. "She sent it after my mom died."

Adrian gasped. "Your mommy lives in the sky, too?"

"Yes. She has for a long time."

"I have this picture in my room too. 'Cept, my words look different. Yours look like little drawings."

Sid couldn't directly translate the words inscribed under the print from *The Little Prince*, but he knew their meaning by heart. "It's a language called Bangla. My mother spoke it."

"What do your words mean?"

"It means that she will be living in one of the stars." Adrian traced over a star in the picture. "And that when I look at the stars—"

"'You'll have stars that can laugh!' I 'member that part because Daddy reads it to me at night before we turn out the lights."

"They say the same thing, don't they?"

"Yes. So, Sid?" Adrian straddled Sid's lap with the biggest grin Sid had ever seen.

"Adrian?"

"I think we should be friends."

Sid ruffled Adrian's floppy curls. "I think we already are."

XV.
AQUILA

SID POSTPONED HIS OWN WORK to make the monster. As he sewed, Adrian drew more monsters "for the next time." Sid consulted and fashioned, stitched and stuffed, until finally he tied a knot in the last hand-sewn seam.

"Voilà! One pocket-sized monster for one pocket-sized human."

"I am not pocket—" Adrian looked at the multicolored doll and, for the first time since Sid had picked him up from the fire station, fell silent. He hopped off his chair and walked to the sewing machine, mouth agape, eyes big and blue in wonder.

As drawn, the monster had a blue body and four pink arms. In two of its hands, it held a flower and a small replica of the sun. Green spikes crowned its head, and a huge velveteen heart decorated its chest. Its smile was huge and fanged, and its swirled and dazed eyes made it look as if it might enjoy marijuana from time to time.

"It looks *just* like my drawing." He took it from Sid's hands and flipped it over and back and upside down to check every millimeter of detail. "Only so much *cooler!*"

When they packed to go to Eddie's house for the rest of the evening, Adrian held his spiky-headed doll like a lifeline. He took it into the grocery when they picked up items for dinner. He clung to it in the car and told new stories of how the monster "took out" the bad guys and saved the good guys.

Eddie called as they finished dinner. Sid laid the phone on the table and put him on speaker. "Tell him, Adrian. How are we doing?"

"Hi, Daddy!" Adrian burped and scooped up his last drop of sloppy joe with his finger. "Sid's sloppy joes are better than yours."

"Sid's sloppy—? That's rude," Eddie said, laughing. "I bet he didn't put any green pepper in them."

"Nope. He made 'em out of chicken, and we put all kinds of spices in them, and, Sid, do we have any more?"

"You've had two sandwiches," Sid said. "Eat your carrots."

Eddie laughed again; he sounded exhausted. "Sounds like you're having fun."

"Yes. And Daddy, Sid has a treasure chest full of pretty fabric, and we made a *monster*!"

"You made a monster? How did you make a monster?"

"With the fabric and stuffing, and he made it look like my picture, but we can't talk anymore. I have to draw a story for Nana with my new monster in it. Sid's gonna write my words."

"Oh. Well. Excuse me! I'll let you get to it."

Adrian got busy in Sid's workroom, leaving Sid and Eddie alone to talk. "Work backlog excluded, it's been a nice afternoon," Sid said.

"I can't thank you—"

"It's fine." And this time, Sid meant it. "You at the station?"

"Yeah," Eddie sighed. "We need to do a debriefing—four townships *and* city. It'll be a while." Eddie sniffed into the phone. "I need to shower before I'm stuck in a car with myself. I smell like apartment fire. "

"Should I get him in bed?"

"Mrs. Crenshaw should be available now. I can have her come so you can go."

"No, no. We're good," Sid said. "He doesn't need another caretaker."

"Yeah, but here's the thing. The other night was a fluke. He's… *difficult* at bedtime. He doesn't like to sleep, so he puts up as many stinks as he can."

"We can kick a soccer ball for a while."

"If you want," Eddie said. "If he doesn't settle, let him stay up until I get there. It's not worth the fight. You've done enough already."

"Okay. Can we, um… can we talk when you get back?" Eddie yawned and apologized. "Never mind. We'll do it another time."

"No. I'll buy energy somewhere if I have to. I owe you more than I can ever pay back."

"You don't. We're fine. If he gets too stubborn, I'll put the monster in charge."

ADRIAN QUICKLY DRESSED FOR BED. He brushed his teeth and took Sid on a tour of his bedroom. After Sid had seen what had to be the very last possible item in his room, Adrian pulled a stool from under his bed. He retrieved a photo from the back of his chest of drawers. "This is my Mommy."

The photo of Maggie, Adrian, and Eddie showed them in much happier, healthier days. Adrian's face was round with extra baby fat. His wispy curls were wispier. Maggie's full mane of long, gorgeous red hair and her look of contentment belied the painful end that awaited her. "She's pretty, Adrian."

"Yes. She's an angel now. And your mom's an angel, too?"

"Yes, she is."

"Yes. And you know Daddy. He's—he's not an angel."

Sid laughed. "No, he is definitely *not* an angel."

"And this…" Adrian put the picture away, climbed on his bed, and walked its length to grab another off the wall. "This is *my* laughing stars poem." He plopped down on his bed next to Sid. "I know some of the words," he said pointing them out. "Sky and stars. Them… and this last one is laugh."

"You know a lot of the words."

"Can you read it to me? Like Daddy does?"

"*When you look up at the sky at night, since I'll be living on one of them, since I'll be laughing on one of them, for you it'll be as if all the stars are laughing.* Say the last part with me since you know it."

"You'll," Adrian started, almost in a whisper. "*You'll* have stars that can laugh." As they finished, Adrian massaged the shoulder of Sid's polo shirt between his thumb and index fingers. "We *both* have laughing stars, don't we?"

"We do. Is that okay that it's not only you?"

"Yes. I like it." Sid hung the picture up and tried to pull back Adrian's comforter. He wouldn't move from his spot on the pillow.

"Let's get in bed now." Sid tugged at the duvet again. Adrian stayed put and crossed his arms around his monster.

"I don't want to lay down."

"Do you normally sit up for your story?"

"No. I don't want to go to bed. I don't *like* sleeping."

They stared each other down, and a flicker of fear in Adrian's eyes pulled Sid out of the potential standoff. "I've got an idea." Sid held out his arms and Adrian climbed in.

"Where are we going?"

"Outside."

Adrian rested his head on Sid's shoulder and twisted his hair in his fingers as they walked. "I'm not supposed to go outside after I have my pj's on."

"Tonight we're going to break the rules." Sid settled them onto a chaise with Adrian resting back on his chest. "You cozy?"

"Yes. And confused."

"It's a clear night."

Adrian looked at the night sky. He sucked in a tiny breath "Oh my goodness."

"Do you know why I brought you out here?"

"To find Mommy's star. There are so *many*!"

"And if we lived farther from the city, you could see more."

"How will I pick? Which one's hers?"

"I think that's up to you."

Adrian sat up and looked around. Starting in the eastern sky, moving west and back again, he mouthed silent conversations with every star his eyes landed on. He settled somewhere in the middle. "That one."

Sid followed Adrian's finger to the brightest star in the area. Altair, at the shoulder of Aquila. "I think that's a good one."

"Which one is your mommy's?"

"Since you and I are friends, I bet our mom's stars are together," Sid said. "What about that softer one up and over?" If it was part of Aquila, Sid couldn't be sure. But it was visible, close to Maggie, and that alone brought comfort.

"I think you're right." Adrian curled into Sid's side and latched onto Sid's hair. "Do you think they're watching us?"

"And laughing. I bet they liked today."

"I bet they liked my monster, and when you let me push the machine pedal with my hands. And when you dropped your sandwich on the floor."

"I *know* that would make my mom laugh."

Adrian snuggled closer and Sid squeezed him tight. "I miss Mommy's hugs."

"I miss Ma's hands. She was tall and thin and her fingers were long and skinny."

"Just like yours."

"Yes, a lot like mine. They curled and stretched and made fabric do exactly what she wanted it to do at the sewing machine."

"Mommies are good guys." Adrian yawned. "I think I'm ready for bed now."

Adrian's weight increased with each move up the stairs. Sid tucked Adrian in and kissed his forehead. "Thanks for a fun night, Adrian."

"Thanks for my monster. And my star."

"Can you do me a favor?"

"What?"

"If you see your mom tonight—"

Adrian's eyes popped open and he gasped. "How do you *know*?"

Sid smiled and brushed a curl from Adrian's forehead. "Ask her to say hi to my mom, okay?"

"What's your mommy's name?"

"Rimi."

"I'll ask Mommy to say hello to Rimi… for my friend Sid."

IN THE DAYS BEFORE FATHERHOOD, Eddie would have slept at the station the night after a huge fire. He would have whipped up a heartburn-inducing snack for everyone on shift, flopped onto one of the rickety couches, and zoned out on whatever the loudest, pushiest idiot on duty decided they were watching. He'd decompress with people who understood. After a good night's sleep, he'd have been able to pull another twelve or enjoy a day off.

Tonight, he started a new pot of coffee for those on duty. He filled his thermos and guzzled half of it before he started his car. He didn't have it in him to wrangle Adrian to bed and he didn't have the courage to call and see if it would be necessary.

Adrian's bedroom light was out. A soft glow shone from the front window. Sid's car parked in the street brought an unexpected comfort. Eddie pulled in the drive and came through the back door. The house was still but for the dishwasher softly whirring in the dark kitchen.

"Sid?" He dumped his duffle of dirty clothes on the floor and stepped on a squeaky floorboard in the living room. A lump on the couch shifted and moaned. Eddie considered leaving Sid until morning, but he recalled his own accidental nights on the couch and the resulting crick in his back. "Sid," Eddie repeated as he shook his shoulder.

"Mmm?" Sid's eyes flickered open. He bolted upright with a litany of apologies. "Oh, god. I didn't mean to sleep. I'm sorry. Is everything—" Sid rubbed his eyes. His grin was lopsided with sleep. "Hi. You're home."

"I am. Looks like he knocked you out."

"Not really." Sid blinked and grinned with the other side of his mouth. "You smell smoky."

"I showered."

"You always smell a little smoky. I like it."

Eddie handed Sid his thermos. "Drink. You're drunk when you're sleepy." Sid groaned into the metal container and took a healthy swallow. "Did he give you any trouble at bedtime?"

Sid stretched and patted the cushion next to him. "He's not a fan of brushing his teeth, but I seem to remember my niece and nephew weren't either."

"No, there's some unwritten children's code that makes them behave as if toothbrushes are torture devices."

"I sang 'Lemonade' while he brushed," Sid said. "He laughed at me because I can't sing to save my life."

"I'm sorry I missed that."

"No. No, you are not. It was traumatic for both of us."

Eddie joined Sid on the opposite end of the couch. Their legs met in the middle and Sid tossed the throw over their laps. As exhausted as he was, Eddie could have sat on the couch all night and watched Sid's hands move as he spoke, watched him nod off and wake up again, just to see that crooked smile and hear his sleep-rasped voice forget to filter his words. "Did he go down easy then?"

"Yep. We had a long talk, and he settled right in."

Eddie was pleasantly surprised until he saw the hint of sorrow, of empathy, in Sid's eyes. "You know his secrets."

Sid nodded. "And he knows mine."

Tears welled in Eddie's eyes, and he quickly brushed them away and kicked his legs out from under the throw. "I must be tired."

Sid stood, stretched, and eyed his bag on the recliner, but did not move to retrieve it. "I should probably head out."

"You said you wanted to talk?"

"I do, but we're both dragging." Sid hooked his bag over his shoulder and put on his shoes. "Another day?"

Eddie needed him to stop, to sit down. Sid had answers. He understood emotions no one else did, and Eddie was tired of being alone with them.

With a soft rattle, Sid's hand was on the doorknob.

"I—I can't thank you enough," Eddie said. A soft chuckle made Eddie look up from the pile of shoes by the door. Sid faced the door with his head lowered. His shoulders sagged. He didn't open the door. "Sid?"

Sid's hand slipped from the knob and he dropped his bag onto the floor. "Eddie…" He turned; his face was unreadable. "I can't do this anymore."

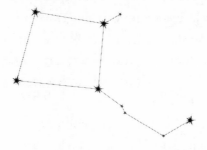

XVI.
PEGASUS

"What?" Eddie's voice was but a whisper; the word was not said to be heard.

"I can't—"

"I knew I shouldn't have called you." A flush of heat, thoughts he couldn't sort, shared smiles that suddenly made no sense, all began to race under Eddie's skin. "I should have pushed Lisbon to reset their chain. I should—"

"Eddie." Sid reached out for him, but Eddie scrubbed his hand through his hair. His eyes focused on the floor as he cracked his knuckles—pop, pop, pop—with each misinterpreted moment. The strudel was just a simple kindness; today's help was the same. "Eddie, look at me."

"I'm so sorry. I thought after the parade… after the fire, the other night, you were—I thought—"

"I'm still here."

Eddie gasped. Sid stood right in front of him, holding Eddie's other hand. "You're still here."

"I'm still here. And I can't keep doing this. I can't keep saying 'I'm still here,' and walk away from you like it's what I want, when it's not, like I'm happier away from you than I am when I'm with you."

"Oh," was all Eddie could summon. He wished for a pun at the ready. He couldn't think of one word to say, let alone a string of them that played on each other.

"I want more underwear parties and peach... everything. I want more rainbow lollipops and kisses at parades. Slow..." Sid's gaze moved from Eddie's eyes to his mouth. "Slow mornings and long showers."

Eddie grinned. His heart raced. "We might have some interruptions with those slow mornings and long showers."

"Well." Sid chuckled and brought Eddie's hand to his lips for a tender kiss. "Yes. We'll adapt. That is—" Sid took another step closer. "If I didn't wait too long and lose my chance."

"Sid?"

"Yes?"

"I know I'm repeating myself, but—" Eddie brushed his knuckles over the curve of Sid's jaw, and a day's stubble scratched under his fingers. "This is where I want to kiss you."

Sid's eyes closed at Eddie's touch; a smile curled his lips and creased the corners of his eyes. "This is where I say yes."

LIKE THE NIGHT OF THEIR first kiss, time disappeared when Eddie kissed Sid. His lips shifted on Sid's, from tender to insistent, from soothing to needy. His fingers slipped into Sid's hair and tugged as he mouthed his way down Sid's jaw and neck.

Sid was breathless but for a laugh that bubbled out when they bumped into Eddie's recliner. "We are," Sid said as Eddie chased him with his mouth, "the worst at this goodnight business."

Eddie stopped. His mouth hovered over Sid's pulse point. "I think we're pretty fucking good at it." He kissed up the length of Sid's neck. His hand was warm on Sid's skin; his lips were wet and soft in a slow kiss. "Upstairs?"

"Yes."

Eddie led the way; the creak of the old house's steps echoed in the stairwell. They stopped at Adrian's door, and Eddie slowly turned the copper knob. "Give me a minute?"

Adrian's door opened with a quiet pop; a corner nightlight bathed the room in a soft blue hue. Eddie bent to kiss Adrian's temple. His voice cracked in sleep. "Daddy, you're home."

"Thank you for helping me today."

"Hmmm?"

"You had a nice time with Sid. That was important to me."

"Is he still here?"

"I'm still here." The declaration felt so much better than the promise.

Adrian flapped his arm in an exhausted wave. "Silly boy," Eddie said before kissing Adrian again. "Love you, buddy."

"Love you, too."

As soon as Adrian's door latched, Eddie led Sid into his room. The stark silence in the old house amplified their stuttered breath and the sounds of rustling fabric. Soft moans echoed when Sid sought Eddie in the dark and kissed him with a soft brush of his tongue over Eddie's bottom lip.

Led by the faint light from a skewed curtain and the streetlight, they shifted closer and pawed and kissed like teens hiding from their parents' watchful eyes. In one swift move Eddie lost his shirt; in another, Sid's flew through the dark room. Sid felt lost in the dark, foreign room, in Eddie covering his neck and shoulders with mind-numbing nips and kisses. "Light. Ed—mmm, god. Where's a light?"

"Behind you." Sid stepped back, their lips connecting as they could—on an ear, a cheek, sucking a bottom lip, kiss-stumble-kiss. With a soft click, a gentle golden glow covered the room. "More?"

"More of you," Sid said and moved Eddie to the bed and onto his back. He wanted more of his body—under him, wanting and desiring, pleasing.

He also wanted more of his *life*, of his heart: more happiness found in the midst of exhaustion; more giggling little boy reminding him that life goes on despite tragic loss; more comfort in the unknown, where sloppy joes and frightening dreams and laughing stars guide day-to-day life.

Sid wanted it all, covering Eddie mouth to mouth, chest to chest, curling Eddie under him: pressure and friction, tongues and soothing hands. The bed softly creaked with each motion. The salty skin of Eddie's neck tickled Sid's tongue; the deep bass of Eddie's moans of pleasure sang in his ear.

Eddie's fingers were quick to brush his cheek and comb through his hair. He stared as if in awe. "You're still here."

Sid smiled down at him. "I'm still here." He reached a hand between them to Eddie's cock that strained thick and heavy in his shorts. "Less clothes; more naked."

Together they scrambled up and stripped down. Eddie frantically dug in a bedside drawer for a condom and lube and fell onto the bed, into the rhythm they'd set: skin on skin; cocks aligned and catching; Eddie kneading Sid's ass; hips, rocking, rocking. The headboard thumped against the wall. "Will we wake him?" Sid asked.

"No. He stirs later—"

Sid quieted Eddie with a deep kiss and a perfectly placed roll of his hips. His focus was on Eddie: his body, churning with deep breath and a subtle move to *kiss me here*, or *do that again*; the sounds Eddie made when Sid wrapped his lips around a nipple and sucked, when his tongue traced the curve of Eddie's muscles where they writhed beneath him; the power of touch, from soft breath over his skin to his grip on Sid's arms, tightening when Sid looked up from his position right over Eddie's cock and smiled.

Sid took his time: languid stripes of his tongue worked Eddie's shaft; for long moments he swirled the drops of pre-come around the pink head, using the slickness for a smooth downstroke, more and over and again until Eddie's hips lifted off the bed to meet his mouth. Eddie's groans turned to pleas.

Sid took his time: a slow massage of Eddie's balls and down beneath, lubed fingers pressing and circling the pucker, taking the head of Eddie's cock into his mouth again, teasing, tasting.

Sid took his time: sinking deep into Eddie's body, hot and tight, with Eddie on his knees, his back a rippled canvas for Sid's hands as he sank in deeper and out and gripped Eddie's hips to rock together, every move intentional.

Eddie looked over his shoulder. "C'mere. I miss your mouth."

Sid curled over Eddie's back and dotted his shoulders with slow, intentional presses of his lips to Eddie's skin. Eddie lifted and curled his hand to bring Sid closer. More breath than connection, more tongue than lips, the awkward kiss barely landed. Eddie pulled Sid's hair as he sat on his thighs and thrust back down onto his cock.

"Want you closer," Eddie panted as he swirled his hips and sank down again.

Eddie's head fell on Sid's shoulder as they moved together. Sid's hand was slick and firm around Eddie's cock. His rhythmic strokes fell, uncoordinated to Eddie's motions on Sid's cock, until Eddie stilled, seated hard on his hips, and, with a groan, jerked and came hot over Sid's hand.

"Don't stop," Eddie said, gasping as he gripped Sid's thighs under him, lifted and sat, urging Sid closer and closer. Sid held Eddie still with the force of his own orgasm, gasped and thrust hard; his strength drained with every glorious pulse.

Eddie fell onto his hands, panting, spent, and stunning. Sid smoothed his hands across Eddie's back, pulled out, and fell onto the bed, taking Eddie with him.

Sid had so much more he wanted to say. But for now, the liquid in their bones, the sweat on their skin, the promise of a new day together said it all.

Eddie awoke in the middle of the night with achy shoulders, a full bladder, and trapped under Sid's long arm. He kissed Sid's fingers and snuck out before his Sleeping Beauty stirred.

When he returned, Sid had rolled over. He was a vision in his bed: dark skin dusted with darker hair, the mop of hair on his head sex-rumpled and twisted. One arm lay over his eyes, and the other under the sheets lazily stroked an inviting erection. "Hi."

If Eddie had to give a play-by-play of the next fifteen minutes, he would have been unable to. Now, heavy with sleep and exhaustion, Eddie found himself loose and satisfied with come cooling at the small of his back and on his stomach. Sid mumbled a sloppy, "Did we do that, or am I dreaming?" into his ear before nipping his lobe. "Your shoulders… do you want a massage?"

"You don't have to—"

Sid's hands were warm on his arms, a firm stroke with a promise. "Let me take care of you."

Eddie cared for others; that had been predestined. But as Sid began beautiful pressure on his shoulders, on the tight muscles of his back, he not only agreed, but told Sid where to find some oil. The scent of jasmine and vanilla filled the room as Eddie rested under Sid's expert care.

Eddie woke at dawn. He glanced at the clock; their couple-fun had come to an end. "Sid?"

"Mmm?" Sid rolled onto his back and smiled. "I like your bed."

"I like you in it. We need to find underwear. We're about to be hit with a tornado of energy."

"Should I be here?" Sid sat up with a start. "I should go. I don't want to confuse—"

"No, it's fine. He obviously trusts you." Eddie distributed the proper boxers. His ass was barely in bed when the bedroom door slammed open.

Adrian blew through the doorway, took a flying leap onto the bed and landed straight on Eddie. "Hi, Daddy!"

"Oof! Hey, buddy. Did you sleep well?"

"I did! I didn't have—" Adrian stopped, looked at Sid—who smiled and waved—frowned, and slipped off the bed. He ran into his bedroom, slammed his door and, from what Sid and Eddie could hear, took another flying leap onto his own bed.

Tears began in earnest.

Eddie sat up and wiped his hand down his face. "Our first miscalculation."

"Yeah. That didn't take long."

XVII.
GEMINI

ADRIAN LAY PRONE ON HIS bed. His cries had dwindled to soft sobs and his raised rump, covered in Spongebob Squarepants briefs, shook with every whimper. Eddie bit back the urge to shush him, to tell him not to cry. Maggie had been clear: Shushing children when they were sad and angry implied that their feelings weren't okay.

He knelt by Adrian's bed and rubbed his back. "Daddy's here."

"I know!" The long and pained "o" echoed through the room. Adrian flattened himself on the bed and turned to face Eddie, blinking through his wet eyes. His cries quieted.

Eddie lowered his chin to the mattress. "What's up?"

"Your room. Daddy…" Adrian sniffed and wiped his nose with the back of his hand. "Your room smells like sick Mommy."

"It smells like sick Mom—oh." Eddie could have sworn the sound of his heart dropping would have rivaled a sonic boom. "It probably does. Daddy didn't think—c'mere." Eddie scooped Adrian into his arms and settled against the headboard. "I am so sorry, buddy."

"Are—are you sick now too?" And with that verbalized fear, Adrian clung, his desperate cries starting all over again.

"Oh, god, no. No, no, no. Ade." Eddie extricated Adrian from his neck. "Adrian, look at me." Adrian sniffled and focused on Eddie's right shoulder. "I am not sick. Do you hear me?"

Adrian nodded and began a fervent tap on Eddie's shoulder. "But, why—"

"Where was I last night?"

"At a big fire."

"Yes. And I was a helper, so I had to hold monster-sized hoses filled with water."

"Did anyone get hurt this time?"

"No. It was a safe fire. But I woke up in the night and my shoulders were sore."

"Like Mommy's tummy?" Adrian looked at Eddie. His bottom lip quivered.

"No, not like Mommy's tummy. Mommy's tummy hurt because—"

"Because it was sick," Adrian said. His tapping finger slowed. "But you used Mommy's special oil to help feel better?"

"Yes. Adrian, I am so sorry. I didn't think. I was half asleep and—yes. We used it to help me feel better."

"And you're not sick." It was no longer a question.

"I am not sick." Adrian's tapping stopped. He curled into Eddie's arms, and they rocked gently while Adrian drew circles on Eddie's legs.

"You're not sick."

"Nope. I'm dumb for not thinking straight." After a few more quiet moments, Eddie said, "I'll take a shower, we'll wash the sheets, and we'll throw that old oil away, okay?"

"No! Don't throw it out." Adrian hopped off Eddie's lap and wiped his eyes. "I could like it someday. Sid's—Sid's house smells like Mommy's house."

"Yes, it does. Did that upset you?"

"No. It was happy Mommy. It smelled like her hair." Adrian squeezed his eyes tight, took a deep breath, and set his shoulders. "We burned skinny sticks when we worked. We're good workers."

"So you're not upset Sid is here?"

"No. But… why is he in your bed without a shirt?"

"We, uh—" Eddie bit his bottom lip and could have sworn he heard Sid chuckling in the neighboring room. "We had a sleepover," Eddie said. "I think we should invite him in so we don't hurt his feelings."

"*Oh*! Yes!" Adrian started toward the door and stopped to turn and whisper, "Does he think I cried because he was here?"

"We'll fix it. I'll wait here."

CONFIDENT THAT HE WAS NOT going to be Adrian's monster's first victim, Sid made himself at home. He stripped the bed, found his track pants from months ago, and blindly thumbed through the news on Eddie's iPad to appear as though he wasn't eavesdropping.

Adrian stood at the doorway. His hair needed its own zip code, and his eyes were red from crying. "Sid?" He stepped into the room, sniffed, and approached the bed. "Can you come into my room?"

"Sure." Sid stood and, before he realized what he was doing, responded to Adrian's lifted arms and carried him across the hall. "How'd the monster do?"

"Good. But I didn't see Mommy."

"That's okay. Plenty of nights ahead."

In Adrian's room, Eddie sat propped against the headboard with his legs splayed out in front of him. He didn't look up. He stared at the stuffed monster in his hand.

"Isn't she *neato*?"

Eddie's eyes shot up from the doll. He dropped it into his lap. "My god."

"What?" Sid asked as he shifted Adrian to the other arm. Adrian took hold of a tendril of Sid's hair and rubbed it between his fingers.

"You're the most beautiful man I've ever seen."

"Eddie…"

"Daddy, is he *finally* your boyfriend? Because I think you ran out of flower colors anyway, and—" Adrian wiggled out of Sid's arms and jumped onto his bed. "Come on, Sid. We all have to sit on the bed."

Sid raised an eyebrow, but walked into the room offering a knowing smile at *The Little Prince* plaque on the wall—a conspirator of spirits.

"So. You guys have a story to tell me," Eddie said, wiggling the monster at Adrian. "Who is this gorgeous creature?"

Adrian took the monster with a huge grin. "This is Rimi! Rimi Monster is a good monster who helps the good guys and takes the bad guys out."

"We have bad guys running around?"

"Daddy, there are bad guys everywhere. Stories are boring without a—" Adrian stopped and looked at Sid who had frozen in place when he heard the monster's name. "Sid, you're not sitting on the bed. It's a house rule when it's story time. That way we're all listening."

"Of—of course." Sid sat on the edge of the bed. That wasn't good enough. They moved and jostled and rearranged until Sid's long legs were completely on the twin bed and Adrian straddled them and Eddie—well, Sid wasn't sure where Eddie's feet landed, but he didn't look comfortable. "Her name is Rimi?"

"Rimi is?" Eddie wiggled his toes under Sid's thigh.

"Rimi is my mother's name," Sid said, in a stupor. Maybe it was hearing her name on Adrian's lips, or the comfort with which he had uttered it, as if he had always known her; or the simple domesticity of the moment, as if overnight this had become his life, not simply a delightful morning after.

"—died too?" Adrian said as Sid tuned in. "That makes us special friends, and now Mommy and Rimi are special friends, right, Sid? They live together in the sky."

"Right." Sid's heart raced, begged everything to slow down so he could catch up. Ma and Maggie and Eddie and so much love, and Adrian, and stories. Adrian looked at him expectantly as if waiting for him to help tell the story of their night. "Tell him how we made Rimi, Ade."

Adrian launched into the tale as if Sid had uncorked a well-shaken bottle of champagne. His voice rose and fell with every exciting turn. He included sound effects and full-body visuals. "I coulda *fit* into the treasure chest it was so big, but I didn't because there was a lot of fabric, and we would have had to put it all back in and we had so much *work* to do!"

Sid leaned against the wall and pitched in when Adrian lobbed him an opportunity. "What are her pants made of, Sid?"

"Brocade," he offered. But his attention was on Eddie's rapt gaze at his son, which Eddie averted long enough to check in with Sid with an unspoken, "Is this for real?" It was on Eddie's foot that had stopped tickling under his thigh and now rested on Sid's lap, where Sid absent-mindedly rubbed it. It was on how, in a matter of eighteen hours, his life, and all of its chaos, had turned right-side up again.

When Adrian finished his story, he tossed Rimi into the air. She landed awkwardly on his lamp and knocked it over. Everyone jumped up for a rescue and saved both Rimi and the lamp.

Less right-side up. Maybe more sideways-upside down. Either way, Sid was filled to the brim.

"You should have been at work two hours ago." From the pileup in Adrian's bed until this moment at the post-breakfast table, there had not been one second of silence: Adrian told more stories about The Best Sloppy Joes Ever and stargazing, about Sid's Bangla words on the laughing stars picture in his workroom, and declared that, since Daddy was the one who dripped milk on the kitchen floor, it was unacceptable for him to ask someone else to please wipe it up.

Eddie disagreed. Adrian wiped—barely—and begrudgingly lumbered upstairs to find some school clothes. "Get a shirt from your drawer, Adrian, not your hamper!"

"I *know*, Dad!" Adrian slammed his bedroom door, and Eddie plastered on a sitcom-worthy grin.

"My son. I think I'll keep him."

"No morning sitter before school?"

"No. I—" Eddie blushed and spun his coffee cup on the table. "I texted her last night somewhere between round one and two." Eddie no longer wore the dad-face Sid had seen all morning. "I had a feeling we might need a slower start this morning."

Sid sipped his coffee, but his eyes stayed on Eddie's. "When do you need to be in?"

"Don't you have a meeting?"

"It can wait."

Eddie looked at his phone, grimaced, and sighed. "In an hour. Besides, you probably shouldn't start putting off work for me again."

Sid stood to collect the breakfast dishes. "You're right." And he was. This was what he'd agreed to, and he had meant every word of it. "We'll have more time."

"You're upset."

Sid turned from the sink. "God, no. Not at all."

"Oh," Eddie sighed. "I'm upset. I'd like to have you to myself a little longer."

"Well, when you put it that way..." Sid grinned and joined Eddie at the table. "I have an idea, but I'm afraid the timing is crap."

"Timing is about to get worse," Eddie said pointing to the stairs. "He's going to come careening down here any minute. You'd better cough it up now."

"I leave for Chicago Friday. Photo shoot Saturday. Home Monday. I would love it if you came."

Eddie narrowed his eyes. "How is the timing crap?"

"Because we've been doing—" Sid pointed back and forth between them. "*This* for what, ten hours? And I'm already trying to find ways to push your child out of the picture."

"Are you inviting me to push Adrian out of the picture?"

"No. Of course not." And then— "Partially?" Eddie grinned at Sid's confession. "A huge part of my life is up there, and I want to share it with you. He can come another time."

Eddie's grin hadn't faltered. "I've never left Pennsylvania."

"How can you—in thirty-three—you've *never*?"

"We were broke. We'd go camping. Once I graduated from the fire academy, she headed west and never looked back." Eddie held up a finger and called upstairs. "Adrian, I haven't heard the water for toothbrushing yet!" A thud followed by quick footsteps sounded from upstairs. "He forgot he had school, started dicking around, and is now frantically making his bed," Eddie explained. "Wanna place a bet?"

"Not in my wildest dreams." A door slammed and the activity moved to the bathroom. Sid stared at their intertwined fingers. "I don't want to miss you when I'm there this time."

"You missed me?"

Sid pinched the skin between Eddie's thumb and first finger. "Don't be a dick; you know I did."

"I don't. You've played pretty fucking coy." That confounded grin remained and grew cockier by the minute.

"Well, I did. I kept imagining you everywhere: cooking in my kitchen, teasing Rue in the studio, holding my hand as we walked from the train to my apartment." Sid stood and massaged Eddie's shoulders. "On my balcony at night," he said, bending to Eddie's ear. "In my bed."

Eddie turned and kissed him with coffee-flavored lips. "I like your imagination."

"Will you come?"

"I'll talk to Sharon. She's been chomping at the bit to get more one-on-one time with him."

"I think I already like Sharon."

"I think I already like Chicago."

Adrian flew down the stairs, hit the floor, and slid into the kitchen. At least, that's what it sounded like; Sid's attention was on Eddie, on his lips and his breath as he chuckled between kisses that promised a memorable weekend.

"Gross. Are you guys going to be doing this all the time now?"

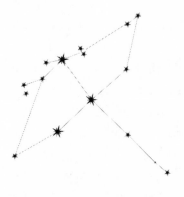

XVIII.
CYGNUS

IT WAS THE MORNING AFTER their second night. Sid's schedule was filled with prep work for his trip and regular visits to his dad's. He dropped by the C-DRT office to make sure the volunteers were set for the weekend and hoped to squeak by without Dottie giving him another task.

"Did someone have a good night?" she asked as she punched numbers into the copy machine.

He had not only failed at squeaking by but, looking down at his outfit, he now saw that he had also failed at dressing. He'd dressed in the dark of Eddie's room long before Adrian woke, long before the sitter arrived.

"Having you here overnight is fine for Adrian," Eddie had explained. "Mrs. Crenshaw? Not so much. She's dear. And old. And buttoned-up. I'll break it to her gently," Eddie threw the pair of sweatpants at Sid's head—sweatpants that had, in their previous life, been victim of a chili cook-off.

Sid was also clad in a Wylie City Fire Department T-shirt that quite possibly had lived a previous life as a dustrag. His shoes were his own.

"I had a great night," he said with a wry grin. "Are we set for the weekend?"

Dottie bent to refill the copier's paper tray. "Is he going with you?"

"Is who going with me?"

Dottie stood up, stared at Sid's shirt, and plucked at the word "Wylie" on his chest. "I'm glad you two got your shit together. I'd suggest wearing a different clown suit if you're going to try to keep the intimate details of your personal life to yourself, though." She slammed the paper door closed and punched in more numbers.

"I didn't tell you," Sid said. "You hate when I don't tell you."

"I do. I don't claim my ownership of your life makes sense."

"I'm in a good mood; we'll call it sweet. And I apologize. I've been… preoccupied."

"Obviously." She hit the print button, swore, stopped the machine, and loaded her original into the feed tray. "Your volunteers are set. You have a CPR class Tuesday morning when you get back. Senior Center—bring pillows for their knees."

"Got it." He watched her run two more originals through the copier and asked, "I'm not making a huge mistake, am I?"

"If you're talking about building your brand based on your appearance, yes. I wouldn't *steal* clothes from you. If you're talking about your heart? That's on you." She looked away from her work and smiled—the kind of smile that had a history, an understanding of who he truly was. "You happy, Zico?"

"Beyond."

"Then go change your clothes and get on with it. A *fireman* isn't going to want to be seen with you looking like that."

* * *

THE DAY THEY HEADED FOR Chicago began at seven a.m.—a ninety-minute gift compared to most weekdays. Adrian crashed into Eddie's room with his typical zeal and started an unending litany of questions.

"When is Nana coming?"

"Between eight and eight-thirty."

"Will she bring the Elmo videos?" Adrian stood on his head on a pillow and slammed his feet up against the wall over Eddie's headboard.

"Did you ask her to?"

"No."

"Then she probably will not bring the Elmo videos." That had been the wrong answer, but when Eddie reminded him that he had written a story about Rimi just for Nana, Adrian settled enough to eat breakfast. After he washed his face and brushed his teeth, the countdown began in earnest.

"It's eight-one-three. Is she here yet?"

"Do you see her?"

"No." Adrian got dressed. For the fourth time, Eddie checked his toiletry bag for deodorant and a razor. "It's eight-one-seven. Is she here yet?"

Sharon arrived at "eight-two-one." Sid wasn't far behind. He smiled politely through Sharon's less-than-discreet evaluation of his worthiness regarding Eddie and Adrian's hearts. Sid earned a kiss on the cheek as they left; he'd passed.

Sid caught Eddie staring as they drove to the airport.

"What?" Sid asked.

Adrian hadn't caused a fuss when Eddie left home this time. His bedtime battles had become the more age-appropriate "I don't have *time* to sleep" variety since Rimi Monster, since Sid had helped Adrian pick Maggie's star. Eddie didn't know how to explain what he was thinking to Sid.

Sid pulled up to a traffic light and took Eddie's hand. "Eddie, what is it?"

He owed him a solid attempt. "You know, I thought I'd lost you. I barely had you to begin with, but—"

"No, see. That's where you're wrong." Sid lifted Eddie's hand and kissed a knuckle before edging his car through the intersection. "You had me the minute you landed in the back of my truck."

"Is that a euphemism, or—"

"Well." Sid grinned. "That didn't hurt matters." He let go of Eddie's hand to maneuver into the sweeping cloverleaf entrance to the airport. "I'm sorry I wasted so much time for us."

"I think a slow-down might have been for the best," Eddie admitted. "Besides, I'm looking forward to seeing your other life."

"It's a different sort of crazy, that's for sure."

Eddie didn't know what to expect from the different sort of crazy Sid spoke of. He looked forward to time together, to seeing a world outside his boxed-in view, to discovering a side of Sid that he knew existed, but had yet to experience.

The discovery began as soon as the plane touched down in Chicago. Normally a man of gentle motion, quiet shifts in direction, a smoothness in diction and a voice whose depth coated his words with serenity, Sid transformed into a man of great intention in the city. His movements became swift and exact, his eye contact pointed and direct. As if on a grand mission, he maneuvered through the airport with long strides and few words.

They stood in line for a cab while Sid apologized to Eddie for answering missed phone calls. After fifteen minutes and little movement, Eddie asked, "Why did we run through the airport just to stand still?"

"Exercise." Sid kissed Eddie's forehead. "Sorry, I sort of hit the ground running here."

The calls and emails continued in the cab as Eddie watched the landscape change from airport to highway to neighborhood. Eventually, Sid pocketed his phone and pointed out landmarks of his life—favorite restaurants, the market with the best produce, the findings store that saved extra zippers for Sid's business.

They pulled up to a nondescript brick three-story with fire escapes on two sides of the building. "Here we are," Sid said as he paid the cabbie.

They climbed all three flights, their suitcases banging loudly on each step. Once inside, Eddie understood why Sid called this place home.

As he looked at the vibrant colors and overstuffed hominess, he searched for something more meaningful to say than the "Wow" that had gusted from his lips. Before he could speak, Sid's bags hit the floor. He slipped Eddie's bag off his shoulder and, with dark eyes, cupped Eddie's face in his hand.

"Hi," Sid whispered as his thumb caressed Eddie's cheek. Eddie gasped before Sid's lips were on his and his tongue teased Eddie's mouth open. Eddie locked his leg around Sid's calf and pulled him closer. He lifted his head as Sid worked his mouth along Eddie's jaw to his ear. "Welcome to Chicago."

"Mmm. Keep this up, and I'll never leave."

"You would get no argument from me." Sid nipped Eddie's earlobe and took his hand. "Let me give you the tour," he said, grabbing the handle of his suitcase. "Make yourself at home, don't ask before you use something—this is our place now, okay?"

It didn't take long for Eddie to figure out that Sid's sublet in Connelly wasn't home—would never be home. But Eddie hadn't expected such an exquisite place here. It was not the kind of exquisite he was afraid to touch—an apple-green couch anchored the living room, for god's sake. It was the kind of exquisite that told of a keen eye, a penchant for "good things," a touch that welcomed. Eddie wanted to fall into the blue and yellow pillows, throw his feet on the coffee table, and forget the world outside.

The world outside entered anyway through huge-paned windows that wrapped around the corner of the living and dining room and added golden sunlight to the already dazzling room. Sid's bedroom ran the depth of the huge apartment. It was crowned by a bed that hinted of cozy nights and daylong stays and was almost larger than Eddie's entire apartment in Wylie. The master bath had a shower for two, with multiple showerheads and a jetted bathtub.

Sid laughed as he kissed Eddie's mouth closed. "Yes, the shower is as fabulous as it looks; we'll visit tonight, okay?"

Eddie nodded and stumbled behind Sid, who tugged him to another bedroom door. "This used to be my studio. This and half the living room." The room was still set up with two sewing machines, a drafting table, and a long worktable in the middle. Another sewing machine with cones of thread on top sat along the opposite wall.

"Serger," Sid said as he walked to it, flipped a switch, grabbed some scraps, and zipped a line of stitches along them. A strip of fabric fell into an awaiting receptor and Sid showed Eddie the work. "Sews and cuts at the same time. Among other advantages."

"You have machines in Connelly, too, don't you?"

"Yep. Some guys buy cars; I buy sewing machines." Sid grinned and pointed to a door across the small hall. "Second bathroom there, kitchen's hiding behind the living room over there, and uh… oh yeah, balcony outside my bedroom."

"How do you ever leave this place? It's… perfect."

"It hasn't been easy," Sid said, as he walked past a beautiful wooden floor cabinet and ran a finger along its molded edge. "Let's see what goodies Rue left us." They found a pan of homemade apple crisp ready to be warmed and devoured, which they promptly did.

"Does she do this every time you come back?"

"Every time. You'll love her."

EDDIE LOVED HER. HIS FIRST impression came when she yelped so loud it could be heard in the hall through the glass walls of Sid's studio. She popped out of her chair. A shock of white-blonde hair sprayed stiff in front of her face bopped along as she ran to greet Sid—Sid, who stood frozen in place, staring at the glass door and its neighboring floor-to-ceiling glass wall.

She swung the heavy door open, squealed, and jumped into his arms. "Isn't it *amazing*?"

Sid spun her around; her nose ring caught the fluorescent lights overhead, and the shaved hair at the sides of her head flashed a shocking green. Sid hadn't spoken, but put her down with a grin bigger than Eddie had ever seen. "Eddie, look." He traced the etched words on his door.

"Bastra: A Marneaux Design Company," Rue read. "You're unstoppable now, baby."

"I don't know about that…" Sid said. "It looks so much better than it does on letterhead."

"And boxer briefs," Eddie offered.

"Not that you've seen those or anything." Rue wrapped Eddie into a tight hug. "By the way, thanks for waiting on this one here," she said as she opened the door and motioned them in. "He can be slow."

"That's enough out of you." Sid groaned at a stack of mail in a wicker basket adorned with his name. "How much of this is junk?"

"Fifteen percent, tops. That's what you get for playing fireman back home."

"If that's all I was doing," Sid grabbed the stack of mail. "You wanna trade? You deal with my dad and sister, and I'll run the business?"

"Can I ride on the fire truck?" Rue clicked a tongue barbell against her teeth.

"I don't get to ride on the fire truck."

"Yeah, but you get to ride on the—"

"Heyyy!" Eddie said before she could complete that thought. "What about Kaitlyn, the medic?"

"Ooh, yeah, Rue. New client from the fire department," Sid said as he stood over the trash dropping in every fourth or fifth envelope. "It's a trifecta: a hot date, my dad, and my sister. I'll give you my plane ticket for Monday."

"No. Thank you. Oh, check the break room; your delivery came just in time." Rue pointed with her nose and grabbed a plate of crackers and a half-eaten cheeseball. "Take a snack with you," she said to Eddie. "You're going to love this."

Eddie took the plate and followed Sid into the break room. "Why do I have a cheeseball?"

"It means she likes you." Sid said as he sliced open the box sitting on the table. "And this…" He peeked in, tossed an invoice onto the table, and laughed. "Means I like you. Put down the cheeseball, Eddie."

Eddie did and caught two bags of underwear. "What the—?" At Sid's mischievous expression, he opened a package to find personalized briefs: "Chief" on one set and "Garner" on the other.

"I couldn't find any with a hose emblazoned on them, but I did find—" Sid tossed two smaller bags to Eddie. "Kid sizes."

Kid sizes boldly labeled "Adrian." "He's going to love these."

"We'll need to phone ahead on underwear party days, though. I'm thinking it might be creepy if we all wear them at the same time."

It seemed odd being moved by pairs of personalized boxer briefs, but nothing about this trip had been what Eddie had expected—and he had been in town a grand total of two hours. "No, no. We have to match on opening night."

SID HADN'T IMAGINED EDDIE WOULD slot into Bastra's machine quite as well as he did. The day before the photo shoot, while a stream of visitors rotated with revolving-door precision, he set to work as if he'd been part of the team all along. He answered the phone and took messages. He learned the small stockroom and retrieved notions and supplies. He ordered carryout before Sid and his staff realized they were hungry and restocked Rue's cheeseballs the minute the last savory smear had been wiped clean.

But best of all, Eddie was ready for a passing kiss whenever Sid had a moment to pause.

After a late lunch, Sid glanced at the schedule and showed it to Eddie. "Remember when we talked about the transformative power of clothes?"

"Yeah—it's been amazing to watch all day."

"My favorite is next."

Iseul, a stocky, soft-spoken Korean woman, came in for her fitting. She was dressed for her job as an insurance adjustor in khakis; an oversized, bland T-shirt; and an expression that said, "Is it five o'clock yet?"

On the hanger, her outfit for the shoot—perfectly tailored trousers, a beige dress shirt, and the rust-colored vest Sid had made with Adrian at his side that loosely draped at the bust with a single button at the waist—appeared somewhat ordinary. A steampunk bow tie added a special touch, but when she came out of the dressing room, she no longer wore the long face of a bored insurance adjustor. She stuffed her hands firmly in her pockets, jutted her chin proudly, and stood with one leg in front of the other as if she was ready to take on whatever awaited her. She was confident, bold, and shining with a bright smile.

That's what made this whole juggling act of his life worth it.

Late into the evening, Shianne, his last model, arrived. She had been a client, model, and friend since Sid's college days. A tall Trini woman with short-shaved hair, she had dimples deep enough to carry Adrian's Cheerios and a voice rich enough to make the floor vibrate. When she took her outfit into the dressing room, Sid laughed and pushed up Eddie's chin to close his mouth. "You're going to start drooling. It's unbecoming."

"Fuck, she's stunning."

"Wait 'til you see her in this outfit."

When Shi came out, she struck a pose, flashed a smile, and laughed in delight. "You make me powerful, Sidney Marneaux." Her accent curled around his name; he wished his brand could be audible with her voiceover: "Bastra: Be powerful."

Sid slipped the trench coat from Shi's arms and draped it over her shoulders. "You don't need me for that. Turn around."

Shi spun and tossed a look at Eddie. "Who's the cutie joining you today?"

"Shi, this is Eddie Garner. He's an excellent Girl Friday and popped-button finder."

She strutted over to him. The lining of her coat swished and swayed over her thick hips. "You're the man he cried for," she said as if it had been imprinted on his shirt.

Sid looked away before Eddie could catch his eye and pulled off the trench coat. He fussed with the vent in the back of her suit jacket, removed it, and asked permission before smoothing his hand over the round of her backside.

"Of course, you can touch me. Feels snug at the waist."

Sid put a pin at the seam and marked her chart. She continued to study Eddie until Sid returned her coat and stepped between them. "We'll see you tomorrow, Shi."

She smiled and stepped closer. "Did I embarrass you?"

"Yes, and you know it." He smiled. "Go home before you do it again."

Sid began to tidy up. He rolled stray tape measures, stacked empty hangers, and checked the dressing room for leftover accessories. He stepped outside the dressing room and right into Eddie, who offered an empty wicker basket for the flotsam in his hands.

"You cried for me?"

Sid dropped his items in the basket. He had no choice but to meet Eddie's sad, reverent gaze. "She, um—has a way of asking the right questions."

"I'm sorry I hurt you." Sid could have stayed in Eddie's kiss all night as Rue shut down the studio and the city quieted around them. Instead, Mitchell arrived and broke the spell with one snide sentence.

"Well, aren't you two cute?" Mitchell said, looking Eddie up and down as if he might have a plague. He inspected a retracting tape measure from Sid's basket. "So now we bring the boyfriend, so we can be distracted here too?" He looked at Eddie as if he had slam-dunked him with the greatest junior high insult of all time.

"Mitchell, it's after dark," Sid said, snatching the tape measure. "Don't you have a nightclub to crawl or something?"

"What? I'm not *wrong*, am I?"

Eddie stepped forward and offered his hand. "Eddie Garner. I understand you're largely responsible for Bastra's success. It's been a joy seeing it in action today." A stranger wouldn't have caught the evil glimmer hiding in Eddie's smile. Sid, however, almost choked on his stifled laugh.

Mitchell took Eddie's hand, stared at Sid, and shook it. Glaring, he mumbled some form of gratitude and stood in front of Sid. "This is an important weekend. Don't fuck it up."

"If you promise to stay in the background and let me do my job, I guarantee there will be no fuckups." Sid looked over Mitchell into Eddie's smiling eyes. "You ready to go?"

"You have no idea…"

"Mitchell, I'm locking up. We'll see you tomorrow morning."

"I have a key—"

"We'll follow you out."

EXHAUSTED, THEY WALKED TO THE train station. Eddie's fingers were loosely twined with Sid's; on the train, his head dropped to Sid's shoulder. It wasn't until after the train hit a solid clip along the rails that Eddie spoke. "Am I supposed to like that guy?"

Sid laughed. "I'd be worried if you did." After two more stops Sid said, "He's not the devil, but his concern for other people stretches as far as his own nose." Sid sighed. "Or his cell phone. He reminds me of my brother."

As they approached Uptown, got off the train, and went into a corner store for fruit for breakfast, Eddie couldn't get close enough, couldn't touch enough. His day—the sweep from five-year-old feet on his wall to his first flight and first exit from Pennsylvania, from his simple muted life in Connelly into Sid's vivid, rich life in Chicago— buzzed under his skin, an irresistible seduction.

"I loved today," Eddie said as they lumbered up the stairs to Sid's apartment. "You're surrounded by amazing people."

"I am. I'm lucky."

Eddie slipped his hands around Sid's waist and rested his head on Sid's back as Sid unlocked his door. "You're not lucky."

The turning knob echoed in the empty hall, but Sid spun in Eddie's arms before stepping in. "No?"

"No. You've made this… you've worked for it." Desire spread through Eddie the moment their lips met, shooting sparks down his arms as he walked Sid backward. A muffled giggle bubbled between them when he kicked the door closed. "You make people feel good about themselves."

"You seem to be feeling good." Sid said between kisses.

Eddie moved the mop of hair covering Sid's ear and skimmed his lips up Sid's neck. "I'm overwhelmed." With a soft suckle of Sid's earlobe, he confessed the most ridiculous, but burning, thought of all. "And that little weasel man is making me feel…" Eddie breathed into Sid's ear, groaning when the skin of his arms raised in gooseflesh. "Predatory."

Sid moaned and held Eddie close as his hands steadily stroked Eddie's back. "Why?" Sid's voice splintered. "You already have me."

"I do. Sometimes it's hard to believe it's true." Sid's life was full, rich. And yet he was here in Eddie's arms, willing to share in Eddie's ordinary life.

Sid took Eddie's face in his hands. "Well, if that's the case," he said with a wicked grin, his dark eyes alight with mischief, "sounds like you need to take me again."

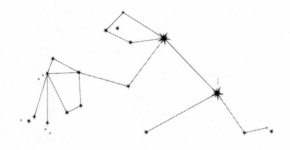

XIX.
AQUARIUS

SHARON: A JOKE FROM ADRIAN: Why was it called the Dark Ages?

Eddie read the text to Sid as they meandered around Montrose Beach looking for the perfect grassy spot for their picnic.

"How does Adrian know about the Dark Ages?" Sid asked, dropping his bag where they were. A cool September breeze blew at their backs; the water *looked* cold.

"A friend's older brother told him that's when dragons lived. It's all he needed to hear." Eddie said, typing: I don't know, buddy. Because no one could find the lightbulbs?

Sharon: No, DAD. Because there were so many knights!

Sid's phone buzzed and Eddie took over unloading their food.

Sharon: You get one too, Sid. So, Adrian crashed his car yesterday.

Sid: We've been gone 36 hours and he already has a car?

Sharon: It was a tyrannosaurus WRECK!

Sid tossed his phone onto the blanket and yanked the package of sliced sopressata out of Eddie's hand. "You do realize you're the one who put the 'weird' into that kid."

"You didn't know Maggie; it could have been her."

"But it wasn't, and everyone who ever has to deal with that boy's dad jokes for the rest of his life knows it." Sid grabbed his phone and pulled Eddie in for a selfie. "Stick your tongue out; I'm sending it as a reaction." In minutes, Sharon sent a similar picture of her and Adrian.

After a toast, they ate in companionable silence. A dog walked its owner to the dog park farther north on the beach. Runners jogged by, oblivious to anything but the music in their ears and the rhythm of their feet on the sand and gravel-covered path. Eddie stopped Sid from taking a bite of cheese and kissed him. "I was so proud of you today."

"It was a good day, wasn't it?" Sid was proud of *everyone* after the photo shoot: Rue's excellent work behind the scenes before he arrived, and his girls—his clients and models, one and the same, but ultimately, his heroes for the day. "I cannot *believe* how turned on my girls were to those new designs."

"I think—I could have been dreaming, but—I think I saw Mitchell smile."

"He probably caught a glimpse of his reflection in his phone." At "his phone," Sid's buzzed against the wine bottle. "It's Anna?"

Eddie kissed his forehead and started cleaning up. "I'm sure it's fine."

"Hey, Anna," Sid answered, feigning nonchalance. "What's up?"

"Sid?"

Sid grabbed Eddie's wrist in a flash of panic. "Dad?"

"It's Sunday evening, Sid. Where the hell are you? You have homework."

Sid flipped the phone to speaker. "Dad, I'm in Chicago. Where's Anna?"

"Anna? She's at her dorm where she belongs."

Sid reached for his glass of wine. "I'm sorry. Ma. Where's Ma?"

"She ran to the store. You're avoiding the question, young man. You said you'd be home at six."

"And it's…" Sid looked at Eddie's phone and adjusted for the time difference. "Yes, it's almost six-thirty. Did she leave you there alone?"

"Of course—I'm not a child. You need to get your ass ho—"

"Dad, hang on a minute. I need you to get your calendar."

"I don't need a goddamned calendar to tell me you're late *and* in a heap of trouble. If you think you're going to that soccer party this weekend you've got another think coming."

"I know. But, I'm in Chicago, Baba. Please get your calendar."

"I have it right in front of me." Sid heard Lou's finger drum against a counter, and imagined him poking a date. "Today is… Saturday, not Sunday. You're in Chicago?"

Sid took a deep breath and tried to focus on Eddie's steady hand rubbing his back. "Yes. I'm in Chicago. Go back one day. What does it say in blue?"

"Your color is blue. It says, 'Sid in Chicago.' Oh." Sid looked to the sky. His eyes filled with tears as his dad processed his mistake. "Did you have a soccer tournament? Did you win? You'd have called me if you won, right?"

"We, um. We play tomorrow, Baba."

"Oh. Well. Good luck then." Lou breathed heavily, erratically, into the phone. "Sid, I'm confused. I don't feel like myself."

"That's okay. It happens sometimes." Sid said, frustrated and bordering on frantic himself. "Is Anna home, yet?"

"I told you, she's at school."

Sid reached for Eddie's hand and squeezed when he caught it. "Ma. Is Ma home yet?"

"No, and she's been gone for hours." Keys jingled in the background. "I'm gonna go find her."

"*No*! Dad! No…" Eddie quietly shushed him and mouthed "Stay calm." Sid swallowed and tried again. "She'll be home soon. You know how crazy the grocery is on Saturdays." The back door rattled, paused and rattled again. Sid had never been more grateful that the summer's plan to fix the sticking door had been forgotten.

"How—how are you going to get there, Baba? Ma has the car, doesn't she?"

"I'll walk."

"Dad, it's six miles."

The door rattled again, and Lou swore. "Why won't this fucking door—"

Sid motioned for Eddie's phone and typed a number into it, whispering to Eddie as he finished, "Can you call my brother, please?"

"Does he know who I am?"

"Doesn't matter. Tell him what's going on and I need him to go to Anna's. Don't ask; *tell*." Sid turned his attention to his dad. "Do you have your scarf, Baba? It's getting chilly."

"And if he resists?" Eddie asked, standing.

"Tell him I'll tell Dad it was him who was driving when their car got totaled, not Ma."

Eddie muffled a laugh and stepped away to make the call.

"Where *is* my scarf? I like that green one."

Sid sighed. He skipped the fact that his dad's green scarf had been thrown out last year. "Did you look on the floor of the closet, Baba? Or wait, I bet you hung it on your bedroom doorknob."

"Oh, I bet I did."

Sid directed Lou from the bedroom to Anna's closet, to the kitchen and the coat closet where a rack stored Anna's family's hats and scarves.

"I found my gray one; it's okay," Lou said, winded. "Okay, I'm leaving to—where was I going?"

Andrew's voice cut through. Sid mouthed a "Thank you" to Eddie while confusion ensued on the other end.

"Would you let me—" Sid heard, and then a scuffle. "Hey, Sid," Andrew said, his irritation evident.

"Andrew. Thank you so much. Where in the hell is Anna?"

"I don't know. Why would I?" Andrew spoke off the phone to Lou, guiding him to something on television. "She asked if I could come over about an hour ago. Something about running out of Dad's cottage cheese."

"And you couldn't bother to do that?"

"I'm working."

"It's Saturday. You couldn't take a fifteen-minute break?"

"You wouldn't understand."

"I understand perfectly, Andrew. I understand that you and Anna both know I'm straddling two cities here. You need to be available to pitch in when I'm gone. He *cannot* be left alone in that house. We've been over this."

"She hasn't been gone that long. Why the fuck are you so—hey, wait. I have a call."

"Don't you *dare* take that call. I've been on the phone with him for more than a few minutes, and he was already scared and confused," Sid said, pacing, wandering away from Eddie and his earnest, but unwelcome, attempts to calm Sid down. "This isn't some game. You have got to help when I'm gone, or we're going to have to look into some sort of assisted living."

"Which is what should have happened to begin with. I did not agree to be his caretaker."

"He is your *father!*" Eddie's gentle touch on his arm stopped Sid cold. He focused on Eddie's eyes and found a steady calm. "Andrew, he could have walked out, gotten lost, been hit by a car—"

"Okay, okay. I get it. I'm here. I'll stay until she gets home. We found a *Mythbusters* marathon; he's good."

"Do *not* leave until she gets home."

"I know what to do, Sid."

"If you knew what to do, this wouldn't have happened."

"I *got* it, Sid. Fuck, it's not like you're around all the time—why are you suddenly the hero?"

The warm press of Eddie's lips to Sid's temple kept him from firing off a litany of frustrations that spanned many years. "Thank you for going over." If they hadn't wanted a hero, why did they throw the fucking bat signal?

"Whatever." Andrew said. "Oh. Congrats on the boyfriend," he added, bordering on friendly for the first time in years. "That's impressive he called me."

"Thank you. Call me if anything changes."

Sid flopped onto the blanket. The high of the day soured as though it had never happened. Eddie, a quiet strength, lay next to him.

After a long silence, Sid wiped the lone tear dripping down the side of his face. "He confuses Anna and Ma all the time. When is he going to forget me?" Sid blinked at the clouds and rolled his head to look at Eddie. He found such genuine concern in Eddie's eyes he had to close his own—Eddie's easy hope read like a lie.

"It was just the two of you for a long time, Sid. He won't forget you."

"You think?"

"I'll hope. It's all any of us can do."

Sid took Eddie's hand and twined their fingers. "Why would she leave him alone? And without her phone? I've been there for *weeks* helping out—more than usual. I don't understand."

"I don't know, sweetheart."

"Whatever her reason, I hope it's a forgivable one." As they rested, the air bit with the promise of autumn; the ground beneath them grew cold. Sid curled into Eddie's side. "I wanted tonight to be beautiful."

"It is beautiful." With a tender kiss to Sid's temple, Eddie sat up. "Come on, look. Your city is beautiful. You're beautiful."

"Stop."

"No." Eddie kissed the bridge of Sid's nose. "What do you want to do? Do you want to stay here?"

"We came for a sunset picnic. Ma said sunset was when the gods painted the sky."

Behind them, the sun began its descent into Uptown. "Looks like the show is about to begin. Take care of yourself for once, huh?"

Sid leaned against Eddie's body, warmed by his arms, his heart, his understanding concern as the setting sun splashed the sky with a million shades of pink and orange and purple.

ON THE WAY TO SID'S apartment, they detoured into a favorite neighborhood bar where they drank too much and ate a huge vat of truffle macaroni and cheese. They drank more.

As they walked home, Eddie flopped his arm over Sid's shoulder.

"You, my handsome man, had four humongolious drinks." Eddie lingered on "go" long enough that Sid had to hip check him to get him out of the stall. "I think you're drunk."

Sid snorted. His body moved two seconds behind his brain; his mouth opened to speak moments before words came out. "*You're* making up words. Definitely drunk."

"Humongolious is so a word," Eddie said. "Three-alarm fires: humongolious."

"I'm surprised you can say it without tr—tripping over your tongue." Sid's left leg crossed over his right as he tried to find footing on the moving sidewalk.

"I could stick my tongue in your mouth. Then I wouldn't trip over it." He leaned over and licked Sid's neck. Usually Eddie's tongue on his neck was pleasurable; tonight, it felt slimy.

Sid grabbed Eddie's hand and pulled him close for a proper kiss. But it too was sloppy and wet and hot—so hot he hooked his ankle around Eddie's legs and leaned against a light pole. Eddie cupped Sid's face in his hands, the kiss deepened, and Sid forgot they were outside, after midnight, one step shy of removing each other's shirts.

They stopped for air. Sid looked around and laughed; Eddie furrowed his brow in question. "We're here," Sid said, pointing to the building behind him. He cupped Eddie's face and gave him one more quick kiss. "Three flights of stairs and we can be naked."

They tripped up Sid's apartment stairs, laughed too loudly down the hallway, and pit-stopped for one more make-out session. Sid had forgotten what Eddie tasted like. "We should," Eddie mumbled between nibbles at Sid's jaw, "sober up first."

"I dun wanna. Numb feels good." Sid's his key worked in spite of his questionable dexterity. He groped for Eddie in the dark room, but Eddie grabbed his wrists and held them to his chest. He blinked slowly as if to focus his thoughts along with his eyes. Eddie's touch was remarkably skillful considering how many apple-cinnamon old-fashioneds he'd drunk.

"We're going to sober up first. You've had a big—" Eddie burped. It smelled like truffles. "'Scuse me. A big day. We've tried to drink it away, but tonight… I'm going to love it away. And I want you—" Eddie planted soft kisses along the curve of Sid's neck and up to his ear—"to remember *everything.*"

WITH A SATISFIED GRIN, EDDIE set two glasses of water on the counter. "Let's get some music," he said as he started thumbing through his phone. "I thought we could have an underwear party."

Sid bent to sit on the coffee table. "I love—" Sid missed the coffee table and sat on the floor. "Oh! I love underwear parties!" He took a huge swig of water, wiggled out of his *kurta*, and flung it across the room.

"I know you do!" Eddie joined him on the floor, so it was convenient for Sid to yank off his shirt.

He crawled into Eddie's lap and fell limp against him. "We're not in our underwear."

"No, we're not." They swayed to the music anyway. Lights from the street shone through slats in the blinds and striped the room in a golden glow.

"I don't know if I'm not moving because I'm drunk or because you make me feel so amazing," Sid said, snuggling closer.

"I think it's mostly that you're drunk." Eddie untangled himself from Sid's arms and offered water again. "Drink. I want to dance without breaking our faces."

Sid might have nodded off—he wasn't sure—but when he became aware of his surroundings again, he was less wobbly in Eddie's lap. "Take off your pants, Garner." He sat up and kissed the smirk right off of Eddie's stupid face. "Let's dance."

Pants flew. Eddie changed the music to a 90s playlist that took them back to the days when there were no bills, jobs or kids, no sick parents or dead best friends. Back to the days before they knew each other when they danced to the same songs and lived separate lives on an unknown trajectory right into each other's arms.

They danced and twirled, sang at the top of their lungs, and pushed away everything that hurt, everything that weighed them down. The rhythmic, driving music played on, but their bodies slowed and swayed. They moved across Sid's living room, draped onto each other, and into slow, lazy kisses that woke their fuzzy brains.

Sid's legs hit the foot of his bed. "Can we turn off the music now?"

"Sure," Eddie said, his fingers tangling in Sid's hair. "You okay?"

"I will be. I don't want anything else here but us."

Eddie lowered Sid onto the bed with such care Sid had to touch Eddie's face to make sure he wasn't dreaming. Eddie's warm lips on Sid's skin eased every spot of tension, erased every worry. And when Eddie had him in his arms—Sid's thighs pressed to his own chest, Eddie buried in him, filling him, his hot breath chanting Sid's name with each thrust, every motion a prayer—the world outside the room evaporated.

Eddie untangled himself from Sid's legs and rested his elbows at the sides of Sid's head. He studied Sid's face, tracing his cheeks, along his jaw, and across his lips until Sid gently sucked his finger in. The soft clap of their sweat-slicked skin echoed in the room, building in intensity until Eddie took Sid in his hand. At a practiced twist of the wrist, a whispered "Sweetheart," ghosted in his ear, Sid's orgasm unraveled as slowly as they moved, and brought pulses of pleasure with each stroke, each breath in his ear.

The prayer changed lips as Eddie's pace sped. He scooped Sid into his arms, buried his face in Sid's neck and, with Sid's soothing kisses, his motions stuttered and he came. Sid hooked his ankles more tightly around Eddie and suckled the crook of his neck. Eddie shifted.

"No," Sid said. "Keep moving. Don't leave me yet."

"Oh, sweetheart." Eddie pumped slowly, slick and softening. "I don't know how long—"

"I don't care." Sid held on tight and cupped Eddie's ass to push him in again and again. His prayer was now a plea with each slow, deliberate thrust, "Stay. Please. Just stay."

Eddie stayed and shared loose-lipped kisses until he could stay no more. He lifted over Sid, slipped out with another kiss, and gathered Sid in his arms as he fell to his side.

Cocooned in Eddie, Sid focused on the weight of Eddie's arm on his waist, the rhythm of his chest as it rose and fell with each breath, and the curl of his coarse chest hair under his scratching fingers. Eddie soothed Sid's scalp and kept his mind on the two of them. *Stay. Please. Just stay.*

But as each moment passed, worries from the conversation with his dad crept in and marred the beauty and ecstasy they shared. He took a shaky breath.

Eddie kissed Sid's forehead. "Hey… you okay?"

Sid nodded wordlessly, but tears threatened. "I'm sorry."

Eddie lifted Sid's face to his. "Why the tears?"

Sid met Eddie's eyes; his gaze was an anchor. "I didn't want to come back."

"Come back?"

"Come back from where you take me."

"Oh, Sid." Eddie pulled him in, and Sid nestled into the crook of Eddie's neck, a perfect place to rest his head. "Sweetheart, we don't have to come back."

"We already have." Echoes of his conversation with his dad, crashed into the space he and Eddie had so gloriously made for themselves. His brother's impatient tone, the realization that the only reason his dad didn't escape was because Sid hadn't fixed the stupid back door muddied their peaceful moment even more. He gave in to quiet tears, to fear, to worrying about what awaited him.

"Come on, now. Let me take you away again."

Eddie kissed Sid's tears as they fell to his cheeks. He mumbled reassurances and affirmations until Sid had to confess, "I'm so scared."

Eddie sat up, and Sid joined him, embarrassed at his tears, yet so grateful that if they had to be shed it was with this man.

"It's scary. The rocks in our lives aren't supposed to crumble right in front of our eyes." Eddie's fingers soothed as they combed through Sid's hair. "But tonight? *Nothing* will make it better."

"I don't think it's going to *get* better."

"Your dad won't. But how you and your family cope with it will." Eddie took Sid's hands in his and kissed Sid's palms. "And tonight Anna has him. He's safe. Work is buttoned up for a few days. So, let me take you away until you can sleep… even if it takes all night."

"Can I draw us a bath?"

Their lazy sponge bath settled into a sudsy warm slosh of water over skin and quiet glances over the rims of wine glasses filled with a deep red pinot noir—a perfect prescription for Sid's aching heart.

"You feeling better?" Eddie asked, stroking Sid's thigh with his foot.

"As long as I don't look beyond this moment, I'm great."

Eddie nodded, put his wine glass on the floor and rubbed his hands over Sid's calves. "Can I ask you a question—about Shi?"

"She rattled you, didn't she?"

"A little," Eddie confessed. "By the way, she needs to be a professional model; she owned that shoot today."

"I know. But I don't want to suggest it; she'll leave me forever."

"I don't know. She seems awfully loyal to you." Eddie continued stroking Sid's calves. "Last night, you told me that she asked you the right questions. What did she ask?"

"When I came home after—" Sid looked up, still embarrassed at his knee-jerk behavior those months ago.

"After Adrian. It's okay."

"After Adrian. She asked if I loved you."

"And that made you cry?"

"Yes."

"Why?"

Sid and Eddie's affair had been short, followed by weeks upon weeks for Sid to get his head screwed on straight. And now they'd had a short time together again. It had been too soon for this feeling then, and it was possibly too soon now. But Sid had bit it back too many times already—too many times on this day alone. He eyed his wine and chose to look at Eddie's eyes instead. "Because the answer was yes."

"Sid."

"And if you had kept the most important part of your life from me, I was convinced that you wouldn't ever love me back."

"But I did," Eddie said, sitting up, his caress moving up to Sid's thighs. "It was too fast and too soon and it got away from me because… it was too big to catch." Eddie took Sid's wine from his hand, put it on the floor, and chuckled before he spoke. "You were a riptide that pulled me under." Eddie smiled; he blushed. "I do love you. More now than days ago. Less than I will tomorrow."

A laugh bubbled out of Sid before he could stop it as relief and ridiculous joy erased all the stress and worry that had blurred the edges of their time together. "Where did you learn such poetry?"

Eddie smiled, and Sid knew. "From the one who told me not to say it for the first time…" Eddie looked down at his naked body. "When naked."

"Oops?" And then—"Maggie doesn't need to know you broke her rules."

"Somehow, I have a feeling she knows and is laughing her ass off right now."

Sid tried kneeling, to kiss, to hold, to love. He toppled over in laughter until Eddie pulled them out of the tub in a dripping-wet tangle of limbs and lips. His need was so desperate that Sid had Eddie bent over the counter and was sinking into him before towels could be considered. They watched each other's reflection in the mirror as they fell apart and chanted more naked confessions of love until they were spent, messy, and in need of yet another bath.

"I don't think you *really* love me," Eddie said as they dried off. "You're trying to kill me."

They vowed to stop touching for at least an hour. They continued to negotiate the vow as they got dressed.

The ripple of muscle on Eddie's back as he bent to step into a pair of his "Chief"-emblazoned underpants made Sid's dick twitch. An hour was absurd.

"Forty-five minutes," Sid offered.

"Fifty-two minutes," Eddie mumbled between kisses and a pinch on Sid's ass.

"Okay, this is dumb. An hour." Sid stepped away, threw a T-shirt over his head, and walked into the kitchen. "I have gelato. Something else to stick in our mouths."

"Mmm, gelato. Creamy and drippy and sticky... we could—"

"Eddie! We're not going to be able to walk tomorrow. Stop it."

Eddie kissed Sid and lingered longer than necessary.

They'd touched again, already. In fact, they hadn't stopped. "We didn't last five minutes without touching, Eddie."

"I'm humongoliously sorry."

Sid grabbed two tubs of gelato and one spoon. "You're not infinitesimally sorry."

"No. No, I'm not."

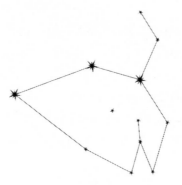

XX.
CEPHEUS

AFTER VISITING THE PHOTOGRAPHER'S STUDIO to check proofs from
Saturday's shoot, they filled their final day with touristy stops: The Bean
at Millennium Park, Navy Pier, and an evening trip up Willis Tower
to overlook the city in its nighttime glory. Through it all, Sid's focus
remained on Eddie—until the panic he'd heard in his dad's voice, the
lack of concern in his brother's, the absence of his sister's, stopped him
cold. Every time, as if he felt the air shift, Eddie held Sid's hand, and,
without a word, took him away.

On the flight home, Sid's dread at dealing with whatever awaited
him grew. "You're not going to believe me, but—" Sid started as they
walked to his car.

"You can't wait to see Adrian." Eddie said with a grin.

"He has a way of seeping into your bones. I'm also not ready to
face reality."

When they pulled up to Eddie's house, Adrian tore out of the front
door. He held one of Rimi's arms tight in his grip as she sailed behind
him and bopped Sid in the back with the force of Adrian's hug. Sid
soaked up Adrian's energy, fueling his tank for the rest of his day. Rimi

had a new outfit, courtesy of Nana, and telling the story of getting it made took three long paragraphs spoken in one run-on sentence.

Eddie must have sensed Sid's exhaustion; he tossed Adrian onto his shoulders and carted him into the house. Sid stood propped up against his car and stared at a weeping cherry sapling. Sharon approached him with a maternal grace he hadn't realized he needed.

"Eddie said you had a scare with your dad. Everything okay?" Sharon rubbed his arm; he leaned into her touch.

"I have no idea. I don't know if I'm dealing with a crisis or a Saturday." Sharon's sweater jacket blew in the breeze and made her collection of long, draping necklaces clink and tangle together. The peace that surrounded her helped clear his mind. "I'm probably being too impatient with my sister. I get to leave town. I work when I'm there, but we played a lot this weekend," he said. "She's in the trenches. He thinks she's Mom. I take off, and he always knows me."

"Can I share—from my experience with Maggie?"

"Please."

"The day I let a nurse in, the day I let Eddie *help*, and not only visit, was the day I became a better caregiver for my daughter."

"How do I convince Anna of that, though? We *tried*, Sharon. She will not listen—"

"You may not convince her. But I'm telling you so you won't carry around guilt. You're doing the best you can. She wants control; she has it. It's all on her."

"At Dad's detriment."

"More likely at her own," Sharon said as the front door opened and Adrian tore outside and ran toward the back of the house.

"He's gonna *eat* me, Sid!"

Eddie followed, "claws" bared, snarling and bug-eyed, in pursuit of his curly-haired victim.

Sharon pointed him to the side yard, but continued with Sid. "I don't want your sister's issues to take away from what you have going here."

They heard a roar and a child's melodramatic squeal.

"I have *two* children here, is what I have," Sid said, as she joined him against the car.

"Did you have a good weekend otherwise?"

"The best. We got some beautiful pictures of my girls for next season. Our press kits are going to be amazing. Hopefully our reach will grow—"

"But did you take time for the two of you?"

"Yes. Thank you for letting us."

Bug-eyed Eddie peeked around the corner. "I think I lost him," Eddie whispered.

"That'll make for a quieter evening," Sid said as Eddie disappeared with another roar. "Would Maggie approve? Of me loving him?"

Sharon gasped and rested her head on Sid's arm. "She'd be over the moon." Her voice cracked, and Sid wrapped his arm around her. "Adrian can't stop talking about you. I haven't seen Eddie happier."

"I see a lot of happiness here considering how much you've all lost."

"All Maggie ever wanted people was for people to love each other. So, while you're dealing with your family, let Eddie love you."

Sid's mind flashed to the previous nights, to Eddie's tender care: he had made love to him all over the apartment; had slotted into the fabric of Sid's work life as if he belonged; had poured the wine before their nightly visit to Sid's balcony; had listened when Sid needed to talk and allowed silence when he didn't. "He makes it easy."

The bush behind Sid's car rustled. Hearing Adrian panting, Sid held a finger to his lips before he ducked and crept closer. He caught Eddie's eye, and Eddie backed off to let Sid make the capture. With a deep roar, Sid swooped his arm around Adrian's waist and hiked him onto his hip like a sack of potatoes. Adrian screamed, Sid roared louder, and Eddie cackled as they ran to the back of the house. Sid spun Adrian in a circle and plopped him in the chaise with an evil grin. "Gotcha."

"Sid, you *scared* me. I almost peed my pants."

Before Sid sat, he kissed Eddie in a long and lingering silent word of gratitude for the weekend, for everything.

"What were you and Nana talking about?" Adrian asked.

"Adrian, that's not polite," Eddie said, sounding so paternal and downright *aged* that Sid laughed, destroying any authority Eddie had tried to exude.

"We were talking about what a shithead your dad is."

"Sid. That is a bad word."

"I'm sorry." He glanced at Eddie and was relieved to find him biting back a laugh. "You're so smart, I forget how young you are. We were talking about what a *stinker* your dad is."

"Oh. Well," Adrian said as he sat with his hands behind his head— the vision of a cocky, well-educated man. "Everybody already knows that."

* * *

THE FOLLOWING MORNING, WITHOUT EDDIE at his side, Sid's bed seemed to swallow him whole. His mind filled with the burden of visiting Anna and getting answers—or worse—getting none. Had the phone call in Chicago been a sign of a shift in his dad's mind and health? Would it be an opening for him to convince her that some form of outside care would be the best for all parties?

He barely remembered showering. He'd lost his appetite. He had ninety minutes until he had to leave for Anna's, so he took refuge in his workroom. As he breathed in freshly lit incense, he soaked in the calm that came from afternoons with Ma in her sewing room. She'd taught him not only the craft, but the mindset necessary to see yards of fabric and envision a garment. She taught the importance of measuring carefully, cutting precisely, and respecting the union of fabric, thread, and machine.

His chest of fabric sat along one wall, still open from Adrian's digging over a week ago. His eye was drawn to a swath of muted blue *jamawar* silk. After a quick sketch, he laid the fabric across his worktable to succumb to his scissors, to his whim of an idea. Before an hour passed, he had fashioned it into a fitted, mandarin-collared vest to dress up an ordinary *kurta*.

Satisfied and replenished, Sid went to his sister's. His dad was nowhere to be seen. Anna skittered between the kitchen and living room, fussing over invisible chores. Tired of her nervous energy, Sid took a side door into the conversation. "Do I smell your blueberry muffins?"

"Yes." Anna put down the basket of remote controls and joined Sid in the kitchen. "Dad likes to toss the blueberries in the flour."

"You let him help you?" He meant nothing by it, but the glare she shot him as she shoved the container of the muffins into his hand indicated that he had missed the mark. He opened the lid, sniffed deeply, and pulled out two muffins. "Where's Dad?"

"Watching *Cosmos*," she said, pointing toward Lou's bedroom.

He shoved the muffins into the microwave, focusing on the numbers of the control pad more intently than necessary. "So. Saturday," he said, turning to her as the microwave whirred. "What happened?"

"You don't know what it's like, Sid. You have *no* idea, so you can't just waltz in here and judge me for—"

"I have been here as much as humanly possible since last winter. How do I still have no idea—" Sid took a deep breath and started over. "I'm not here to fight, Anna."

"Well, maybe I *am*." The microwave beeped. When Sid pulled the muffins out and turned to her, he almost laughed. She stood with her hands on her hips and her lips pursed—a fourth-grader ready for a playground battle.

"You're angry with me." He grabbed butter, sat down, and pushed a chair out for her with his foot. "Let's have it. I'm tired of dancing around everything."

She softened long enough to sit and eat a loose blueberry. "You *don't* know what the constant care of him is like: the doctor appointments, the ups and downs of his moods. He grabs my breasts!"

"He thinks you're Ma."

"Sid, he never did that to Ma… in front of people?"

"It's the disease," Sid said. "The doctor's—"

She charged on as if Sid hadn't said a word. "He's clumsy, and at least once a day I'm on all fours cleaning up a mess. It's day in, day out, and at the end of a day I think has gone well, he's yelling because the dishes aren't done."

Sid had cleaned up his share of their dad's messes. He'd been yelled at for how cluttered the living room was. He'd taken him to plenty of doctor appointments in the last months.

But he'd also witnessed how much more patient their father was with Sid—how he was more loving, more centered and focused with him around. Anna's stress bled like a fresh wound around Lou, but Sid was welcome direct pressure, firm and solid. Though Lou was often confused in Sid's presence, Sid balanced his scattered brain. It had to cause resentment.

Fighting her wasn't going to fix anything. Sid searched for solutions.

"I know Claire's back at college, but Tyler's home. Can he be of any help?"

"They're teenagers. How many dishes did *you* do as a teenager?"

With one question, Anna brought to light the chasm that had always existed between them: the difference of growing up with Ma and without. Because Anna had already started her own family by the time Ma passed, she'd never quite grasped the burden Lou and Sid lived with every single day. Sid's desire for solutions evaporated. He pushed his plate aside and leaned closer to make his point.

"I did *all* of them," he said, anger burning bright under his skin. "Every night unless I had a match. Then I did them first thing in the morning. I kept my room clean. I helped with laundry. I vacuumed and kept the bathrooms clean. I mowed the lawn and cooked a few meals a week. I kept a three-point-eight GPA, held a part-time job, won multiple soccer awards, and earned *two* scholarships to college. You know why?"

"Sid, I'm sorry. I forget—"

He didn't care that she "forgot." He needed her to remember. "Because Ma taught me to work hard, and Dad and I had to do it *alone*."

Anna crumbled a piece of muffin. "D—do you want something to drink? I'm suddenly thirsty."

"Water is fine, thanks." While she worked, Sid continued. "I'm doing *everything* you'll allow me to do with Dad. I concede to your decisions because, frankly, I have no legal choice. But what we're doing is not working, Anna. You won't let him do anything, and you and I both know the doctors want him more active. You left him confused and frightened. I can't imagine anything you needed that couldn't have waited."

"We were out of his cottage cheese. Do you *know* how worked up he gets if he doesn't have it?"

"I do."

"What the hell was I supposed to do?"

Sid tried again. "Where was Tyler?"

"He was at a friend's. He needs a break from him, too, Sid."

"And he couldn't have stopped by the store on the way home? Don't you *see*, Anna? If you can't get your own family to pitch in, if you're never happy when we *do*, you need outside help."

"If you'd have been here—"

"But I wasn't. And you knew I wouldn't be. You've had the dates of my absences."

Anna had barely sat down and was up again, pacing, flailing her long arms as she talked. "You want me to get outside help so you can be free to go off and live your creative life—have your *business*…"

"Yes, please. Let's make this about me doing exactly what Ma and Baba encouraged me to do. To follow my own damned path… like they taught *all* of us."

"No, Sid." Anna spun around, still but for her wagging finger. "That's where you're wrong. We weren't raised by the same woman, you know." At Sid's confused look, she continued. "Oh, the DNA matched, but when Andrew and I were children, there was one goal in this house—to be smart and to succeed. Our whole purpose was to prove to her *dead* parents that she'd made the right choice by coming here."

Sid chilled. "What?" Certainly, Anna's view of her childhood had warped over the years. "That's not fair."

Anna scoffed and motioned to the chaos around her. "Life isn't fair."

As if Sid didn't already embrace that truth: Mothers died before their lives were complete; little boys were left to be raised by grieving fathers; cancer happened; dementia stole the minds of brilliant people. In the midst of it all, families sacrificed and fought and splintered.

"Haven't you ever wondered why you work so fucking hard, Sid? Like you're trying to *prove* something to some unknown entity?"

"I'm not trying to prove *anything*. I'm just trying to make a mark. To make Ma—" *Proud. To make Ma proud.*

"See?" Anna said. "They got you too. Except *you* got the charmed life. You got the best of them: sitting for hours at the sewing machine with her hair on your cheek; days in the backyard with Baba and a soccer ball; nights under the stars." Anna's tension rose as Sid's anger intensified—*charmed life*. "And I?" Anna picked up a stack of papers from the counter—Lou's calendar, her notebook of notes from doctor visits, drug inserts, ephemera—and slammed it to the floor. "I get *this*."

Papers spread across the kitchen floor. Lighter pieces fluttered before landing in far corners. A pen scurried from the fray like a scared mouse. It ignited a memory from weeks after their mother died.

Lou had been as strong as anyone would expect; Sid had been as strong as anyone would expect. Their dinner had burned, and they'd missed an important soccer meeting, which might have cost Sid his spot on the traveling team. Sid yelled; Lou yelled. Like Anna, in his inability to put words to his fury and grief, Lou had taken a stack of papers from the counter and flung them against a wall. Sid hadn't seen his father that angry before—nor had he since.

Sid had cried for the first time since the casseroles and flowers had stopped arriving. Lou cried with him. Sid slept in his dad's bed that night. Lou let him skip school the next day. They saw a movie and ate ice cream for lunch. Though that would have made a day of sweet victory for a typical child, for Sid it had been a day of cavernous loss, a loss that, no matter how fulfilling Sid's life had since become, would never be completely healed because Ma would never see it happen.

Charmed life. Best of her. Ma's hair at his cheek.

He looked at his sister, at her graying roots and rage-filled eyes. He picked up his dad's calendar and the stray pen and put them on the counter next to her as resentment vibrated under Sid's skin. His mother would beg him to think before he spoke, but she wasn't here to stop him. The fury in his heart made his voice shake. "I had the best of her? Don't you *see*? I would have taken *half* of her to have had her as long as you—"

"That's *enough*!" Like teens caught with a smoking bong, Sid and Anna froze. "Both of you! Go to your rooms."

Sid and Anna swore in unison and stepped away from one another. Lou held onto the doorframe. There was a smudge of blueberry at one corner of his mouth. "Baba, I'm sorry," Sid said first. "We, uh—"

"Got out of hand," Anna continued. "Here, let's get you into your wheelchair."

"I'm gonna…" Sid sighed as his dad yanked away from Anna's approach. "I'm going to go."

"You're not leaving this house, young man."

"Dad, I—" Sid caught his sister's gaze. He took a mental walk through his calendar for the day; every task could take a backseat, and if it couldn't, it would. "Anna, why don't you go see a movie this afternoon? Call some friends for dinner? I'll stay with Dad. We can talk later." Lou's planisphere peeked out of papers on the floor, and Sid scooped it up. "How about we head to the park this evening, Baba? It's supposed to be a clear night."

"Well… that might be nice."

Lou shuffled off to his room. Sid picked up the rest of the sprawled papers. "When you called me in February, you said I wanted the best for him. And I do; we all do, Anna."

"I seem to be the only one that wants him *back*."

"He's not coming back. And I can't give you another chance to prove your worth to him—or to Ma." Sid stacked the papers, reached for the muffins, and handed Anna her plate. "But I can give you today."

She took the plate; her eyes softened, and she cupped his face in her hand. It was the most maternal she had been with him since Ma's death. "I'll bring you some *rasgulla* from that place on Thornton."

"Bring enough for Baba, too."

*   *   *

LATER THAT WEEK, SID TOOK Lou to his appointment with Dr. Martin, who, he came to learn, had been speaking to Anna about alternative full-time care options for some time; he had pamphlets and recommendations at the ready. When they got home, Anna listened and took the pamphlets. Sid counted it as a major score.

The following night, after bedtime stories, bedtime giggles, and a soft kiss before Eddie began snoring softly beside him, Sid wrestled with a moment of guilt. While Anna was at home dealing with their dad, walking through a bedtime routine with the man who'd taught her how to brush her teeth, Sid had this.

As he reached to turn out his bedside light, the doorknob turned, and Adrian peeked in. "Daddy?"

"Ade? C'mere, buddy. Daddy's asleep." Adrian stood by the bed and chewed on one of Rimi's head spikes. "What's up?"

"I had a bad dream."

"Oh, I'm sorry. What was it about?"

"I don't want to talk about it."

Sid waited for Adrian to say more. When he didn't, Sid started out of bed to take Adrian to his room. But Adrian gasped and bit more frantically on his doll. Sid was tired; he wanted peace and quiet. Adrian was frightened.

Anna's words of accusation spun in his tired mind: *You had the best of her.* And he had. A focused, calm, and spiritual version of the woman who had grieved the loss of her homeland and family while raising her older children.

He reached for Rimi and scratched the spikes Adrian wasn't sucking on. "What does Daddy do when you have a bad dream?"

"He lets me sleep with him. But you're here."

"Yeah, but…" Sid picked Adrian up and sat him between their pillows. "You're tiny. Will you sleep?"

"I promise." Adrian lay on his side, and Sid curled around him before he realized what he was doing. Adrian's curls brushed his nose. Eddie snored. "Oh my goodness."

"Nudge him. He'll stop."

Adrian nudged. Eddie snorted—loudly. Their laughter would have woken the dead.

"Mmm, buddy?" Eddie rolled over. Sid and Adrian shook the bed trying to stifle their laughter. "What have we here?"

"We have a growling bear, Daddy. You *snore!*"

"He had a bad dream," Sid said. "Is this okay?"

Eddie's sleepy smile was all the approval Sid needed. "Did you see Mommy again?"

"No. I fell into a fried egg." After a long moment of silence, Eddie and Sid roared in laughter. Adrian sat up and roared Rimi back at them. "It's not *funny!*"

"Oh, buddy. Yes, it is," Eddie said wiping his eyes. "Now that you're awake, think about it."

"Was it over easy or hard?" Sid barely got the question out before he started laughing again.

"The runny kind," Adrian said, his anger giving way to the giggles. "And cold and sticky."

"Eww. Will you ever eat an egg again?"

"Not tomorrow." Adrian flopped onto his back. "I'm sleepy. And hungry." Sid and Eddie fluffed their pillows and held the sheet up until Adrian got comfortable. He turned toward his dad and heaved a huge sigh. "Sid? Can we be spoons tonight?"

Sid pulled Adrian to him and nuzzled his nose into his curls again. "Instead of a spoon, I could pretend to be frying bacon." Sid ran his fingers up and down Adrian's belly. "Tsss. Tsss. Tsssssss."

"Sid, you're a big old meanie head."

That might be, Sid considered. But at least he would be the *best* big old meanie head.

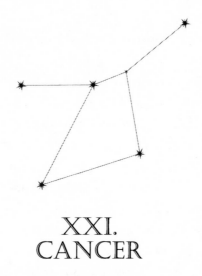

XXI.
CANCER

IT DIDN'T TAKE LONG FOR the excitement of having this new life, this new built-in family to wear off. No longer an amusement to Adrian, Sid had gone from Dad's fun boyfriend to the occasional "boss." And while usually kind and well-behaved, Adrian could also be incredibly five-years-old.

He could be belligerent:

"But I don't *like* macaroni and cheese when it's white," Adrian said one evening while Sid covered Adrian duty so Eddie could attend a community meeting. "It's supposed to be *orange.*"

"They taste the same. Color doesn't change flavor." Sid poured the powdered cheese into the pot and pulled Adrian's stool to the burner. "Stir."

To Adrian's credit, he did, albeit with complaint. "I'm not going to eat it."

"Then you're going to be hungry." Sid got out two plates.

"I don't like you anymore."

"At the moment, I don't like you either." Adrian ate three bites of macaroni. When Eddie came home he claimed Sid wouldn't feed him dinner.

Adrian could also be dictatorial, even with his father:

"The water's too hot."

"You had no problem when I started the bath," Eddie said. Sid, answering Bastra correspondence from bed, heard Eddie slosh the water around the tub.

"Now, it's too hot. I'm not getting in."

"This isn't a democracy, Adrian. You're taking a bath. I've added some cool water. Get in."

"No."

If Sid had any policy, it was that he was not going to get in the middle of Eddie and Adrian's occasional bickering. He stood to investigate anyway. When he got to the bathroom, he had to pop his hand over his mouth to stifle a laugh.

Adrian stood naked in the middle of the bathroom with a blue submarine in one hand and a pink-haired alien in the other. A plastic triceratops was tucked under one arm. He had to hand it to Eddie; taking Adrian's demanding tone seriously when he was in such a state had to be difficult.

Adrian did get bathed—in a standing position—and Eddie ruminated on his qualifications to be a father after all. "I'm not sure why lifting a naked five-year-old who had committed to his argument was something I had to do. Why did I think he would miraculously bend at the waist?"

Sid kissed him, helped him remove his soaked shirt, and, in trying not to laugh, chewed his own bottom lip almost raw.

"Parenting should be relegated to professional... parents? Or wrestlers." Eddie shook his drenched hair like a wet dog. "Someone other than me."

Adrian could also be temperamental in the completely unpleasant, flailing way that children have when they aren't getting their way:

"I don't *want* this book." Adrian flung the book across the room.

Sid's day had started with his dad losing a shoe and then his remote control. It ended with a heated phone call with Mitchell. The call had started well enough: Out & About had called; they loved the new line. They had snooped the website and wanted to talk more about the business. But then the call ended with Mitchell saying, "It would really help if you were here, Sid. I'm sure your dad—"

Sid had never hung up on anyone in his life; Mitchell got to be his first. Reading *Clifford the Big Red Dog* for the fifteenth time in half as many days was not something he would fight for.

"Then lie down and go to sleep without one."

"But, I'm supposed to get a story before bed!"

"You threw a book," Sid said and pulled back Adrian's blanket. "You lost your story tonight."

Adrian stood on his pillow. "*I get a story before bed!*"

"Not tonight. I'm sure your dad—"

"Well, you're *not* my dad." With the word "not," Adrian punched Sid in the arm. He wound up to smack Sid's chest; Sid grabbed Adrian's wrist and held his gaze.

"But I'm in charge—by order of your dad—and you and I both know this is *not* how he expects you to behave."

With his hand pinned, Adrian kicked Sid's thigh. He flipped backward onto his pillows, and whacked his head onto his headboard. Tears flowed. Sid bit back his anger and reached to comfort him, but was met with more flailing limbs and more awful words: "And you're not my mom either, so *leave!*"

Sid walked out, letting Adrian rage until blessed silence filled the old house. He made a cup of tea, helped himself to some of Adrian's sketch paper, and sat at the kitchen table. He tried to tell himself that the words hadn't hurt. But they had—in a way he couldn't have imagined.

Sid knew no one could replace Maggie. He wouldn't dare try. Attempts from well-meaning neighbors—and his sister—to fill his mother's shoes had never seemed genuine, or as though they were made with Sid's interests in mind. They were made to help the "helpers" reconcile the unfairness of the world.

An hour later, when Eddie returned from his meeting, Sid had a stack of unoriginal sketches and a cup of cold tea to show for his evening.

"The honeymoon is over," he said as Eddie kissed his forehead. Sid selfishly wished Eddie had been fighting a fire. He longed for the sweet scent of a house fire to fill his senses and ground him, through the man who made nights like this worth it.

"You look like you've been run over by a train."

"The Adrian James Express."

"Oh, shit." Eddie sank into the chair and listened to every detail of the evening.

By the time Sid finished, Eddie promised him the moon, the stars, the planets, *and* the planets that had yet to be discovered in exchange for his lousy evening.

"I'm so sorry, Sid. You know he didn't mean it."

"I know. I think." Sid sipped the last of his tea. "Are we pushing too much on him? I mean, I'm here a lot and taking care of him more—which I love, don't get me wrong—but I have to wonder…"

"I don't know. I don't know what the hell I'm doing. How do you ask a five-year-old what's right?"

"By watching him, I guess. He's been acting out more lately."

"He hasn't said anything negative about you. He likes you more than me half the time."

"I don't buy that." Sid gathered his sketches and rinsed his mug.

"Let me talk to him tomorrow. The bottom line is, you're both my life. We're going to have to figure out how to make it work together."

Two nights later, Sid returned, invited by Adrian himself. He and Sid shared Sid's special recipe for sloppy joes. They ate, bundled in sweaters, and sat on the back porch by the light of two team-carved jack-o-lanterns. Adrian didn't eat much; Sid wasn't sure he had stopped talking long enough to be bothered.

Adrian opted for a *Franklin the Turtle* marathon over kicking around the soccer ball. Adrian read *Clifford* to them at bedtime. Short hours later, Sid slipped into Eddie's bed, into his body, and later slept in his arms, sated, satisfied, and at peace.

"*Daddy! Daddy!* Oh my goodness, *Daddy!*"

"Oh, god. That's the…" Eddie bolted up and grabbed underwear from the floor. Sid looked at the clock: 2:15 a.m. The groan Eddie emitted when he opened Adrian's door could have vibrated the floor. "Sid! I, um… I could use your help."

Sid slipped on lounge pants and entered the hall, where the scene hit with full force: the sound of whining and sniveling; the sight of a boy being carried face-first into the bathroom; the sickeningly sweet and sour smell of vomit. He peeked into Adrian's room to avoid seeing the volcano erupt again as Eddie barely got him into the bathroom.

"I'll…" Sid gulped. "I'll get the sheets."

"Thank you. Oh, buddy. It's okay. It's okay."

Sid ignored the disgusting noises coming from the bathroom and piled everything from Adrian's bed to take to the basement. "Quick, toss his nightshirt up here." He caught the soiled shirt on the sheet pile, then got everything downstairs and into the laundry.

When Sid returned upstairs, Adrian sat in bed. Eddie had covered his mattress with a well-loved, worn blanket. "You okay?" Sid asked him.

"I throwed up."

"I noticed." He instinctively felt Adrian's forehead. Hotter than a radiator. "What can I get you?"

"Daddy's getting ice chips." Adrian's voice was ragged and shaky. His naked arms and chest were covered in gooseflesh. "Can I have a hug?"

"How about another nightshirt, too?"

"Please?" Sid dug in Adrian's drawer and jumped when Adrian coughed; he was afraid another eruption might happen. "I have an orange one with a flower on it."

Sid pulled out a faded orange shirt dotted with a few holes and a barely-there flower on the front. He paused before slipping it over Adrian's head. Their eyes met; Adrian's were sunken and dark. His attempted smile pushed away threatening tears.

"It's Mommy's."

"The perfect hug for when you're sick." Sid wiggled it onto Adrian's head, guided his arms into the sleeves, and held him close. "Need another blanket for on top?"

"Yes. I'm cold. And I'm sorry."

"For what?"

"For being a big old meanie head to you yester-night."

"It's okay." He kissed Adrian's hot temple and rubbed his hair. Adrian moaned at his touch. "I was tired, so I probably made mistakes too."

"This boy at school was being mean to me. It made me mad."

"Does your dad know?"

"He does now. And the teacher."

"I'm sorry that happened."

Adrian cuddled closer, and they sat silently while Adrian rubbed Sid's hair between his fingers. He sighed like a troubled old man and said, "You're *not* my mommy…"

"Of course not."

"But Sid? You make me feel good like she did." He sighed again. "You hug like her."

Eddie cleared his throat when he came in with a bowl of ice chips. He kissed Adrian's head, and, with eyes looking into Sid's, mouthed "I love you." He offered the bowl to Adrian. "For when you're ready— don't eat a lot, now." Adrian didn't budge; his confession had knocked him into a deep sleep.

In Eddie's bed, Sid stared at the ceiling, unable to absorb the evening—the simple joy that led to chaos. The honest, easy, unexpected *love* that drifted through the house like a ghost of goodness and warmth.

In the silence, Sid had a confession of his own. "I love him, you know."

"I know." Eddie rolled to his side and tugged Sid close. "I won't tell anyone."

* * *

TWO DAYS LATER—CHICAGO

Sid: Daddy? I throwed up.

Eddie: What? Oh no…

Sid: Remind me, did Adrian die? Because I think I'm going to.

Eddie: He's alive and well. Did you make it all the way to Chicago?

When Sid didn't answer for another fifteen minutes, Eddie began to worry.

Eddie: Sid? Sweetheart? You okay?

Sid: Oh my god… yes. Barely made it into the apartment.

Eddie: I'm so sorry. At least he got over it quickly?

Sid: He puked twice? Slept for twelve hours and watched Disney all day. I think he got the wimpy version.

Eddie: What can I do?

Sid: Find and kill patient zero. I'll lie here and blast disgusting fluids out of my orifices. And whine.

Eddie: I probably shouldn't be laughing, should I?

Sid: I hate you. And that child of yours. Which doesn't matter because I'll be dead in a few hours.

Eddie: Okay. When I speak, I'll speak highly of you.

Sid: You're a gentleman and a hero.

*   *   *

SID RETURNED FROM CHICAGO, FLU-FREE and with a budding relationship with Out & About. As Mitchell had said, they'd loved his Trial Line and his custom order line and had offered to host a trunk show. A successful trunk show could change the entire course of Bastra, but with the constant pull to care for his father, Sid wasn't ready to commit. Mitchell balked. Sid dug in and flew back to Connelly and found that nothing at his sister's house had improved.

"Have you looked at—" Sid tapped the assisted living pamphlets that sat on her counter while Anna tidied the perfectly clean kitchen.

"No, Sid. I have not." She shoved them under the infamous stack of papers. "I can't. It feels like I'm reading about someone else's life, not my own."

"It *is* your life, Anna. It's ours. It's Dad's. We have to—"

"*There's* my boy!" Lou said, appearing in the kitchen so quickly he had to have been eavesdropping. "Are you staying for dinner?"

After dinner, Sid took his dad outside. Necks bundled and hands gloved to fend off the early October chill made holding and pointing field glasses more complicated than usual. Lou's breath ghosted in front of his face when he spoke. "Ma tells me you have a boyfriend."

Sid's grin was instantaneous. "I do."

"Is it that fireman?"

"It is. His name is Eddie."

"You gonna marry him?"

"Oh, I don't—we've been together a few weeks." Minus, of course, the weeks and *weeks* when Sid was being an idiot… and falling deeper in love in spite of himself.

Lou lifted his binoculars and squinted into them. "I asked your mom before we hit the American shore, you know?"

"You did not." Sid lowered the glasses from Lou's eyes. "How did I not know this?"

"She turned me down. Broke my heart, that Rimi Gayen."

Sid stared at his dad as if he had never known him before. "It obviously didn't stop you."

"Well, I couldn't let her go. She kissed good!"

The evening stretched out before them, warmed with conversation and chai. Lou, in his slow but clear speech, spoke of his journey to America with Rimi. He told of her insistence that Lou find her a job at the college, "Or I'll turn myself right around, Louis Marneaux. I will *not* be your housewife."

After a contented silence, Lou asked again. "So, are you going to marry this fireman?"

"I'll tell you what, Baba. I'll agree to not let him go. He kisses good, too."

"Mmm, I think I should meet him." Lou lifted the field glasses and aimed right at the horizon: an eighty-year-old astrology buff's attempt at coyness.

"Why, are you planning on telling him about some gross childhood habit of mine to scare him away?"

"Oh, I'll scare him away all right," Lou said. "I'll spill my dinner and yell when he cleans it up wrong."

"He has a five-year-old. That won't scare him."

Sid arranged for the three most important men in his life to meet. Three days later, they sent Anna off on a night with her friends. Adrian fidgeted and asked when Olivia and her parents would be over to get him. Sid showed Adrian his phone. "It's five-one-five; they'll be here at five-three-oh. I want you to meet my dad first."

As if on cue, Lou walked into the room. "Who are all these people in my house?"

"Dad," Sid took Lou's arm and guided him to the couch. "This is Eddie and his son Adrian."

Lou nodded at Eddie and slowly lowered himself onto the couch. He patted the seat beside him as he eyed Adrian. "Hop up here, young man. Let me get a good look at you."

Adrian climbed up, caution apparent in his every move. Sid wondered if he might have *over*-warned Adrian about how sick his dad was, but as soon as Adrian's bottom hit the couch, he pulled Rimi from under his arm and sat her on his own lap—an offering of conversation.

Lou took the bait. "What do we have here?"

"This is my monster. Her name is Rimi!"

Lou's face blanched. "Rimi?" His voice boomed. "Why would you name her that?"

Adrian gasped. He tucked Rimi close and stared at Eddie and Sid with huge eyes.

Sid took the doll from Adrian and winked. "Dad, Adrian and I made Rimi together." He sat on the ottoman to look directly into his father's eyes and told the story of how Rimi was made and how she had been a great friend to Adrian in his new home. "She survived the flu-pocalypse."

"So, she's a good monster?"

"The best monster," Adrian said. "She helps me sleep sometimes."

Lou grunted and took the doll from Sid. He ran his finger over the velveteen fanged heart on Rimi's belly. "She looks like she might know a few good jokes." He handed Rimi to Adrian with a crooked smile. "Do you know any good jokes?"

"I know a lot of good jokes." Adrian lifted to the doll to his own face and spoke in a silly voice. "Why did the pig stop sunbathing, Mr. Sid's Dad Lou?"

Eddie laughed and leaned against Sid. "We should have worked harder on the name."

"I don't know, I sort of like this one," Sid said, nudging Adrian to tell the punchline.

"He was bacon in the heat!" Adrian barely got the answer out before he fell backward on the couch in laughter. Lou's smile was slow, but landed right between Sid's eyes.

"I like this kid."

The doorbell rang and Sid took his dad's hand while Eddie and Adrian spoke to Olivia and her parents on the porch. "I like him too," Sid said. "He and his dad make me happy."

Adrian ran inside to say goodbye and was off before Lou caught up to what had happened. Halfway through dinner, Lou looked away from his food as rice fell from his fork. "Where did the boy go?"

"He had a hot date, Dad. You're stuck with us tonight."

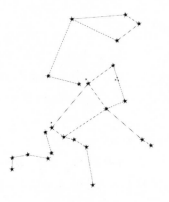

XXII.
HERCULES

EDDIE WOULDN'T ADMIT TO BEING nervous about meeting Sid's dad, but that didn't make it any less true. Considering that Lou was a well-educated man who was losing bits of his mind every day, had a weak heart that kept him on his ass more often than his feet, and was stuck living with his controlling daughter, he was enjoyable company for an evening.

Lou rubbed the spices over the sea bass for dinner. He set the table and misplaced only one fork and one drink. He praised Sid's fish curry and compared it to Rimi's, then went on about a night he had upset her because he burned it.

While Sid cleaned up from the meal, Eddie and Lou sat in the living room. The Marneaux Inquisition began.

"Where did you go to college?" Lou started.

"No college," Eddie said. "I took off for the fire academy after high school."

"What, didn't you like school?"

"I liked English."

"Ah, like Rimi." Lou shouted into the kitchen. "Sid! When is your mother going to be home?"

"Soon, Baba."

"Have you finished your homework tonight, young man?"

Sid peeked through the pass-through and caught Eddie's eye. "Yes, before Eddie came over."

To Eddie, Lou said, "You look like an athlete. You into sports? Football?"

"Basketball, mostly. Did you play?"

"I dabbled. Played second base for Mordell, 1957," Lou said. "But Sid's the real athlete in the family. He's going to play soccer in college."

"I've heard he's pretty good. Adrian plays. Sid's been a great help."

"Who's Adrian?"

"The little boy who was here earlier—with the blue and green monster?"

"Oh. Yes. Sid's a great soccer player." Lou's expression was blank—no recollection of Adrian.

Eddie tried to lead the questioning, but Lou picked up a magazine and a magnifying glass and began to read. They sat quietly; Sid took a call in a back bedroom. Uncomfortable with the silence, Eddie stood to finish the dishes.

"Where do you think you're going? I'm not done talking to you."

Eddie sat down. "I'm sorry, sir. I thought I'd help Sid."

Lou grunted and read his magazine. After Sid returned, Lou smacked his rolled magazine on the end table and looked Eddie squarely in the eyes.

"Do you like my son?"

"Mr. Marneaux, I *love* your son."

"Good." He unrolled the magazine and tossed it onto the couch. "Don't get any ideas about playing hide the sausage under my roof, young man."

Something dropped in the kitchen, followed by a mumbled "Shit." Any remaining nerves Eddie carried broke free right along with the dish that hit the floor. "No, sir. I will make sure to keep my sausage out and visible at all times."

"That's a good boy."

When they visited a few nights later, Lou misplaced his pocket protector. It resulted in a near catastrophic panic that stopped all conversation, all dessert eating, all function outside of finding the "fucking thing—that cost me a fortune!" Afterward, Sid took a breather in the basement with the laundry. Eddie settled in with Lou, who checked his shirt pocket one more time to make sure he hadn't lost the protector yet again.

"Thank you for finding this," Lou said. "I got out of sorts."

"It's okay. We all have safety nets."

Lou looked at Eddie, narrowed his eyes, and grinned. "I like you, Eddie."

"I like you too, sir." And he did. He liked that from the nose up, he could see what Sid would look like as an older man. For an eighty-year-old man, Lou still had a thick thatch of gray hair. His brow was strong, his eyebrows also thick and gray. In lucid moments, his hazel eyes emoted just like Sid's.

In spite of Lou's gruffness, the warm man Sid spoke of so fondly still shone through. The bonds they had created while living without Rimi's tender care were palpable in the way Sid touched his dad, in the way Lou looked to Sid for assurance, in the way Lou's body visibly relaxed as soon as Anna left the room.

Eddie understood. Sid had the same effect on him: around Sid, he felt a quiet assurance that—bumbling as he was as a dad, unprepared as he felt running Connelly fire department—with Sid by his side, he could quite possibly do anything.

Lou sipped tea from a straw and sat back with a satisfied sigh. "Sid doesn't need me to look after him anymore, you know. He hasn't for a long time."

"No, he's pretty independent."

Lou nodded, his focus seemed to phase out. "I've been talking to Rimi lately. So, I'm asking this for her, you understand."

"Of course."

"Do you love him? I don't mean a for-now kind of love. Do you *love* him?"

Lou's concern for Sid's happiness touched Eddie. It also reminded him of someone who obsessively checked the stove, the iron, the locks before leaving on vacation. But Lou's departure wouldn't include a return trip.

Eddie smiled. "I do, sir." Lou looked at Eddie as if waiting for him to elaborate. "He's creative and smart. He laughs at my dumb jokes and finds some of his own to keep up. Adrian loved him the instant he met him. I did too, in many ways. He makes me feel like I can do anything." Eddie stopped and blushed. "I'm sorry—I should tell him this, not you."

"You'll have your chance," Lou said, patting Eddie's hand. "All that good stuff? It comes from his mother."

"Oh, I don't know. I see your sparkle in there, too."

"She lives in him, Eddie." Lou sat up, a clarity in his eyes Eddie hadn't seen before. "After she passed, Sid and I stumbled around a lot. I couldn't cook. I couldn't care for him like she did. I could kick a soccer ball and get him dressed, but I had no idea how to *love* him."

"It's scary as hell some days."

"Yes, but Sid found a kind of peace. I don't remember a lot, but I remember that day. He'd had a rough soccer practice. He walked into the house, stopped right inside the door. He took this huge, deep breath—I thought he would scream or cry, but no. He took a deep breath… and he rested. I knew right then, that was Rimi. She found her final home in him."

"He needed her the most."

"He did. And he's who you love because of it."

Eddie considered how Adrian's dreams about Maggie no longer frightened him, how he found as much comfort in Sid as he did Eddie, how he now talked to teachers about mean kids at school instead of acting out. "Maggie lives in Adrian too, doesn't she?"

"Maggie is?"

"Adrian's mother. She died earlier this year."

"Yes, I remember now." Eddie believed him this time. "I wonder where I'll land."

"Mmm, I have an idea…"

"I keep asking Rimi, and she hasn't told me. What have you got?"

Eddie listened as Sid put clothes into drawers in Lou's bedroom, a task of love in these circumstances: love for his father, his sister, and his mother. "Anna. She can't seem to work hard enough, can she?"

"That's my fault. I missed so much when they were little." Lou reached for Eddie's wrist. "Don't do that, you hear me? Pay attention to that boy."

"I've got 'em both, sir. I'm not letting go."

"Good." Lou closed his eyes and traced the upholstery on the arm of the couch. "I need to know he's in good hands before I go."

*　　*　　*

"So," Sid said, running his finger along the seam of Eddie's flannel lounge pants. He elongated the "o" and batted his eyelashes. It was the third morning of this game.

"I'm not telling you anything." It was the third morning Sid had tried to use his masculine wiles to find out what Eddie and Lou had talked about.

"You shared secrets with my dad while I did laundry. It's rude." Sid poked; Sid prodded. Kisses and licks remained unsuccessful. Tickles irritated and threats fell flat. Eddie would not be moved.

The previous morning, Eddie had indeed offered to hide his sausage under Sid's roof. Sid had cracked a reluctant smile and, by the end of the day, conceded to the offer.

On the fourth morning, Sid tried disarming Eddie with an elaborate breakfast, complete with a hurry-before-Adrian-misses-us blowjob. Eddie wouldn't talk.

"We spoke father-to-father," Eddie had gasped when Sid unbuckled his pants. "And taking my pants off isn't going to... oh. Jesus."

Sid's curiosity eventually quieted, and life pressed onward. Sid began to bounce back and forth from Chicago to Connelly with increased regularity. The new web design had lured in more clients; the latest Trial Line had been their most successful. Rue and Sid confessed they needed to reconsider the benefits of holding a trunk show—regardless of Sid's ridiculous schedule. They made press kits, line sheets, and used every picture from the photo shoot to their advantage. Mitchell was happy. Sid's head spun.

As a continued nod to his dad's service, Sid kept himself on the volunteer schedule for fire runs when he was in Connelly, but asked Dottie to please hire someone for the office, to refill the gaping hole that Lou had left and Sid could never fill.

The domestic life, a life he had never sought for himself, brought an unexpected balance amidst the chaos. Adrian and Eddie enjoyed visiting Mr. Sid's Dad Lou even though Adrian had to reintroduce himself every time. He was direct with Lou in a way adults were afraid to be. "I just *told* you that!" he would say, exasperated. Lou would bristle, and, with patience beyond his years, Adrian would repeat himself, or change the story altogether until Lou caught up again.

On a quiet Saturday afternoon, Sid and Eddie watched from the kitchen as Adrian launched into a new story. Lou sat on the couch and, as directed by Adrian, held a piece of paper taped to a stick. He held his hand on his stomach—a castle door that opened upon Adrian's command.

Eddie leaned against Sid and took a shaky breath.

"What's up?"

Eddie kissed Sid's jaw and busied himself with drinks. "Ade used to do that with Maggie," he said with a broken chuckle. "She was a great flagpole. He learned so much patience with her."

As October came to a close, patience became more and more necessary for everyone. From one visit to the next, Lou's speech began to slur, his movements slowed, and the delay from question to answer lengthened. Lou cried whenever Sid and his family left. Anna stopped feigning interest in getting outside help. One evening, Lou threw his field glasses onto the picnic table because he couldn't find Aquila. They broke on impact; Sid and Anna fought about the need to buy him a new pair.

Sharon offered to take Adrian to Wylie for Halloween to see his old friends. Adrian jumped at the chance to show off his costume: a Sid-made replica of Rimi Monster, complete with a spiked green hood, a velveteen, fanged heart on his belly, and an extra set of arms protruding from his sides.

Ready to enjoy a rare date night, Sid had just buckled himself in Eddie's car when his phone buzzed. Assuming it was Rue with yet one more point from their daylong conference, he ignored it and planted a lewd, suggestive kiss on Eddie's mouth—*in* Eddie's mouth. The phone buzzed again.

"Get it, so we can move on," Eddie said with a growl. "Why are we leaving the house at all?"

Sid looked at his phone and grabbed Eddie's hand. "Hey, Andrew. What's up?"

"It's Dad. He's collapsed. I don't know what to do."

"How does a grown man of forty-six years not know what the—" Eddie instinctively reached out to brace Sid in his seat and came to an abrupt stop at a traffic light. "Why didn't I drive the station truck tonight?"

"Because you're off duty." The intersection was empty. "Run the fucking light, Eddie."

With a quick glance both directions, Eddie floored it and picked up where he'd left off. "What the *fuck* to do when someone—with a *heart condition*—passes out? How do you go through life and have no goddamned idea how to—"

"What, call 9-1-1? I cannot believe—" Sid gasped as Eddie ran another yellow light and swerved to avoid a car turning left across their lane. "I had to tell him to do it. Turn right here. Back way; no traffic lights."

"If we beat the squad, I've got a mask and—" Eddie blindly reached for Sid's hand. "Does he have a DNR?"

"No. Anna talks him out of it every time he brings it up."

"Christ. Forgive me for wanting to kick both of your siblings' asses."

"Forgiven. Left here and you know the rest of the way."

Eddie pulled into the drive and was out of the car in a flash. He flung his trunk open and grabbed a small red tackle box. Sid stopped Eddie; his eyes were wide in panic.

"Eddie?"

"We're going to be fine. The squad will be here any minute."

"Why don't I hear one? His station is up on Monterey."

"I don't know, but I have *got* to get in there." Eddie walked inside and toward the back hallway. "Andrew?"

"In the bathroom." Andrew stood at the doorway. Lou lay on the floor on his side.

"How long has he been down?" Eddie hit the floor, opened his kit, gloved himself, and rolled Lou onto his back. He quickly checked for a pulse, and, swearing, tossed a facemask to Sid as he entered the room. "No pulse. I'll start chest compressions."

"Fucking—Baba…"

"You okay to do this?"

"I have no choice." Sid knelt and cupped the back of his dad's neck to open his airway. He kept a quiet count of Eddie's compressions and slid the mask over his dad's mouth.

"I don't know what happened," Andrew said, as callously as if he was reporting a minor fender bender. Eddie tried to capture the important words as he counted: "Tired all day… barely ate… bathroom… heard him fall…"

"Twenty-eight, twenty-nine, thirty." Eddie paused for Sid to give rescue breaths. "How long has he been down, Andrew?" Eddie asked again. He resumed heavy, steady compressions on Lou's chest.

"Ten minutes? I called Sid right away."

"And you called the squad?" Sid asked.

"Yeah, a second ago."

"A *second* ago? What the fuck were you *waiting*—"

"Sid," Eddie said, breathless with exertion. "Later." He lifted from Lou's chest and looked at the mask. "Thirty. Go, give me two."

He and Sid fell into a rhythm of compressions to respirations, switching places so neither would get too exhausted. Andrew stared and offered excuses explaining why this was not the emergency it clearly was.

"He was breathing, so I thought he fainted and—" Lou expelled a rattling, agonal breath. "See? Won't you hurt him if he's breathing?"

"Andrew," Sid stopped compressions while Eddie provided another rescue breath. "Shut the fuck up and go wait for the squad."

Within moments, the team from Paulson Township arrived, stunned to find Chief Garner working on their patient. Eddie filled the team in on the circumstances while Sid continued the chest compressions. "He's their patient now, Sid; let's get out of the way."

Sid kissed his father's forehead. "I love you, Baba."

"Come on, sweetheart," Eddie said and pulled him into the kitchen as the team resumed chest compressions. "You did great, everything you could." Andrew leaned against the stove, furiously typing into his phone. "You, on the other hand—" Eddie stopped himself; this was not his family. "Have you notified Anna?"

"She had to go to Tyler's school. I guess he got hurt in cross-country or something."

"Which answers why you're here," Sid said trying to get a glimpse down the hall. He jumped when the sounds of a portable defibrillator snapped.

"What's *that* supposed to mean?" Andrew asked, buried in his phone.

"It means—"

Eddie tugged Sid back into the kitchen, shutting him up with a kiss on the cheek and as paternal a look as he could manage. "It means that we're all worried and upset and probably shouldn't talk anymore."

A call from the bathroom stopped all three men. "We have rhythm!"

Eddie held up a finger to keep Sid and his brother in the kitchen and stepped to the bathroom. A paramedic handed Eddie an EKG strip. "It's not great, Chief, but it's something."

"Pulse?"

"Pulse and blood pressure present, but weak. We've secured the airway."

"Call the hospital."

Like a defiant child testing his limits, Sid stood at the edge of the kitchen and peeked into the hallway. His eyes begged for good news.

"It's weak. But it's there," Eddie said.

"He's been down too long, hasn't he?"

"He was down a long time, but knowing him, if he has more to say he'll figure out a way to say it."

They wheeled Lou to the ambulance. Andrew followed them with a litany of questions on insurance and billing. Sid stood frozen in the kitchen. His breath came in shallow puffs; he stared at the front door.

"Sid? You need to hold on, okay?" Sid nodded and took Eddie's hand, squeezing Eddie's fingers as if soaking up every ounce of strength Eddie could offer. "We should go."

"Let me—" His grip tight on Eddie's hand, Sid walked to his father's room. He grabbed Lou's robe. "In case he's okay? And..." Sid's eyes were desperate, seeking answers Eddie didn't have. "In case he wakes up cold."

Eddie smiled sadly and pressed a kiss to the corner of Sid's mouth. "Good plan. He's going to want to see you."

* * *

SID FLINCHED AND BATTED BLINDLY at the buzzing noise that interrupted his already fitful sleep. The overhead fluorescent lights stabbed his eyes like daggers and, when he sat up, his entire body ached in protest.

He grabbed his phone and found an empty corner in the ICU waiting room. "Yeah, this is Sid."

"Baby. What's the news?" Sid heard the crackle of Rue's inhaled cigarette through the phone. Her voice and the ever-present cigarette sent relief through his entire body.

"What time is it anyway? What *day* is it?"

"It's Monday morning. Seven o'clock your time." It hadn't been twelve hours, yet Sid felt as if at least a week had passed.

"What are you doing awake this early?"

"Worrying about you. What's the *news?*"

"It's not good. They put in a stent and a balloon pump… thing. Or one of those? Rue, I can't keep it all straight. I know he's on a ventilator and they keep checking to see if he responds to anything. I wish everyone would leave him alone."

"I'm so sorry."

"I'm sure the damage is irreparable. I want to wait to see if he wakes up, but—"

"What can I do? Is Eddie with you? Do you want me to fly out? I feel helpless."

"Rue, my god. Stay put and—" Sid gasped. "Fuck. Rue. The trunk show. We were supposed to get that on the calendar."

"Fuck the trunk show, Sid. You have one priority right now and it doesn't involve any of us."

"Mitchell is going to—"

"Sid, stop. He's the assiest of assholes, but he'll understand this." Rue sighed; her cigarette softly crackled through the phone. "I hate that this happened. I know how much your dad means to you."

"He liked you." The floor-to-ceiling windows of the waiting room overlooked a small courtyard. As the sun began to rise, the death of autumn's landscape mirrored Sid's heart.

"Let's not talk past tense yet," she said. "You promise me you'll call if I can do anything?"

"I promise," Sid said. "I'll keep you updated."

Sid pocketed his phone and reveled in the silence, a stark difference from the incessant whirrs and pops and clicks of machinery in his dad's room. He wished he'd replaced his dad's field glasses and found one more night to sit beneath the stars and let Lou dream his way to his wife.

Sid ran his hand through his hair and braced himself to go back. A crack of radio transmission interrupted Sid's quiet. Eddie stepped behind him and slipped his hands around Sid's waist while pressing his lips to Sid's neck. "Hi," was all Sid could summon.

Eddie rested his head on Sid's shoulder and swayed them gently, in tandem with the dwarf trees blowing in the courtyard below. "How you holding up?"

"You. You're holding me up."

"I'm happy to do that for you. Did you sleep okay?"

Grateful for the gentle rhythm of their bodies, for Eddie's quiet strength, Sid spun in Eddie's arms. "I'm not sure I'd have slept well at home either." Obligated to return to Anna, Sid stepped back. His *desire* was to go home with Eddie and let him spoil him with a beautiful meal, a sudsy soaking bath, warm skin, and firm hands. "Wait. You're on duty. Why are you here?"

Eddie tapped his radio. "On duty. Reporting to Connelly General to take the most handsome man in Pennsylvania to breakfast."

A less-than-beautiful meal, no sudsy bath, and definitely no skin. But Eddie. Eddie would be enough. "Are you inviting me to dine at the exquisite hospital cafeteria?"

"Would you go with me if I was?" Eddie didn't wait for an answer. He grabbed Sid's hand and walked them to the elevator.

"I don't know," Sid teased, typing a note to Anna. "Do you put out on the first date?"

"You *know* I do."

"Fourth date, Eddie. That was our fourth date."

XXIII.
VIRGO

"*SID!* SID! COME QUICK! SID!"

Eddie lay perfectly still. If Sid wasn't already going through the storm of his life, he might laugh that his son had called for Sid, not him.

He had felt victorious in convincing Sid to come home with him at all. Because of a promising neurological test result, the family sat in a holding pattern to see what Lou's body might decide to do. Anna and Sid had both spent every moment at his bedside. After twenty-four hours and no change, the nursing staff had urged them to go sleep in their own beds.

Except now, at 2:47 a.m., no one was sleeping.

At Eddie's back, Sid twitched and moaned. "Is he calling for *me?*"

"Yep."

"This is why you asked me to stay here; it had nothing to do with getting a decent night's sleep, did it?"

"You found me out."

"*Sid!*"

Eddie lost his battle. The bed shook with his laughter.

"You're enjoying this entirely too much," Sid said as he curled into Eddie in a way that implied nothing about middle-of-the-night childcare.

"In light of the circumstances, I should apologize."

"Asshole."

Eddie rolled over and kissed Sid's shoulder. "Rumor has it, Sid Marneaux likes assholes."

"*Sid!* I'm calling for you!"

"You know how to get him to shut up?" Eddie said, pointing to the door.

Sid whined. "Get out of bed and see what he wants."

"It's worked for me. I'd offer to go and all, but last I checked my name isn't Sid."

"Rumors are only partially true, you know. I like *certain* assholes. It's not looking good for you." Sid flipped the covers from his body… and Eddie's.

"That wasn't nice at all."

"Mmm. If I find vomit in there and he's calling for me, I'm hanging you from your station's cherry picker." Sid stood and hovered over Eddie's face. "By your balls."

"Promises. Promises."

"At City Hall." Sid kissed him, renouncing his threat with one peck.

"*Sid!*"

SMELLING NO VOMIT, SID STEPPED into Adrian's room, where his fuzzy curls cast a ridiculous shadow on the wall. "I'm here. You okay?"

"Yes! I'm—I saw her, Sid! It's been for*ever*! I saw her!"

"Your mom?" Before Sid's ass hit the edge of Adrian's bed, Adrian had climbed into his lap. "Whoa…" Sid scooted them against the wall. Rimi Monster's spikes tickled his chin. "How do you move so fast in the middle of the night?"

"Well, it took you like ten years to get here."

"I was sleeping."

"So was I. That's how dreams work, Sid."

"You are a smart aleck for someone who woke *me* up from a good dream." Eyes wide in anticipation, Adrian stared at him in the dark, blue-hued room. "You're going to explode if you don't tell me about this dream. Go."

"She was in a line, like every time. But this time she turned away before smiling at me. I got scared she wasn't going to talk."

"She never does, does she?"

"No." Adrian flicked the spikes on Rimi's head. As this was Adrian's tactile comfort whenever he had something important to say, a few spikes had weakened at their base.

"Do you know why she turned away?"

"To show me someone across the room… the place." Adrian huffed. "I'll draw a picture tomorrow. It's like a big blue space with fog and flowers. Someone was sitting at a table."

"Who was it?"

"I was afraid it might be that boy from the fire—that she had a new boy—but it wasn't him."

"You're her only boy, buddy."

"Yes." Adrian rested his head on Sid's chest and swirled a finger over his arm. He whispered his question. "Sid, what does your mommy look like?"

Sid stopped stroking Adrian's back. "Have you seen the picture in my living room?"

"No."

"No, it's up pretty high. Let's go see Daddy—I have one in my wallet. Climb up." Adrian climbed onto Sid's back, and, when he stood, Sid groaned at his weight. "They're feeding you something funny at school. You're getting too big for this."

"I'm the littlest in my class."

"That's because everyone else has to stretch to be awesome. You already are." When they got to Eddie's room, Sid hefted Adrian right on top of Eddie. "Incoming!"

Adrian squealed and landed in a fit of giggles. "That wasn't nice either, Mr. Marneaux." Sid turned on a small table lamp. "Seriously? It's three in the morning."

"This is important, Dad. I think I saw Sid's mom."

"What?" Eddie sat up and attempted to open his eyes. He achieved Popeye, with one eye closed to the bright light. "Do you know what she looked like?"

"No, but…" Adrian sat on Sid's pillow. "You said you have a picture, Sid?"

Sid pulled a small photograph from his wallet. Even though it was faded and worn at the edges, it was his favorite picture of her—how he remembered her. "Before I show you, tell me what she looked like in your dream."

"Her hair was black like yours." Adrian tilted his head and squinted at Sid. "It fell on her shoulders like pretty puddles. And, she had dark eyes like you, a skinny nose, dark skin, and a big smile. Sid, she's *so* pretty."

Sid swallowed and handed him the picture. "Like this?"

"Oh my goodness." Adrian stared at the picture. "And she was wearing a baseball hat with 'MC' on it, like the stone sign by your house. She gave me a big thumbs-up." Adrian showed them with both thumbs and a huge grin.

Sid started to talk and stopped. When he found his voice it was a quiet monotone. "We used to go to basketball games at Mordell; Dad had students on the team. She never got the hang of the game, but cheered when we did. After she died, he didn't go back."

"Did anything else happen, Ade?" Eddie asked.

"Nope. Mom moved up in the line, and Sid's mom disappeared after I waved at her. And I woke up."

Sid glanced at the photograph in Adrian's hands and kissed both of his boys on the cheek. "I'm going to go downstairs to get something to drink." He changed direction and grabbed a sweatshirt from the closet. "Sit outside."

EDDIE COULD HEAR THE STAIRS of his old house creak with every step Sid took. Kitchen cabinets popped and clicked; the backdoor squeaked open, and the blinds smacked against the window when Sid closed it.

In the silence that followed, Adrian asked, "Did I make Sid sad?" Adrian teethed one of Rimi's spikes and rubbed the flower in her hand.

"No, buddy. He's worried about his dad. I'd guess that makes him miss his mom."

"She looked happy, Daddy."

Eddie cupped his son's face in his hand. Nowadays, his longing for Maggie revolved around his wish that she could see her boy show a heart as lovely as hers. "I know. He knows too. Let's get you to bed so I can go make sure he's okay, though."

"Can I stay here?"

"Not tonight. We'll plan a bedroom movie night soon, okay?" Adrian nodded and asked no more questions. He climbed into his own bed and kept Rimi close to his chest. "I'm glad you got to see Mommy again."

"Me too. She looks happy every time I see her now."

"She was her happiest with you, buddy."

Eddie followed his nose to the kitchen, where the cinnamon, anise, and cardamom scents of Sid's chai lingered. A pan sat on low heat in silent invitation to make a mug and come outside.

Sid sat on the chaise under a throw; steam from his tea billowed around his face. He reached for Eddie's hand and hooked their fingers together to swing between the chairs.

Sips of tea and contented hums of pleasure filled the night's silence. Sid let go of Eddie's finger and gripped his mug with both hands; his gaze was intent on the cloudless sky. Eddie asked, "What's that big group of bright stars straight out?"

"That's Orion. The three stars in a row make his belt. His shoulder is to the left… I can't remember the name of that star. His knee is to the right. I think… Rigel?" After more silence, Sid added, "Pity Aquila isn't visible."

"What's special about Aquila?"

"It's where Maggie and Ma live." Sid spoke as if it were scientific fact. "I know that sounds insane."

"No more insane than Maggie and Ma starring in my son's nighttime movies."

Sid kept his attention in the sky. "She's waiting for Baba, isn't she?" he asked, clearly not looking for an answer. "I'm not ready to let go of him yet."

"I don't think anyone ever is… not really."

"He's eighty, for god's sake. A year ago he was tormenting volunteers in the C-DRT office. He'd text me his cycling mileage, his speed. 'Beat *this,* Zico,' and I couldn't. I didn't have the time." The last word slipped out on a whimper. "I didn't have the *time* to come visit him once Anna took him in. He told me to stay up there. To make my mark. Make him and Ma proud, so I'd stay."

"He is proud of you, Sid. Even if in his mind you're a still a high school soccer star."

"I know," Sid said, pulling his attention back to the patio, to Eddie. "He deserved more from me this year."

"If your success was a gift to him, then you're doing exactly what he wanted."

Sid quieted again, turned as if shutting the stars out of their conversation. "He's not coming back to us, is he?"

Eddie could utter the most medically sound guess, which was a solid no. He could exaggerate the slight pupil response the neurologist had found forty-eight hours before. But Sid begged for reassurance. "I don't like to walk away from hope."

"Anna finally signed a DNR. He's going to arrest again. I'm going to have to figure out life without him at the sidelines."

Eddie tugged Sid's hand and pointed to the sky. "Who says he won't be on the sidelines? Your mom has never stopped cheering for you."

"And we're back to that boy's dream," Sid said on a sigh. "Is it selfish that I wish she would have visited me instead of Adrian?"

"She knows you're not ready yet."

"She's probably right." He stood and held his hand out for Eddie to take.

Loving Sid's heart, wishing he could protect it, Eddie kissed Sid's temple. "Good moms usually are."

*   *   *

THE NEXT MORNING, ANNA MET Sid in the hospital hallway. She greeted him with a softness in her face that Sid hadn't seen in well over a year. Sid pulled her into his arms. She swayed and lingered there, combing her long fingers through his hair.

"Today feels heavy and it's only eight a.m.," she said into his neck.

"Did you sleep okay?"

"Better than here. Thank Eddie for insisting."

"Did the doc come by?"

"Yeah. We need to make a decision by tomorrow morning. He wants to give it one more day… just in case."

"You're okay with this?" He didn't need to ask. The peace about her said everything.

"Yes." She leaned against the wall and gripped his fingers. "I'm sorry I've been so blind to everything. I wanted—"

"We both wanted what was never going to happen. He's been walking away from us all year."

"For the smarter of the two of us, it sure took me long enough to figure that out." Her eyes twinkled; she was as beautiful as their mother.

"Wisdom doesn't come from books, Didi."

"Zico…" She cupped his face and kissed his forehead. "You haven't called me that in years."

He hadn't. The name—Bangla for "older sister"—hadn't fit. A sister who stressed, who judged, who demanded in ways a sister shouldn't made using the name beyond Sid's reach.

"You're my sister." Sid said, feeling it in his bones. "My much, *much* older sister."

"Don't get sassy. I can still find a way to ground you."

That afternoon, Andrew agreed to relieve them for a few hours. Welcoming the idea of not seeing his brother—who hadn't bothered to come to the hospital since Lou's attack—Sid joined Eddie at the firehouse for a county-wide safety meeting.

He sat with Eddie and poked through the soupy pasta salad Lieutenant Parker's wife had slopped onto his plate. Food hadn't tasted right in days.

"Any news?"

"Still hanging on. We have to give the doctors a decision tomorrow morning." Sid doodled a gallows to begin a game of hangman. "Distract me." At Eddie's pause, he nudged. "Seriously. Please."

"Dirty?"

"Why else play?"

Thirty-five minutes into the meeting, they had already filled a page with numerous hanging stick figures and naughty words. Sid's phone buzzed.

Eddie: What should you do if your boyfriend starts smoking?

If anyone ever questioned Sid as to why he loved Eddie, he would point to this moment as an example.

Sid: Snub the offending cancer stick on the thick of his muscular, delicious thigh.

Eddie: I have muscular, delicious thighs? I thought that was your job.

Sid looked at Eddie and licked his lips, sufficiently distracted. He guessed the letter "A" in their game. Eddie added a right arm to the victim and picked up his phone.

Eddie: You haven't answered the question. Safety training. What should you do if your boyfriend starts smoking?

Sid: Tell me, Chief. What should I do?

Eddie: Slow down and use a lubricant.

Sid tossed his phone onto the table, looked at the hangman puzzle, and picked his phone up again.

Sid: You misspelled frottage, which I'm guessing is your hangman answer. Coincidentally, it's also my request for—

Sid stopped typing and hit send. Hangman and naughty texting weren't working after all. The idea of that sort of intimacy seemed irreverent.

About an hour into the meeting, Sid's phone vibrated again.

"Eddie... Dottie's glaring."

"It's not me this time, sweetheart."

"Shit." He was chilled to see Andrew's name opening a text message.

Andrew: hospital. now.

"Go." Eddie kissed him. "I love you."

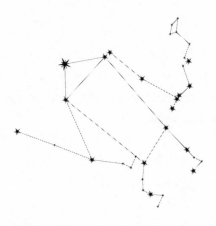

XXIV.
OPHIUCHUS

Sɪᴅ ɢᴏᴛ ᴛᴏ ᴛʜᴇ ʜᴏsᴘɪᴛᴀʟ in record time. His favorite receptionist waved him into the all-too-familiar ICU unit—down this hall, to the right, third door on the left. An unrecognizable alarm rang from his Dad's room. As he rounded the corner, it went silent. Sid stopped cold. The entire unit seemed to stand still.

"Baba... *no.*"

The curtain was drawn around his father's bed. He gripped the hideous fabric and pulled it open. Andrew sat along the far edge of his father's bed and met Sid's gaze. He whispered Sid's name; tears filled his eyes. Anna curled over the hospital bed; her soft cries sighed through the otherwise silent room.

Lou's breathing tube had been removed. His mouth sagged open.

A nurse at the head of the bed turned from his duties. "I'm so sorry," he said to Sid. After jotting a note onto a clipboard, he made a point of touching each of them on his way out. "Take as long as you need."

Sid couldn't move, couldn't breathe. A need gripped him like a vise, and he typed a quick phone message. He backed out of the room—right, to the left, down the long hall—and turned into the waiting room. In his quiet corner, he slid to the floor.

SID: I NEED YOU.

"Shit." Eddie was out of his seat and on his way to the hospital.

Before he got into the ICU, he caught sight of Sid's boots in their far corner of the waiting room.

"Sid …"

Sid sat on the floor with his legs splayed in front of him. He stared at the floor; Eddie got on his knees in front of him.

"Sweetheart?"

Sid took in a quick breath and, instead of speaking, let it out in a soft huff and looked at a new section of floor. His eyes slowly filled as he breathed unevenly through his parted lips. He blinked and tried again, this time looking straight into Eddie's soul.

"He's gone," Sid said simply. A tear slipped down his cheek. "He's gone, Eddie." As Sid drew in more erratic breaths, the reality of his words sucked the air out of their private corner. "He's gone, he's gone."

Eddie ran his hand up Sid's arm and, at that simple touch, Sid collapsed into him. Soft sobs echoed as Eddie held on. Sid's cries intensified and then quieted as he tried to speak words where words didn't exist. Eddie held on for Maggie and for Rimi, tossing up a wish upon a star that they would indeed be waiting for Lou, that in time that belief would bring comfort.

Sid loosened his grip; his stuttering sobs slowed as he grabbed tissues from a box that had magically appeared on the floor. "The tissue fairy came," Sid said before blowing his nose. A pair of white shoes disappeared around the corner.

"She did," Eddie said. "I wonder if she's in cahoots with the tooth fairy."

Sid's attempt at a smile failed. "This hurts more than I ever imagined. I knew—I *knew*, and it's still like a knife… like it's stuck." He clasped at his chest and twisted, closed his eyes, and pulled his T-shirt as though trying to yank a knife out. "I don't know what happened. I took off."

"He'd already passed?"

Sid nodded. "I must have missed him by seconds."

"I'm so sorry. Are Anna and Andrew with him?"

"Probably." Sid leaned his head against the wall and sighed. "I should go and—" Sid pulled his knees to his chest and quietly wept.

After Maggie had taken her last breath, Eddie hadn't been able to think. Inappropriately-timed jokes had softened the blow. Mundane conversation had redirected the overwhelming grief. Tears would hit mid-sentence, and walking away mid-conversation had become acceptable behavior. Anticipated feelings of relief for the dying now seemed like betrayal. During it all, Eddie had wanted one thing: a silent companion. So that's what he offered Sid.

Sid blew his nose and chuckled as the noise echoed. He smiled weakly and moved to stand. "Will you walk me down?"

Eddie fired off a quick text to his second-in-command and made sure he had turned off his radio. "Whatever you need, I'm here."

"I love you." Sid bit back more tears, then swallowed them away. "He loved—I'm so glad he got to see that I'm happy."

"It's all he ever wanted for you."

Sid held Eddie's hand and started down the hall. "You helped make that wish come true."

Eddie smiled in memory of his conversations with Lou. He vowed to be all that Lou had asked him to be for Sid. "It's been my greatest honor."

* * *

SID SPLAYED ACROSS THE LENGTH of Anna's couch, sure that if he stayed there for five more seconds, he could sleep for a week. Eddie knelt on the floor next to him and fiddled with Sid's hair. "What do you want to do?"

"I want to go home; can you come with me?" Sid smiled sleepily at Eddie. Reality hit. "Adrian. Shit."

"Sharon, remember?"

"God, you *are* a prince." Sid moaned and groaned his way upright. "Does Ade know?"

"Yeah. I'm not sure what he grasped. I'd interrupted a serious game of Sorry."

"Was he winning?"

"Doesn't he always?"

As Eddie drove him home, questions and concerns spilled from Sid like a river flooding its banks. He listed people he needed to notify and backtracked, wondering if the obit in the paper would be satisfactory. "But they'll want to hear it from me, won't they? Dottie was so—I don't want to make her tell the volunteers. She's a mess too."

And then, "I'm going to have to help Anna go through pictures. I don't know why funerals have to be a fucking "Life and Times" production nowadays. Won't the people there already *know* his story?" After a moment's silence, he added, "No. I guess they wouldn't. They should know his story."

"It's a good one."

At a traffic light, he opened and closed the glove box. He found gloves, an umbrella, napkins, and a manual—no answers. "Who does the dinner after the funeral? Where are we going to have it? Do you think the college would have a place? Why didn't Anna and I *talk* about this all those fucking hours at the hospital?"

After he had exhausted all of his options, he said, "I don't know how this all works. I want to take a bath and drink wine."

Eddie turned into his own driveway. "Eddie? I thought you were taking me home."

"If you don't want this, we can leave, and Adrian won't know we were here. I thought—"

"Adrian hugs," Sid said. "Yes. Please."

"He's a good little healer."

"It's Maggie. Inside of him."

Eddie took Sid's hand in his, leaned across the gearshift, and kissed him. "Yes. Like another little boy who lost his mom." Eddie healed, too.

Sid stared out the front window. "Baba's gone, Eddie."

"I know, sweetheart. I'm so terribly sorry."

Either Adrian had been coached or he was the real angel among them. He waited patiently while Sid and Eddie toed off their shoes. He accepted the head rub Eddie offered on his way to the kitchen.

Sid sat on the couch and patted his lap. Adrian's nose was red and cold from playing outside. He nuzzled in the crook of Sid's neck and said nothing. In moments, their breathing matched. Adrian took his own comfort rubbing Sid's hair between his fingers.

"You smell like fall," Sid said.

Adrian sat up and outlined the pocket on Sid's shirt with his finger. "What's fall smell like?"

"Little boys. Burning leaves. Apple cider." Sid mimicked Adrian and traced the stripes on Adrian's sweater. "Wool sweaters."

Adrian looked into Sid's eyes. "Your eyes are sad, Sid."

"I'm sad all over, buddy."

Adrian nodded and outlined Sid's pocket again. "I don't know what words to use."

"That's okay. Words aren't important right now."

"Are hugs important?"

"The most important."

"I do those good." He fell on top of Sid, snuggled close, and launched into a quiet story about his day. He talked about the block city he and his friend built at school. They had populated it with dinosaurs, but when the teacher wanted to use the sandbox underneath, they had to tear it down. The story got better when, after laughing at their city and their frustration, a mean girl had to help them put the blocks away. "And Sid, we had a *lot* of blocks!"

"I bet you did. You build the biggest cities."

"I do. 'Specially with Isaiah. Then we—" Adrian sat up and whipped off his sweater, leaving himself in an undershirt and dark green corduroys.

"Hot?"

"Yes. And itchy. And hot."

As he launched into part three of his story, Sharon came in from the kitchen with a mug of hot tea. She took one look at a barely clad Adrian and shook her head. "I know with this kid, it's best not to ask."

Sid sat up and popped Adrian on the bottom. "Buddy, go get dressed for bed before you start griping about being cold."

"But I'm not done with my story!"

"You're never done with your story. Put some clothes on, you streaker."

Sharon joined Sid on the couch and scooped his socked feet onto her lap. "How are you doing, sweetie? I'm so horribly sorry."

Sid shrugged. "Numb. And thank you."

"That's how you get through the first few days when people are everywhere. Otherwise, you'd probably take a few of them out."

Sid chuckled. This family brought him hope in the form of block stories, foot rubs, and warm concern. "I feel like I've lived a week in a day."

"That's because you have." She rubbed his feet as they sat in shared grief, an emotion time couldn't alter. Eddie came in with a stuffed overnight bag. She pushed Sid's feet off the couch with a tender pat. "Now, go home. Let Eddie take care of you, and call me if you need anything."

"You're already doing more than enough."

"Someone did it for me. Now it's my turn."

"Sid! Wait! You can't leave yet!" Adrian jumped down the last three stairs to the floor with a pounce and a somersault. He ignored his father's stern, "Adrian James!" and launched himself around Sid's legs. Sid stumbled, dropped his shoes, and scooped Adrian up by his ankles.

"Why can't I leave yet?"

"Because. We have some—" Adrian hung upside down; his nightshirt flipped inside out and over his head to bare cartoon briefs and a pale belly. He wiggled and squirmed to right himself, but gave in to his lot. "We have some business to take care of."

Sid looked at Eddie and Sharon for insight; evidently they had none. "Business? I think you're dilly-dallying to avoid going to bed."

Adrian wriggled out of Sid's grasp and stood with an irritated huff. He twisted his nightshirt into place before explaining. "Yes. Business. We need a blanket." He grabbed a throw and took Sid's hand to escort him to the back patio where, if not in Adrian's bed, all serious discussions happened in this house.

They took their places on the chaise: Sid first, Adrian second, blanket third.

Eddie peeked out. "Is this private business?"

"You can come too, Daddy." As Eddie took a seat in the lounge chair, Adrian explained the rules. "You have to be quiet, though. And you can't stare at Sid. We're looking at the sky."

Sid held his breath. Though he believed his own advice to Eddie about grieving in front of Adrian, this seemed different somehow. Adrian wasn't grieving; he was soothing.

"Do you remember our star poem, Sid?"

"I think I do." Sid reached for Eddie's hand. "You'll help me?"

Sid started, and Eddie's mellow baritone joined in with Adrian's voice adding words as he knew them.

"*When you look up at the sky at night, since I'll be living on one of them, since I'll be laughing on one of them, for you it'll be as if all the stars are laughing. You'll have stars that can laugh!*"

Sid couldn't hide his tears, and Adrian didn't seem to mind. In a broken voice, Sid asked, "Remind me, which one is your mommy's?" Aquila sat far in the western sky this night and was blocked by neighbors' trees. Finding the right constellation wasn't the point, it wasn't the point at all.

"It's this way," Adrian said, twisting his body. "And your mommy's is right there."

"Yes, it is. And… what do you think? See that one above them? Not quite as bright yet?"

"Is that your daddy's?"

"I think so."

"I think so, too. So, now they're all friends. Laughing friends."

Sid took a deep breath and nuzzled Adrian's loose curls; his tears dampened Adrian's hair. "Can I tell you something I haven't told you before?"

"Yes."

"Sit up," Sid said. "I want to see you."

Sid fit the blanket around Adrian's shoulders, clasped Adrian's hands, and tugged him close to touch foreheads. "This is sort of a long sentence, but it's important."

"Okay."

Sid said the Bangla words slowly, not only for Adrian's benefit, but his own. "*Ami tomake bhalobashi.*" His mother's voice echoed in his head; the memory of her touch soothed as he cradled Adrian's tiny fingers in his own.

Adrian mouthed the last syllables, his eyes on Sid's. He gasped and a slow smile spread across his face. "I love you too, Sid."

Sid grinned and kissed Adrian's forehead. "How did you know what that meant?"

"That's what Daddy and Mommy look like when they tell me." His smile unwavering, Adrian glanced at Eddie. "Teach me how to say it that way."

Word by word, Sid spoke the sentiment, and Adrian echoed the words until he had the phrase under his tongue. "*Ami tomake bhalobashi.* It's so pretty, Sid."

"Love is pretty."

Long moments stretched before them. Bedtime passed, and no one moved until Adrian yawned. He kissed Sid and Eddie goodnight, and left them to the quiet of the evening.

Eddie reached across for Sid's hand. His exhaustion was visible now, too, in darkened eyes and sleepy lids. "I knew it then, but I believe it now. Your dad was right."

"About?"

Eddie shook his head and stood to pull Sid up to standing. He leaned in for a soft and tender kiss. "He just was."

*   *   *

"WORDS I DIDN'T THINK I'D ever say in my life: This suit feels fantastic." Eddie stretched his neck. Sid tightened his tie and continued to fuss at the shoulder seams. He made Eddie spin for a final inspection.

"And here you fought me on the importance of owning at least one custom-made suit."

Sid had started the ensemble for Eddie weeks before Lou's heart attack, after Eddie had confessed insecurity about looking too "blue collar for the menu" at Sid's favorite restaurant in Chicago.

"I've been making and tailoring suits my entire adult life," Sid had said. "A nice hunter-green wool… You'll be stunning."

As Sid finished getting ready, Eddie remembered the day of Maggie's funeral. In his grief, he'd been sure his dream of having a family had died right along with her. And yet, Adrian and Sharon's laughter soared through the vents. Sid's red toothbrush joined his blue one in the cup on the bathroom sink. A steady rotation of Sid's outfits took up space in his closets and dresser drawers. The kitchen filled with scents less familiar and again with old favorites. Adrian's stories infused the loose floorboards of their old house with reminders of Maggie's joy.

A family had formed right under his nose.

Sid stood in the doorway of the bathroom and fiddled with the hem of his sleeves. He wore a crisp ivory *kurta pajama* and a slate-blue waistcoat that fitted his body from shoulder to hip. The vest buttoned to a mandarin collar and was adorned with matching glistening threads of embroidered design. Sid had meticulously trimmed the stubble on his chin; the shaggy waves of his hair framed his face and teased the collar of his shirt.

Eddie could barely say his name. "Sid."

"Is it too much?" Sid looked into the dresser mirror and smoothed his hand down the front of the vest.

"No. Where did you—I haven't seen that before."

"I made it... in a fit of anxiety about Dad." Sid turned to Eddie and fussed with the embroidery on each side of the placket. "I've been adding details off and on ever since."

"It's stunning. You're stunning." Eddie kissed him once and again. "We probably need to go."

Sid grabbed Eddie's arm before he got to the door. "You okay?"

"Yes." Eddie bit back his lie and confessed. "I'm nervous. You were right... about it hurting more after losing someone."

"You know, I have plenty of people." Sid brushed imaginary lint from Eddie's shoulders. "Rue's here, Dottie, my family. Don't feel like you have to be—"

"I'm here for you. Today is about you."

"I'm saying it doesn't have to be. She's not been gone a year, and I'm going to need you more when everyone leaves. When we've eaten the last fucking green bean casserole."

"When no one notices that he's gone anymore."

"Yes. Now, I want you to be okay."

"I'm okay." Eddie smiled and hoped Sid believed him. He was wobbly, but for Sid, he would do anything.

As they walked downstairs, Adrian's voice filled the stairwell. He was headlong into a story that involved a pickup truck, a dozen cakes, and a crooked—he stopped with a gasp before Eddie could figure out who was crooked.

"Oh my goodness! You look so *handsome!*"

"You act as if we aren't normally." Eddie grabbed his pocket items from the end table near the door.

"Daddy..." Adrian looked them over as if giving a final inspection before a runway show. "Why aren't you wearing your uniform? You always wear it for dress-up times."

"Because today, I'm not Chief Garner. I'm Eddie."

"You're Sid's Eddie, not Sid's chief." Sharon cleared her throat and nodded toward the recliner where Rimi Monster sat. "Oh! Sid, I have something for you. A…" He glanced at Sharon and she mouthed his missing word. "A loan. That means you have to return it when you're done."

"Okay." Sid took a seat on the arm of the couch.

Adrian grabbed Rimi from the chair and hid it behind his back. "Because she helps me be brave." With a tentative smile, Adrian handed Rimi Monster to Sid.

"She's wearing a tie," Sid said.

"Yes. Nana says that we dress up for funerals to show that we loved the person who—who died."

"And Rimi loves Lou." Sid mouthed a thank you to Sharon. Eddie stared, breathless at the effortless love—Maggie's love—that shone through his son.

Eddie hurried Sid out to the car before they decided to skip the whole event and listen to Adrian's stories for the afternoon. Sid held Rimi on his lap and straightened the handmade tie and the elastic band that kept it on. He traced the heart on its chest, the shape of the flower in one hand, and the sun in the other: strength and kindness, love, and, looking at the silly spikes on Rimi's head, a nice helping of craziness.

"You going to take her in with you?" Eddie asked, knowing Sid's answer, wishing he could answer the same for himself if the roles were reversed.

"Yes. It's the next best thing to having Ma."

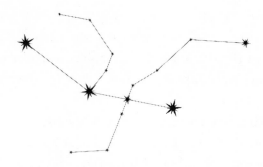

XXV.
ANDROMEDA

When Sid had come home from his mother's funeral, his father's sister had rambled on and on about how *glorious* the day had been and how *lovely* it was to have seen so many people there, to catch up, to reconnect.

"I didn't expect to feel so full. Don't you feel full, Lou?" she had said while kicking off her shoes and flopping, uninvited, into his mother's favorite recliner. Sid hadn't met the woman before, and as her fat butt warmed his *mother's* chair, he decided he would be fine never seeing her again.

When his dad agreed with the woman, Sid had fled to his room. "Feel full," were they kidding? He felt emptier than he ever had. He felt so empty he didn't know the word for it. It ached worse than the time Jason Waters aimed a goal kick right at Sid's chest in practice for Claremont County Junior Intramurals. The force of the impact had flattened Sid to the ground, earned him his first encounter with an EMT, and blessed him with a grapefruit-sized bruise that lasted for two weeks.

Full was not an emotion he could begin to comprehend, then. Now, nineteen years later, the concept remained out of reach. He sat at his father's service sandwiched between Eddie and Anna. He "listened" to former colleagues and friends tell stories, but Sid's mind wandered to all the joy he and his father had shared—without Ma. To how much life had been lived in her absence.

And with Eddie's solid presence at his side, and the little boy waiting for their return—the boy who lived every moment as if it was the most important moment of all—Sid ached, knowing how much life would be lived without his father there to witness it, to guide his decisions, to cheer his successes.

"Full" did not compute.

Innumerable friends had come to pay their respects to a man many of them had never met. Dottie stuck by his side, a magnet of support when Eddie slipped away to use the bathroom or check in with the station. Professors and colleagues from Mordell, C-DRT volunteers, firemen, and Olivia's parents all came. The family that lost their little boy in the fire those months ago even came in gratitude, as they'd told Sid, for his generous care on that most horrible day. Most touching of all, some of Sid's girls from Chicago—his models and longtime clients—caravanned in to assure Sid that he wasn't alone.

Rue and Mitchell were the last to leave. Rue, Sid, and Eddie stood outside for close to an hour telling stories, trying to avoid saying goodbye. A new world awaited, and Sid wasn't ready.

Mitchell paced and sent so many frenetic texts, Sid began to believe he was talking to imaginary people. Finally, he pocketed his phone and joined them, interrupting Rue in the process.

"Out & About called with an offer the other day," he said, all pretense of awareness of a funeral, death, loss, and friendship gone.

"Mitchell, that can wait." Rue flicked her cigarette butt into the grass. "Let him breathe."

Mitchell should have been an attorney. The sentence had been uttered; he knew it would flutter around in Sid's mind until the whole story was out. Sid had experienced his manipulations enough in the past to know that Mitchell had banked on that.

"It's fine, Rue. Just out with it, Mitchell. What'd they want?"

"A holiday trunk show. Share in profits, of course. Based on its success, they want us in their store."

At any other time in Sid's life, this would be a goddamned coup, an open door with more opportunities inside. "Holiday? That gives us *no* time, Mitchell. I hope you told them—"

"If we don't do it then, they're going to pass."

"For good?"

"For now." Mitchell shrugged. "You know how this business works—if you don't jump when the offer is there..."

"Mitchell, fucking shut up." Rue lit up again. "He needs time. I'm sure Anna—" She looked at Sid. "Doesn't Anna still need a hand? Isn't there a ton of shit to do?"

"Yes. I was hoping for two more weeks." Sid leaned against his car and typed a reminder into his phone. "I'll call them tomorrow."

"Sid..." Eddie said. His eyes pled. He was right, but Sid didn't know what else to do.

"Do not fuck this up," Mitchell said. "This could be the break you've always dreamt of. We all have."

"Yeah, *my* dream, Mitchell." He turned his eyes to Rue. "If they call again, you send them to me. No decisions." He shot a glare at Mitchell. "No agreements will be made without me."

"I'm so sorry, Sid... I *told* him—"

"I know." He hugged Rue and kissed her cheek. "Thank you. We'll talk soon."

The impact of Mitchell's announcement lay dormant between Sid and Eddie. They carried on the following week as if Mitchell had spoken in a foreign language. Eddie returned to work. Sid tried to work—he had so much extra time now—but mostly he sat with his sister, drank tea, and feigned interest in going through their father's belongings. The first weekend after the funeral, Anna joined Sid and Eddie to cheer Adrian on in a season-ending soccer game. At the end of each day, he and Eddie shared wine, a bath, and each other... as if Lou was alive.

As if everything wasn't about to change.

A week later, Sid tossed his toiletry bag into his suitcase to head back to the Windy City. For the first time, no calendar marked a return date. "Family obligations" no longer required it. Sid and Eddie ignored the ever-growing rift between them all the way to Eddie's cursory "I'll see you later" kiss that morning.

Sid dropped his car at the station house. He had less than an hour to patch the divide before Eddie took him to the airport.

Eddie greeted him warmly enough. They sat in his office with Styrofoam cups of too-strong coffee and meaningless small talk that finally dwindled to silence. Feeling more like a child reluctant to perform for his piano recital than a grown man in a war between his heart and his career, Sid uttered the one clear sentence in his head.

"I don't want to go."

Eddie nodded and sipped his coffee.

"Eddie, we've always talked if—"

"I've been trying to give you space," Eddie said, still not looking away from his cup.

"You have. You've been wonderful, but… I can also see you're unhappy. I'm not all that happy either."

"I'm not unhappy." Eddie finally looked up. His normally bright eyes showed little emotion. "I'm angry."

"At?"

"I haven't decided, which… is why I haven't said anything."

"Tell me what you're thinking. I don't want to get on that plane if you're angry."

"You may have to."

"Eddie…" Sid reached for Eddie's hand. Eddie leaned back in his chair, separating them even more.

"Have I been naïve, Sid?"

"About?"

"Don't act like you don't know what's going on here. Your bags are packed. You've shipped boxes ahead—"

"That's fabric. Work supplies." Eddie leveled his gaze in a "challenge me" look typically reserved for Adrian's occasional sassy mouth. "Okay, there are a few personal items—"

"You've been leaving since we interred your father."

"I don't have much of a choice, Eddie. This is my *job*. We knew this was coming."

"I didn't think it would come so soon," Eddie said. "How come we didn't talk about how this would work. *If* this would work?"

"I don't know. I've been a little preoccupied the last few weeks."

"Which is why I haven't—" Eddie sat up and spun his coffee cup on the desk.

"It all happened so fast, Eddie. I thought Dad would be around for so much longer. I assumed I'd have more time after—" Sid's thoughts scattered. He couldn't fix anything in this short meeting... why he'd thought he could escaped him. "You are my family. We'll figure it out."

"We *have* been naïve," Eddie said. He picked at the brim of his Styrofoam cup and flung the pieces onto the desk, as if each piece represented a question he was afraid to ask. "We didn't even mark Adrian's calendar for the weekend you said you'd come back."

"Because I don't *know*. I'm hoping Thanksgiving. I'm doing—"

County Dispatch to Connelly City Fire. Connelly City Fire. We have a residential structure fire at 423 Baxter Street. Repeat, residential structure fire at 423 Baxter Street. Call time 10:42.

"My best," Sid finished, defeated. "I'll call an Uber."

Standing together at the door, Eddie brushed his knuckles down Sid's cheek. It was the first time that day he'd looked in Sid's eyes with something that reflected the love they'd come to share. "I'm not graceful when people leave; I'm sorry."

Sid kissed his knuckles and lips. "I love you. Without question."

"I love you." Eddie opened his office door. "Without question." From the hall, he added, "Let me know when you get in."

Standing on the bridge, Sid lost Eddie in the flurry of activity in the garage. It wasn't until he spotted him in the cab of his fire truck that he could share his most courageous smile. When he blew a kiss, Eddie caught it outside of his open window and backed out of the garage, siren blaring.

Sid's phone vibrated.

Rue: Out & About called. Can we meet with them at 8 am tmrw?

Sid: Let's get this show on the road. See if they're available tonight.

* * *

SID: END OF THE YEAR.

Eddie: This isn't a pun set-up, is it?

Sid: Fine. What do gay termites eat?

Eddie: If they're smart, they'll eat a fully balanced diet with a variety of woods. Wait. Wood is part of the answer.

Sid: Woodpeckers. That was an easy one.

Eddie: That doesn't make sense. Are they eating sexually or cannibalistically? That seems important.

Sid: Well, you know how The Gays are, Eddie. They only think about sex. Also, you're deflecting.

Eddie: They just want to eat wood. Can't they be who they are?

Sid: Are you having a meltdown?

Eddie: Likely.

Sid had missed Thanksgiving. A scribbled mess of crossed-out circles and re-numbered countdowns covered Adrian's calendar. In their few weeks apart, Sid kept his video dates with Adrian, but otherwise stopped asking about him. Conversations that had once started with "I miss you," and "I wish you could have seen…" had all but disappeared.

Eddie shoved department ledgers around his desk, picked up his phone and typed: What does "end of the year" mean?

Sid: It means I promised my partners I would be here full-time after the holidays. The trunk show is tomorrow and after finalizing that, we're all going to take a few weeks to slow down and focus on our families until the new year.

Eddie: That means you won't be home this weekend either, doesn't it?

Sid's face lit up Eddie's phone. Before Eddie could greet him, Sid said, "Home shouldn't be such a complicated concept."

"Yet here we are, in two separate cities."

"I'm home with you."

"*Prove it*," swept through Eddie's mind, but regardless of how impatient he felt, the sentiment rang childish.

"I can't do this over the phone," Sid said to Eddie's silence.

"So, let's talk about something else. Has your weather been as shitty as ours?"

"Shittier. I don't want to talk about the weather," Sid said. Eddie heard a sewing machine and chatter in the background. He imagined Sid pacing his studio with a tape measure around his neck while Rue offered him a cheeseball that he'd politely decline. "I had lunch with Mitchell yesterday. He kept his phone in his pocket and talked like a normal person."

"That's because you're making him money."

"I don't want to talk about Mitchell, either. I probably shouldn't have called."

"What do you need from me, Sid?"

"I don't *need* anything, Eddie. I *want*. I want you. Now. January first when the picture blurs again. It'd be nice to know you want that too."

Eddie wanted, too. He wanted his family back together. He also *desired*: touch, smell—the taste of Sid's mouth on his after sipping a hot mug of chai.

As Eddie licked his lips in memory, Sid said, "I've got to go. I shouldn't have called."

"No, wait. I'm sorry. I'm—" Eddie sighed, cracked his knuckles. "Can you at least tell me when you'll be home?"

"I'm looking at Tuesday. I'll fly home after lunch."

Tuesday. He'd have to explain to Adrian again...

"Do you *want* to come back?" As soon as the words left Eddie's mouth, he regretted them. The question seemed reasonable, but now that it had been spoken, it stretched the miles between them even farther.

"That's not fair. I *told* you." Eddie heard a huge metal door close, and Sid's voice echoed as he spoke. "This isn't some whim, Eddie. This is my *life*; these are the things I've worked for."

"Sounds like home isn't such a complicated concept after all, then, is it?"

"Eddie, please. I'm trying. You *have* me—full stop. I'm trying to figure out how to find a balance, but it's going to take time and effort and—"

The metal door slammed again, and Rue's voice came through the phone. "Shit, there you are. Your three o'clock interview is here."

"Eddie, I'm so sorry—"

"Tell you what. When you land—whether that's Tuesday or... or two weeks from now, you call me then, okay?"

"Eddie!"

"Have a good show tomorrow." Before he could second-guess himself, Eddie hung up. He collected everyone on duty. "Call your families; we're having a chili party tonight. Josh, get in touch with the aux team and C-DRT too. Everyone's invited."

SID BARELY REMEMBERED THE INTERVIEW for their new social media manager. Afterward, he stared at her résumé: Bala Nath, twenty-nine years old, marketing graduate from Chicago State. She'd worn a jacket from Sid's last year's fall line to the interview. He thought she mentioned that her wife had worn one of his suits for their wedding. He did remember that he liked Bala, that he'd probably hire her.

As Sid's train pulled out of Sheridan station, the numbness that had lingered since Eddie hung up began to morph into anxiety, a feeling of being split in two. Sid hadn't intended to take Eddie for granted. He had spent their entire relationship taking refuge in Eddie's love, in

Adrian's joy, as he bounced from one priority to another. He'd tried, in the midst of it all, to return a fraction of the love and joy they had so freely given. But since his dad died, they hadn't communicated; his good intentions weren't enough.

He walked from the station with long strides that bordered on a jog, then sprinted up the stairs into his apartment. As if he could lock the anxiety out in the hall, he swiftly closed his door. His work bag slid to the floor with a lazy thud. A golden glow from a streetlight outside his living room window shone a hazy spotlight on his mother's *mandir*.

In Sid's childhood eyes, performing *puja* renewed his mother from within. Worship, like the changing of her clothes, transformed her from a stressed-out, busy mother into the most beautiful woman filled with light and peace.

With anxiety still coursing through his veins, Sid kicked off his shoes and fetched a box of matches and a damp cloth from the kitchen. He stood in front of the wooden cabinet and ran his fingers along the molded trim along the top edge. Forgotten prayers and burning incense would do nothing to quiet the grief Sid had been ignoring since he got on a plane to Chicago. It wouldn't give him answers to the lingering questions about home and family, success and happiness.

But it just might bring peace, clarity, connection.

As he opened the cabinet, he recalled a morning late in Rimi's life. He had knelt beside her, lit the incense, and listened as she prayed. After she blew out the incense, he had asked her, "What do you pray for, Ma?"

"I pray for your happiness," she had said.

"But I am happy!" And he was—ten years old, his mother at his side, not a care in the world.

"Happiness doesn't always come easily; sometimes you have to work for it," she said. "I pray you will always work for happiness."

Sid had the work down. He had been happy with Eddie, even in the midst of all the surrounding stress. If Ma was right, the two could coexist. Opening himself to whatever answers he might find,

Sid cleaned the one remaining *murti*—a framed picture of the god Vishnu—with the damp cloth. His hand hovered first over the bell and then the matches, unsure which item he should tend to next.

"We're inviting the gods into our home, Zico. Be still," she always reminded him when he fidgeted at her preparations. Now, he rang the bell and lit the incense. The thin plume of smoke hit the edge of the *mandir* and drifted up to the ceiling.

With a deep inhalation of sandalwood, Sid focused outside himself. He reached for his mother's tranquility, his father's wisdom, his own inner balance. He grieved their loss. He listened for answers. And he prayed.

* * *

THE TRUNK SHOW WAS A success. He would meet with the owners to crunch numbers before he left for Connelly, but based on outward appearances—sold samples, multiple orders, queer-press coverage and positive reviews—Bastra would end the year on a positive note. Tuesday was only one calendar block away. He and Eddie would talk on Tuesday, touch on Tuesday. Family would be redefined… on Tuesday.

Tonight, he had a date with his tracing paper and a new trouser design that had been tickling his brain for a week. With a free moment to play, he armed himself with warm chai, proper music, and the scent of patchouli wafting through his workroom. As the curve of a pocket formed on the paper, his phone rang. He considered ignoring it, but took a step closer; it was Sharon. *Oh, shit.*

"It's Eddie," Sharon said. She sounded winded. "The department called; they've taken him to Connelly Medical."

XXVI.
ORION

WHILE WAITING FOR SHARON TO call back with more information, Sid tried to concentrate on his pattern. He waited before booking a flight back, for which he was grateful. As if he had put his hand to a burning coal, Sharon barked a desperate "No!" when he confessed his idea.

"It's not a big deal, Sharon." It was a huge deal—he had promised his full attention to Bastra through Tuesday, when they would wind up the administrative year, eat one final cheeseball, and sail off into the sunset of holiday celebrations. He needed to be in Chicago.

"Stay put. He's fine. Besides, he'll kill me." Sharon groaned. "You're not supposed to know."

This conversation needed wine. "Well, now that I do know," Sid said, turning off the light in his workroom, "what the fuck happened?"

The accident happened when Eddie got itchy at a fire scene. Instead of trusting his crew to get their assigned job done, he'd nosed around. An unsecured bookshelf had lost stability in the heat and toppled onto him. With a broken left fibula, he sat pouting at home in a short leg cast.

"He didn't get a scrape on that pretty face of his, either," Sharon said.

"I'm sure his ego is bruised." Sid couldn't decide if he should laugh or scream. He had swallowed half of a glass of wine while Sharon told him the story. He topped it off, grabbed a sweater, and sat on his balcony. The stars hid behind thick fall clouds. "How's Ade?"

"He has a new drawing surface, which is fun. He's also making sure everyone knows that 'Daddy is not sick,' about every hour."

"He's frightened."

"He'll be okay. I'm sure by morning, he'll have figured out a way to make Eddie into a prop for his stories."

"Oh, please let me come back so I can kill him."

Sharon laughed and, irritated as he was, Sid did enjoy the image of Eddie acting as a flagpole while Adrian bounced plastic dinosaurs off the slope of his reclining chest.

"You may *not* kill him," she said. "I'm supposed to be twilighting my twilight years with a rich old man who likes aging hippies, *not* raising another child." After a brief pause, she added, clearly delighted, "That means you'd get him!"

He could think of worse options. The idea of life without that boy—or worse, life without Eddie—distressed him enough to give up on murder as a valid solution almost instantly. "Did he do this impulsive, reckless shit in Wylie?"

"Let me tell you something about Eddie," Sharon said. "I don't know how much you know about his background."

"Bits and pieces; he doesn't like to talk about himself."

"No, he doesn't. His mother had a reputation in town, so he was born with one. Maggie took a shine to him, and I dreaded it when he came over. He had no discipline, no respect for other people's space or property."

"I can't wrap my head around that."

"I know. He learned very early in life that people left—that nothing was promised. His dad never showed up, his mom left him alone to be with other men, and then his 'stuff' left when their house burned down. The fire department couldn't save their house, but they saved Eddie."

"And then he saved Maggie," Sid said.

"Yes, when he saved people, the ground wasn't so shaky anymore." She paused and took a deep breath. "But then, he couldn't save her."

"So he saved Adrian," Sid said with a sigh. "Sharon, I don't need to be saved. This is crazy. I just want *him*."

"I know. He was exhausted when you met, Sid. Losing Maggie... Adrian... You're the one that saved *him*. It had to have been a relief."

The full moon peeked out from the moving clouds. He wondered if Eddie might be outside watching it, too. "He's afraid I'm going to leave him, isn't he? That's why he's doing dumb shit."

"Are you?" Sharon asked.

"No. I don't know how I'm going to make it work, but... I love him. I know that more than anything. I just haven't acted like it much lately."

"Well, get it together soon. He's going to run out of limbs to break."

*   *   *

THE FOLLOWING MORNING, BEFORE HE trekked to the studio, Sid sat in prayer. Again, his mother's words floated from the plume of incense: *Happiness doesn't always come easily; sometimes you have to work for it.*

He made a phone call. "Dottie Mulligan, my sweet."

"Tell me you're coming back," Dottie said. "I finally filled your dad's position and I'm already regretting it. She brought homemade cupcakes today."

"That's bad how?"

"She decorated them individually to represent first aid protocols. One had a bleeding marzipan arm strapped to a popsicle stick by licorice strips."

"Immobilization. Clever... were there double-sugared ones for diabetics gone hypo?"

"It's not funny. I want you back," she said. "And I want the best for you, so you see my dilemma."

"Thank you for the segue," Sid said, wondering what kind of cupcake décor would represent falling for a reckless fireman. "Remember in college when I considered starting my business in Connelly?"

"Yes, when you were young and stupid? I recall tons of those moments."

"Thank you. I'm considering. Again. I could work remotely, couldn't I? Have studio space here for local clients. Keep up with the online orders. Like I've done while Dad was sick." Sid sighed. Hearing his ideas out loud amplified their absurdity. He was shooting blind into an empty barrel, but at least he was shooting. No idea started at the point of completion.

"Like you've been doing since college, you mean. I thought you were done working out of your bedroom."

He ignored her. "I mean Mordell alone has to have potential clientele, doesn't it?"

"It's not like there's been some massive lesbian cavalry since college," Dottie said. "Pity—this town needs a good dyke bar again."

"Wait, what happened to Bernie's?"

"Goddamned hipsters. I fell in love, blinked, and missed the takeover."

"So, what? You need to grow a beard or wear a scarf to get in?"

"And agree to drink your beer while sitting on a fucking wine barrel that poses as a stool. Oh, and eat your kale-laced nachos served on a wooden board with a tiny shovel for the extra salsa."

"Oh, shit. No wonder you didn't take me there while I was home."

"I don't know what's worse, Sid: kale or you wanting to take a step backward to get the guy. What are you *doing?*"

"I told you; thinking. That's all."

"Let me think for you. Last time we talked you said Bastra was killing it. Should you be putting your heart before your career?"

"I don't know what I'm doing, Dottie," Sid said. "My mother followed her heart eight *thousand* miles and never looked back."

"And your parents died very happy."

"They did. And Eddie makes me happy," Sid said. "But so does my work—you have to come and see. Ma and Baba would be so proud. It's everything I've been working for, you know?"

"I do know. If anyone in our class could have done it, it's you."

"I—thank you. But it's come at a cost. None of it brings me the kind of happiness Eddie and Adrian bring."

"Okay, you sap. I'm a sucker for a good love story." Dottie said. "I'll knock around, do you a solid and dress up more for work. Will that help? We have a couple butch girls in the program; they have friends. I'll be a walking advertisement instead of saving it for special occasions."

"I can make you more clothes. I *will* make you more over the holidays. Are your measurements the same since the catalog shoot?"

"I'm only doing this so you'll save me from the cupcake princess."

"Ask her if she needs some dress shirts. You know a guy."

"She wore a miniskirt her first day, Sid. I can't wait to see the feedback from her first CPR class. 'Instructor's panties were too pale blue for my taste.'"

"Provided she wears—"

"Hanging up. I like the idea of you coming back permanently; watching you eat nachos from a shovel will be worth it."

*　　*　　*

EDDIE SAT IN HIS RECLINER while Adrian chattered away on his lap about something something stegosaurus and something something monster, and, as he began to nod off, something something *tidal wave*!

Eddie jerked alert. Adrian caught the T. Rex that toppled from Eddie's chest and the die-cast Delta airplane that that fell from the T. Rex's mouth. "I should make monster movies, Daddy!"

Based on the die-cast's arrival, Sid had to have sent it Fed Ex the moment they hung up from their last phone call. It pissed Eddie off and reminded him of his previous dunderheaded partners. "Here's a token for the kid. Let's make up."

Of course, since Eddie's accident, he'd been pissed off a lot: about his damned cast and how it would—and had—handicapped him at work; about how complicated it had made Christmas shopping; that no one had bothered to send a set of inflatable crutches and a T-shirt that said, "I do my own stunts." If he was going to continue to do stupid shit, the least his crew could do was to torment him for it. And the most annoying short of all, of course, was that Sid wasn't *around* to torment him, or draw him a bath as Eddie had so many times for him after Lou's heart attack.

While Eddie sat and pouted and became a permanent Adrian prop, he convinced himself that Sid was more married to his job than Eddie had ever been. Eddie knew "married to the job" in an intimate way. Before Adrian, he had once volunteered for so many twenty-four hour shifts in a row that his landlord assumed he had skipped out of his lease and put an ad in the paper for his apartment.

But by the end of his second convalescent day, Sharon's loving words—"Stop being such an idiot; my grandson deserves better," and "Who's the dunderhead now, Eddie? You are"—finally cut through his fog of self-pity. Her grandson deserved better, and frankly, so did her grandson's father. And "better" meant getting off his ass and going after what he wanted... crutches, bad attitude, and all.

Tuesday, Eddie bought a dozen orange roses on the way to the airport. He took PTO for the day and remained unavailable for emergency calls until Sunday. Olivia's parents took Adrian for his first-ever sleepover.

Eddie's cast started at the bend of his knee and ended just before his toes. To keep his toes mostly warm, he covered his foot with a cheap, hard-soled, oversized slipper. He liked to think it looked like he'd sustained a heroic sports injury. Glancing down at his old jeans, sliced open at the leg, he knew that he more closely resembled a clumsy suburban dad who'd fallen off his roof instead of calling a professional, the way any reasonable human being would do.

With a grunt of disgust at his own stupidity, he propped himself and his crutches against a thick column outside baggage claim. He lifted the bouquet to his nose: Breathe in patience; breathe out worry. Sid *said* he wanted Eddie. Eddie knew he wanted Sid.

When he opened his eyes to peek over the apricot petals, his heart skipped a beat. Heat coursed through his body from head to toe. Tears prickled his eyes in such relief, he almost took off toward the concourse without his crutches.

Sid's hair fanned behind him as he walked briskly out of the concourse. He focused on his phone, was frantically thumbing a message. Eddie's phone vibrated in his pocket. Sid hiked his bag onto his shoulder and yanked a troublesome scarf from his neck. With his towering height, dressed in a burgundy *kurta*, blue jeans, and gray overcoat, he stood out—striking, indescribably handsome.

Eddie pushed himself away from the column, balanced himself on his crutches, and eased into Sid's line of view.

Sid spotted Eddie. His mouth opened; his eyes widened. He skipped a step and another until he was in Eddie's arms. The crutches crashed to the ground; Sid's bag followed as orange petals flitted around them.

"You're here. I didn't expect you," Sid said. Eddie clung, but Sid eased his way out of his tight grip. A tear stained his cheek; a smile made it shine. "I didn't think you'd be here."

"I know. That's why I am." Eddie wobbled, and Sid bent to grab a crutch for him. "I'm so sorry, Sid."

Sid smiled and picked up the other crutch. "I am too. We need to—" Sid kissed Eddie instead of finishing. The minute their lips touched, the weight of the previous weeks lifted. Home couldn't be found on a map; home lived and breathed in this man. "Do you need to sit down?"

"I'm fine," Eddie glared at his cast. "You don't seem too surprised at my new addition." He swapped the crutch for the bouquet of flowers.

Sid winced, but focused on the flowers, inhaling them dramatically. "Sharon told you."

"Sharon told me, and you're not allowed to be mad at her."

"You're in charge of that now?" Eddie teased as he settled both arms around the crutches.

"Should I cancel my Uber—can you drive?"

"Yes to both." Eddie jerked his head to encourage Sid to stand in front of him. When he did, Eddie awkwardly tugged Sid closer for another kiss. "I need you to trust me."

"I trust you."

"Like… this minute, trust me. I'm not taking you home."

"Where are we going?"

Eddie grinned and leaned in for another kiss. He stayed there, letting their lips brush as he spoke. "Trust me."

THEY DROVE FOR AN HOUR. Sid nodded off, but whenever Eddie took a turn Sid hadn't expected, he perked up. "Eddie…"

"Sid…"

"A hint?"

"Trust me."

Once into the winding foothills outside of Mayfield County, Eddie turned in to a steep, deteriorating driveway. Crumbling concrete crackled under the tires of the car. They came to a stop, and his engine virtually sighed in relief. By the time Eddie unbuckled, Sid had climbed out to gape at the manor—Ridley Mansion Bed and Breakfast.

"Eddie! This is beautiful!" He helped Eddie out and handed him his crutches.

"I used to see this on the way to our favorite campsite when I was little," Eddie said. "I've wondered what it was like inside." A large turret climbed three stories of the stunning refurbished brick building. Every detail had been meticulously cared for on the outside; the inside promised more. "We only have tonight, I'm afraid."

"Wait. I'm entirely out of clothes."

"I brought some—I came prepared."

"Ooh, a fireman *and* a Boy Scout. If you'd have told me that earlier…"

As Eddie had hoped, the entire building had been perfectly redone: carved wood moldings and trim framed every room. Wood floors amplified each footstep—especially Eddie's wobbly ones. Victorian furnishings made the space warm and inviting.

Eddie cussed and grumbled as they clumped to the second floor, but his frustration disappeared as soon as he opened the door to their room and Sid gasped.

"It's the turret room." Sid kicked off his shoes, dumped his bags and walked straight to the bed nestled in the arc of the turret. The bed was stunning—a four-poster, wrought-iron beauty that fit the windowed nook so exquisitely it looked as if it had been built on-site. Sid yanked the curtains open and spun to Eddie. "Is it too gay to say I feel like a queen in her tower?"

"It's pretty gay. Fortunately, I like that about you."

Sid jumped as if to launch into Eddie's arms, eyed the crutches, and approached more gingerly. He peppered Eddie with kisses and thanks yous, pausing to toss his scarf and shake himself out of his coat. "You're still—" With a gentle nudge, Eddie leaned on a small work desk. Sid slipped his hand into Eddie's coat. "Aren't you hot?" Sid fidgeted and kissed and fussed to work around Eddie's coat. He stepped back with a huff. "Is this like the first time? I have to take your clothes off of you all over again?"

Eddie groaned, tossed his crutches and, button by button, Sid opened Eddie's coat and slipped it from his shoulders. When the weight of the wool hit the desk, their eyes met. The stillness of the manor, the romantic surroundings, and the absence of all that burdened them sent a charge from Sid's fingers to Eddie's chest.

"Why did you bring me here?" Sid asked.

"Because I love you. I hate how the last few weeks have gone, and I thought if we got away, we could lay everything out. Stop questioning."

"My heart is always with you," Sid said. "There is no question."

"I've questioned," Eddie admitted. "And you've questioned me. I don't ever want you to doubt how *desperately* I love you." Eddie hooked his fingers into the opened collar of Sid's tunic, unbuttoned a button, and pulled him close for a sure, unquestioning kiss.

"Make love to me, Eddie."

Eddie chuckled as he kissed down Sid's jaw. "This could be a challenge." He unfastened the final button at Sid's chest, skirted his hands to Sid's hips and walked the length of the tunic into his fingers. He kissed and nipped Sid's revealed skin and ran his tongue along the valley of his collarbone.

Sid lofted his shirt across the room and hissed as Eddie reached between them and cupped Sid, hard and thick, in his hand. "I'm up for a challenge," Sid said, groaning. "You?"

"Always."

In the days before Sid left for Chicago, even as they'd avoided Sid's departure, sex had been a healer. It had needed to be—"Make me feel so I'm not numb," and "Make me numb so I don't feel." But here, between giggle-filled kisses and awkward stumbles over a lame leg, the weeks of separation disappeared.

As Sid slid tight and hot into Eddie with their bodies slick and so perfectly fitted together, Eddie released the doubt and insecurity that had gripped him while Sid was away. It was Eddie's name that Sid called in moments of bliss and ecstasy. It was Eddie's body Sid kissed and surrounded, caressed and sank into.

It was Eddie's heart that had healed as Sid wove his loving care into his life, into Adrian's life. This gorgeous man now bending to nuzzle his neck was his. Of that, there was no question.

XXVII.
CANIS MAJOR

THE SCENT OF SAUTÉED ONIONS and garlic pulled them out of bed for a communal meal downstairs. Guests passed baskets of loaves of the most amazing pumpernickel bread and hand-churned butter. Everyone chatted amicably until the last drop of sweet tea had left the hostess's pitcher.

After dinner, Eddie followed Sid upstairs. As if words were intrusive, complicated, Sid silently stripped him naked and mapped his body with soft kisses and gentle bites as each inch of skin was revealed. He took Eddie in his hand, in his mouth, working him with stripes of his tongue, glorious suction, and twists of his fist around Eddie's length until he dripped with spit and pre-come.

Sid smiled up at him as he tongued the slit of Eddie's dripping cock. "Give me your hand," he said, and Eddie did, willing to cut it off for him if necessary. "Take over for a second," he said as he removed his own pants. "Leg okay?"

"What leg?"

Eddie barely managed to get a condom on, he was so taken with Sid straddled over his thighs with fingers slick and squelching into his own ass, waiting and moving as if he didn't need Eddie for the pleasure.

But his eyes, dark and needy, didn't leave Eddie's; his mouth whispered words of love and impatience and *need*, and, once Sid lowered himself onto Eddie's cock, a smile of pure contentment spread across his face as his ass wiggled on Eddie's hips. He rode Eddie—gracefully danced above him. Every motion was a new promise, a new commitment to each other, to making it work, to reducing miles, to finding a way.

They came with Sid hanging onto the post behind Eddie's head, quiet moments gone in the rattle of the old bed frame and the creaks and cracks of its wooden legs against the floor. Deep groans of release lifted high to the ceiling and echoed around them as they breathlessly curled into a heap.

After long moments, Eddie shifted. The bed moaned. He got the giggles.

"What?" Sid asked before nipping Eddie's shoulder.

"That couple—the woman with the—" He motioned around his head, as if patting a tight beehive hairdo. "The *hair*, that had the necklace with the ashes of their dead dog. I hope to hell they're not underneath us."

"No, love." Sid pointed to their surrounding windows. "Turret, remember? We're over the dining room."

"Oh, so we traumatized everyone. Excellent." Eddie said. "Maybe they're down there nibbling on shortbread."

"Let's hope so."

Eddie remembered little after he tried to get comfortable to nap and clubbed Sid with the cast. He remembered the laughter and the apology and the lame attempt at a cold cloth "ice pack," but once they settled down, Eddie checked out until much later, when Sid bolted upright, wide-eyed and out of breath.

He reached for Eddie, ran a hand through his own hair, and fell backward onto his pillows. "Did I wake you?"

Sid's skin was clammy. He fought to control his breath.

"Are you okay? Let me get you some water."

"No, you'll fall and kill yourself, I'm fine. I um—I saw Mom and Dad," Sid explained. "And Maggie."

Eddie sat up. His cast bounced inelegantly and shook the mattress. "Are you kidding me?"

"They were having a picnic. Maggie is stunning."

"Yes. She is." Eddie understood some of Sid's feelings after Adrian's dream. *Why won't she visit me?*

"She waved. I knew I couldn't go where they were, but she pointed me to a picnic table. Ma sat next to Baba—they were holding hands and he was wearing that Mordell hat from Adrian's dream. Ma took it off and kissed the top of—" Sid bit back tears.

"Oh, sweetheart…"

With a shuddered breath, Sid pressed on. "She kissed the top of his head. He *giggled*, Eddie. Do you know how long it's been since I've heard that? Since it wasn't attached to him grabbing his own daughter's ass?"

"How lucky you got to hear it again."

After a long silence, Sid said, "I wonder if Ma smells the same."

"If she's been hanging around Maggie…"

Sid sat up and took Eddie's hand. "They're not sick anymore."

"Nope. Maggie got her hair, your dad got his laugh…"

"He needed Ma to find it," Sid said, kissing Eddie's shoulder. "You helped me find my laugh again."

"You'd lost it?"

"I think I forgot about it. I was so busy making Ma and Baba proud, I forgot that all they wanted was for me to be happy." Sid closed his eyes and smiled as if remembering the sound of his mother's laughter. "I don't want to forget again, Eddie."

Eddie quietened, regretting his role in their time apart. They'd have been in separate cities, but they wouldn't have been so *detached*, so completely disconnected—"I've let you down," Eddie said. "You told me you needed me after the circus of the funeral and… I wasn't there for you."

"What? No. You were there as much as I let you, but I *left*."

"You had to."

"I did. But I took *off*. I didn't take care of us."

Eddie chuckled and knocked his shoulder against Sid's. "You're more like your sister than you realize."

"Do you *want* to get laid again? Because I can arrange—"

"We made up; don't be a jerk." Sid kissed Eddie softly, the way no jerk ever could. "Your parents taught you all a great work ethic."

"With tunnel vision. I forget the people that matter." Sid rested his head on Eddie's shoulder. "Has Adrian told you he's mad at me? He wouldn't talk to me when Sharon called."

"He's mad at me too." At Sid's questioning look, Eddie pointed to his cast. "And he's afraid we broke up. He's mad I wouldn't '*pologize*."

"What should you apologize for?"

"For being upset that you did what you had to do."

"I did it thoughtlessly, though." Sid hiked up on an elbow, his hair mussed and draping one side of his face. "Life is too fucking short to work it away."

Torn between taking Sid apart again and resting in the simplicity of the moment, Eddie pushed a tendril of Sid's hair behind his ear. "What are we going to do?"

Eyes bright with a ready answer, Sid grinned, sat up, and straddled Eddie. The floral sheet draped over Sid's thighs so seductively that Sid had to flick Eddie in the chest to get his attention up where it belonged. "This is all pretty simple, you know."

"Is it?"

"I see three possible solutions." He counted them on his fingers. "One, we consider this a one-off. A good time, great sex, some laughs—"

"That choice sucks. Number two?"

"Two, I come back. Part-time. Full-time." He flapped his hand. "Something. I've been snooping around. I sustained myself with tailoring for years. I can do it again, open a pilot location at Mordell. Dottie has a way with the community and—"

"You hate Connelly."

"I do not *hate* Connelly," Sid said. "I just—"

"Love Chicago. It's where you came to life."

"I love Chicago. And I love Eddie. And I love Adrian, which leads to number three." Sid grinned. "Come to Chicago."

Eddie chuffed. In Sid's absence, it had been his one consideration, impossible as it may have sounded.

At Eddie's silence, Sid pressed on. "You know what I learned on this trip?" Sid didn't wait for him to answer. "Chicago has fires. They have fires so amazing that they're *known* for one of the country's biggest and most destructive fires."

"They are." Sid might have forgotten his laughter along the way, but Eddie had never known how to jump into life as he jumped into fires. Sid could teach him.

"They also have *firemen* who put those fires out."

"Sid…"

"And do you know what else they have in Chicago? Schools. Some of them are excellent. They teach math and history and art. In fact, that school right around the corner from my apartment? Art-focused."

Eddie didn't try to counter anything Sid said. He sat on top of Eddie like a king: proud, cocky, and full of sarcastic authority.

"They have parks. And beaches—they're pretty decent in the summer. They have one of the nation's finest zoos *and* some of the nation's finest museums. With dinosaurs."

Eddie laughed—at Sid's wistful dream, at his belief that it was this simple. "In fact," Sid added, "I might go out on a limb and say that there's more for Adrian in Chicago than there is in Connelly. Or Wylie. Or Pittsburgh. Put together."

"That all sounds fine and good, but—" It sounded amazing.

"I know it's insane. You have a new a mortgage and you guys lost Maggie and Ade's barely in kindergarten, and I'm asking the entire world of you, but Eddie, you and Adrian? You are my *life*. My work, it's my blood, but you… you are my heartbeat." He kissed Eddie's brow. "Come." Kissed his left eye. "With." Kissed his right. "Me."

Eddie kept his eyes closed and breathed deeply, until Sid sat back and traced the line of Eddie's clavicle. He took Sid's hand, and Sid met him with such trusting, expectant eyes he wanted to scream. "It sounds like an amazing plan. Please don't take my silence as a rejection; I'm not closing any doors."

"I know you're not." Sid bit his lip and looked out the window behind their bed.

"I love you," Eddie said, more sure of that than anything else.

"I love you." Sid looked into the room, into Eddie's eyes. His excited hope had barely diminished. "I don't expect an answer right now. We have time."

"We only have this month."

"Can we try something? Let's go there for Christmas—with Adrian," Sid said. "A trial run."

Eddie's heart fluttered. "Oh, god, I've been so anxious about—it's our first without her. Yours without Lou."

"Wouldn't being away make it easier?"

"Yes." Eddie said. "Yes, it'd be perfect."

"And then, we'll talk and plan."

"We'll get it right this time."

*   *   *

Connelly City Medic 2 to County Dispatch. Heading to the station. Time out: 13:28

    County Dispatch copy.

    Garner to Medic 2. Can you guys grab some chips on the way in?

    Medic 2 to Garner. Copy. What brand, sir?

    Parker's asking for them, so it better be Utz or he'll birth a small farm animal.

    Medic 2 to Garner. Copy. Utz potato chips for Parker. Out.

Sid sat alone in the C-DRT offices and cackled. Dottie had asked him to serve a few hours so the volunteers could have a break at the holidays. As a reward, the idiots of Connelly City Fire Department entertained him by accidentally sending their private radio conversation to the county network.

Sid: Tell Parker his taste in chips sucks.

Eddie: What? Oh shit. County got that?

Sid: No, I'm telepathic.

Eddie: I'm surprised the mayor's office hasn't called to give me shit.

Sid: Give him time. Besides, do you gentlemen need chips?

Eddie: A chip-less firehouse is an inefficient firehouse.

Sid: Do you have enough dip?

After a long silence, Eddie's voice rang over the radio: *Garner to Medic 2. Don't forget the French onion dip. Out.*

Medic 2 to Garner. Copy that.

Sid: County. Again.

Eddie: That was just for you.

Sid: You ran down and checked to see if you needed it, didn't you?

Eddie: I'm not an idiot.

Emergency signals broke through the droning static of the dispatch radio.

County Dispatch to Connelly City Fire. Connelly City Fire. We have a residential structure fire at 1572 N. Elizabeth Street. Repeat, residential structure fire at 1572 N. Elizabeth Street. Call time 13:57.

Eddie: See you there?

Sid: Sounds like it. Be careful. I love you.

Sid was dispatched an hour later, and the fire was already well under control. Sid argued with the rear stairs of the truck and jumped around puddles to get to the chief.

His chief.

He would miss the giddy feeling that washed through him whenever he saw Eddie standing there, official and heroic—although the crutches comically diminished the image—in his turnout and white helmet.

Because he knew, underneath it all, he was simply… Eddie. The man who filled all the empty spaces in his life.

"Hey." Sid tugged on the lip of Eddie's helmet. "What do we have?"

"Hey, love. Space heater, dry Christmas tree. One room." He pointed to a house across the street. "Family of four. Mom and Dad are at sixty-seven."

Sid ducked under Eddie's helmet and kissed his cheek. "You entered the property again. With your cast?"

"Barely inside the entryway. How'd you—" Eddie grinned. "C'mere, stud." Eddie pulled off his work gloves and licked his thumb to wipe a smudge of ash from the center of Sid's nose. "You're making me lose my staid professionalism, Mr. Marneaux. Maybe you should go speak with the family."

"Maybe I should. See you at home?"

Eddie wiggled his hand into his glove and grinned. He tipped his helmet as he hobbled to the house to assess. "Whatever the hell that means."

CHAPTER XXVIII.
CENTAURUS

WHEN SID WAS EIGHT YEARS old, his parents took him to Disney World. His sister had just finished college and was livid she hadn't been invited. "You have a job now, a life," Ma had explained. Sid had promised to buy Anna a set of mouse ears. She'd responded by calling him a spoiled brat. He didn't buy her mouse ears.

Of the many memories made that trip, one flashed fresh in Sid's mind as he buckled his seat belt on the plane bound for Chicago. Adrian sat between him and Eddie and hadn't stopped talking since his eyes had opened at five-fifteen that morning.

On Sid's flight to Orlando, his dad had reached the end of his patience. "Sidney Pravit, I will pay you one dollar for every minute you are quiet," Baba had said, punctuating his words with the click of his airplane seatbelt.

"Louis! You cannot *pay* the child to stop acting like a child," Ma had said.

At age eight, Sid had preened at his mother's support.

But this morning, he considered paying five hundred dollars per minute to not only *the child* but also his father, the flight attendant, the pilot, and that wheezing man in seat 2C if any of them could get Adrian to shut up.

The plane pulled away from the gate, and the sudden movement took Adrian's breath away long enough to silence him. He sat wide-eyed as they taxied, gripped Rimi Monster, and vacillated between holding Sid's or Eddie's hand with his free one. Once in the air, once Adrian had closed his mouth from the delightful lift from the ground, he started again. "Oh my goodness, that was so much fun! When can we do it again?"

They broke though the light cloud cover and Adrian said, "Sid! Daddy! Look! Now we're in sunshine. It's like *magic!*"

Two hours later, after informing the sweet, patient flight attendant of their plans to go to the top of the Willie Tower—the correction of which they could *not* get through Adrian's head—and see the Christmas market and Santa Claus, after furiously chewing on sticks of gum once descent began, his relentless yammering continued. "My ears. I think I need more gum." The plane wobbled. "I don't like landing at all. Are we on the ground?" The rear wheels hit. "*Oh!*" And the front. The engine noise increased, and force strong enough to slow a speeding bullet pressed them against the seat. "I guess we landed. I don't like the landing part so much."

He retold the tale of the perilous flight all the way to the rental car. He talked during the entire drive to Sid's apartment. And as they found parking, the jabbering stopped because now that they had to carry their luggage up three flights of stairs, the little shit was sound asleep.

"You know," Sid said as he hiked Adrian's dead weight into his arms. "I think I might be able to tolerate the *Willie* Tower lines if we have a promise that we could leave him there and no one would arrest us."

"Hey, now. He's our free ticket onto Santa's lap."

Sid side-eyed Eddie and held the door open for him as he hobbled in with a softer cast and a rolling suitcase. "There is so much wrong with that, I don't know where to start."

"You've lost your inner child, Sid. And during the holidays. I'm disappointed."

"I don't need an inner child. I have an outer child right here, falling asleep and drooling on my scarf."

"Merry Christmas!"

*   *   *

IT HAD BEEN THE MERRIEST of Christmases. Eddie and Adrian took to Chicago as if they'd been there a million times before. Adrian picked up the 'L' system like a champ, often outsmarting Eddie as to which train would get them where. After a stop at Bastra to show Adrian the treasure *closet*—"All this fabric will be *clothes* one day?"—they dove into the touristy portion of the trip: the Shedd Aquarium, The Field Museum, and Christkindlmarket, where the famous Christmas markets of Germany are brought to life in the heart of Chicago. They took a train up to the Lincoln Park Zoo, and froze their toes to walk the Zoolights Festival. To end the day, they headed back downtown and rode to the top of the Willis Tower to see everything from above.

After looking out this side and that, after stepping out onto the glass-floored sky deck, they huddled together at a window that overlooked Lake Michigan. Adrian leaned against Sid as his eyes roamed the vast view. After a short time, his body stiffened and he tugged on both of their coat sleeves. "Daddy? Sid? Is… oh my goodness."

"What's up, buddy?" Eddie asked.

"It was a sunny day, right?"

"Yep," Sid said. "It's supposed to be pretty our whole trip, why?"

"Well." Adrian hummed and pointed to the black sky. "Sid? Are there stars in Chicago? Because I don't see any."

"There are, except—" Sid took Adrian to a city-facing view. "Look down at the street. See how bright it is down there?"

"Yes?"

"It's light pollution. All the light on the ground drowns out the light in the sky."

Adrian pursed his lips and heaved another long-suffering sigh. He squeezed his eyes shut and opened them. He crossed his arms in front of himself. "I'm not so sure I like Chicago after all."

"The stars are still there, Ade," Eddie said. "They are. Mommy's star and Rimi's star. Mr. Sid's Dad Lou's star. They're there even if we can't see them."

"I don't like that. I'm ready to go to Sid's house so I don't have to think about it anymore."

Sid squatted to bundle Adrian against the cold. He didn't try to reason with the boy. He understood. Sometimes, belief wasn't quite enough.

"Think we could change our plans for tomorrow night?" Eddie asked at the apartment. Adrian was blissfully asleep. Eddie and Sid had enjoyed a glass of wine, and now they wobbled in a lazy dance around Sid's living room.

"I don't mind at all. What's the plan?"

"Tomorrow night, let's take him to the stars."

*   *   *

SID CALLED ANNA THE NEXT morning. Being away would have made the holiday easier on her, too, but she had opted to stay home for her kids.

"I have a Christmas gift for you," she said. "For us. You don't even need to be here to get it."

"Oh? I'm curious."

"You know I'm going back to teach after the holidays," she said. "I've been talking with the astronomy department. They're replacing their telescopes. I bought one for Baba."

"Anna... how many do they need?"

"A few more reflectors. Do you want their info?"

"Yes. Thank you. That's perfect. Do you think Andrew would, too? They could all be for Baba."

"He did it yesterday. I wasn't supposed to tell you."

"Merry Christmas, Didi. We love you."

"Love you too, Zico."

That evening, they drove to Dearborn Observatory. While they were all exhausted, Adrian's tiredness manifested itself like a well-shot pinball: bell to lever, bumper to turnstile while Eddie and Sid took turns being the flippers. But once they arrived and Adrian's eyes landed on the telescope, all exhaustion lifted.

"It's *monster*-sized! We should be able to see the entire *universe!*"

After a short lecture and patiently listening to the proper directions, Adrian stepped up to the telescope. With one huge gasp of air, Adrian no longer had words. Now he could see the stars.

"How can I *find* Mommy's?"

"You can," Eddie said. "You'll know hers above all the others."

Adrian chose one. He found Rimi and Lou's and he was done. Happy.

"You were right, Sid. They're there when we can't see them!"

"All the time, buddy. Anywhere you go. Any time of day."

Eddie bundled Adrian up while Sid waited for his own turn at the telescope. When the view came into focus, he was sure he whimpered. The view blurred as tears filled his eyes; he blinked them away.

Lou had taken him to an observatory a few years after Ma died—he had been in junior high. That evening, he and his father shared the same view with two different telescopes. Then, as tonight, the stars and planets appeared so dense and numerous, constellations became impossible to identify. His dad had tried to point them out, and Sid had tried to see, but it had been too much, too beautiful, too overwhelming.

"Ah, there's Aquila, Sid. To the east, can you see it? Find the brightest— what's it called?"

"Polaris. I know that one, Baba."

"Okay, smarty-pants. Forty degrees. Vega. Find Vega."

Sid couldn't differentiate Vega from a speck in the telescope's lens. But he knew the formations he should be seeing, so he fibbed. *"Up there? Altair, right? At Aquila's neck?"*

"Atta boy."

"And Vega is part of Lyra, the harp. Twenty-six light-years away," Sid added, *sealing his genius.*

"So much beauty, huh, Zico?"

"Too much, Baba. It's too much."

A gentleman behind Sid cleared his throat. Embarrassed, Sid jolted. He wiped his tears, nodded an apology, and found his family in the lobby. That night, when Sid and Eddie tucked Adrian in, he asked for his laughing stars poem.

"I changed my mind about Chicago," Adrian said as he curled around Rimi and sank into his pillow. "It's pretty magical after all."

*   *   *

ONCE HOME, SID AND EDDIE worked out a temporary arrangement. Sid would come home for an extended weekend every three weeks. It was far from ideal, but knowing the schedule, what to expect, and that they were both fighting for the same things, made it workable.

Bastra hired a fourth tailor. From the spring pieces Sid had designed, a casual, experimental line—Rimi—would be featured exclusively at Out & About. The Trial Line grew. Custom-order numbers increased. Sid's business boomed, but an old loneliness—homesickness similar to his first year in college—became a constant companion.

The time Eddie spent in his cast, unable to jump at the first sign of crisis, taught him to trust his crew. He led from the side with authority and respect. He and Dottie joined forces to push for another levy that would restore the funds to support two medic trucks for Connelly City. In early March, the levy passed.

Two weeks later, Sid came home for a long weekend. Dottie invited him to join her on a fire call in Waterson Township. "I know you miss Eddie," she had said, "but I miss you, too."

The ERV bumped down a barely paved county road when she finally revealed why she'd invited him. "So, how's the long distance romance going?"

"I like it better when I'm here," Sid said.

"Zico, there's no way you two can keep this up. It's crazy."

"I know, but he doesn't want to move Adrian again; he's fitting in well at school, has friends. I can't ask them to sacrifice if I'm not willing to put myself on the line, too."

"True."

"Which leads me to asking…"

"Nada. The one I sent you—Devin—she said she loves the trousers. She'll probably order again." That wasn't enough. They rode a few more miles in silence as the wooded foothills unfolded before them. He loved this part of the county: tree-lined streets, protected parkland. As much as he'd fought it since he left for college, Connelly *was* home. He might have come alive in Chicago, but the seeds had been planted here.

"Is Eddie considering?" Dottie finally asked. "Maybe after the school year or something?"

"Chicago Fire Department has a lottery… with over seventeen *thousand* people waiting. His experience doesn't seem to hold any weight."

"Jesus, Sid."

"I keep hoping for a sign, for the incense to spell out a word in smoke or something."

Dottie turned onto a gravel road. An orange glow peeked through the barren trees; this fire was a doozy. "Is it okay if I root for the Pennsylvania angle?"

"I need you to be happy for me if I end up in Chicago. And promise you'll come model for our catalog."

"Take me to the Willie Tower?"

Sid laughed and slipped into the back of the truck. "I'll do you one better. I'll take you to my favorite bar; we have real chairs."

"Blow up the air mattress. I'm there."

XXIX.
BOÖTES

"He's home, Daddy! I heard his car door. Where should I go? Should I get Rimi? We didn't talk about—"

The knob on the back door rattled, and the old wooden door popped open. As Sid took off his heavy work boots, they thudded against the linoleum; Eddie's heart thudded in tandem. In the living room, Sid looked at Eddie, at Adrian fidgeting. "You two look guilty."

Eddie plastered on a less-guilty-looking grin—he hoped. "Not guilty. We're... happy to see you."

Sid gave them a look and headed to the stairs. "I'm going to take a shower. We walked the property and I smell like... you."

"No! Wait! Um—could you—" Eddie sighed; this was going beautifully so far. He pointed to the stairs. "Could you have a seat?"

"On the stairs?"

"Yes. Sure." Eddie turned to Adrian, who had bounced from the overstuffed chair to the ottoman to the couch and back again. "Ade, the stairs will work, don't you think?"

"What*ever*." Adrian climbed onto the bench by the stairs, grabbed two spindles, and rested his head between them. "This is good. Go."

"Right." Eddie smiled again as Sid sat with doubt and distrust written all over his face. "Going."

"You're freaking me out," Sid said, but a smile quirked at his lips.

"No freaking out." Eddie sat below Sid, took a deep breath, and began. "So, I've been thinking." He paused and waited for a reply before realizing that he hadn't said much of anything. He tried again. "I've been thinking about your parents and how your mother followed her heart, how she made an entirely new life for herself knowing nothing more than that she loved Lou. It was enough. And I've been thinking about Maggie and how she would tell me over and over again that I might need to leave the tiny box of Wylie if I wanted to find happiness. And I did." He took Sid's hand and looked at Adrian for some extra bravery—but Adrian had flattened himself backward on the bench. "Ade, your support needs work."

"I didn't know you would give a *speech*!"

Sid's patient smile became pained.

"So, thinking," Eddie continued. "I know you've been looking to stay here." Sid took a breath to interject, and Eddie stopped him. "You and I both know it's not going to work, and… you won't be happy here long-term."

"I'm happy with you. I don't like Chicago anymore."

"It's winter. Who likes Chicago in the winter?" Sid conceded—no one in their right mind, that's who. "So, with all the thinking, and the knowing, and the missing you, Adrian and I have come to a conclusion." Adrian sat up and pressed his face against the spindles. "We want to move to Chicago."

Adrian jumped backward off the bench and danced, but Eddie's eyes were on Sid. On the smile that spread across his face. "You'll come? To my apartment, and Adrian will go to that arts intensive school around the corner, and—" He laughed, as if in disbelief. "You'll *come?*"

Sid scooted down to Eddie's level and cupped his face in his hands. His lips were cold, but perfectly soft and wet and vibrating with contained noises of joy. "You're moving to Chicago?"

"We're moving to Chicago."

He accepted Sid's kisses that slowed as he paused and looked at Eddie. "I want to make you so happy you won't regret it."

"Well, that's convenient because we have two requests. In exchange... so to speak."

Sid sat back and waited.

Adrian wasn't as patient. "Two? Oh my—how much longer until you—"

Eddie shot him a glare and smiled at Sid. "The first—I want him to finish his school year here. I hate this arrangement we have now. Even though it's working, we miss you like crazy. But we know when you'll be home; we can make it a few more months."

"Yes. Totally fair. He's had enough change for one year."

"Right." Eddie looked at Adrian, who had already started dancing around the living room, singing a song under his breath about Chicago and the zoo and the stars and the water. "And the second—Adrian, come over here, buddy. We're a team on this, remember?"

"*Oh*! Yes. Is it time? Because, Daddy you talk a lot." Adrian climbed the few stairs and sat next to his dad. "I'm here."

Sid looked at them as if they had lost their minds. And... as if he had figured out what they were up to. Eddie would not be deterred. "I'd also like to request—" No. That sounded as though he wanted extra towels and pillows delivered to his hotel room. "I would be *honored*, Sid, to seal this all up... if you would agree to be my husband. Will—will you marry me?"

Adrian began to tap Eddie's shoulder. He had coached Adrian to wait. "He might say no," Eddie had warned.

"He won't say no, Daddy. He likes that gross tuna noodle... pea... thing you make. He loves you."

Sid didn't say no, but he didn't say yes either. He simply whispered Eddie's name, "*Eddie...*" as if it was the last word he would ever utter.

"Look, I know what we have is real, and strong, and true. But Ade and I will be uprooting *every*thing. And the truth is, I'd uproot *more* than everything, if I had it, to be with you."

"Eddie…"

"But I don't have more than everything. I only have this simple life to offer you. And this crazy kid…"

"Hey!"

"So, I want to offer all of it. Every last corner of me, of our life."

"Eddie…"

"So, will you? Will you be my husband? And make me the happiest man alive?"

"Of course! *Yes*! Of course!"

Eddie straddled Sid's lap. He held his face in his hands and nudged one more time. "Say it again."

"Yes. I would be honored to be your husband."

As their lips met, hard and gasping, clinging to the promise they made, Adrian jumped off the stairs. He whooped. He hollered. He shouted to the world that his daddy was getting married; he was moving to Chicago; Sid and Eddie were sitting in a tree, K-I-S-S-I-N-G.

Sid and Eddie's celebratory kisses dissolved into a fit of giggles, which dissolved again into quiet smacks of more gentle kisses. After one final kiss, Eddie slipped off of Sid's lap and looked down at his son with a smile. Adrian had quietened and plopped himself on the floor, and was gazing up at them as if watching an epic romantic movie.

"Ade. You're on. Go."

"Oh my goodness! I got too excited. Sid, don't move."

When he disappeared, Sid brushed his knuckles against Eddie's cheek. "What about work for you? Even if you get *in* with Chicago, you're going to lose your rank."

"All the way to the beginning—a simple fireman."

"And you're okay with that?"

"Sid, I've been miserable as chief. I'm not a paper pusher. I'm not one to stand and watch other men do the job. I became a firefighter because I love fighting fires."

"You're a good chief, though. The station loves you. The city. Dottie—you've done so much!"

"Thank you, but I'll be happier as a fireman. And, they said I'd move up to lieutenant pretty quickly—possibly after my probationary period."

"Wait. You've been hired?"

"I have to take the tests. I wouldn't start until summer anyway. I'll start at five years' service instead of losing all my tenure, too."

"You've been working on this." Sid's grin grew bigger.

"While you were with Adrian and Santa at the fire station, I poked around. Made a few quick friends."

"Why didn't you tell me?"

"Because it looked hopeless until a few weeks ago. I have Evanston in my back pocket if this falls through."

They shared another kiss. Sid almost lost his balance as he bent to Eddie and then jerked up with another thought. "Oh! Oh my god, what about Sharon?"

"She's thinking of coming up, too—there won't be anything here for her anyway."

Before they could discuss it further, Adrian arrived with a navy blue velvet bag. He plopped it into his dad's hand and grinned at Sid. "You thought we were done, huh?"

"I should have known better."

Eddie bounced the bag in his hand, felt the weight of it, of what they were doing. Of the memories inside and the promised memories yet to come. "This has a story." Eddie dumped the contents of the bag into his hand and closed his fingers around it. "This was Maggie's."

"No. Eddie…"

"Story. Shush." He unfurled his fingers to reveal Maggie's ring. "It's sort of beat up because we found it at the Wylie Antique Mall. We don't know how old it is, but she fell in love with it. 'Three diamonds for the three of us,' she said. She must have cycled around to look at it ten times that day wondering if it was weird to wear a man's ring."

"She loved her big jewelry." Sid said. "I remember from pictures."

"She did." Adrian brushed his finger over the ring, then slipped a finger in and out of it. Eddie shared a sad smile with his son, kissed him, and continued. "At the end of the day, she got caught up in a bidding war with some guy on a green glass... *thing*."

"Your juice vase?"

"Yeah. Is it valuable?"

"Depends." Sid looked down at the ring in Eddie's hand. "Story. Please?"

"Right, so I snuck off and bought it for her. She wore it on her thumb every day. A month later, she metastasized, and when it got too big she put it on a chain. About a week before she died—" Eddie voice cracked, and he stopped.

"It's okay, Daddy. This is what she wanted."

"It is." Eddie kissed Adrian's temple. "A week before she died, she gave it to me. She said I could wear it myself, which I refused to do. I could give it to Adrian when he was big enough. Or—" Eddie pulled his eyes away from the ring, from its three glistening diamonds, and looked at Sid. A tear stained his cheek. His eyes darted from the ring to Eddie to Adrian. "Or, she said I could save it. For the man who would come along and make us a trio again."

"She voted for the last one, Sid." Adrian picked up the ring and slipped it on his own thumb, carefully spinning it around.

"We've become a pretty awesome trio," Eddie said as he plucked the ring from Adrian's finger and kissed it. "So, it would mean the world to me, to us, if you'd wear this. We can get something newer or—"

"No. Nothing newer. Nothing—" Sid lifted a shaky hand and Eddie slid the ring onto his left ring finger. Adrian watched as though magic might happen. And maybe it did. It fit perfectly.

"It's beautiful," Sid said after hugs and more tears. "You're beautiful. Both of you. I want to find a ring for you, too."

"Soon."

"Tomorrow. I want everyone to know."

"Okay. Tomorrow." Eddie took Sid's hands in his, feeling—as he usually did when Sid's hands were intertwined with his—grounded, sure, focused, and true. "So. I think I have one more request."

"I'm not sure I can take anything else."

"This one's easy," Eddie said as his thumb brushed over the face of the ring. "This is where I want to kiss you. *Really* kiss you."

"This is where I say yes. Always yes."

XXX.
CORONA BOREALIS

"Sid! Come look! It works!"

Sid turned off the burner on the stove and rushed into Adrian's bedroom. Adrian dragged him inside and slammed the door closed. Light-blocking curtains covered the windows of the pitch-black room.

"Give it a second," Adrian said, sounding more like a patient parent than a newly six-year-old boy.

Sid looked at the ceiling and grinned—more like a six-year-old boy than a patient parent. "Oh, Ade. It *does* work. Look at that."

"It's better over here." Adrian hopped onto his bed and huddled close to the wall. "If you lie down, it's like being outside."

Sid joined him, flat on his back with a cascade of "stars" overhead. It had been a whim of an idea that turned into a passionate plan, and now a brilliant welcome home for a little boy whose heart aimed toward the sky.

In the months between "Will you marry me" and "Welcome home," when Sid lived in this space alone, when his business continued to blossom and gain space in the city, he'd stewed at night about the little details, or, in this case, big details, like Adrian's concern over the lack of visible stars in the Chicago skyline. He researched. He considered. When he brought the idea to Eddie, he had sweetly teased him.

"Can't we get a couple packages of those stick-on glow-in-the-dark stars?" Eddie said. "He's *five* for god's sake."

"We cannot. They're tacky and he'll *be* six by the time you get here, and he deserves—"

Eddie had cut him off with his soft chuckle and consent to give it a try.

And now Adrian's ceiling had been painted by people who loved stars and constellations as much as Lou had, who understood the comfort in them as much as Adrian did. Using a luminescent paint that charged by daylight and glowed at night, a replica of the summer sky covered Adrian's ceiling. Aquila, Lyra, Hercules and Virgo, Ursa Minor—because of course Polaris guided them all—Pegasus and Aquarius all appeared to an eye trained to find them.

"Can you find your mom's star, Ade?"

Adrian took Sid's hand and directed it to a spot over his dresser: Aquila. Right where he had found Maggie's star a year ago. "That's hers. And Rimi's is there..."

"And Lou's is right above it. Of course."

"I hope I can sleep tonight. I might stare and stare and stare."

"I hope you can too; you turn into a boogerhead if you don't sleep."

"*You're* a boogerhead."

They quieted down and stared. Adrian took Sid's hand and ran his finger over the ring. It hadn't left Sid's finger except for the week when a jeweler made a match for Eddie, and again on the day Eddie and Sid became Mister and Mister—long enough for Eddie to put it right back on his hand. "I like Mommy's ring on your finger."

"I like the promises she made that we get to keep."

After long moments, Sid thought Adrian had fallen asleep. In the darkness, muffled by his pillow and Sid's chest, Adrian started to speak and stopped. He had to try three times before he could ask what was on his mind. "Sid? When do we go back to the wedding place? The courthouse? So—so you can be my daddy?"

"Soon, buddy. Go get your calendar and we'll count."

Adrian turned the light on without warning. "Goodbye, stars," he moaned and Sid joined him, "Goodbye, eyesight."

For months, Adrian's calendar had been a colorful array of circles and arrows, squares and exclamation points: Sid's arrivals, Sid's departures, wedding day, *sixth birthday*, last day of school, moving day. It had all whittled down to one final countdown: Adoption Day.

Adrian counted. "Fifteen! That's *too* many days." He flopped onto his back and heaved a sigh. "It'll *never* get here."

"Get up here, you boogerhead." Sid flipped the calendar back two, then three months. "Look how long you've already waited."

Adrian counted again. With so many days, he lost track and had to start again. "Fifteen doesn't sound so bad," Adrian admitted, giving up. "Can we turn the lights off again?"

As the tiny "stars" looked down on them, Adrian blurted out, "What am I going to call you? 'Daddy' will get confusing."

"You can call me Sid if you like."

Adrian hummed. "I don't like. Sid is my friend, which I do like, but you'll be more than my friend. You need a special name."

"I suppose you could call me Boogerhead."

That had to have been the funniest thing Adrian had ever heard. He fell forward. He laughed and he laughed and Sid laughed because Adrian kept laughing. Adrian slid off the bed and dangled there until he found enough breath to say, "I could call you Stinkybutt," which sent him into another fit of laughter.

Sid yanked him on the bed by his ankles and started a tickle attack that triggered a juvenile and ridiculous list of playground names. Between gasping laughter, they tossed names around and grasped for each other's bellies and armpits until their name-calling had deteriorated to nothing more than yelling names for bodily fluids. Sid put a gentle stop to it and focused on the ceiling again. "Show me the North Star."

"That's easy—the handle of the Little Dipper."

"That's right," Sid said, deciding to study—stop relying on his memory, but *teach* Adrian the way his dad had taught him. Distance closed when you knew you were beneath the same stars, and Sid knew that in the blink of an eye Adrian would be gone, traveling the world, capturing the stars with his own hands.

"What did you call your dad, Sid? You had a special name."

"In Bangla, Dad is *Baba*."

"Baba. I like that." Adrian quietly practiced the name, whispered it, adding "Daddy and," to see how it fit. "Do you think—can I call you Baba?"

"Oh." For a long moment, that was all Sid could get out. "I think that would be nice." Sid took a shuddering breath and held Adrian close.

"Did I make you cry? I didn't mean—"

"Happy tears, buddy. Happy. I miss Baba. I can't wait to be yours."

"Well. I was thinking we could start now? Because fifteen days is a long time and you taught me how to say 'I love you' like your mom—" He sat up and patted Sid's chest. "*Ami tomake bhalobashi.*"

They had been so engrossed in their own private world, neither Adrian nor Sid had heard Eddie come home. He opened the door and shut it behind him as he stepped in. "Look at that, Ade! It's almost like the real thing!"

"I know." Adrian squeezed Sid's hand and proudly said, "Baba picked the right thing."

"Y—yes, he did." Eddie bent to kiss Adrian, then Sid, lingering at Sid's temple. "I'm going to shower. I'm smoky."

On his way out, Eddie tapped Maggie's queen of hearts card, which had moved with them onto Adrian's dresser mirror. Adrian picked up right where he'd left off. "Love's the most important part, isn't it?"

"Yes. The best and most important."

Later, after Adrian had been tucked in for the night and Eddie had prepared the perfect iced chai, they met on the balcony. The stars were faint, like the waning crescent moon that sent its last light into the sky.

"Baba, huh?" Eddie asked as they leaned on the wrought-iron rail. "When did that happen?"

"About when you hit the second floor landing, I'd guess. Came out of nowhere."

"You okay with that?"

Sid scoffed—how wouldn't he be okay? "Yeah. I wonder if I'll be able to live up to it, though. It's a huge name."

"Sid… sweetheart. You became that boy's baba the night you showed him his mother's star."

"It's so much, when I take it all in. You giving up so much to be here, his trust in me. Yours. I've spent my life looking out for myself."

Eddie hummed and sipped his tea. "Remember the night your dad and I talked?"

"Yes, and you still haven't told me anything," Sid teased, pulling the folding chair from the wall to sit. He would stay out here all night if sleep weren't so damned important.

"I had to wait for the right time." Eddie said. "He told me that your mother lived in you—that she took her rest in you, that everything I love about you came from her."

"Oh, he's in there too, you know."

"I do. I'm glad. Which means… you're big enough. For Adrian. For me. For your own dreams."

Sid took another drink as he looked out across the sky. He focused on the warmth of the spices as they hit his tongue and on the chill of the liquid traveling down his throat into his stomach. "I guess we never die, do we? Maggie's here, Ma, Baba."

"If we keep them in sight, they're not that far away."

Sid reached for Eddie's hand, rested his head on Eddie's hip. "They're even sneaky matchmakers."

"It's been their plan all along."

ACKNOWLEDGMENTS

To the team at IP, I offer the deepest gratitude for the opportunity to continue this odd, unplanned journey. Candy, for your relentless behind the scenes action that gets our books out from behind the scenes and into the world. Annie, for your patient guidance, gentle instruction and creative mind that helps sculpt our books—and to your awesome support editorial team as well. Wizards, you are. And CB, in the words of Adrian, oh my goodness. You created a cover, like you so often do, that made me want to step up my writing game even more. You're a wizard too, aren't you?

To my family, always patient and frequently filled with fast food, I can't express my gratitude at the space you give me to reach for this. Alex, you are a prince among men. To my friends and family on the outside of this ride looking in—Mom, Dad, Cindi, Jen, Toni, Becky— your cheerleading is forever with me when I'm alone in my room typing away. And my IP family, especially Georgie, Brew, Axe, Jude, Knits: I can't imagine getting through those I Can't Do This days without you, and I wouldn't want to celebrate the good days with anyone else.

And finally, to Smita Vijayan and Dr. Julia Durrant… my thanks beyond measure for your time, your knowledge, and your caring touch in refining the details that helped bring this book, and its characters, alive.

ABOUT THE AUTHOR

LYNN CHARLES' LOVE OF WRITING dates to her childhood, when thoughts, dreams, frustrations, and joys poured onto the pages of journals and diaries.

She lives in Central Ohio with her husband and adult children where a blind dog and his guardian cat rule the roost. When she's not writing, Lynn can be found planning a trip to New York or strolling its streets daydreaming about retirement. Her previous novels from Interlude Press include *Chef's Table* (2014) and *Black Dust* (2016).

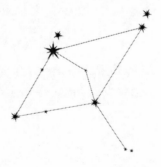

interlude  press
you may also like

Black Dust by Lynn Charles

Fifteen years after a tragic car crash claimed a friend's life and permanently injures his then-boyfriend, Broadway musician Tobias Spence reconnects with his former love. As Emmett and Tobias explore their renewed relationship, the two men face old hurts and the new challenges of a long-distance romance. Will Tobias lose his second chance at love to the ghosts he can't seem to put to rest?

ISBN (print) 978-1-941530-63-4 | (eBook) 978-1-941530-64-1

Chef's Table by Lynn Charles

Chef Evan Stanford steadily climbed New York City's culinary ladder, but in his quest to build his reputation, he forgot what got him there. Patrick Sullivan is contented keeping the memory of his grandmother's Irish cooking alive through the food he prepares in a Brooklyn diner. The two men begin a journey through their culinary histories, falling into an easy friendship. But even with the joys of their burgeoning love, can they tap into that secret recipe of great love, great food and transcendent joy?

ISBN (print) 978-1-941530-17-7 | (eBook) 978-1-941530-20-7

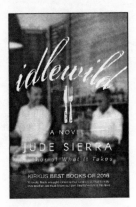

Idlewild by Jude Sierra

In a last ditch effort to revive the downtown Detroit gastropub he opened with his late husband, Asher Schenck hires a new staff. Among them is Tyler Heyward, a recent college graduate working his way toward med school. When they fall for each other, it's not race or class that challenges their love, but the ghosts and expectations of their pasts.

ISBN (print) 978-1-945053-07-8 | (eBook) 978-1-945053-08-5

5/17

CPSIA information can be obtained
at www.ICGtesting.com
Printed in the USA
FSOW01n1718070417
32731FS